TULIP

TULIP

ALICE L. LUMBARD

ALDM Publishing

TULIP is a work of fiction. Any references to historical events, real people or real places are used fictitiously. Other names, characters, places, and events are products of the author's imagination, and any resemblance to actual events or places are used factiously, and any resemblance to actual events or place, or persons, living or dead, is entirely coincidental.

ISBN: 978-0-578-74097-3

Published by ALDM Publishing
aldmpublishing@outlook.com ALDM Publishing P.O. Box 104 Quilcene, WA. 98376

Cover design by selfpubcovers.com /John Bell Art

Printed in the U.S.A.

Author's Note

Audrey Hepburn, May 04, 1929-Jan.20-1993

British actress, Hollywood movie star, humanitarian. As a child, Audrey Hepburn lived in the Netherlands during the Nazi occupation. To avoid prolonged bouts of hunger she scavenged tulip bulbs from the muddy fields to serve as food. Her story of survival was the first I had ever heard of tulip bulbs being edible. Shortly after learning of this curious possibility, the novel TULIP sprang almost fully formed in my mind, the imagined powerful side effects of consuming the tulip bulbs becoming the centerpiece of the novel TULIP. And although Audrey Hepburn's story is true and the novel TULIP is pure fiction, both stories share the common thread of hardship. Audrey Hepburn's bright spirit is reflected in one of her favorite quotes, "Nothing is impossible, the word itself says "I'm possible!"

I

1886 Springtime

A wooden bench rests on the banks of a raging river opposite gigantic images of ancient deities carved into a sheer cliff. The bench affords a comfortable viewing seat for those wishing to pay homage to the Gods. It also marks the termination of a well-worn path. To arrive at the bench, the path travelled through a verdant river valley and the prosperous village at its center. And before that, it switched its way down the perilous side of a scree-covered foothill. Midway on the slope, the path encountered and crossed a man-made terrace. And it was above the terrace, behind a massive pillar of rock, that the path was seemingly birthed from a fissure of such size it had apparently split the foothill's summit in two.

A human skeleton lays scattered on the pillar's flat top. Vultures have been at it. They've done the work of stripping and eating the flesh from the corpse, leaving it free of identity, free of the past and all the weighty responsibilities attached to the complicated job called human life. The skull has detached from the vertebrae and is resting near the skeleton's hands. The finger and the toe bones appear to be missing, the little bits of bones more than likely kicked over the pillar's edge during the raucous feeding frenzies of the vultures.

Colorful Buddhist prayer wheels have accompanied the meandering path the entire way, always staying on the sunny side. Comprised of eight panels, each with three tiny fins, the prayer wheel's construction is unique to the region. Paper strips inscribed with blessings have been wound around each wheel's spindle and when the wheels are spun the blessed words are set loose to fly across the universe, helping each and everyone and everything they encounter, especially the ill-tempered humans. The people of the valley have renewed the blessed prayer strips every full moon, every year, back so many generations they've forgotten how long they've been at it.

The nearly continuous sounds of spinning prayer wheels provide a titillating bonus. United in chorus, they mimic the rhythm of squeaking beds, the exact same sound lovers create while indulging in the mutually satisfying, bringing it home kind of sex. It's a pleasing sound. A most desired of sounds. A sound that makes the ancient Deities sit up and take notice.

Below the pillar of rock, the man-made terrace is fully revealed. A high rock wall surrounds all but the narrow strip of path running along the southern edge. Mid-way along the graveled path a gate adorned in glowing golden bells appears in the wall. The gate opens onto a flagstone walkway that leads to an ancient, rickety one-story rock and timber framed cottage. Installed in the walkway is a large mosaic designed as a compass rose. It's so new the white dust from the mortar still mars the edges of the green, gold, and black tiles.

A woman of indeterminant age stands at the very center of the compass rose. She's deliberately facing northwest. Long tendrils of lush spring growth push against her toes, but she doesn't notice. Honeybees brush against her face as they flit about collecting pollen from the beckoning flowers, but the woman fails to react. Brightly colored singing birds fly about her head as they gather twigs and dry grass to use in the building of this year's new nests, but the woman doesn't care, she's far too busy waving a personal, hand-sized prayer wheel before her open, unblinking eyes. The woman's prayer wheel's spin is different, the exact opposite of the rotation of all the other prayer wheels in the valley. And that change makes her prayer wheel selfish, and in that sense truly evil. The backward spin adds an extra note of an entirely different pitch, the sound still that of sex, but unnatural enough that the ancient Deities are drawn like flies to the source of the sound.

The woman makes use of the anomaly to communicate with the Gods. It's her undisputed right to do so for she is, in fact, a real Shaman and has been so since shortly after the sudden death of her father. And to ensure that outcome, mere moments after his death, she left her father's side and descended the foothill to the valley down below to search out his four closest, oldest friends.

She found the men at various locations, and one by one she brought them to the entrance of the community's meeting hall. And once she had them all together, she informed them of her father's sudden passing. She waited a moment or two for the shock to wear off, then politely insisted they immediately conduct the traditional sky burial. And furthermore, they were to perform the ceremony on the flat top of the massive pillar of rock located just above the terrace.

To a man they knew it was wrong to do what she had asked. The proper procedure was to carry the Shaman's corpse to the mountains for a sky burial, altitude being especially important for a man of his stature. The break with tradition would surely upset the people of the valley and perhaps, more importantly, endanger the Shaman's spirit. They hesitated, then flat out refused to honor her polite request. After all, at that point she was still just a mere woman.

The Shaman's daughter gave them just one chance to change their minds. Then she asked, "Are you certain of your decision?"

And once again, to a man, they said they would not, could not, do what she had asked. She gave them the old chicken eye, then promptly called their bluff by ringing the meeting bell the exact number of times it took to call an emergency session. A short while later every one of the inhabitants of the valley had gathered in front of her, including the babies. To their credit, her father's four best old friends had stayed by her side, looking solemn and sad, and just a bit chastised.

Once the people of the valley had slowed down the sharing of whispered speculations, she informed them of their beloved Shaman's unexpected passing. Her initial sob and her short jag of crying added enough drama to the telling that people's heartstrings were pulled.

After a few minutes of communal grieving, she got down to the real reason the meeting had been called. The dead Shaman's bones held residual power, powers that were needed for the continued health and prosperity of the valley's people. And that was why it was so imperative his corpse remain within the confines of the valley. The flat top of the massive pillar of rock would make an adequate substitute for the mountain ledge normally used in a Shaman's sky burial, but her father's burial must be done today, right now, as it was unusually hot, and his corpse would soon begin to rot and leak and stink.

By the end of her plea, she was so intense she scared the villagers. It was quickly whispered about that she was to be the next Shaman, and no one wanted to be on the wrong side of that. And so, the community did the smart thing and held a vote. Right hands went up for yes, left hands went up for no. And of course, everyone's vote was for a yes including the babies and the dead Shaman's best old friends.

And that was that.

The four old men, those best dear old friends, let it be known to all that they would now perform the sky burial. And to prove it, in front of the watchful eyes of everyone, they left the meeting and trudged up the path to the terrace. When they entered the garden, they found their dear old friend lying on the ground next to his favorite teacup. They carefully examined his body before daring to declare him stone cold dead alright, no doubt about it.

Each man stood next to one of his limbs, then briefly stood still as a show of deep respect. Then, as one, they reached down and grabbed hold of his upper arms and upper thighs and lifted. They adjusted their grips to hold him as close to their bodies as possible, then proceeded to carry him. But they did it slowly, for it was awfully hard work to carry the dead weight of a dear old friend.

They huffed and they puffed their way up the steep slope, the path's zigs and zags helping to ease the climb, but still the sweat poured down their brows and stung their eyes, rendering each man temporarily blind. By the time they arrived at the pillar's base, they were exhausted and had to lay their dear old friend down and take a rest.

As soon as everyone's breathing had returned to normal, they picked the dead Shaman up again, this time by his wrists and ankles. And in one smooth, unpracticed move they swung him back then forth and tossed him on top of the more than ten-foot tall, massive pillar of rock.

Of course, the forward action caused a reaction. The old men took a few unintended backward steps towards the path's edge but as they lost their footing they reached out and grabbed hold of each other's hands and elbows, forming a chain as they sat down hard. And in that way, they prevented the most vulnerable of their group from slipping over the cliff. Throughout the whole ordeal, their eyes never once left the dead Shaman. They watched in awe as he landed at the exact center of the flat top of the pillar of rock. Surprisingly, he even managed to stay upright as he settled into a tidy, motionless heap. The dead body toss was spot on. The four best old friends might be old, but they were still in the game. The unexpected success gave the exhausted men the adrenalin rush needed to climb the sheer side of the pillar of rock and finish the ritual of sky burial.

As they free climbed, the sharp edges in the hard rock viciously cut their fingers and bare toes. Worse yet, the awkward angle of their feet caused their old men's heels to crack open and bleed. The blood ran down the pillar's face, combined, then ran in rivulets, clumping into drops, reminiscent of tears, the whole creating the illusion the pillar was crying real tears of blood.

The four old men barely noticed. In fact, the added slickness seemed to give them an extra boost in their ascent. And once on the top of the pillar, after they had stopped their old man shaking and caught their ragged breath, they proceeded with the sky burial. On his knees, the eldest removed the Shaman's pantaloons then spread them on the ground so they could be used to create a bundle. And then he stood back and allowed the other men to take their turns removing the remaining clothing. Each took their time removing every bit of bone, bead, feather, and braided headband from the Shaman's sacred body. They sniffed each object, smelling their dead old friend's musk for one last time before stacking his meager possessions on top of his worn-out pantaloons. His rhythm makers, those precious bangles of beaten gold and silver, were slid from his frail ankles and wrists and gently laid on the pile.

And finally, it was time to patiently untie and unwind the Shaman's magic medicine pouches from around his neck, east to west. It was common knowledge the contents of the pouches had been handed down for a thousand years or so and were the true source of his powers. And although it was hard, they resisted the temptation to peek inside to find out what actual power and magic might look like. And so it was, the medicine pouches became the last items added to the pile.

Touching the ancient pouches made each man disappear inside himself to that secret star dust place beyond even the ancient lizard brain. It lasted but for a moment, and then each man came back to the here and now. Suddenly anxious to finish the ceremony, everyone gave a hand at wrapping the pantaloons up and over the Shaman's possessions. After they made sure to tuck everything in, good and tight, the youngest of the old men secured the bundle by tying the Shaman's long belt crisscross fashion around it.

And then the bundle was set aside, and the men went about the sad task of arranging the dead old man's limbs. His head was tipped back, and his eyelids pushed open, so his unseeing eyes were obliged to stare at the sky, and only the sky. To ensure this outcome they tied his head and limbs in place with strips of fabric they tore from the hems of their own clothing. It was understood the rays of the sun would eventually cause the ties of bondage to completely disintegrate, and their dear old friend's spirit would be set free of his earthly bounds.

After they had unbraided the dead Shaman's thin white hair and finger combed it loose so the lightest of breeze could lift it, they bowed their heads, prayed their thanks, then said their good-byes. And when they were done with that, the eldest of the old men stood up, picked up the bundle, and dropped it over the edge of the pillar of rock.

And of course, the bundle landed in the waiting arms of the Shaman's daughter. She promptly ran down the path to the cottage, all the while silently laughing. Once inside the garden, with the gate securely shut behind her, she celebrated her victory by holding the bundle aloft and twirling round and around. And this time, she laughed out loud, delighted she had so easily acquired the magical medicine pouches.

Soon enough she settled down and entered the cottage. But after only a few steps in her knees gave out and she collapsed to the floor.

As she laid on her side, she hugged the bundle and pretended it was really her father come back to her, that his death was just a bad dream. And then the truth won out and great shuddering sobs consumed her as she felt for the first time the great loss of her beloved father.

But it wasn't long before she sat up, wiped the tears away, and assumed a cross legged position. After a few deep breaths she unwrapped the bundle and removed the magic medicine pouches. She dangled them by their strings, admiring them, but she knew better than to untie the bags and peer inside. Instead, she wrapped and tied the medicine pouches around her neck all the while reciting the prayer that transferred all the power of a thousand years of Shamans into her body and soul.

And just that quick, in less than the blink of an eye, she became a Shaman. She felt not a bit of remorse about lying to her father's best old friends and the lovely people of the valley about the sky burial. After all, they weren't the ones that needed the Shaman's residual powers, they just needed good management to prosper. She was the one who needed his naked dead body close by so her pet vultures could consume his flesh and thereby become supernatural. The vultures were, after all, an essential part of her plan of revenge.

It was that same need for vengeance that led to her poisoning her elderly father's mid-morning cup of tea. She had even managed to smile an encouraging smile as she watched him take the sip that would instantly stop his heart. But she wasn't completely heartless, she genuinely loved her father and so had deliberately chosen the quickest, kindest way to kill him. His death was not personal, but a necessary means to an end.

The villagers suspected something was off. They whispered and wondered about the coincidence of her father, their perfectly healthy, most beloved of Shamans, suddenly dropping dead within a day of her return, but none dared accuse her of actual murder. And since her mother had been a Tibetan witch, they felt there was a good chance her powers were more than likely doubled. And while his sudden death made them somewhat cautious, they also hoped she would bring a much-needed boon to the valley.

And that's exactly what happened. The first harvest after the Shaman's daughter had taken charge provided an overabundance of food. The valley's inhabitants suddenly had enough leisure time to increase the manufacture of their traditional embroidered panels. The trade goods were packed out of the valley by mostly young, childless lovers, happy to be associated with the exquisite embroideries. The couples used front packs and back packs and sometimes carried the goods balanced on top of their heads. And after they had walked or ridden in carts for quite a distance, they would arrive on the banks of the Indus River where they would pay for passage on a steam powered vessel. And in this way, they were able to travel the almost thousand miles to the bazaars of the far away city of Karachi, situated on the coast of the Arabian Sea, in little more than a month's time.

The finest of the embroidered fabric panels were sold to the representatives of the European royal families for exorbitant prices. The centuries old practice of hiding little silk pouches filled with hand cut precious gems disguised as curtain weights was continued. Smuggling was the only way the highest quality diamonds, emeralds, and rubies could leave the country, and the only way the second-best quality gems could avoid paying taxes. Occasionally, the silk bags full of gems was all that was wanted, and the curtains would be returned and re-sold without bothering to repair the hems.

With a portion of the profits the traders would buy the small luxury items their fellow villagers had requested along with the raw materials necessary to create the next round of trade goods. The return journey on the river took much longer. After all, they were going against the current and carrying more than they had left with.

When the river became a stream and was no longer navigable, the traders would hire a few Buddhist monks to help them pack the goods the rest of the way to the valley. The new-found prosperity made absolutely everyone glad that the woman was now the valley's Shaman.

Comfortably settled in her father's cottage, the woman spends her days tending to the people of the valley's spiritual and medicinal needs, tending to her personal food garden and the essential herbs needed to make medicine. The rest of her time she spends embroidering on the very finest of the available fabrics. Her specialty has always been landscapes, preferably on large hanging panels for use as room dividers, curtains really. She marks the top corners of her work with bouquets of red and yellow tulip flowers, it's her one and only identifier. Her embroidery is the most skillful of all the valley's inhabitants and her finished goods fetch the highest of prices, even without the hidden jewels sewn into the hems.

But always, no matter what she is doing, day or night, she keeps an eye on the path. The villagers understand she is waiting, it's that obvious. Some think she is waiting for the return of her handsome husband, while others believe he will never return. It was no secret he despised the confines of the valley and the dirt of the fields. It was why once they were married, he insisted they leave the valley for the busy seaports and the clean, open waters of the welcoming sea.

She was so crazy in love with him that she willingly abandoned all her of friends, her father, and most of her easily replaceable possessions. When she left the hidden valley, she carried just two packs; a backpack stuffed full of embroidered panels, the hems loaded with precious gems, and a front pack containing a meager collection of personal items and clothing.

The reason for her sudden return five years ago remains a mystery to the valley people. The morning of her return, a mated pair of Himalayan Griffin vultures appeared and let loose a series of obnoxious, ear-splitting screeches as they circled above the terrace and the massive pillar of rock. The people suddenly stopped what they were doing and looked towards the source of the horrendous racket.

At first, they saw just the vultures, but then the regal silhouette of a woman against the rock face of the pillar stood out. The good people of the valley instinctively knew they were looking at their beloved Shaman's long-gone daughter at long last returned home.

Beginning almost immediately after the sky burial and continuing every day after for one complete cycle of the moon, the villagers watched with a mixture of horror and curiosity as the vultures consumed every bit of the flesh on the Shaman's corpse. And then, the vile creatures disappeared and were not seen again until three moon cycles had passed. But once the vultures returned to the valley, they remained.

The villagers knew there was not enough death, at least not enough big death, in the whole of the valley to sustain the vultures, and yet they seemed to thrive. It was whispered about that they were kin to the magic tortoise of ancient Chinese folklore and thus could live on nothing but air. And soon enough, the speculation that the pair were supernatural creatures became accepted as fact and their continued presence became part of the background of everyday life.

Today, on this most special of days, the woman has dressed in a shimmering emerald-green blouse and a bright, crimson colored skirt, each made of different grades of silk, both articles of clothing worn years earlier by her mother during her witching ceremonies.

The drape of the sleeveless, single strap blouse exposes a tantalizing view of the woman's right breast, the thin silk of the blouse proving to be very pliable. As a finishing touch, the skirt's hem is tied in an overhand knot, the knot's ends tucked into the skirt's waist band, all done to display her naked, perfectly shaped legs. The soft mass of the overhand knot rests smack dab over her precious mound of

Venus, drawing the eye and inciting the mind to the possibilities of easy access, easy pleasure.

The woman's moon shaped face and prominent, rounded cheekbones reflect her mother's Tibetan heritage. Her jewelry is a further testament to her unusual and elevated status, the noonday sun proving the point. Glittering gold hoops pierce the edges of her dainty ears. Sparkling rubies, emeralds, and diamonds held in golden and silver filigree chains wrap round her long, slender neck. And beneath it all, the ancient magical medicine pouches lay against her rapidly beating heart, all but hidden, yet utterly useful.

As she waves her personal prayer wheel back and forth, she steps up and down, but just enough to cause her wrist and ankle bracelets to clink against one another, the collision of the different precious metals producing a hypnotic sound. Tiny braids threaded with her mother's Tibetan silver and turquoise beads swing in and out of her long, blue-black hair, all in rhythm with the up and down steps.

Suddenly, the woman's trance breaks. She ignores the flitting birds and the buzzing bees and instead focuses on the patch of unusually large red and yellow tulip flowers growing near her feet. She lays the prayer wheel down upon the ground and retrieves a wooden bowl filled with a flour-like, gritty substance. She shakes the powder around the base of each flower stem. Then, using a sharp pointed metal digging tool forged in the shape of a dagger, she scratches and pushes the powder deep into the soil around each flower stem.

Deliberately, she leaves two flowers unfertilized. One is red, the other yellow. She stares at the two flowers for a long moment, then makes her choice. She jabs the digging tool into the ground and buries it up to its hilt. She leans back hard on it, putting her slight weight behind it. The action unearths the entire tulip plant, and it lands against the length of her arm. The plant is so tall the flower rests behind her left ear. And it is there the flower looks most at home, nestled up against the golden earrings, laid into the soft bed of her blue-black hair, the flower kissed by the turquoise and silver beads of her little braids. As she stands up, the plant slides down her arm and drapes across her palm, the stem in the middle, the dirt encrusted bulb hanging off to one side, while off the other edge of her palm the flower droops down, her choice now obvious, the flower's a deep crimson red, the color of freshly spilled blood, the whole a perfect illusion of a mortal wound. And all the while she has been about her business, she has hummed an ancient hymn, every now and then slipping into the hymn's lyrics, the words begging the valley's ancient deities to come help her now.

2

Lotus and the Botanist

It was the sudden, overwhelming need to piss that compelled the man to pause midway up the foothill, at the base of a thorny thicket. An unlikely place, the thorns making it a somewhat dangerous place to pull it all out, but what the hell, nature was calling.

Out of habit, he glanced down at his feet to make sure his stream was missing his boots and it was then he noticed the faint signs of what appeared to be a seldom-used path. As he shook himself dry and buttoned his trousers, he thought about it, then made the easy decision to abandon the route indicated on the map and follow the path instead.

Emboldened by an abundance of curiosity, he pushed his way through the narrow gap in the brambles. The spring growth was a fearsome opponent, his passage an almost impossible feat, the thorns catching his clothing and scratching his face and hands, drawing pinpricks of blood as he made his way through.

Fifty or so feet later he stepped out of the thicket and onto a cleared, level landing backed by a rock face split in two by a sizable fissure surrounded by carvings of fearsome one-eyed winged creatures. Just half his size, the carvings were of such ancient origin that black lichen had long ago filled the grooves.

He found it an unexpected sight for neither the path, the carvings, nor the fissure were marked on his map, though the map did identify the foothill as Notch Pass. A quick glance at the summit confirmed the fissure as the cause of the notch in the ridgeline.

Sudden shadows fall on him, surprising him, and his eyes are drawn to the sky. Two vultures circle overhead, flying so low he can easily identify them as Himalayan Griffins. He finds their presence odd as their usual haunt is in a far-away land called Tibet. He sniffs the air but fails to detect the smell of rotting flesh nearby and so he dismisses the vultures as just another anomaly in yet another strange land.

His gaze drops back to the fantastical carvings flanking the fissure. The carvings create the illusion of a door frame surrounding a wide-open door. Intrigued, not overthinking it, he follows the path into the throat-like passageway. A near absence of light forces him to take his time. He uses his staff to search for hidden traps and possible voids, careful to check each step before taking it.

Suddenly, the passageway lightens. He rounds a sharp bend, steps out into the daylight, and finds himself face to face with a massive pillar of rock. It blocks his way forward and his view of what lies beyond. Momentarily frustrated, he looks to the ground for answers and discovers the path continues around the south side of the pillar. He has absolutely no idea where it might lead so he leans his back against the cold rock of the pillar, careful to stay hidden while he takes a break to think about his next move. A few seconds later, bored of all the thinking, he pokes his head around the pillar to see what's what.

An enormous circular shaped valley backed by a scree covered foothill lays spread out before his eyes. A raging river runs along the foothill's base until it disappears under a gigantic rockslide. Something odd midway along the base of the foothill tweaks his interest so to get a better look, he retrieves his telescoping spy glass from his coat pocket, rotates it open and holds it against his best eye. He looks directly across the valley at the sheer rock face rising from the raging river. It's covered in gigantic carvings nearly identical to the images he saw as he entered the passageway. A viewing bench is positioned across the water on the bank of the river directly opposite the carvings. The path leading to the bench appears to be a continuation of the very path that he is currently standing on.

And that's when he finally gets it. The hidden valley is an outdoor temple for the ancient deities depicted on the rock face. He remembers dating the lichen in the grooves of the carvings at the entrance to the passageway at well over two thousand years old. The deity carvings would impress his fellow professors, but he's not really that interested, he's looking for something much dearer to his botanist's heart.

He pans the spyglass across the valley floor until the sight of a field of enormous red and yellow tulip flowers catches his eye. It's exactly as he was told it would be, there can be no doubt now. He has finally found the birthplace of the fabulously valuable origin tulip, the two primary colors positive proof.

He takes a deep breath. Relaxes. Looks around some more. Verdant fields of red rice, millet, lentils, and barley cover most of the valley floor. He guesses the region's legendary diamonds and all manner of other valuable gemstones are the reason for the small mine at the center of the valley. Orchards in full bloom are growing behind the modest dwellings lining the path. Beehives dot the landscape, the bees busy servicing the fruit trees and the fields. Chickens and ducks wander around loose, excluded from the vegetable plots by wattle fences so cleverly made of orchard pruning, the pruning have managed to take root and become functional, fruiting espaliers.

Outhouses and communal baths are tucked in here and there behind the dwellings, the baths made obvious by the soapy bubbles floating in the drainage ditches. A large meeting hall dominates the center of the community, a huge golden bell having place of honor next to the double doored entryway. And behind the meeting hall is a dozen round silos and an equal number of storage bunkers. Many centuries of use have worn the access paths into unintentional trenches.

He sees children running naked and free, the sounds of their loose laughter making him laugh too. People are gathered in mixed groups here and there along the path, gesturing and talking. Both sexes are dressed in vibrant colored silks. Their behavior indicates they live as equals and have plenty of leisure time. But best of all, not a single weapon is in sight.

And that's all he needs to know about that. Finished with his survey, he twists the telescoping spy glass closed and drops it back into his pocket. And then he spends a moment thinking about the unusual geology of the valley. In his mind's eye, he can see what happened.

Eons ago, the hidden valley was once an enormous active volcano. And long after the volcano stopped spewing fire and brimstone, long after it became extinct, the rim of the volcano began to erode. The scree filled the volcano's caldera, the top layer eventually eroding into usable, friable soil. More time passed, and a river found its way inside the crater, carving out a channel north to south, before being swallowed by the earth. And to this very day, the volcano's rim is still collapsing and too dangerous to attempt to cross. And so, the valley remains effectively sealed from the outside world.

He gives a quick look over his shoulder. The leveling of the passageway's floor and the widening of the walls makes perfect sense now. Clearly, it is the only safe way in and out of the valley. He knows from experience that disturbing people living in such an isolated and hidden fashion carries inherent danger. He becomes hyper vigilant, standing ready to retreat if needs be.

The two vultures reappear and circle above the pillar of rock. They squawk and screech so loud he covers his ears to damp down the sound. They act as though he were disturbing a newly dead, meaty corpse. And sure enough, as he looks up, he catches the flutter of a piece of cloth and the gleam of a sun-bleached bone on the verge of falling off the edge of the pillar.

Curious, he drops his staff and free climbs the side of the pillar. He peers over the edge and sees a substantial pile of bones mixed with wispy white hair, undeniably human in origin. The skeleton was picked clean of rotting flesh so long ago the bones have lost the smell of death. But something about the skeleton appears off. He gives it another once over and discovers the finger and toe bones are missing but not the rest of the hands. But it's really no surprise, the carrion eaters are known for crunching and sucking small bones to get at the marrow. And after the bones are crushed, they soon become dust and are never seen again. And with that minor mystery solved, he lets go of the edge, drops down to the path, and steps boldly out into the open where he can be seen by anyone so inclined to look his way.

He stands shoulders back, as any man of confidence would, and takes stock of the cottage on the terrace just below the massive pillar of rock. The pillar of rock, the cottage and the terrace were described to him a little over a month ago at a bazaar in Karachi, on the coast of British West India. Chance had brought him to the stall of an attractive young couple selling embroidered fabrics. Brilliant bouquets of red and yellow tulips adorned the top corners of the magnificent panel they had hung for display purposes.

Excited by the possibilities, he slipped a yellowed, torn missive from his pack, unfolded it, and pointed to the painted renditions of red and yellow tulip flowers adorning the opposite corners of the letter. He pointed back and forth between the flowers and asked, in the official language of trading, "Do you know where I might find the land where these flowers grow naturally?"

Of course, they understood him. Like all seasoned traders they could speak the King's English. The couple shared a quick look, then held their hands out, palm up. He took the hint and gave them each a gold coin. They wiggled their fingers, indicating more, and so he continued the payout until they smiled big smiles and closed their fists.

It was the woman that took charge and pointed him upriver, advising he travel by steamboat as far as he could, and once he reached the headwaters (a trip of nearly a thousand miles) he was to search out the local Buddhist temple. As she wrote the temple a note giving permission to share the valley's whereabouts with the Botanist, she explained the monk named Rabbit had often helped the couple pack goods to and from the valley and he also was by far the best map maker in the region.

After more than a month of arduous travel, he managed to locate the Buddhist temple, find Rabbit and give him the note. After reading and pondering the note for what seemed an ungodly amount of time, Rabbit agreed to draw the map. Another monk provided the Botanist with a simple meal, and soon after eating his fill, the exhausted Botanist found a dark corner, spread his bedroll, and promptly fell asleep until the next morning when Rabbit gently shook him awake and handed him the completed map.

The map was compact and folded lengthwise in thirds. It was a stunning, if primitive, work of art. The mountains and the nearby landmarks were fully illuminated in gold leaf and green paint, delicately outlined in sensuous black brushstrokes. A simple, practical compass rose had been placed at the bottom right-hand corner, a tulip at its center. He promptly paid the monk in as many gold coins as it took to make the man smile, then gifted the temple a few gold coins, too.

Then, after a quick breakfast, and an expensive resupply of provisions, he left the monastery and faithfully followed the map until he reached the base of the foothill called Notch Pass. The map then directed him to cross the foothill's scree covered slopes. The scree was the most dangerous of sorts, so unstable that one wrong slip of a foot could cause a man's death, but to the Monk's credit, the faint animal trail marked on the map passed close enough to the shortcut that the Botanist was able to spy out the hidden path, bypass the danger, and end up exactly where he needed to be.

The Botanist retrieves his staff and follows the path downhill, passing scores of spinning prayer wheels along the way, taking little notice. He sees the village in the distance, but he has no interest in it for he sees what he wants, and it is much closer than the village or the fields. The noisy crunch of his heavy boots on the loose gravel announces his impending arrival as he walks down the short path to the cottage gate, but he doesn't care, he wants to be heard.

He arrives at the closed garden gate and rests his hand on the wooden bar that acts as the gate's only lock. He takes a long, measured look at her, then whispers under his breath, in the language of the Dutch, "Thank God, it's only a mere woman."

The woman is not surprised by his sudden appearance at her gate. She's had her eye on him since she heard her pet vulture's cries of warning. She nods her head yes, giving him silent permission to enter her garden. As he unlocks the gate and pushes it open, the movement causes the many clusters of glowing golden bells to ring as he enters.

Once inside the garden he removes his wide brimmed hat and holds it over his heart, the hat's absence revealing his greying head of thick black hair. Being this close to her, he can't help but bow down to her, the woman's commanding presence demands it.

He quickly resumes his upright stance, not wanting to appear subservient. He tries his hardest to appear aloof, but her overt sexuality distracts him to the point that he gives in and gives her an obvious up and down look. A whistle slips through his lips followed by a lop-sided grin of admiration.

The woman continues to hold his lively gaze as she ever so suggestively rubs a dirt encrusted tulip bulb against her skirt. She abruptly stops and violently twists the stalk of the blood-red flower free of the bulb, then casually opens her fingers and wiggles them, laughing as the debris falls to the ground. She makes a show of peeling the bulb free of the protective papery tunic, throwing the pieces up in the air, laughing as they lift and float on the light breeze. She even purses her plump lips and blows on the floating pieces, puffing them along, till they finally sink to the ground.

With a wicked little grin, she puts the tip of the perfectly prepared tulip bulb in her mouth and repeatedly takes the tiniest of bites until she has consumed nearly half of it. He watches as the excess juice dribbles over her plump bottom lip, then licks his own lips in response to his overwhelming desire to lick hers.

The shape of the tulip bulb and the bright color of the juice somehow reminds him of a strawberry, the bulb's texture resembling that of an apple. He watches as she sucks on what is left of the bulb, sucking the sticky juice, her cheeks working in and out in rhythm, all the while directing his attention to her ruby red lips, making him want her to suck on him, too.

She pulls the half-eaten bulb free from her lips, the breaking of the suction audible. Her black, black eyes meet his honey brown gaze. A moment passes. She takes a deep breath and as she exhales, she begins to glow, pulse, and shimmy. The single strap of her blouse slips off her shoulder. As it falls, she catches the collapsing fabric in the ready crook of her elbow, preventing the full reveal of her breasts.

The woman bends down, and as she does so, she sticks the half-eaten tulip bulb back in her mouth and bites down hard on it, holding it in place with her perfect little white teeth. With both her hands free she takes up the digging tool and shoves it deep into the ground, up tight against the stalk of the single yellow flowered tulip she has deliberately left unfertilized. She leans back on the handle and puts her full body weight into it causing the bulb to pop free of the loose garden soil. She quickly prepares the tulip bulb for consumption, then offers it to him with an encouraging smile. She casually takes a little bite of her own half-eaten tulip bulb, indicating it's a normal food source in her hidden valley.

In all his many travels, he has always eaten whatever foods he has been offered. And although he has never eaten a tulip bulb before, he doesn't hesitate to reach out and take it from her hand. Their fingers brush, and the contact incites an electrical charge that radiates all the way to their hidden sex. The sudden bulge in his trousers reveals the desire he feels, but he shakes his head no. After all, he's a disciplined man and he's here on serious business.

Big money business.

Taking a step back from the sexual attraction, the sweet woman scent of her, he drops his staff and slips off his backpack. He kneels and unbuckles the pack, lifts the rain flap, and pulls out a tucked in, rolled-up oilskin. He unrolls the oilskin and removes a folded, worn, and slightly torn missive. To conduct the business of his acquiring her exceptional, origin tulip bulbs, he unfolds the missive and holds it up with one hand for her to examine.

Dominating the missive is the portrayal of a blood red tulip flower at the upper left-hand corner, while at the lower far right corner is a much smaller, though more luminous painting of a yellow tulip flower. Both paintings include the leaves, the bulbs, and the roots of the flowers. Placed between the lovely botanical paintings are words written in the language of the Dutch. The bold script reads: Wanted, the Holland Horticultural Society will pay ten thousand English pounds for tulip bulbs recovered from the place of origin believed to exist somewhere west of the Tien Shan Mountain range and north of the northern most region of India. Must provide proof of origin location.

He points to the tall patch of tulips flowers growing in her garden, then points to the paintings of the flowers on the missive and says, "I'll pay you three gold coins for a bundle full of those tulip flower's bulbs."

With his free hand, He reaches into his trouser pocket and pulls out three gold coins. As he holds them out to her, he begs, "Please, I really need your tulip bulbs."

Then he points at each individual flower in the tulip bed, slowly counting out twenty-six, as though she can understand his unfamiliar language. He shrugs his shoulders and waits for her response.

She stares at him. He stares at her.

They gaze at each other for a long, long time.

She's beyond lovely and she's pulsing, and it will not be denied. Shrugging her shoulders in a practiced way, she causes her blouse to fall to her waist. Lifting her arm out of the single strap, she frees her breasts of their last restraint, exposing the deep blue veins feeding the enlarged nipples, tempting him to reach out and touch.

He drops the missive and slides the coins back into his pocket, but before he can act on his baser instincts, she pushes the hard bulb of the yellow flowered tulip into the palm of his right hand, then points to his mouth, indicating he needs to eat it now. She consumes the rest of her bulb slowly, sucking the juices, taking small, delicate bird bites, all the while peering up at his great height, willing him to come closer.

She's captivated him. She owns him. He's unable to take his eyes off her willing body. Enthralled, he willingly takes a bite. He can't help it. He takes another bite, then another, and yet one more.

She's finished her bulb now, and slowly, suggestively, she sticks one of her fingers in her mouth and sucks on the sticky residue that clings to it. Stimulated, encouraged, he quickly finishes his bulb. But wickedly, mischievously, he makes her wait for it as he slowly licks the tulip juice from his own sticky fingers. He tortures her a little bit longer by slowly dragging his eyes across her half naked body. He rests his gaze for several heartbeats on the knot hiding her precious mound of Venus before finally dragging his eyes slowly back to hers.

She returns his look, a question in her eyes. She squirms in anticipation. She licks her lips, becoming impatient for what will surely come. She steps up to him, close enough that she feels his panting breath against her cheek. She sucks his breath in, her action triggering some deep reaction within the man.

And then it happens. His lizard brain explodes with lust. The need, the desire for sexual satisfaction overtakes him. The peculiar act of eating the tulip bulb has made him forget all about his mission. He has but one purpose now, one thought left in his man's mind.

He's wracked by a great shudder and the very air between them becomes charged with an energy expressed as an intense vibration, a thrumming akin to the stroked string of a musical instrument. They move towards each other, reach out and touch each other palm to palm. Their bodies meld together as they suck on each other's swollen lips.

Hands desperate and greedy, they rub and stroke every part of each other. As they spin round and around, they come closer and closer to the cottage until finally they bump into the door, and it swings open. And it's there they collapse and lay across the cottage threshold, in and yet out.

She opens his trousers releasing his throbbing manhood. Drops of semen squirt from the engorged head and land on her belly and breasts. Desperate for complete release, he pushes her skirt aside and enters her, covering her body with his, covering her high, firm breasts with his hands, rubbing her aching nipples round and around with his thumbs, loving how hot and plump they've become under his soft stroking motions.

Belly to belly, the man and woman move against each other, with each other, opposing and completing, finding the right rhythm so quick it's as if they were born to be lovers, as if it were their fate. She rocks herself into a bow like arch and cries out. He grunts in a deeply satisfying way as he aims and shoots his wad. Together, they reach mutual climax.

Hot and sticky, done now, they separate and glance at one another. They exchange satisfied smiles, both proud of their quick success. Helping each other stand, they step apart and arrange their clothing. He buttons his trousers as she slips her arm through the single strap of her blouse. Her skirt's hem falls to the ground, covering her bare legs, the knot having come undone during their wild coupling. Together, they step away from the entrance of her home, never once having been inside.

The sexual tension resolved the Botanist remembers why he came to the hidden valley. It's to purchase the origin tulip bulbs, of course. The bulbs are to be the last and most important of all his acquisition. And once the origin bulbs are safely in his pack, he can return home to Holland and reunite with his motherless son.

First things first, though. He looks at her and smiles, then points to his chest and proudly introduces himself, "I am Jacob, (he pounds his chest, pauses a second, then says louder, with greater authority) I am Jacob Vandermeer, the world-renowned botanist."

Laughing, nodding her head in agreement, she points at him and says, "Jacob." She locks eyes with him, picks up his hand, places his palm on her heart and breaths her name out as a secret that only he should know. She whispers, "Lotus." Her warm breath carries her name into his nose and open mouth, saturating him with her essence. She pauses, drops his hand, leans in close and pokes his heart twice as she again slowly blows the two syllables of her name into his opened mouth.

Jacob sucks her name in, unable to resist. He's suddenly immobilized, and for many long moments, hypnotized. He's finally released from her spell when a seizure rolls through him and frees his mind. Not realizing he has lost time, he nods his head in agreement and responds, "Of course your name is Lotus. It means a flower rising and blooming above the murk to attain enlightenment. Well, my little darling, you got a rise out of me. But now I need us to get down to serious business."

With exaggerated motions he points to the tulip patch and flashes both hands twice adding an additional six fingers to indicate the quantity of tulips he wants. He points to the tulips again, emphasizing his determination to complete the purchase.

Lotus vigorously nods her head yes, wanting him to know how eager she is to accommodate him. She takes her digging tool in her hand and bends to the task, quickly digging up twenty red and six yellow flowered tulips, all still attached to their bulbs. She lays all twenty-six plants in his arms, points to them, and clear as a bell says, "SHANGRI-LA." Retrieving her personal prayer wheel from the ground, she places it on top of the pile of plants. Patting the prayer wheel, pushing it into the pile of tulips, pushing him, she forces him take a step backwards towards the open gate. She nods her head yes and points her finger up the path. She wants him to leave, and she wants him to leave now.

Well, alright then, he will. Jacob drops his armful of plants on the ground next to his pack, then spreads the oilcloth on the ground to use as a base for the bundle he must make. He turns his attention to cutting the leaves and stems free of the tulip bulbs, tossing the debris aside before gently brushing the clinging dirt from each bulb, careful to preserve the protective papery tunic. He makes a pile of the bulbs at the center of the oilcloth, then adds the prayer wheel and missive to the top. It's obvious the pile is too high and way too wide. The twenty-six bulbs have taken up too much room. He returns five bulbs to the lovely Lotus, and he's left with twenty-one bulbs, a manageable amount.

He bends, folds, and tucks the oilcloth around the pile until everything is secured. For added insurance, he double ties the bundle with thick twine. Then he stuffs the bundle into his pack and pulls the pack's rain flap into place. He cinches and buckles the outer strap as tight as it will go, thus securing the most precious acquisition he has made in all his years of collecting unique botanical specimens. And all the while he's been about the business of packing up, he's grinning from ear to ear.

When the pack is ready to go, he picks it up and swings its cumbersome weight around, using the weight to help slip his arms through the straps and settle the pack comfortably on his back and hips. He adjusts the bedroll under the hard edges of the bottom of the frame, preventing the heavy pack from digging in on his skinny hipbones. When everything feels right, he buckles the waist strap.

He's about ready to leave except for one little thing. He must pay for the tulip bulbs, it's how he conducts his business, no exceptions to the rule. The tulips have tremendous monetary value, and he considers not paying for them akin to common thievery. And no one, not ever, will have reason to accuse him of that most vile of destructive acts called common thievery.

Jacob reaches into his pocket and retrieves the three gold coins. Once again, he presents the coins to her, and once again she deflects by shaking her head no and hiding her hands behind her back, clearly refusing the payment. But her pathetic act of refusal doesn't matter much to him, he's so much bigger and stronger than she is. He pulls her right hand out from behind her, then ever so gently pries her clenched fist open and drops the coins into the center of her palm. He quickly folds her fingers around the gold coins, gently squeezing both his hands tight around hers for long enough that she understands she must keep the payment. She gives up and gives in, acknowledging the surrender by looking him dead in the eye and nodding her head yes. He sighs with relief.

They gaze into each other's eyes and grin. It really has been so much fun.

The Botanist bends down and retrieves his floppy, faded brown hat and his staff. He slaps the hat on his head and adjusts the fit till it shades his face just so. He turns his back on her and walks through the garden entrance. Then he turns around and pulls the gate shut, all to the joyous sound of the tinkling golden bells. He slides the heavy wooden bar into its slot, locking the gate, locking her in, protecting this special one. He looks at her fondly and blows her a goodbye kiss.

And then he struts his way up the path towards the massive pillar of rock, feeling better than good. Once more he passes the many spinning prayer wheels and the shiny white human skeleton. He rounds the pillar, disappears behind it, and enters the near pitch-black of the passageway. But then he does something unexpected. He stops, spins around, and sneaks back outside into the daylight. Staying hidden behind the pillar, he retrieves his telescoping spy glass from his coat pocket, pulls it open, and directs the single lens onto the satisfied woman he has just left behind.

He watches as Lotus rubs her belly round and around, a blissful smile playing across her still swollen, blood red lips. It dawns on him he might have given Lotus more than just the three gold coins. And wasn't that really what the woman was wanting? She clearly had an agenda. After all, she had no real interest in taking the money.

Lotus tilts her head to heaven, her lips moving in prayer to some ancient, unseen Deity. She gives her flat belly a final pat, then steps over to a large mortar and pestle. After removing the covering cloth from a nearby earthen bowl, she dumps the skeleton's missing finger and toe bones into the mortar. Then she takes the pestle in her hands and proceeds to grind the bones into a flour-like dust.

Finished with the gruesome task, she uses the digging tool to poke five holes in the dirt of the tulip patch. Then she pours the bone dust into the bottom of each hole, followed by a bulb. Unexpectedly, she pricks her finger on the thorn of a nearby rosebush then holds her bloody, dripping finger over each bulb, squeezing the prick to encourage the blood flow, and then after each bulb has received her blood, she takes the side of her foot and pushes the dirt back into the hole, covering each one. She follows by doing a foot stamping dance, her arms raised over her head, her hands twisting in complicated patterns.

And all the while she has gone about the gruesome task of the bloodletting and the performance of the strange dance, she has sung sweetly, imploringly, as if she were calling a spirit to hurry home, to come and join her now.

Naturally, her song floats up hill, and Jacob hears every note of it along with all the odd, foreign sounding words. Suddenly, he finds himself shivering uncontrollably. The hair on the back of his neck stands up, and a moment later the hair on both his arms brushes backwards. It's as if unseen hands had stroked him and not in a good way. The sensation quickly passes and the implications of what he has just witnessed dawns on him. The origin tulip's fertilizer recipe might be repulsive and unacceptable in Holland but if he substitutes animal blood and bones for human, the recipe would be technically correct and worth a tidy sum to the horticulturists, perhaps he'll even write a paper on the subject suitable for publishing.

And it's no wonder Lotus called the bulbs Shangri-La. The Buddhists use the word to express ecstasy and bliss, and he can surely attest to that fact. But really, why should anyone know of their power or that they are even edible? He might tell his son, though. It would be quite an unusual present to give him, especially now that he has come of age.

Jacob lets loose an accidental whoop of joy in celebration of his good fortune at finding the origin tulip bulbs. He is especially pleased at having sexual pleasure so easy, so free. The world-renowned botanist gives one last appreciative look at the exotic beauty, then turns on his heels and vanishes into the fissure behind the pillar of rock. The pair of Himalayan vultures scream their lament for the dead, the many prayer wheels squeak their wonderful rhythm of sex, and all in all the sounds create a marvelous farewell song as he exits this magic, fantastic kingdom for the ancient silk road and home.

3

Early Fall

At a dock in Holland, on the river Maas, deckhands finish the job of off-loading cargo from the hold of a merchant sailing ship equipped with the latest model of the supplemental steam engine. The ship has recently returned from the Indian Ocean via the man-made wonder called the Suez Canal.

Jacob Vandermeer, the world-renowned botanist, exits the ship, crosses the dock, and stops beside the stack of crates the deckhands have assembled. Out of habit, he looks to the sky and then at the crowns of the nearby willow trees for the pair of Himalayan vultures that have been his constant companions since he took his leave of the lovely Lotus and her secret valley of the tulips.

Sure enough, the creatures are nearby, perched on the top branches of the largest of the weeping willow trees. In fact, the vultures are looking down on him as if he were about to die and become their next bloody meal.

But Jacob doesn't think so, he's got places to go, people to see. Besides, he's become so used to their continual presence that he's no longer intimidated by their eager looks. And to prove the point, he turns his back on them and casually examines his immediate surroundings.

He was told the main purpose of the dock was to provide support to the warehouse of an import export business, but the warehouse is nowhere in sight. However, there are two small buildings across the narrow road. The larger of the two has a simple sign above the window declaring it to be the shipping office. An open lean to, barely large enough to stable a single horse, is attached to the building's side. The second, smaller building is set back and further away, it's obvious it's the privy.

It's just as the captain warned, there is no other service here, not even a little tavern with dock whores for the sailors to enjoy. And according to the charts and maps he looked at, it's a good, long distance to the nearest village.

But he doesn't care. Once he saw the words Miller's Wharf marked on the chart, he knew it would be his destination. He informed the ship's captain of his decision and within a day he had received word that the shipping company associated with the wharf would be glad to handle his cargo, all for a hefty fee of course.

Unfortunately, the local office was manned just one day a week, and without exception that day was always on a Monday. It gave the ship's arrival time little room for error, but the navigator thought it could be managed. The captain notified the main shipping office via telegraph of the ship's arrival date and the approximate time the ship would dock, weather and tide permitting. He knew the captain had also requested cargo transport be made available and sure enough a horse harnessed to a two-wheeled cargo cart was tied to a nearby hitching post, ready for his use.

The sight pleases Jacob no end. Everything was going exactly as planned. Out of habit, he pulls a dented gold watch from his vest pocket and checks the time. It's getting late, it would speed things up if he had help loading the crates. Usually, there were men for hire at a dock, and he looks around hoping to see one now, but there's no one in sight.

An open sign hangs on the office door. Adjacent to the door a bicycle leans against the wall. Above the bike, nailed to the southern corner of the building, a large wooden arrow points to the nearest village. The paint on the arrow is so old the name of the village is barely legible, but he thinks it says Miller. The road leading towards the village looks well maintained indicating it probably has frequent use. In the opposite direction though, once the road passes beyond the privy, the road looks seldom used. It suggests the road services very few people and probably dwindles into a path that terminates in the useless marshes of the hinterlands.

He pulls his attention away from the big picture and looks at his cargo. As always, Jacob is obsessed about the possibility of thievery. And while visually the crates appear to be secure, he doesn't trust his eyes. To satisfy his worried mind he runs the tip of his index finger around all the seams of the crates to see if the subtle grooves carved into the wood still line up. They do. He checks to see if the six long, narrow custom stamps glued over the seams of the six lids are still intact. They are. He takes a deep, satisfied breath and smiles a real smile. All's well in his small world and best of all, he's one step closer to seeing his son and going home.

But the feel good doesn't last long. Something sneaky climbs up his back and over his neck. It's the eyes of someone watching him. He looks around and spots a man in a bright blue hat standing across the road between the lean to and the privy. He's sure the man wasn't there a few moments ago. The man appears to be waiting for something to happen.

Jacob gives it to him. He points at the man in the blue hat and yells, "Hey you in the blue hat! Come over here!"

As the man approaches, Jacob takes his measure. The man has a pronounced limp, caused no doubt by the obvious bend in his lower right leg. He's of similar height and build to Jacob, but he appears to be a good ten years younger. And despite the man's clothing being worn thin and oft mended, he has the confident bearing that suggests an upbringing of wealth and privilege.

The man in the bright blue hat stops a few feet in front of Jacob and politely asks, "Yes Sir, what can I do for you. Sir?"

Jacob replies, "I'd like to hire you. I want you to load each one of these six crates marked with the Holland Horticultural Society stamp onto that cart over there." He slaps each crate as he issues his orders ignoring the physical fact of their lone existence, for there are no other crates on the dock. More tellingly, Jacob's actions imply he thinks the man for hire is so stupid he couldn't possibly be able to count, let alone read. Adding further insult, Jacob points to the only cart and horse in evidence and continues with his instructions, "Mind you, make sure you stack the crates in that cart three deep, two high. I expect the job I've given you to be done by the time I return though it shouldn't take long for me to pay my bill and send a telegraph to my son informing him of my arrival.

The man for hire nods in agreement and politely answers, "Yes Sir, alright Sir, I'll have it done right away, Sir. Thank you so very much, Sir."

Jacob abruptly turns his back on his hired help and strides off in one hell of a hurry, not quite at a jog, but almost. He arrives at the door of the little office and flings it open without bothering to knock first. Then he barges right in, allowing the door to slam shut behind him.

The man for hire carries the crates the short distance to the cart and creates a new pile. Then he sets about loading the crates on the cart, shoving them forward as far as they will go, making three stacks in all, two crates high, just as the Gentleman had instructed. But as he lifts the final crate, the two vultures leave their perch in the willow and swoop down over the horse. The vultures come so close their wings brush against the horse's mouth, his eyes, and the top of his head before sliding down his neck to his rump and tail. Then the vultures lift off and fly out of sight.

Of course, the horse startles. He takes a quick step forward, then one more step, causing the post to wiggle like a loose tooth. But somehow the post manages to hold fast to the ground, and the horse is brought to a sudden, jarring halt.

The horse's unexpected forward motion and sudden stop has caused the last crate to miss the mark. The crate teeters on the top edge of the bottom crate, the balance all wrong. And before he can stop it, the crate topples over, hits the ground, and lands on its side. Upon impact, the crate's lid pops open.

The man for hire shrugs. Accidents happen. He tips the crate upright and realigns the lid. Then he double folds the hem of his felted woolen vest and lays the side of his hand on it to use as a kind of glove as he hammers his fist down on the lid's little nails. He pounds each nail back into their hole, putting everything back just as it was. He even checks the custom stamp and finds it remained intact, the thick paper acting as a hinge instead of ripping apart.

Fixed now, ready to go, he lifts the crate and heaves it into place. The thought that something might have spilled from the crate suddenly occurs to him and so he searches the ground but finds nothing. Relieved, he relaxes and whispers to himself, "Oh well, no damage was done, nothing really happened here. There's no need to mention it to the Gentleman, no need at all." Moments later Jacob exits the shipping office, the loud slam of the door announcing his return. He stops in the middle of the road and makes a big show of giving the agreed upon signal to the ship's Captain that all is well. Someone on the ship's deck barks an order and the deckhands slip the hawsers free of the wharf's pilings. The whistle toots three times and the sailing ship disappears around the river bend under the power of the new-fangled supplemental steam engine the shipping company so prudently installed a few years ago.

With the last and only business of the day finished, the clerk exits the office and flips the sign over to say closed. For the benefit of the man for hire, the clerk makes a great show of locking the door, even shaking and turning the handle several times to prove that it's securely locked. Satisfied he has made his point, the clerk grabs the bicycle, settles into the seat, and peddles off in the direction of the village without so much as a thank you, a goodbye, or a backward glance to either man.

Jacob finds the clerk to be rude, saying goodbye is good manners, it just shows respect. He damps down his rising anger and hurries to the cart. He does a quick count of the crates, then checks each one for the stamp of The Holland Horticultural Society. Satisfied all six of his crates are now on board the cart, he finally acknowledges the man for hire by saying, "I see it's all done. Thank you, my man, I believe this pay is more than adequate for the job."

He pulls a handful of coins from his trouser pocket, picks out five silver coins and drops them into the waiting palm of the man with the bright blue hat. Then Jacob boards the cart, settles his bony ass down on the hard narrow seat, and politely asks, "Will you untie me my man?"

The man in the bright blue hat slips the coins in his pocket then unfastens the horse's reins from the hitching post. He keeps one hand tight on the bridle as he hands over the reins. They nod in agreement, and he lets loose the bridle and slaps the rump of the skittish beast. The horse moves off at a brisk walk. A moment later, the Gentleman whips the horse's flanks and sets him to a trot.

The man for hire examines the hitching post. He finds it odd that it came loose like it did, it was sturdy enough last Monday. And why did the two vultures suddenly appear out of nowhere and harass the horse? It makes no sense. Vultures are carrion eaters, not predators.

He pulls the coins out of his pocket and counts the value. He thinks of what the coins will buy and how it will never be enough. He needs more, a lot more. And he could certainly use a bit more luck about right now. And with that thought rolling around his worried mind he notices something lying on the ground where nothing should be.

He gives it the old once over. It's an oilcloth bundle double tied with sturdy string. But a corner has torn loose, and an almost apple sized tulip bulb has escaped through the hole and rolled free of the bundle. He picks it up and examines it, marveling at its size. He retrieves the bundle and tries to peer inside, but another large tulip bulb is blocking the hole. So, he does the next best thing and runs the tips of his fingers back and forth across the surface of the oilcloth to get a sense of what lies beneath. His fingers slide over more oversized bulbs but then he feels something oddly configured of hard edges, clearly created by man.

Time passes, and he wakes as if from a dream. He's still standing, still holding the bundle, still mindlessly stroking the manmade object. He knows he's lost time but not how much. He struggles to break contact with the hidden object and once free, he shakes his hand out, trying to get rid of the sticky feeling, the dirty and somehow used feeling. And then he immediately forgets all about the peculiar experience.

The ship, the clerk, and the Gentlemen are long gone. No one is left to take charge of the bundle. The office is locked, and it would be improper to leave the bundle propped against the office door until next Monday. Nor does it feel right to leave it in the open lean to. Either choice would almost guarantee overnight destruction by the ever-present wild critters. The privy has a door, but it has never, ever kept the ravenous river rats out., they would eat tulip bulbs in a heartbeat.

He's unable to think of a single safe place to leave the bundle and it's far, far too late in the day to chase after the Gentleman. He seriously doubts the bundle of tulip bulbs will ever be missed. After all, this is Holland, the land of tulips. He clutches the bundle to his chest as he limps his way to the backside of the privy where he has stowed his bicycle. He drops the loose bulb in his pocket and mounts the bike and peddles off, traveling down the seldom used road,

4

Monday, Late Afternoon

A short distance from the dock, the road curves away from the river and all its many working windmills. Beyond the bend the man in the bright blue hat crosses a bridge spanning a canal lined with graceful weeping willow trees. Not long ago, the bridge was re-named the Bridge of Sighs due to its proximity to the blackened foundations and ash heaps of a home and warehouse, a sad reminder of the horrendous fire that destroyed lives and the family's business.

Once his home, once upon a time. He stops for a long moment, honoring the memory of all that happened and all that was lost that tragic night.

The horrendous fire occurred a little more than five years ago, during a fast-moving storm that came out of nowhere and carried no rain. What it did carry was plenty of thunder and lightning. It was the sound of a crackling boom directly over his bed that woke he and his wife. A second later they heard breaking glass then felt the very air being sucked from the room. Instinctively, he knew the window in the staircase had been blown out by lightning. And then they smelled smoke.

In a panic, they jumped out of bed. As usual, they'd been sleeping in the nude and so precious time was lost as he pulled on his pants and his wife threw on her nightgown. They ran to the bedroom door and slowly, carefully opened it only to see the flickering red glow of a growing fire in the stairwell. He shared a worried look with his wife, silently acknowledging what must be done. And then she headed down the hallway towards their daughter's bedroom, as he headed in the opposite direction towards his parent's bedroom.

As he sprinted past the stairwell, he held his breath .The air was thick with the smoke caused by the flames consuming the steps. He saw the stairwell was now a death trap. And that's when he knew there was no other choice. If his family were to survive, they would all need to jump from the windows.

When he arrived at his parent's closed bedroom door, he didn't bother to open it, but instead pounded on it and yelled at the top of his lungs, "Poppa! Momma! The house has been hit by lightning! The staircase is on fire, and I can't put it out! Listen to me, listen to me poppa! Don't open your door, if you do your room will become like a chimney and the fire will come in and we will all be burnt to death. Poppa, I need you to open your window and throw your bedding out, and then you and momma jump out the window. Promise me you'll do exactly as I say, poppa. Promise me you'll do it right now!"

The unexpected pounding on the door and the fear and panic in their son's voice was enough to alert both his parents to the immediate danger. His father shouted from behind the closed door, "Oh my God! Yes, yes, Vonder, we smell the smoke. You hurry back to Neola and Letty and make sure they are safely on the ground. Don't worry about us. Momma just threw the bedding out the window. We'll shove the top mattress out and land on it. We'll be on the ground in a moment."

By now, the ravenous fire had followed the smoke into the hallway. It presented a challenge to Vonder's survival. He took a shallow breath, held it, and sprinted through it. The flames licked him, causing blisters on his neck and naked torso. His thick head of hair caught fire and to save himself he did a strange sort of dance, his feet jumping over the hot spots, his elbows jutting out every which way as he slapped at his head to put out the flames. It took just seconds for him to arrive at his daughter's bedroom door, but by then his naked torso had sustained serious burns.

He opened his daughter's bedroom door a crack and slid through, quickly closing it on the hungry flames. He found his wife waiting for him, as he knew he would. Letty was out of her bed and clutching her momma. She was sobbing, her eyes wide with terror. Neola had wrapped their marriage quilt around Letty's little shoulders and was busy stroking her hair, trying to calm her down.

Vonder knew there was not a moment left to spare. He threw open the narrow casement window and ordered his daughter to climb onto the sill and jump, but she refused to let go of her mother.

Just then, flames erupted under the gap at the bottom of the closed door. Frustrated, running out of time, he locked eyes with his wife and with a look asked what to do. She jutted her chin towards the window giving tacit approval. And so, it was he who jumped first. A second later his wife threw their screaming daughter out the window into his waiting arms.

He caught their daughter then set her firmly on her feet. The quilt had slipped from her shoulders, and he spent precious seconds wrapping it tightly around her, all the while whispering reassurances. When he felt he had her complete attention, he pointed her towards the road and gently pushed her in that direction. When she arrived at the road, he yelled for her to stop and wait, and that's exactly what she did.

And then he turned his attention back to the window. He waited for his wife to leap from the window ledge, anticipating catching her in his arms, but she failed to jump. She was at the open window, he saw her plain as day, but she stood frozen, as if hypnotized, her eyes locked on the crowns of the distant weeping willow trees. She was so far gone she failed to notice when the curtains burst into flames, nor did she react as the hungry flames reached out and licked her back.

Her utter indifference was a fearsome thing for him to see. There was no way he could get to her. How was he to save her? Desperate, panicked, he screamed, "Neola! Neola! Look at me darling, look at me. You need to jump! Jump out the window! Do it now, Neola, do it now!

Somehow, someway, his desperate words managed to break through the powerful spell she was under. The tiniest of seizures shook her, the physical disturbance freeing her mind. Her blank look evaporated and was replaced by one of sheer terror. She scrambled onto the windowsill and leaped, the back of her thin cotton night gown catching fire at that moment, the flames blistering the skin of her back, her long, loose hair disappearing as the firestorm consumed it.

He caught her in his arms, but they were off center, and the awkward angle of her sudden weight drove him down into the soft ground, twisting and splintering the long bone of his lower right leg. The broken tip pushed through his skin resulting in an open fracture. The broken bone split the fabric of his pants and dirt entered his bleeding wound contaminating his blood.

They both heard the crack of his leg bone as it broke. Neola understood it meant her husband would not be able to walk. At the same time, she realized she was on fire. She fell out of his arms and rolled back and forth on the dew-soaked grass. The heavy night dew extinguished the fire and cooled her burns in the process. As Neola rose from the ground, her nightgown fell apart, dropping from her body in burnt fragments. Naked and blistered, shiny wet with dew and very nearly bald, she spun in a circle taking everything in, passing quick judgement on all that was happening around her.

The two carriage horses passed within ten feet of them, running wild eyed, their broken teethers dragging on the ground. Her husband was on his back, his lower right leg horribly bent, a bone projecting from the tear in his scorched pants. She heard a tremendous crash and jumped back as the heat suddenly increased ten-fold. Without stopping to think of what to do next, she just did it. She grabbed her husband by his wrists and pulled him away from the scorching heat and licking flames of their burning home.

Vonder remembers how hard he struggled against her, the absence of his parents now of major concern. But his struggles didn't last for long. The pain of his shattered leg and the loss of blood caused him to pass out from shock. His unconscious state had the unexpected benefit of making it easier for his wife to drag him across the slippery, dew-soaked lawn.

Days later, Neola told him all that happened after he passed out. She had just managed to drag him halfway to the road when their daughter walked past them, all empty eyed, heading straight for the inferno.

Neola screamed, "Stop, stop." But Letty paid no heed. Neola had no choice but to let go of Vonder and run after her. She managed to grab hold of Letty's hair and pull her back just as the roof collapsed in a shower of sparks. As they came alongside Vonder, Neola reached down and picked up his wrist with her free hand while still holding on tight to a fistful of Letty's hair.

And then the real struggle began. Dragging two dead weights was almost too much for the very petite Neola, but she managed to move them another fifty feet or so before their home imploded in a huge shower of sparks. The hot embers rained down on all their heads and Neola was forced to stop and wage battle, slapping the burning bits off her husband and daughter as fast as they landed.

She was sloppy and hard about it and that was all to the good. The hard slaps managed to revive Vonder and lift the strange glaze from Letty's eyes.

It was all the sign Neola needed. She dropped her hold on her daughter's hair and grabbed both of her husband's wrists. And then she ran backwards, hard on her heels, skidding him along on the night's slick dew till she arrived at the spot on the road where Letty had dropped their marriage quilt. Letty had followed close behind her father's feet, but she was visibly shaking, her state of shock obvious.

Once Vonder was safely at the road, Neola let loose of his wrists and recovered the quilt from the roadbed. She shook it free of grit and draped it around Letty's trembling shoulders. And then she calmed her daughter by breathing in sync with her, deliberate in slowing their breathing down just as she'd done when Letty had temper fits as a small child. Neola gently stroked her daughter's hair, tucking it behind her ears, all the while cooing comforting words. Soon enough, Letty stopped shaking, her constant crying becoming an occasional sob.

From his prone position on the ground Vonder waited for his parents to emerge from behind the burning home and join him, but they never did. After a short while he gave up all hope and accepted that one or both were trapped by burning debris, for he knew the one would not have left the other, their love was too great for each other.

Thousands of sparks floated up from the collapsed home. The fire wind carried the sparks onto the wood shingled roof of the nearby warehouse. Within minutes the roof ignited, and soon after the whole building was engulfed, the wicked flames feeding on the inventory of fabrics, tea, and spices stored within. The combined burning of the two buildings created a great towering column of fire and smoke.

The pungent smoke drifted in the direction of the nearby village. Eventually, it settled on the land and seeped through the cracks of all the homes along the way until it reached the village proper. The smell of smoke woke every man, woman, and child. They ran out the doors of their homes fearing it was their own roof on fire. They looked around, taking stock of the buildings, the fields, and the sky. To the north they saw a huge red glow in the distance, and it was then they realized the import export warehouse was on fire.

The good folks rushed to the rescue, but it took a bit of time for them to harness the horses to the carts and wagons, load the kegs of water, and get moving. When the first man arrived at the scene it was already too late, of course. Nothing could be done. Others arrived moments later, and they were just as powerless. The would-be rescuers watched from a safe distance as both buildings became nothing but glowing heaps of embers and ash.

Someone wondered out loud, "I see the young couple and the child but not the old folks. Does anyone know where are they? Has anyone seen them?" The crowd searched for the elderly couple, even looking in the outhouse, but they could not be found. And so, it was presumed the elderly couple had died in the fire and were now nothing but bones and ash.

Helpless to help, but determined to do something, the women went on the hunt and recovered a carriage blanket they deemed clean enough to drape over Neola's naked body. The rough wool blanket rubbed against Neola's blistered skin, popping the blisters, the pain so excruciating it dropped her to her knees. She very nearly passed out, but the stakes were too high, and she managed to hold on to consciousness. A scant moment later she rose back up, ignoring the pain. With the blanket clutched around her, she thanked the well-meaning women for their kindness. Then she turned and scanned the considerable crowd and calmly demanded splints to stabilize her husband's broken leg, a litter to carry him, and transport to the Village Inn.

The local drunk handed Neola his nearly full bottle of cheap whiskey. Neola knew full well the useful power of spirits and so she nodded her thanks, then dropped to her knees next to her injured husband. She uncorked the bottle and took a few tiny sips, then put the bottle to her husband's lips and tipped it up, forcing him to gulp several mouthfuls. When Neola decided Vonder had had enough, she recorked the bottle and secured it between her naked thighs.

She scanned the crowd again, her eyes landing on a sheath hanging off the blacksmith's waist. She calmly held out her hand and asked him for his knife. At first the blacksmith hesitated, but she was so intentional he found he could not refuse. Neola whispered her thanks, then set about cutting her husband's pants right off him. When she was done, she returned the knife, then uncorked the bottle again and splashed a liberal amount of the purifying spirits on the splintered bone protruding through her husband's skin.

Moments later, four men appeared and unrolled a thick, woolen triage blanket beneath Vonder. While they were at it, Neola crawled to her husband's feet, all the while hanging on tight to the precious bottle of whiskey. Somewhere along the way she had thrown off the blanket and was naked once more. She felt eyes boring into her and looked up. The four men were still there, looking at her, standing at attention, accepting her authority, awaiting further orders.

Neola knew what needed to be done and thought the four men probably did too, for their posture and behavior had betrayed them for what they really were, soldiers recently returned from some distant war.

Without hesitation, she said, "Men, I need you to hold onto his shoulders, his hips, and the leg that's not broken. I need one of you to hold the upper thigh of his broken leg and keep it from moving. Hold him in place until I tell you not to."

To a man they accepted her command and immediately assumed the necessary positions. She uncorked the bottle of whiskey and splashed a liberal amount of it on her husband's protruding bone. She stowed the nearly empty bottle of whiskey between her thighs and grabbed hold of her husband's broken leg by the ankle. As quick as she could she pulled back hard. The bone sucked in, and she gave it a hard twist. And then Neola felt the strange sensation of her husband's broken bone slipping back into place.

Working quickly, she pushed hard against the heel of his foot with one hand, while gripping his ankle with her other hand to prevent it from twisting, all in the hopes of keeping the bones locked in place. And then she waited. The four soldiers waited as well. They held their positions without a sound, their job made easier as Vonder had once again passed out from the pain.

It wasn't long before the cabinet maker and his wife pushed through the crowd and knelt by Vonder's side. The man carried three freshly carved splints made of white willow in his arms, while his wife clutched a roll of bandage material that looked suspiciously like a ruffle that had just been ripped from her own underskirt. The couple bent over Vonder and went to work. The cabinet maker laid the splints on the sides and back of Vonder's broken leg and held them in place while his wife rolled the bandages in a crisscross pattern, securing the bandages from the heel of Vonder's foot, up his calf, and all the way over his knee so it couldn't bend. She was careful to leave an opening over the wound. As soon as the ends of the bandages were tucked and pinned into place, the couple stood up and got out of the way.

Impressed with the expertise of the bandaging, Neola let go of her husband's ankle and immediately splashed the last of the purifying alcohol onto the bleeding wound. It had the unexpected consequence of reviving him. His sudden piercing screams caused most of the crowd to drop what they held in their hands and cover their ears. Thankfully, he once again passed out and lucky for everyone he stayed that way.

Neola indicated to the soldiers they could let go now of her husband and so they did. And then they took hold of the reinforced edges of the triage blanket and lifted. The blanket cradled Vonder perfectly, as they knew it would. In their war addled minds Vonder had become one of their own. They became overprotective and muscled every man, woman, and child out of the way as they carried Vonder to the blacksmith's wagon.

Anticipating the need, the blacksmith had built a ramp using the two planks he kept stored under the wagon's seat for loading purposes. The four soldiers walked up the ramp (oh so careful, oh so respectful) and onto the bed of the wagon. And when they were all aboard and in their proper places, they gently laid him down. Then they exited the wagon bed and returned the ramp boards to their proper place before heading for their tethered horses.

And once again, the women offered the naked Neola the blanket. She understood her nakedness made everyone in the crowd uncomfortable, and so she allowed the blanket to be draped over her shoulders once again. This time she anticipated the pain and was able to stand up under it without collapsing. She held her shoulders back (mostly to hold the blanket away from her blistered skin) and walked to the wagon, her dignity left intact. She climbed aboard without help, and as she kneeled at her unconscious husband's side, she took his hand in hers and kissed each one of his fingertips.

Letty, still wrapped in her parent's marriage quilt, had followed her mother onto the wagon deck, but she felt a powerful need to protect her poppa's leg and so she knelt at his feet.

The blacksmith took his seat, picked up the reins, and got the horse and wagon slowly moving towards the village. He drove as carefully as he could, hoping to avoid the potholes and the subsequent jostling and jolting they caused, but it was an impossible task as the half-moon's inadequate light cast confusing shadows across the roadbed.

Being the first group to arrive at the Village Inn, it fell on the four soldiers to arrange for a downstairs room. The Inn Keeper's bejeweled wife obliged and prepared the room for the family while the four soldiers patiently waited on the porch for the arrival of the wounded man. Within a moment of the wagon coming to a creeping halt in front of the door, the four soldiers had retrieved the boards, set the ramp, and helped Neola and Letty walk it down. Then the soldiers clambered aboard the wagon and carefully lifted the four corners of the triage blanket, lifting Vonder in the process. Slowly, they proceeded to carry him into the downstairs bedroom behind the Inn's kitchen.

Neola and Letty followed, sticking as close as possible to their man. Once Vonder was safely laid on the bed the soldiers carefully removed the triage blanket from beneath him. The oldest of the four soldiers took charge of it, folding it in a practiced, practical fashion so that it would be easy to transport, yet ever ready for use.

Neola graciously thanked the soldiers and the blacksmith for their help. The thanks embarrassed the men, for they had only done what was needed, as anyone would have. The Inn Keeper's wife served everyone in the room two fingers of brandy, Letty and herself included. And after it was drunk, she sent the four soldiers out of the room to fetch the doctor. The blacksmith accompanied them, to help with the directions.

Within minutes of the men's exit the Inn Keeper's wife had cleaned and put salve on Neola's burns and fetched a clean cotton nightgown for Neola to wear. Then she offered the homeless family free room and board for the next month and help with the nursing. Sobbing uncontrollably, Neola accepted the more than generous offer.

Insurance paid the outstanding debt on the lost inventory in the warehouse, but little else. They had made the common mistake of being underinsured and overextended. They lacked enough money or credit to rebuild the business or their home. And it was all because of a single bolt of lightning Thrown by God, God's will be done.

When it was time, the church congregation moved he and his family into the ancestral one room cottage Neola had inherited just a few months earlier when the sad news arrived that her father's merchant sailing ship had disappeared in a storm in the Indian Ocean, near Karachi. Sadly, everyone on board was presumed lost at sea including Neola's father.

Once Vonder was able, and it took a long time to be able, he worked the dock on Mondays. Most other days he carved fanciful clothespins, wooden shoes, and other useful household goods. The family sells his carvings along with orchard honey, jam, seasonal fruit, and flowers at the Saturday market in the village. Neola has a regular group of people that buy her herbs and healing tinctures.

The windmill on the ancestral property operates as a gristmill and earns a bit of money, but only in the fall. Mostly they barter for a share of flour or grains when a farmer's grain needs grinding. So far, they've had enough oats for breakfast and plenty of flour for breadmaking. But none of it gets them ahead, how can it? It's all just small change, like the petty cash the Gentleman at the docks paid him today. It's been over a week since he spent the last of the family's savings and all that he has managed to scrap up since that day is the paltry five silver coins he just earned. It's time now, well past time, that he faces the bitter truth.

Soul sucking poverty is just one wrong move away.

5

The Family

Vonder's stomach rumbles, reminding him that supper is waiting for him at home. He resumes pedaling, but soon his arm goes numb from clutching the bundle so tightly to his chest. He manages to ignore the discomfort of his arm, but after a few miles his crippled leg cramps and he's forced to drop the bike and stomp around to release the spasm. The stomping gets rid of the cramp but now he needs to give the leg a rest.

Fortunately, the huge flat-topped boulder marking the lane to the Peterson's farm is just a few steps ahead. He plants his bony ass down on the cool stone and massages his aching leg. He tries to get a good look at his neighbor's farmhouse, but his view is mostly blocked by a tangle of branches. He doesn't remember the lane being so overgrown when he checked on the elderly couple. Somehow, everything has grown out of control in a little more than two weeks. It must be from the last push of summer growth; it is that time of year. Funny the old folks never bothered to say anything about it at church services yesterday. Too proud to ask for help he guesses. He knows that feeling, he remembers it well.

The last time the lane was pruned was just after the spring flush. It was a memorable work party hosted by his church. An abundance of good food and music made the hard work of pruning seem like play. They saved the pruned wood for kindling and burned the leaves to make ash to spread in the garden. The Peterson's small woodlot needed thinning, so the blacksmith and the butcher took on the job of cutting down the weakest and most crowded of the trees. Before they left, they had cut and stacked the wood so it could dry in the summer heat. The men promised to return in the fall and move the dry firewood to the old couple's woodshed.

Vonder decides to arrange for another work party. It shouldn't be a problem. Everyone in the congregation loves the old Peterson's almost as much as they love a party, especially if they can entice the fat old fellow to bring his accordion again. He'll mention it next Sunday at the church's social hour or maybe sooner if he ends up going to the village before then. Really, there's no telling what the next week will bring and Sunday is such a long way off.

A shadow passes over head, then another. He looks up and finds two vultures circling directly above him. Their presence confuses him. He knows vultures are rare in these parts, usually appearing when a large domestic animal has wandered away from a farm and been caught in the deep muck of the marshlands and died. He sniffs the hot, still air for the scent of decaying flesh but smells none.

Oddly enough, Vonder has lost all memory of seeing the vultures earlier that day, nor does he remember the trouble they caused with the horse at the wharf. And now he just shrugs them off as if they are of no account. He mounts his bike and peddles off. After a half hour of steady cycling, he comes upon a gentle hill lush with of all manner of useful trees and shrubs. Like always, his crooked leg makes it impossible to pedal uphill and so he dismounts and walks the bike up the gradual slope.

At the top of the hill, he stops to take in the sight of his wife's ancestral windmill. Constructed of granite rocks and thick wooden beams, the windmill is three stories tall, narrow and circular in form. Attached to the vanes are adjustable, triangular pieces of canvas painted a bright white. Permanent scaffolding encircles the windmill just below the vanes providing a sturdy platform to stand on when the canvas and vanes need adjusting or repairing. The mill's purpose is to grind the local farmer's grains into flour though these days the constant flooding of the fields has reduced the grain yield so there's not much need of the gristmill.

Nearby, but well out of the reach of the windmill vanes, an enormous English oak tree grows. The family lore claims the tree was planted on the same day construction of the windmill was completed. Planting the oak tree was a good choice, two hundred years later the tree is still providing firewood for the cottage.

While Vonder inspects the mill, the two vultures land on a couple of sturdy branches near the oak tree's crown. After they tuck their wings in just so and settle their asses comfortably down on their chosen branch, the vultures peer around the premises, checking the layout for possibilities.

Vonder fails to notice.

He rolls the bike inside the mill and leans it against the wall next to the door. A quick look around the tidy space is all it takes to convince Vonder the mill is just as he left it. He exits the mill and heads across the road. His family's small flock of red hens and a lone rooster attempt to walk before him. But he's too fast and before long they resort to darting in and out of his legs trying to avoid being stepped on. For his part, Vonder hops, skips, and jumps over them as he makes his way to the cottage gate, trying hard not to laugh out loud and give his presence away. He takes a moment to stop and admire his wife and daughter while they work side by side in the kitchen garden.

They have their backs to him, and he can tell they don't know he's there. Hoping to surprise them he slowly opens the gate. But as usual the gate's rusty hinges squeak a warning. In unison, the women straighten and turn in his direction. Upon seeing who it is they break out in radiant smiles, the love expressed in their eyes genuine and welcoming.

Their expressions please Vonder. He walks into the garden smiling a smile all toothy and wide and with a smidgeon of pride in his voice he declares, "I have good news! A ship delivered a Gentleman and his cargo of six crates to the dock this afternoon and he paid me to load the crates onto the little cart for hire. Oh, and I found a bundle in the middle of the road."

Vonder briefly struggles to pull the bundle loose from the hollow of his chest. It breaks loose with a sickening sucking sound, but no one seems to notice. When he drops it onto the counter of the garden shed next to a small blue enameled wash basin the bundle goes thump, thump, thumps as it lands, but once again no one notices. And oddly enough, the memory of his strange attachment to the bundle evaporates the very instant he loses contact with it.

Vonder eyes his wife, and always up for some fun, he throws his chest out in imitation of the rooster. He struts his way to her and grabs her by her tiny waist, lifts her up, and swings her round and around till she throws her head back and squeals with delight. The tidy bun Neola had so carefully crafted that morning comes undone and her long hair escapes and swings out behind her. The rays of the late afternoon sun strike her auburn locks just so and the ends brighten. It all comes together to create the illusion of a giant fire within a halo, and it all surrounds Neola's head as she is being twirled around.

All the swinging around he's doing makes Vonder somewhat dizzy. Worried he might lose his balance and drop his wife he comes to a sudden stop. Besides, he has another, better idea of what to do and so he holds his wife still while he attempts to give her a proper kiss. But because he's still so dizzy, the kiss slides off to the side, all sloppy and wet.

Laughing, done for the moment with trying to kiss her, he attempts to set Neola safely down upon her dainty feet. But she's not having any of it. She felt her heavy wooden shoes slip off during all the energetic twirling and she absolutely refuses to touch the ground now because above all else, she hates to get her leather footies dirty, he should know better by now. To make her point, she tucks her feet under her butt, and hard as he tries, she refuses to drop her legs and stand on her own two feet.

He soon realizes her shoes have fallen off (it took him long enough and it is his fault) and so he kicks her wooden shoes beneath her. But it's still not good enough for Neola. She stares hard at the ground beneath her butt until Vonder pushes her shoes directly under her, tips them upright, and points them in the proper direction. She makes a slow show of dropping her legs and sliding her feet into her heavy wooden shoes. They both laugh at her stubbornness, her silly antics. Really his too, he was the one that started it all. They love playing games.

Because he is tall, and she is not, Neola steps back and tilts her head up so she can get a good look at him. He catches the wanton look in her eyes, and it gives him another, even better idea. He pulls her tight up against him, belly to belly. Then he drops one hand down on the cheek of her ass and firmly cups it. At the same time, he slides the big finger of his other hand along her bottom lip before reaching up and caressing the side of her face. She trembles at his touch, and he loves her more for it.

Vonder's rumbling stomach suddenly interrupts the tender moment. Everyone heard it, it was that loud. And mistaking it for hunger he declares, "You know what Neola? I am one hungry husband. I hope supper is ready. I really do. Because you know the rule, I get to eat your pretty little hand if it isn't." Vonder picks up his wife's dirty little gardener's hand and pretends to take a big bite. His antics are so ridiculous she laughs all over again.

Still playing the game, he turns to his daughter and declares, "And you, my little baby girl, only you have the power to save your momma's hand from being devoured. I demand you tell me my supper is ready to eat this very instance or else. Vonder sticks his wife's tiny hand halfway into his wide-opened mouth, apparently ready to take a real big bite. To emphasize his point, he wiggles his bushy blond eyebrows, daring his daughter to deny him.

Letty giggles. She can't help it. She claps her hands and declares, "Oh, stop it poppa! Stop being so silly. You know we made you supper, we always do." She grabs his free hand with both of hers and skips backwards, pulling him away from her momma and towards the open door of the cottage.

But Neola, the boss of the family, holds her free hand up, palm out. Well trained, Letty and Vonder dutifully stop and patiently listen as Neola issues her orders, "Hold on you two, no one's going anywhere just yet. The chores need to be finished, no exceptions."

Vonder's guts suddenly roll so loudly the trouble in the sound cannot be denied. The unripe apple Vonder so eagerly consumed earlier in the day is now on the verge of escaping in the foulest of ways. Vonder rushes off to the outhouse, not bothering to excuse himself for he hasn't the time.

While Vonder is busy doing his necessary, the women fill buckets at the well and set them down by the door. And because the dreaded rust never sleeps, Neola washes and dries the garden tools. Letty does her part by rubbing the tools down with an oily rag before storing them in the garden shed. Just as they finish, Vonder's return is preceded by the loud clap of the outhouse door slamming shut behind him.

He rejoins the women, but he only has eyes for his wife. He patiently waits while she fills the wash basin with water from the nearby rain barrel. The second she hangs up the ladle, he steps up behind her and leans the whole length of his body against hers. He pauses, savoring the touch, then a moment later he reaches around to pick up the homemade bar of gritty soap. He takes her hands in his, dips their hands in the water, and rubs the soap round and around, covering every inch of their dirty hands as he slowly creates a wonderful cleansing lather. His motions are erotic and sensual, and Neola can't get enough of his wondrous touch.

The couple reluctantly pull themselves apart and step aside so their daughter can take her turn at the wash basin. When she finishes, she picks up the basin of dirty, soapy wash water and makes a show of high stepping while tiptoeing to the far side of the garden. Her game and her goal are to not spill so much as a single drop of water. When she arrives at a designated spot, she slings the dirty water in a great sweeping arc out and over the rock wall. She looks over her shoulder to see if her parents are watching. But as always, they only have eyes for each other. Letty shrugs, and skips her way back to them, not done with having fun yet. She holds her wet hands over her head and strikes a pose, then flicks water droplets at her mother. The drops hit the side of her mother's face and instantly gets her attention. Neola breaks into a spectacular smile and mirrors her daughter's pose. Then the mother and daughter perform the silly, shimmy dance her mother learned while at the river Narmada's dock in Broach, India. They do the dance to please themselves but also to make their man laugh.

And of course, just like always, Vonder laughs as he watches the bumping of butts and the bumping of bellies. The women twirl round and around, up and down, shaking their hips and shoulders until everyone is laughing so hard, they nearly fall over.

Neola is the first to quit laughing. It's proof she really is the boss of the family. Once again, she orders them about by saying, "Come on you two. Time to go inside now."

Neola does one last spin, falls back in a swoon and lands in her husband's waiting arms. She looks up at her husband, bats her long lashes, and in an overly theatrical, bedroom voice, she invites, "Vonder my man, follow me." It's all a part of a game the couple have played many times for many years. Laughing, he stands his wife upright and retrieves the bundle. Together, twinning, they each pick up a bucket. As they walk along Neola takes hold of her husband's elbow and pretends to guide him. But really what she is doing is indulging in her desire to touch him. Letty follows her parents at a respectful distance, instinctively maintaining her parent's obvious need for intimacy.

As soon as Vonder enters the cottage he heads to his usual place at the table and tucks the bundle under his chair. Then it's just a few short steps and he's in the kitchen where he promptly sets his water bucket down between the hearth and the kitchen cupboard.

That done, he takes the three steps needed to arrive at the mirror and shelf hanging on the wall next to his bed. He removes his bright blue hat and his grey woolen vest and carefully hangs them on their accustomed hooks under the shelf. And it's then he smiles a pleased smile. He loves the way his work clothes look next to his good coat and Neola's best shawl. Neola's fancy going to town hat hangs separate and aloof befitting it's importance. The gradation of the earthy tones, colors and the textures are so subtle, so fine. He has no idea why, but he suddenly envisions ancient velvety black lichen growing in the cracks of volcanic stone, a cloudless, bright blue sky overhead.

Above the hooks, a shelf holds an almost brand-new Bible. It was a gift from the congregation meant to replace the family Bible lost in the fire. But it couldn't. All the recorded family history was lost in the fire, everyone knew it, no one talked of it because it hurt too much. His dead father-in-law's chess board and ebony and ivory pieces occupy space with the family's hairbrush and set of ivory combs (one big toothed, the other fine). A carved wooden box takes up nearly half of the shelf and contains Neola's essentials along with her sewing needles and such. The only mirror in the cottage happens to hang above the shelf. It's hung so Vonder and Letty can see their faces reflected in it if they stand with normal posture, but Neola is so petite the only way for her to see her pretty face is for her to stand on the wooden step currently tucked against the wall under the hanging clothes.

Removing his hat releases Vonder's thick head of hair. Each corkscrew curl seems to have a life of its own, going this way and that. He looks in the mirror and sighs. His hair is so long it makes him look like a clown, thank God for his hat covering his hair today, otherwise the Gentleman might not have hired him, he looks so unkept. And his five o'clock shadow needs to be attended to first thing in the morning, but not the trimming of his moustache, he can leave that for early Sunday morning, he wants to look extra sharp when he makes his proposal to the congregation about having another work party at the elderly Peterson's property.

His neck is painfully tight. He rolls it and it obliges by crunching. The lifting and stacking of the Gentleman's crates has caused the scar tissue on his back to itch and burn. He's had lots and lots of experience with this specific pain and knows it will soon pass if he just ignores it. He kneads his neck in time with his steps as he walks back to his chair at the table.

He arrives just in time to grab his wife by the waist as she slips from the chair she's standing on. He guides her upright and holds her steady so she can resume the task of lighting the kerosene lantern hanging from the beam above the table.

He feels a stab of annoyance. Neola could have been hurt. She should have waited for Letty to light the damn lantern, Letty's plenty tall enough to do it. Or he could have done it, his wife's impulsiveness is always getting her into trouble, he wishes she would slow down and think before acting but he knows she never will, it's not in her nature.

Vonder surprises his wife by lifting her off the chair and swinging her around in a tight little circle before gently settling her bottom safely down upon the chair's hard, wooden seat. Impressed with his finesse, she gives an intimate promise in her smile, making direct eye contact, reinforcing the notion. It's not a hard thing to do, locking eyes with him. His eyes make her want to. That thick black ring surrounding the light blue iris always drops her down deep and makes her belly tingle. His eyes are wolf eyes, head of the pack eyes, family eyes. Letty's eyes are the same. They even have the same corkscrew curls, though Letty's are a lighter blond. Father and daughter, so perfect, both so tall and strong. Nearly identical.

Vonder becomes restless waiting for Letty to serve them supper. He expends his pent-up energy by taking stock of their home. The cottage is so primitive, way too primitive, what on earth had he been thinking? He feels shame for allowing his family to descend to this level of poverty, their simple home nothing more than a one room, mice ridden hovel.

He rubs his hands back and forth over the oily surface of the old, scarred table, then stretches his arms from side to side, measuring the shabby old thing. He knows if he bothers to lift the lid on the table's bench seat, he'll find there's just a meager store of dry goods. He catches his wife looking at him, shaking her head no. Somehow, she knows the night's not normal, otherwise she would have spoken to him, expressing her worry Instead, she is speechless.

Vonder feels the same way. He's unable to explain his distracted air to himself, let alone to his wife. The odd feeling sticks with him and compels him to examine every nook and cranny of their home. He sees movement out of the corner of his eye and turns and catches Letty messing around at the kitchen cupboard. She's shuffling through the utensils in the only drawer in the whole of the cottage. He hopes his daughter's not looking in the drawer for the soup ladle because she'll never find it in there. He can see it hanging on the wall next to the fireplace, in its usual spot.

A pitch pocket explodes inside the hearth. The sound makes him flinch and the sudden increase of light draws him in. He sees the stew bubbling over. It's time the crane should be swung away from the fire. He forces himself to relax, it's not for him to do. He knows Letty will take care of it.

His gaze just naturally travels to the smokey green vase decorated with lotus flowers sitting on the mantle. It's an especially nice piece, the gold outlining of the flowers an especially fine touch. He remembers the moment Neola found it hidden inside an old, chipped crock in the back of the garden shed. She was sure her father had left it there for her to find some day. Playing hide and seek with precious objects was a special game they played whenever her father came home from the Indian Ocean. The cottage was their favorite place to play the game. Neola keeps the vase full of flowers and herbs all year long whether fresh cut or dried. He especially appreciates the way the sweet smell of flowers and the scent of the tangy herbs covers the sour, dusty smell of their slowly rotting old home.

At the center of the table is a leaded glass crystal bowl. It's there most every day. Today, it's filled with white and pink lilies floating in water. Neola discovered the bowl tucked inside one of the large pots stored on the bottom shelf of the kitchen cupboard. She told Vonder that she didn't consider it to be part of the hide and seek game she played with her father. Instead, she thought it was probably something her father had stowed away for his personal use once he retired. His wife makes such a lovely home, always making the best of the worst, she deserves so much more than he can ever give her.

Hovel it might be, but the form and function of the cottage is near perfect. The old, scarred table is the heart of the home, the fireplace backs it up, and they line up exactly with the only door in the whole of the cottage.

The opposing walls each have a bed and a casement window large enough to escape from if needs be. He really, really appreciates that design feature, there'll be no burning alive in this home. The frames of the beds are made of stout oak, rope netting attached to the ends and sides, allowing the mattresses to be held off the floor about hip high, a practical design Neola's father brought home from the Orient.

Each bed has a mattress and pillows stuffed with goose and duck down. And underneath each soft and forgiving feather mattress is a second mattress filled with straw. The straw is rigid yet somehow soft and forgiving all at once. Both beds are big enough for two people to comfortably occupy. The church members were kind enough to change the rope netting and stuffing in all of the mattresses along with providing down comforters and pillows on the day they moved in. And of course, their wedding quilt is covering their marriage bed, the one and only possession that survived the fire.

Life was hard after the fire. He was barely alive due to an infection that persisted most of a year. Still, when he was conscious, he tried to be of some use by applying liberal amounts of honey and soothing balm to Neola's blistered back. Neola tended his more complex injurie and somehow, they managed to survive and heal. But poor little Letty ended up doing most of the fetching and carrying, the cooking, and the gardening. She was barely eleven years old, and she always did as she was told, but she could not do it all.

The firewood was an especial problem. The local church congregation stepped in and provided split firewood, brought to the cottage every Sunday afternoon, kindling included, and they did it for well over a year. And it was that one kind act that ensured his family's survival. The church congregation also made it possible for he and his wife to make love again. While snooping around in the cottage, the minister's wife discovered four large curtain panels stored inside the table's bench seat. Once the curtains were hung, two separate sleeping alcoves were created resulting in privacy from Letty's curious eyes.

The curtain's fabric is a heavy silk colored a midnight blue. The fabric is lavishly embroidered. Scenes of stars and moons traversing the dark blue sky, of peacocks strutting across lush green lawns and lines of turtles crossing bridges spanning ponds filled with lotus blossoms are on each panel on both sides. So are scenes of bright gold and silver fish jumping in streams colored the jade green of glacier melt and scenes of mountain landscapes include a tiny couple holding hands in front of a cottage at the center of a terrace. A massive, ominous pillar of rock looms over the couple. All the upper corners are marked with tiny red and yellow embroidered tulip flowers.

The curtains are worthy of royalty, yet here they are, hanging in this hovel. Since that day, Neola has found many other essentials needed for comfortable living. Her father had carefully prepared for the day when he would retire and move into the cottage full time. Unexpected tears fill Vonder's eyes. He misses his father-in-law. It feels like a dull ache, a heavy weight. He blinks the tears away, not wanting Neola to see.

Vonder's restless eyes move on and land on the seventeenth century free-standing walnut wardrobe pushed tight against the wall opposite the kitchen cupboard. Original to the cottage, it was built in place and is far too big to ever fit through the cottage door let alone any of the windows.

The wardrobe is a genuine work of meaningful art. Carvings of fat, smiling cherubs adorn the four upper outside corners. The cherubs symbolize protection of the innocent. And at the bottom four corners, angled outward, are carvings of fierce, fire breathing dragons defending the ground. Carved flowers and leaves twine up and down the edges of the wardrobe's frame, their purpose to join protection with defense obvious. The extraordinary wardrobe is worthy of the finest of manors, would be welcomed in a castle, yet here it is, confined to this hovel, unable to leave. It makes no sense.

The sight sinks Vonder into a deep state of melancholy. A memory surfaces of Letty spending hours and hours hiding in the cupboard and behind the curtains. It was a game she played nearly every day during the first year they lived in the cottage. She declared herself the winner of the game when she heard her parent's surprised laughter when she magically reappeared and said "BOO." But her favorite game of all was enacting a silly fantasy of a prince and a princess living happily ever after on a mountain terrace in a tiny cottage above a river valley. And it's only just now that he realizes the embroidered scenes on the curtains were the inspiration for her game.

A sense of unease overwhelms him. He feels deep in his gut that something is horribly off in their small, sheltered world. He begs silently and prays secretly to his Christian God that no matter what happens, his lovely little Letty gets her happily ever after.

His feeling of unease leads him to memories of the cure Neola devised for the depression he suffered after the fire. Neola came up with the brilliant idea of his building a chest for Letty's meager pile of possessions. She scrounged dry planks of oak for the body of the chest and collected pieces of purpleheart, rosewood, lilac, and ebony wood, along with a large jar of mismatched mother of pearl buttons to use for a decorative inlay. She found all the necessary woodworking tools stored in the windmill. She relocated them to a portable bench within easy reach of his bedside.

Because he was bedridden, he had to lay on his side or sometimes his belly and work the wood, holding the boards over the floor as he sawed and planed and sanded. The day came when the dovetails all fit and with the help of his wife, he put the chest together. The inlay on the lid took much longer. Neola traded four jars of honey and a basket full of fresh sage leaves suitable for sausage making for a single large jar of collagen glue the local butcher had recently made. Vonder carved grooves in the lid and affixed tiny pieces of exotic woods and mother of pearl buttons until bouquets of stylized flowers appeared, all banded by darker geometric shapes.

As soon as he was done, and it took a long, long time to be done for he was gravely ill most of the year, Neola declared a party. The guests brought plenty of food and music. Two able bodied men, farmers by trade, carried Vonder from his bed and set him down on the chair at the head of the table. The same men placed the chest against the wall at the foot of Letty's bed. Everyone oohed and awed over the intricate inlay. But the best moment came when Letty was told the chest was to be hers and she reacted by doing a spontaneous twirling dance of pure joy.

The happy memory fades. The accounting of their home is finished. The elegant simplicity of their lives is obvious now. An odd sense of pride creeps into his heart. But the feeling quickly fades away as another wave of panic overtakes him. With considerable effort he forces the feelings out and away by doing what he has always done. He reaches out to his wife and takes both of her hands in his.

6

Letty

Vonder watches as Letty hooks the fireplace poker over the arm of the crane. She swings the stew pot away from the heat and the stew stops bubbling. Not missing a beat, she picks a few pieces of wood from the stack next to the fireplace and feeds the small fire. The wood sparks, then catches, throwing off an abundance of heat and light. She strips a long splinter from a piece of kindling and lights it on fire then uses the flame to light the beeswax candles sitting on the mantle.

Vonder can't help but marvel at his daughter's economy of movement and her never-ending willingness to be of use. But Letty doesn't stop there, there's lots more to do. She swivels around, unlatches a glass door above the kitchen counter, and takes out three wooden bowls. She fills the bowls with stew and sets one each before her parents and one at her own place at the table. Then she returns to the kitchen cupboard and picks through the jumbled mess in the drawer until she finds three ornate silver soup spoons.

The spoons glow, they shine, and most importantly, they mirror. Letty instantly becomes distracted. She holds the spoons up and turns them round and around until the light hits exactly right and a distorted version of her face pops into view. Encouraged, she stretches her mouth wide open and sticks her tongue out, wiggling it, amplifying the monstrous illusion. Mesmerized by the image, she forgets what she's supposed to be doing until she hears her mother's frustrated cry of hunger. The harsh sound breaks her concentration and ends her silly game. Letty shrugs sorry and skips her way to the table. She lays the soup spoons down beside the bowls of stew, all except for her mother's. Instead, she makes an exaggerated show of handing her mother the spoon while saying, "For you, your Highness, only for you." She finishes with a deep curtsy and is rewarded by her mother's forgiving laughter.

Encouraged, Letty walks backwards while scraping and bowing. She secretly counts her steps until she knows she's in front of the glass doors above the kitchen counter. Then she positions her hands just so over her head and claps twice to punctuate the perfection of her timing (and to get a smidgen more attention) before she spins around. Then, without missing a beat, she slips the latch on the glass door on the right side of the cupboard and swings it open while exclaiming in a perfect French accent, "Voila, voila."

With a dramatic flapping of her elbows, she takes a cutting board from a shelf and places it on the kitchen counter. The board holds a loaf of bread wrapped in a flour cloth and as she removes the cloth her fingers get all oily and slippery from the butter slathered over the crust. Behind her mother's back, Letty quickly licks each one of her greasy fingers clean before she adds a bread knife and a crock of butter to the cutting board. After placing the cutting board before her mother, she brings three metal cups and a copper pitcher full of fresh drinking water to the table. She fills her parent's metal cups, then her own, before setting the pitcher within easy reach of her poppa.

Done with her duties for now, Letty plops down on the bench

and takes possession of her usual spot, her back to the door. She locks eyes with her parents and as one they bow their heads, steeple their fingers and close their eyes.

Vonder prays out loud in a deep clear voice. He repeats the same supper prayer he learned as a small child, but slowly for now he is the man of the house and no longer that impatient boy of yesteryear.

In measured, reverential tones, he proclaims, "God is great, and God is good. And we thank him for our food. By his hand we must be fed, give us Lord our daily bread. Amen."

In perfect harmony, Neola and Letty add, "Thank-you God, Amen."

After a short, meditative pause, they all look up. Vonder and Letty's eyes gravitate to Neola and the loaf of bread. The white knuckled grips they have on their spoons signals their desperate hunger. Taking the hint, Neola cuts three thick slices of bread and slathers each one with butter before handing the first one to her husband and the second to her daughter. She leaves the smallest slice for herself.

They eat slowly, in measured bites, relishing the savory stew. For every bite they take, they dip the bread into their bowls, The butter melts into the stew, further enhancing the meal. Neola is the last to wipe her bowl clean with her final bit of remaining bread, finishing their lovely meal with the beautiful firelight, the sweet-smelling flowers. But Vonder returns to scraping his empty bowl and Letty jumps up and refills it, placing the full bowl in front of him, happy to return to her old game of giving him a deep curtsy, then a manly bow. She squeaks out a high-pitched, "Your Highness." Then, bowing her way backwards, she proclaims in a deep bass voice, "Your Majesty, Your Majesty." Immensely pleased with herself Letty just naturally giggles, the joyous sounds float away like so many musical notes in the air, her youthful exuberance impossible to contain.

Neola ignores her daughter and prepares a second piece of buttered bread for her husband even as he shakes his head no in refusal. She hands the bread to him anyway, and pleads, "Vonder, really. You need to eat more than our little woman's share, and I am sorry there are no eggs. No matter how hard we looked for a nest today, we couldn't find one. It's so annoying. The hens have been constantly moving their nests. It really makes no sense. I know they have no fear of us, they never run away when we walk among them. I wonder if they are hiding their nests from that red fox. That vixen has probably weaned her kits by now and the little foxes must all be looking for food. It is that time of year. What do you think?"

Vonder looks up from his second bowl of stew and instead of answering he takes her hand in his and gives it a quick squeeze to reassure her, and maybe himself. He bends his head over his bowl and resumes eating, making short work of his second helping. Finished, he shoves the empty bowl away and leans back, satisfied with his supper, and for the moment, satisfied with his life. He gives a loud belch and follows it with an embarrassed, lopsided grin.

Letty begins the after-dinner cleanup. She wraps the cloth around the leftover bread and stores it away in the cupboard along with the butter. That done, she sticks her hands inside a pair of thick felted mitts, takes hold of the hot handle on the stew pot, and lifts the pot free of the fireplace crane. She sets the heavy cast iron pot down at the end of the hearth where the leftover stew can cool. She leans the pot's lid against the pot, prepping her mother's final chore of the night.

The dish water needs to be heated, so Letty hangs a small tin boiler full of water on the crane and pushes it slowly over the fire, mindful not to rock and tip it, careful not to spill a single drop of water on the precious fire. While she waits for the water to heat up, she plays a game with the water pitcher, pretty much the same game as the spoon game. The hammered copper distorts differently than the smooth curved silver of the spoons, allowing for truly terrifying faces. She makes the face of a tortured angel, then that of a bug-eyed wild woman. And finally, she pulls her hair and imitates the hideous face of the legendary Medusa, her own corkscrew curls aiding in the illusion. She wiggles and giggles, until she dissolves into outright laughter. So much fun, in so little time, she can make a game out of anything, anytime she wants.

She tests the water and finds it's comfortably hot. She slowly swings the crane away from the fire and careful to use the mitts again, she lifts and slides the handle of the pitcher off the crane, then pours half of the water into the wash basin that lives on the kitchen counter. With practiced strokes, she shaves soap into the warm water, then swishes her fingers until the surface is covered in tiny bubbles. The popping bubbles ride up her fingers, roll over her knuckles, and hug up her hands till it feels just like she is being tickled. She reacts by giggling.

Then, after a few seconds of playing with the feel-good sensations, Letty returns to her chores. She pours the leftover hot water into the water pitcher, mixing the hot with the leftover cold. Then she proceeds to wash each item, rinsing them over the slop bucket, laying each item upside down on a towel laid flat on the counter. Finally, she pours the dirty dish water into the slop bucket then rinses the basin with the last cup of rinse water left in the water pitcher.

They'll need water come morning. Swinging an empty container in each hand, she skips her way out the door and to the well. She plops the containers down on the pea gravel, side by side under the spigot. Then she furiously pumps, deliberately overfilling the vessels, purposely flooding the ground, making the one mess she never has to clean up. She makes the mess most every night. She loves to do it. It usually makes her feel like she's in charge of the world. But not tonight. Tonight, she feels uncomfortable and doesn't know the reason why.

She hurries back inside with the overfilled water pitcher and tin boiler and returns them to their accustomed spots, no fooling around this time. Her last chore of the day is to empty the slop bucket. She picks it up by the handle and slow walks it to the door, keeping it steady, not spilling so much as a drop. It's a serious game she plays, because to lose would mean she'd be on her knees cleaning up the mess.

Once outside, she follows the mica flecked flagstone path to the wall just beyond the outhouse. She avoids every third stone, stretching her long, skinny legs in crisscross patterns just because she can. And once again, the goal and the game are not to spill as much as a drop. She declares herself a winner upon her arrival at the wall.

And still she's not done playing games. She lifts the heavy slop bucket to shoulder height and carefully picks her target. Quick and sharp she throws the dirty dish water out and over the wall as far as she can, away and downhill from the garden. It's another game she plays most every night, but it's the most challenging when it snows. To help her with the game, her poppa had pounded wooden stakes painted bright white into the ground in a random manner for her to aim at, the farther the stake the more points she wins, but they tended to blend in with the snow.

Just now, even though it's months away from snowing, she's managed to lose the glistening water's tail end, so she looks extra hard to find it. A movement catches her eye, maybe a moth or a bat, and she looks up and over to the eastern sky at the exact moment the full moon breaks the horizon.

The sliver of blinding light stuns her. She stops, all still now, games all but forgotten. One or two heartbeats later and she's falling in love with the sight of the rising sliver of bright moonlight. A memory bumps her mind, and she realizes the sun should be setting at the same moment. She turns to face due west, only to find she's too late, the sun has already slipped behind the hill.

It doesn't matter. She knows on this day full dark will never really have a chance. Her grandfather explained all this to her years ago, but she had forgotten all about it until now. Strange to think of her seafaring grandfather tonight, it's been more than five years since his ship was reported missing and presumed sunk somewhere in the Indian Ocean.

Her eyes find the ghostly glow of the white sails of the windmill. Next to the ancient structure an old, oak tree stands. The branches form a skeletal foreground against the gathering clouds. Two large birds, eyes glittering an evil yellow, perch on the branches near the crown of the massive tree.

Letty frowns at her sinister thoughts. A skeleton? Why would she even think of that? She's never thought of a skeleton before in all her life and can't imagine what has caused the upsetting thoughts now. And what kind of birds are even that big? She's sure she's never seen their like before. And they seem to be looking directly at her. She shivers so quick and hard, the hairs on her arms and the back of her neck stand up all on their own. It's not normal, not at all.

An owl hoots once, and a bat flies at her face. She tries to dodge out of the way, but she doesn't move quick enough, and the bat's wings brush up against her cheek. She reacts by taking an awkward step and her legs tangle with the empty slop bucket. She trips and falls and lands so hard on her tailbone it knocks the breath right out of her. It scares her, the not being able to breathe. She's barely sucking air at first, but then she's able to take a few deep, shuddering breaths. Finally, she's breathing so normal she forgets to pay attention to it. When she regains her footing, she hurries back inside. Once the door is shut tight between her and the spooky outside, she begins to doubt her own fears. She decides not to mention any of it to her parents and so she goes about putting the dishes away and hanging her apron in the usual spot. Then she gives each one of her parent's a quick kiss on the cheek and heads to her sleeping alcove.

Once there, she gazes out the window above her bed. The two

large birds are still perched near the crown of the tree, still looking at her, their eyes still a ghastly shade of bloody, bruised yellow. She turns away, determined to ignore the ugly creatures because they're not fun, not at all. She unties the bed curtains and pulls them closed. She slips off her wooden shoes and her leather footies and rolls her elastic garters and stockings down till they pop off her toes and roll away like little balls. She relaxes and giggles, then wiggles her toes, glad to have them free at last. She retrieves her balled-up stockings and bounces them on the floor a couple of times, playing games again.

A moment later she grows bored with the game and tosses them into her wooden shoes. She slips off her outer clothes and hangs them on the hooks above her shoes. She leaves her muslin chemise and underskirt on; she prefers them as nightclothes. There is no corset. Letty doesn't wear one, not ever. Neither does her momma. They have no need of corsets for they both have fine, firm figures of just naturally the right size. Letty doesn't bother to wear drawers either, except for that time of month. She likes to feel the rough fabric of her chemise and underskirt rubbing against her breasts and butt cheeks, but it's a secret pleasure, a newly found pleasure. It just feels right.

She slides under her covers and calls out, "I'm in bed now. I'm going to sleep now. Goodnight, you two lovebirds."

Her parents answer in perfect harmony, "Goodnight, baby girl, sleep tight."

But Letty doesn't sleep tight. She keeps her ears open and her eyes peeking through the perfectly placed hole in her privacy curtain. It gives her a full view of the entire cottage. She started spying from it about when the buds of her breasts bloomed. But she doesn't really think of it as spying. After all, she's sixteen years old and just wants to know about the world she inhabits.

7

Vonder and Neola

Vonder retrieves the bundle from under his chair and places it on the table between them. He pulls the five silver coins from the depths of his pants pocket and fans them out on the surface of the old, scarred table.

Neola looks at him with a twinkle in her eyes and asks, "Do you have anything else in your pants for me, husband?"

Vonder chuckles. "You are wicked, aren't you?"

Neola bats her lashes and responds in a put-on husky voice, "I learned it from you, I learned everything from you."

They laugh, understanding the night's anticipation of pleasure is no longer a promise.

Neola picks up the coins and rubs them together. She grins and exclaims, "Money, money, money! I love it! I just knew something would come our way. I had that odd notion when I woke up this morning that our luck would change. Remember I told you so? These coins are the start of that change, I just feel it!"

She pours the coins back and forth between her hands a few times, then spills them back onto the table. They shine, they glow, they're real enough to buy cheese and butter and maybe some sausage. Neola's pleased, seductive glance is not lost on her husband.

He smiles knowingly and covers one of her hands with his. He begins the pleasuring of his wife by rubbing his thumb slowly along the outside length of her thumb, sliding his thumb up her wrist, travelling slowly inside the wide sleeve of her shirt waist towards her long, slender neck. He rubs the tender spot on the inside of her shoulder at the edge of her breast, teasing, circling round and around, slowly sliding his way towards her swelling nipple until finally she gasps, and he stops.

As he withdraws his hand, he smiles the slow and lazy smile of a man who has just won a prize. Vonder whispers to his wife, a decided twinkle in his eye, "Look at you, so perfect, so ready, so pulsing with wanton desire for me." He rubs her wrist gently, again with his thumb, in a circular motion on her pulse point.

Such simple words and so simple a move cause a wonderful tingle in all of Neola's pleasure parts. Her husband has always been good at knowing the right moves, this moment is no different. She wants more. She's hungry for a kiss. A sloppy, lazy, take me to bed right now kiss. She leans forward in anticipation.

But before she gets too close, he places his finger on her lips and gently slows her down. "First things first," he says. "Let's see what's inside this bundle."

Vonder cuts the twine and unwraps the oilcloth. Inside is a worn, folded piece of paper and a foreign looking man-made object partially covering a pile of enormous tulip bulbs. The object appears to be made of eight metal panels cleverly assembled to appear as a cylinder. A wooden spindle runs lengthwise through the cylinder's center allowing it to freely rotate. Tiny fins, meant to catch air, are randomly placed on each of the cylinder's panels. He flicks one of the fins and the cylinder spins so fast the colors bleed into one. It's dizzying, mesmerizing. The speed of the cylinder's rotation creates a repetitive, squeaking sound. It's pleasant and somehow familiar. He quickly recognizes the universal sound of sex, and chuckles.

Still looking at the strange object in his hand he asks, "Neola, what is this? Do you know what this is?"

When he doesn't get a response right away, he looks up at his wife. He finds her with her hand over her heart, her face twisted in agony. He watches helpless to help as she struggles to catch her breath even as she speaks in a frightened whisper, "Oh my God Vonder, I feel like I'm being stabbed in my heart. Oh God, it hurts, it hurts. I want it to stop. Please make it stop."

Vonder lays the foreign object down and takes her free hand in his. He gives it a squeeze, it's the only thing he can think to do. He's never known his wife to have this problem before and it's concerning. The moment he lets go of the object Neola's eyes go wide in surprise and she whispers, her voice all broken and raspy, "It stopped, Vonder. The pain has gone."

It takes Neola a moment or two of clearing her throat before she fully recovers her voice. She thinks about what just happened and declares, "I think my chest pain is what the old folks would call the heartburn, probably caused from too much garlic and pepper in the stew. It just means I'm getting old. I'm sure it's nothing to be worried about. And now to answer your question. That strange-looking object does look familiar. If I remember right, it's called a prayer wheel. I used to watch people buy and sell them all the time at the ports my father's ship visited. This prayer wheel looks like it belonged to someone special, maybe someone wealthy, possibly a woman or maybe a child. I wonder should we give it to Letty?"

Painted in three colors, the most dominate being a brilliant, luminous green, the prayer wheel's second color is a deep, blood red, while the third color appears to be real gold beaten into miniscule grooves.

Vonder reluctantly hands it to his wife. She thoughtfully examines each portion of it, then waves it in the air. She flicks the fins, and as the cylinder spins her eyes go blank. Vonder reacts by wrappings his hand around the spinning cylinder, stopping the motion, putting an end to its hypnotic power. He loosens her grip on the handle, one finger at a time until finally he gently removes it from her hand. He watches with amazement as Neola's eyes regain focus.

"No," he says, "No, it's not a toy for our Letty. I don't think it's a toy at all." He's leery of it now, and since the novelty has worn off, he sets it aside, out of her reach, and they forget about it for the moment.

Instead, they stare at the pile of tulip bulb. He takes the errant bulb from his pocket and adds it to the heap. Together, they count the bulbs and arrive at the same amount at the same time. As one they shout, "Twenty-one." Too late they realize they've become too loud, and not wanting to wake Letty, they lean in towards each other to whisper. But instead, they end up kissing long and deep. Once they come up for air, they share the job of separating the two colors of bulbs into two piles, silently counting out sixteen red tinted bulbs and five bulbs blushed yellow. They whisper their wonder to each other over the size of the bulbs, and how very odd of the bulbs to be blushed red or yellow, for it's not a normal trait.

Letty's been spying on them from the comfort of her soft feather bed. She's fascinated by the prayer wheel and sorry to see her poppa set it aside. She watches her parents take turns counting a pile of boring old tulip bulbs. When they finish counting, her mother picks up the dirty old piece of paper and carefully unfolds it. Letty catches flashes of red and yellow at the paper's opposing corners. To get a better view she leans out of her bed, but she goes too far, and she's forced to throw her hands down on the floor to keep from hitting her head. And it's then she accidentally bites her tongue so hard it bleeds and swells. The swelling's so bad it makes her talk funny for the next few days. But somehow, she manages to keep from crying out, she's that intent on keeping her spying a secret.

Still whispering, Neola reads out loud, "Wanted: HOLLAND HORTICULTURAL SOCIETY will pay ten thousand English pounds for tulip bulbs recovered from the place of origin believed to exist somewhere west of the Tien Shan Mountain range and north of the northern most region of India. Must produce proof of origin location.

Neola rereads the letter out loud again for Vonder's benefit. As Neola absorbs the meaning understanding dawns. Her hands begin to tremble and the paper shakes in response. She makes direct eye contact with her husband, holding his thoughtful gaze for many long moments. Finally, she returns her attention to the missive, and after silently reading it again, she lays it down at the corner of the table and promptly covers the tulip bulbs with her shaking hands in a somewhat protective gesture, suggesting an unconscious desire for ownership. Her face reflects the shock she feels as she processes the value of the bulbs now in their possession.

The husband and wife are both quiet, lost now to their internal worlds. They stare at the two piles of bulbs. Then they stare some more.

Neola makes eye contact with her husband. She leans in close, and whispers, "The tulip bulbs are worth ten thousand pounds to the HOLLAND HORTICULTURAL SOCIETY. It's a small fortune. How on earth did you come by this bundle?"

Vonder's visibly upset and suddenly stands, then starts pacing. He hesitates before speaking, for he is a deliberate man, and a mindful one. Not wanting to overthink it, he pushes on, presenting just the physical facts, for it is his fervent belief that truth is always found in physical facts.

Ever mindful of his sleeping daughter, Vonder barely speaks above a whisper as he explains, "Neola, this afternoon when I was loading the last crate the horse suddenly moved the cart and caused the crate to miss its mark and fall to the ground. I saw the lid pop open, but I failed to notice the bundle fall out or see it roll under the cart. By the time I discovered it lying on the ground the Gentleman had already driven out of sight, the dock office was closed, and there was no one left to give it to. And really Neola, everyone has tulips in Holland, you know this. Other than the unusual size, why would I think the bundle was in any way valuable? I thought it was a gift from God for the garden, a little thing, a bonus. But you must know that letter changes everything. I must find the Gentleman first thing in the morning and return his property to him."

Trying to keep her voice down but doing a poor job of it, Neola comes right out with it and says, "It's so much money, Vonder. It could be the answer to all our prayers. We could sell the tulip bulbs and leave this flooded hell Holland has become. We could start all over in the colonies or America. Most everyone we know has already left and taken their children with them. There isn't even one single young man left in this area for Letty to marry! Do you want her to become a sacred sister? What more must we endure? The hand of the good God above reached down and placed those tulip bulbs in front of you for a reason. Please Vonder, please believe it. The bundle was meant for us and that's why you found it."

Letty has heard most every word. It's true the floods and the killing cough have driven most families to the safety of the colonies or to America. Her own family had remained in Holland because they had no means to move. Besides, her mother held the deed to the cottage, so they had a free place to live and there was enough food grown in the gardens and orchards to keep them from starving.

Letty hadn't really noticed a shortage of young men before, but now that it's been brought to her attention, she realizes it's true. And what on earth is a sacred sister? The words sound strict and lonely and not much fun. Hoping for more clarification, Letty leans in closer to the hole in the curtain.

Vonder is lost in deep thought. He shakes his head no, as he paces back and forth, trying to work it out. He comes to an abrupt halt and grabs Neola by her thin, narrow shoulders. He looks hard into her stubborn eyes, searching, desperate for consensus. "How can we sell the tulip bulbs? How would we even do that? And is it the right thing to do? After all, they belong to the Gentleman. I think it's best I find him first thing in the morning and return the bulbs. He'll surely want them Neola, you know he will."

Neola stiffens and shrugs his hands off her shoulders. She responds with a quick flash of anger, hissing, "Whatever are you thinking, husband? We can't give them back. They're for us. God gave them to us, don't you see? They're a miracle, a gift, like manna from heaven, the bible tells us so. Of course, we can be the ones to sell them, it's what we used to do before the fire destroyed the import business. No one will think twice about our selling them. Please Vonder, don't give them back. Please don't do that to us, this is our one and only chance, I just know it."

Neola's green eyes spark, shooting arrows of anger at Vonder, daring him with a look to disagree with her. For many long, silent minutes they glare at each other, trapped in the first serious disagreement of their marriage, neither willing to be the first to give in and give ground. Never have they had a separation of purpose, but now the monstrous tulip bulbs have split them apart, the possibility of money for nothing cracking the shell of their once perfect love.

The sudden boom of a hard knock on the door breaks the impasse. Caught off guard, Vonder and Neola share worried looks. The knock comes unbidden. No one ever comes to their home this late at night. After all, the road dead ends in front of the cottage and becomes nothing but a path that disappears into the marshlands.

Neola jumps from her chair. She holds her hand out to Vonder and he takes it, the tense moments between them all but forgotten because the unexpected is happening now. As one, they bravely approach the door. Without warning, wood pitch explodes in the fireplace and the room blooms a ghastly shade of bruise yellow, exposing the drying herbs hanging from the rafters. Startled, Neola throws herself into the safety of her husband's waiting arms. The room brightens, then dims. Embarrassed, they release each other, shaking their heads at their foolish reactions. After all, this is their home, they have nothing to be afraid of.

And just as they think this, damned if someone on the other side of the closed door doesn't start pounding so hard the door shakes. In fact, the door is bulging in and out from the force of the blows and appears to be on the verge of popping its hinges. A sudden, sharp crack sounds and a split in the upper panel of the door appears.

Vonder puts his finger to his lips to silence his wife, shaking his head no. He gently pushes her to the side, away from the door and out of harm's way. Neola stands flat against the wall, quiet and afraid, but safely hidden from sight.

Bracing himself, Vonder jerks the door open and takes one quick step forward, blocking the entry to his home while bravely confronting his fate. Standing at the door is the Gentleman from the docks. Vonder recognizes the man and tries to speak but he can't quite do it. He's struck dumb by the challenge contained in the man's angry eyes.

Vonder's surprised, yet not.

A gust of wind blows through the opened door and propels the missive off the table and onto the floor. Another gust pushes the missive along until it slides under Letty's curtains. She captures it, not knowing why, just doing it, and hides it under her pillow. Then just as quick as she can she resumes spying on her parents, and now, the Stranger.

The Gentleman confronts Vonder by asking, "You're the workman with the bright blue hat, aren't you? You worked for me this afternoon. You did, didn't you? You were the man who loaded my crates at the docks today. Right? Am I right?"

The man waits for a response and when he gets none, he continues his tirade, "Now I know I paid you good money for the job, you do agree with that, don't you? So where is it? Where is my bundle of tulip bulbs? You stole it, didn't you? And who the hell told you I had tulip bulbs worth a small fortune?"

The Gentleman's aggressive accusation of theft is so shockingly untrue that Vonder is still struck dumb. Vonder's silence further enrages the Gentleman. Raising his voice, he demands, "You tell me right now who it was told you or I swear to God I'll beat the holy shit right out of you right now, you hear me you god damned no good thief!"

Vonder has no idea what the man is talking about. No one told him about the bundle of tulip bulbs. Vonder's confused. He needs a quiet moment to collect his thoughts so he can explain the afternoon's events in a reasonable manner. But unfortunately, the Gentleman has pushed beyond the limits of common civility and is demanding an immediate response.

Vonder remains tongue tied and his failure to respond further unhinges the Gentleman. He loses all semblance of normal. He takes one intimidating step forward, gets in Vonder's face, and screams his accusations, "You're a thief, aren't you? You're a worthless, spineless piece of shit thief! You stole my tulip bulbs, didn't you? Didn't you! Now just admit it god damn it!"

The Gentleman shakes with frustrated righteousness. It throws him off-center, and he stumbles on the uneven flagstones of the threshold of the cottage. To regain his balance, he compensates by stepping ever so slightly to one side.

He grabs the doorframe for support and that one simple move enables him to see around Vonder's large frame and into the home.

When he spies the prayer wheel and the tulip bulbs piled on the table his violent lizard brain comes out of hiding, fully formed and fully unleashed. Spiraling out of control, insane with rage, he uses both his powerful hands to grasp Vonder by the throat.

He wants to kill him. He'll do it. He'll kill that guilty, worthless, subhuman piece of shit. This time he'll not let the thief get away with what he has done.

The accusations and attack have happened so fast Vonder has been caught off guard. He wanted to explain to the Gentleman how he found the bundle lying in the road after the cart had driven off. And how it was his intention to return the bundle to the Gentlemen the next morning just as soon as the Gentleman could be found.

But now Vonder can't. He is being choked to death. He can't breathe, never mind being able to speak. In self-defense, he latches onto the Gentleman's neck, squeezing back with all his might. He tries to shove his elbows inside the other man's arms to break his hold. But he can't. He can't bust loose from the Gentleman's death grip.

They turn and twist and bash each other's heads into both sides of the hard oak frame of the doorway, splitting each other's heads wide open as they fight for dear life. Blood gushes from the gaping wounds on each of their heads, obscuring their ability to see, and still they battle on.

Their legs give out and they collapse onto the floor, and still their death grips remain unbroken. They roll over and over each other until they come up against the heavy oak table. The force of the collision shakes the table so violently that the five silver coins, the tulip bulbs, the prayer wheel, and the crystal bowl full of beautiful flowers slide off and scatter across the cottage floor, the crystal bowl shattering into lethal shards.

And still the men don't stop, they don't let go. They can't. The fierce battle rages on until they end up at the fireplace with the Gentleman straddling Vonder. Using the last of his strength, he smashes the back of Vonder's head repeatedly into the hearth's rough stone edge. In turn, Vonder uses the last of his remaining strength to squeeze the very last breath from his attacker.

Each man's skin and lips turn blue from lack of oxygen. Bright red blood drips from their countless wounds. The home fills with the stench of iron and copper, piss and shit. And still, neither man gives up or gives in until they finally collapse one on top the other. And there the men remain, motionless, without a single twitch to give proof of life.

8

The Stranger and Neola

The cold, white light of the full moon shines through the open door and lays bare the grisly horror. All sounds are absent from the small world of the cottage. No rustlings of animals or calls of the night birds float in on the gentle breeze. The wife and daughter remain as still as marble statues, their frozen hands cover their paralyzed mouths, their unblinking eyes big and round, their breath barely stirring.

The full moon continues to shine through the open door as if nothing at all has happened. Witness to the violence, it remains indifferent to the results, the face of the man in the moon smiling as if the world were still happy and sane.

As if on que, swarms of bats fly from the attic spaces of the windmill, so numerous they become dense as a cloud. The living cloud blocks the light of the moon, establishing pitch black as the sightless ruler of the night. The cottage darkens in a very sudden and frightening way.

But no cloud can hold, and so the bats disperse and release the captured moon's light.

And still no one has moved.

Out of the long, long silence there comes the sound of a heart-wrenching sob. It's the girl, it's Letty. She rolls off her bed and yanks her curtains aside. On bare feet she runs to her mother, ignoring the slimy, slippery blood, not yet aware of the lethal shards of broken glass.

She whispers, "Momma? Momma?" She pauses for a few seconds and when her mother fails to respond, she panics, really panics, and screams, "Momma!"

And still nothing happens, nothing changes. Her mother remains unmoving, a vacant, detached look on her slack-jawed face. Letty latches onto her mother's wrist and yanks on her arm, tugging hard, desperate to get her attention.

Neola wakes to the waiting nightmare. She ignores her daughter and instead whispers her husband's name. "Vonder? Vonder?" She takes three hesitant steps towards her husband's bleeding body. Sobbing, she begs, "Please God no, not my Vonder."

Vonder shudders. Neola frowns at the sight of the blood seeping out from under her husband's head. She wonders at the miracle. She knows he should be dead, but he's not.

She tiptoes to her husband's side and drops to her knees. She clasps her hands in prayer, bows her head, and whispers, "Thank-you God, thank you." She lays across the back of the stranger's inert form to reach her beloved husband's face.

Once there, she kisses his bloody forehead again and again as she whispers, "I'm here Vonder. I'm here. I'll take care of you. I promise you I'll fix you just like I did after the fire."

She cups his face in her shaking hands and kisses him ever so gently on his lips and eyelids. Her hot tears mingle with the blood on his face and flows as rivulets over his chin, rolling down his neck, sliding under his shirt, until finally the rivulet of blood pools on his barely beating heart.

A release of breath and a groan escape from under Neola's belly. A tiny bit of movement, a mere suggestion of some other life captures her attention.

It's that Stranger, the Gentleman.

She's laying on her belly on top of that murderous man holding the love of her life's bloody head in her hands. She's been praying to God for all she's worth to save her husband's life, and what does she feel? That murderous man moving under her. He's not dead, not at all.

The Stranger twitches and groans. Her eyes track his head as it shakes ever so slightly. His arms seek purchase on the floor, and he tries to rise, her slight weight barely a hindrance.

The nerve of that man. How dare he still be alive after all the damage he has done. The blood drains from Neola's face as she stares straight ahead.

Lost and turned inward, her mind wanders to someplace unsafe. Her hands clench and unclench, itching to do something, her eyes desperately search the room for the what to do. Her glance takes in the left-over supper, and white-hot anger explodes with a purpose.

She rears up, a deranged animal, an avenging angel, appearing larger than life. And without a moment's hesitation, she picks up the heavy cast iron stew pot and smashes it into the back of the Gentleman's head with all her fury and might. Again, and again she hits him until the bone in the back of his head cracks with a terrible sound and his head caves in. His blood and brains ooze out and chips of bone fall away.

And still, she cannot stop hitting him. Finally, her strength is used up and she can do no more, she is done.

And the Stranger? Well, he's good and gone.

Neola throws the cast iron pot aside and rolls the dead man's body off her husband as if it weighed nothing.

The heavy weight removed, Vonder rallies. He moans, his eyes flutter. She gently raises him to a sitting position and hugs him, and with that loving act she helps him to stand. Holding him steady she kicks one of his feet forward, then the other.

And in this way, she walks him the few steps to their marriage bed. Holding him steady with one arm wrapped around his waist she strips back their marriage quilt with the other. She turns him around and helps him to sit down. Then she lifts his legs, swings them onto the bed and gently, ever so slowly, she leans him back till his crushed, bloody head is cradled on his soft, feather pillow.

Neola stares into her husband's dilated pupils. She's hoping for some sign of recognition but sees none. She knows yet refuses to believe in what her eyes are showing her.

She decides her eyes are being disloyal and so she looks away but only for an instant. She needs to look at him, her one and only love. But when she re-examines him, she finds nothing has changed. Vonder's eyes are still empty.

Desperate to make a difference, she turns to their daughter and begs, "Bring me some water and a cloth. Make it cold and make it clean. Hurry up now child. Your poppa's life depends on it."

Habit compels Letty to obey her mother. Moments later she sets a bucket of water at her mother's side and hands her a clean cloth. Neola wets the cloth and gently sponges the blood from Vonder's face and hands. She unbuttons his shirt and examines his bloody neck and chest for signs of any injury that could be life threatening. She finds fresh bruises and the old scar tissue from his burns.

As she lifts his head, she touches the back of it. Her heart skips, the natural rhythm becoming as broken as her man. Her face reflects horror as her fingers caress the back of his crushed skull. She feels the dents and bloody splits and something else she shouldn't. She understands the awful truth of it yet pretends she doesn't.

Letty has caught sight of the changing emotions flickering across her mother's face. She's absorbed her mother's fear but doesn't quite know what to make of it. The unknown causes her to take several steps back from the sick bed. She makes a sudden decision and turns towards the open door, ready to bolt.

Out of the corner of her eye Neola sees the movement. She realizes what her child is about to do and reacts by shouting, "No! No! Don't run away. You can't. Your poppa needs you. I need you. Please don't leave us Letty, don't do that. No, no, no, don't go." She drops to her knees, her legs too weak to hold her. She reaches out to her daughter, a supplicant to her minor child.

Letty turns to face her mother, the mention of her poppa enough to turn the tide of her motion. But she can't ignore the violence she just witnessed. Her mother committed murder by crushing a man's head into a bloody pulp and she did it without a moment's hesitation. Letty's afraid now, afraid for her poppa, afraid of the dead man, but most especially, she's afraid of her own mother. She changes her mind again and takes a step backwards, then turns towards the open door, towards outside and far away.

Neola leaps to her feet and chases after her daughter. She grabs Letty by the arm and yanks her so hard and so quick that Letty loses her footing and falls to her knees. She cries out in surprise at her mother's rough treatment.

Neola ignores her daughter's cries and instead pulls her upright then drags her towards Vonder, all the while screaming, "Stop it Letty, just stop it! Your poppa needs you. We're in trouble here and that includes you, too. We're a family for God's sake. Do you want us to all go to prison? Yes, Letty, you'll be put under arrest, too. They're sure to think you helped steal those tulip bulbs and kill that man. Do you really want to go to prison? Do you really want to hang for murder?"

Anger replaces the fear that had gripped Letty a moment ago and she pulls free from her mother's restraining hand. Her hands ball into fists, and she stares defiantly into her mother's crazed eyes, a disgusted expression revealing her true feelings.

At first her mother is confused by Letty's reaction, but then understanding dawns and Neola goes on the defense. "What? What else could I do? He was trying to kill my husband. He was trying to kill your poppa. Your poppa! He would have ruined us. He has ruined us! Oh Letty, I couldn't help myself. I really couldn't. I couldn't stop."

An anguished moan escapes Vonder. The sound draws their attention. They watch as Vonder is overcome by a violent seizure. The mother and daughter move in tandem, forgetting the conflict as they rush to his side. They stand over his bed, helpless to help and when the seizure finally comes to an end Vonder is barely breathing and clearly comatose.

The kerosene lamp hanging over the table picks that moment to sputter out. The fire has burnt down to the last little bit of knotty wood, providing the faintest of light. The oilcloth the tulips were wrapped in is lying near the andiron and a lick of flame reaches out and touches it causing it to ignite. The explosion of light draws the women's attention to the fireplace. The flames reveal a few tulip bulbs at the edge of the hearth and the suggestion of more against the grate. A pocket of pitch explodes and illuminates the battle scene. The dead Stranger can be seen lying on the floor on the far side of the hearth. His blood and brains have leaked from his busted skull and formed a thick pool. The sight brings it all home to them. After all, it's not just truth that is found in physical facts, it's also justice.

Letty whispers, "What do we do?

Neola answers, "I don't know."A horse whinnies and they hear the stomping of hooves. They jump, spooked, and grab hold of each other's hands. They tiptoe to the open door and peer out into the moonlit night. Their fear of discovery dissipates as soon as they see the Stranger's horse and cart tied to a tree at the far side of the mill.

Evidently, the Stranger had approached the cottage on foot, sneaking up on them, they know not why.

Neola shakes her head no, no, no as she steps back from the doorway. Her face clouds with confusion and fear. She moves to the table and collapses onto the bench. Tears stream down her cheeks as she watches seizure after seizure roll through the beaten body of her comatose husband. The keening sound of a wounded animal escapes from deep inside her and she hugs herself, shivering uncontrollably from the shock of it all. Letty remains in the doorway looking out at the moonlit garden. She stares at the cart and horse, finally understanding the problem.

Thinking out loud, Letty- acknowledges, "We need to get rid of the horse and cart, momma, they're evidence. We need to do it right away."

After a long, long silence, Neola drags out a response, "I know it, but how will we do that? (Sadly, softly) I don't know how to do that."

The hopelessness in her mother's voice triggers alarm bells in Letty's mind. Her mind spins with crazy thoughts and gruesome images. She has just enough sense left to know she's teetering on the edge of madness. To ground herself, she takes stock of her home. Her poppa is lying on his back in his bed, unconscious, near to death. Blood, especially blood, broken shards of glass, gigantic tulip bulbs, and spilled stew are strewn everywhere. Near the hearth, lying in a pool of blood is a dead man. Her mother, the boss of them all, has become lost inside herself, unable to make eye contact and barely able to communicate.

And worst of all, an evil atmosphere permeates the cottage, the moon's cold light stretching shadows off the rafters, the herbs hung to dry creating the illusion of multiple gallows

9

The Dead Stranger

In the center of the last piece of burning firewood a knot's pocket of pitch explodes and illuminates the entire cottage. And just as quickly as it burns bright, it burns out. Letty's eyes go wide with the sudden understanding of the what to do.

Bouncing with excitement, she exclaims, "That's it, that's it. We can burn the cart, momma! The cart is mostly made of wood. We can make a big bonfire under it and burn it just like firewood!"

Letty picks her way through the debris to her mother's side. She seizes her mother's trembling hands and expands on the idea, "We can take the cart down the path to the low spot, on the back side of the hill where no one will notice the flames. But we need to be careful, momma. The Peterson's might use their outhouse and see the smoke. What do you think?"

Neola revives just enough to whisper her approval, "What a good idea. But I doubt we need to worry about the Peterson's. They've become so old they probably pee in their slop bucket at night instead of going to the outhouse. You know the burning of the cart will take a whole lot of wood and such. And to draw the air to feed the fire properly we should not only build the fire in the bed of the cart, but we should also build a small fire on the ground. And I must tell you, it's quite possible the metal parts will refuse to burn."

Neola appears relieved the problem of disappearing the cart has been resolved but fails to lift a hand to make it so. Instead, she leans towards Letty and whispers, "But what do we do about the dead man?"

"I don't know about that momma." Letty's voice fades away as she glances at the dead man. Even in the dim light she can make him out. The pool of blood is still expanding. To glance was all wrong, it's all so wrong, she should not have looked. Letty edges towards the door while whispering, "Please, please God, why can't he just disappear?"

Neola suddenly realizes her daughter is on the verge of running away again. Neola's so terrified of being left alone with the hell of it all she leaps off the bench and grabs one of Letty's elbows from behind. She spins her daughter around till they are within an inch of touching noses. Oddly enough, the act of restraining Letty has stimulated Neola's mind and she comes up with an answer to their big problem. Excited, she exclaims, "Letty, Letty. Wait. Just wait for a minute, we can burn him, we can burn him up with the cart and if we do it hot enough, nothing but ash will be left. It might seem harsh, but that's what happened to your grandparents. Remember how the whole village searched through the ashes, looking for their bodies? They couldn't be found because they had become nothing but ash. The reason that happened was because the fire was so fast and hot. We can do the same thing. We can disappear him so he's nothing but smoke and ash. We'll need lots of wood and straw to make it happen. We can do it Letty. I know we can do it!"

Letty absorbs the idea, considering. She holds still, deliberately making her mother worry for the outcome before nodding her head in agreement. And then she makes her one demand, "All right, all right. But I remember the house fire too, momma. You scared me when you threw me out that burning window, you did it so fast. I want to trust you now, I do. But I saw you kill that man, and you did it fast, and you scared me all over again. Now I want you to promise me you are done doing things fast, else I won't help you."

Neola gently pushes Letty's hair behind her ears, stroking that most hidden and sensitive of spots, calming her daughter with the repetitive gesture, calming herself, too. Quite a few heartbeats pass before Neola answers. "Yes, Letty. Yes, my sweet baby girl," she says. "Of course, I promise. But we still have one more problem. The tulip bulbs are worth a small fortune, and when people start looking for the dead man, they'll also be looking for the bulbs. Most likely they'll come here because that mean old clerk at the shipping office will tell the authorities your poppa was working the dock the day the ship was unloaded. But we don't really have time right now to clean the house, it'll have to wait until after the cart is burnt. We'll just have to take our chances that no one will come."

Letty takes a minute to think about it. She's not stupid, and so she challenges her mother by asking, "Really momma? Why can't we just explain what happened? And if they saw the way the house looks right now, they'd know that the Stranger attacked poppa first. There'd be no reason to put us in prison, let alone hang us."

Neola shakes her head no as she replies, " Everyone in the region remembers the fire and they all know how poor we are because of it. It's no secret we're hand to mouth surviving. They would never believe we were innocent, not when they discover the true value of the tulip bulbs. And besides, the dead man was hit in the back of his head, now that doesn't look like self-defense, does it?"

Letty shakes her head no, then takes a new tack, "But momma, I didn't do anything wrong, why can't I just run away? Pretend I was somewhere else when the Stranger showed up?"

Visibly frustrated, Neola lays it all out again. "Letty, Letty. You have nowhere else to go, you have no other family. And besides, you're plenty big and strong enough to help kill a man. You're sixteen years old, old enough in the eyes of the law to know right from wrong. Only the guilty run away, you know that. They would catch you in a heartbeat and hang you from the nearest tree. They wouldn't even bother with a trial."

Neola is so serious Letty believes her. Her response to her mother's words is to throw a tantrum the likes of which her mother hasn't witnessed since Letty was a little toddler. Letty collapses to the floor, her bare butt cheek just missing a viscous shard of cut crystal. At first, she pounds her thighs with her fists. But when that fails to bring relief, she grabs handfuls of her hair and yanks her head back and forth while shouting, "no, no, no, no, no, no, no." Finally, a scream of intense pain mixed with primal rage erupts from her throat and fills the cottage.

Neola instinctively covers her ears and hunkers down, fearing what Letty might do next.

Pulling her hair really hurt something fierce, but it also helped Letty to think. Her mother is right. Everyone knows her family lost all their money in the fire and their business, too. And her poppa is unable to speak his truth. Besides, her momma really did kill that man and Letty would have to say so if she was asked. She's not been raised to be a liar. She can't even think of one lie she's told in her whole life. She lets go of the fistfuls of hair. Her sobs become sniffles.

Letty's surrender is obvious. Neola takes advantage and becomes the boss of the home once again by declaring, "Now, I'll be the one to drag the dead Stranger out to the road, and you be the one to go to the windmill and get the firewood and straw. Collect as many branches as you can and load everything onto the cart. When you think it's full enough get more, go higher. Then bring the horse and cart to the cottage and tie the horse so the back of the cart is even with the gate. Hurry up now child, we need to get the burning done before daylight, we don't want people to notice the smoke and come looking for the cause.

Letty runs across the road to the cords of firewood her father stacked against the windmill's wall. She fills her arms and carries the firewood to the side of the road. She does it six times and creates a sizable pile. Under the old oak tree, she gathers twigs and the little branches broken off by the twisting winds. The dry moss on the twigs and branches will help start the fire. She drops the kindling next to the firewood and moves on to the next task. She enters the dark windmill and wedges the door open so she can come and go without hindrance. The full moon's light spills through the doorway and highlights the natural golden glow of the pile of straw. A six-paned window set at just about head height adds extra illumination and Letty takes advantage of it by looking around, memorizing what's where for future reference. She knows nothing's normal now, every little thing matters.

It doesn't take her long to gather the straw and load it in the cart and once it's done it's time to handle the dead man's skittish horse. Letty approaches the horse slowly while making all the proper soothing sounds. And before she takes hold of the bridle with one hand, she's already gently stroking his forehead with the other. She leans in close and blows warm air into his ear while talking of sweet nothings. The beast falls under her spell and allows her to lead him to the pile of wood. She wraps the reins around a handy limb on the old oak tree and slowly loads the wood in the cart so as not to startle her new friend. When she finishes, she unties the horse and leads him to the cottage.

The moon has progressed in its nightly travels and is well on its way to the western horizon. Cloud's scud across the night sky, pushed by a rising wind. A storm is brewing. Letty shivers and hugs herself, the sudden fear she felt after supper has once again returned.

While Letty has been busy with her chores, Neola has been taking care of business, too. She headed straight for the fireplace and built a small, intense fire to light up the surrounding floor. Then she studied the dead man for a moment before leaning over his feet and yanking off his heavy boots. She shoves a hand inside each boot and feels around, lifting the sole liners, searching for anything out of the ordinary, but finds nothing. She rolls down his hose and pulls it off, and still finds nothing. Finally, she checks the bottom of his feet in case something stuck to his soles, but again there is nothing.

She checks his pockets then feels the stitching of every piece of clothing he's wearing including the band of his hat. She takes nothing at face value and searches for secret pockets built into the garments. She takes her time and is richly rewarded for her efforts. Along with finding a multitude of silver and gold coins loose in his pants pockets she discovers two bags of gold coins plus an old beaten-up Swiss compass in a tiny pocket cleverly distanced away from any other type of metal. While checking the pocket on the left side of his vest Neola uncovers a simple gold watch and chain.

As she unhooks the watch fob from the buttonhole in the vest's pocket, a secret pocket spreads open behind it. Neola slides her fingers in and pulls out a thick stack of newly minted English banknotes. She finds an equal number of banknotes in an identical hidden pocket on the right-hand side of the vest. She consolidates the money in the largest of the two bags then throws the empty bag on the fire. She continues her search and discovers his leather billfold tucked in another inside coat pocket. The billfold contains several documents and quite a few freshly minted English bank notes. She decides to leave the documents in the billfold but adds the banknotes to the bulging bag of money. There's just enough room to add the compass and the gold pocket watch.

Although the bag is plumb full of valuables, she's not quite done with the picking. She unbuckles the dead man's belt, pulls it free of the loops on his waistband, then checks to see if his belt is a money belt, but it's not. The leather knife sheath that was hanging on the belt has slid free and dropped to the floor. She pulls the knife free of its sheath and looks inside the sheath but finds it to be truly empty now. The knife has an inscription etched into the steel just below the handle. The script is beautifully done in delicate curlicues. It's not the usual crude work of a village blacksmith but instead the work is that of a talented jeweler.

Neola mouths the words, "For J.V. Love Always W.V. The initials mean nothing to her and not knowing what else to do she slides the knife back in the sheath. She can't put it in the money bag, it's far too big. Not knowing what else to do with it she places it on the table and immediately forgets about it. The knife's not important right now, big money is talking.

She knows she needs to hide the money bag and the billfold but the only safe place that comes to mind is with her husband. She hurries to her sleeping alcove and stuffs the bag and wallet between the two mattresses near the bottom of her marriage bed. Then she rushes back to the dead man, grabs hold of his bare ankles, and walks backwards while dragging him through the slippery mess of blood and stew.

He's so much bigger and heavier than she is. She can barely pull his dead weight. When she finally manages to make it to the door exhaustion forces her to stop and take a rest. Her back is hurting something fierce, almost like it's on fire again, and she's so short of breath she's gasping for air. While she recovers her breath, she glances about her home.

The fire's glow has illuminated her route to the door. The sight makes her gag. The dead Stranger's lumpy brains have trailed out behind him in a long, stringy train. Chunks of hair attached to little pieces of chipped bones have broken loose from the back of his skull and dropped off along the way, the fragments are glowing an eerie almost ghost-like white. But it's the excessive damage to his head that's of real concern, for she never knew she could be that violent.

She thinks on what has happened and what she's done. There's no going back now, no undoing of the deed. She knows what she is now, she's a murderer and oddly enough the thought gives her added strength. Her breathing returns to normal. Taking a rest was necessary, but the night's quickly passing, and she really needs to get the dead man to the road. And so, with lots of grunts and groans and wiggling of his pockets and waistband to bust him loose from every little bumpy jagged edge of the flagstone path he somehow manages to get caught on, she gets him to the gate.

And once again that's about all Neola can do. She drops his ankles and stays bent over, her hands on her knees, her back to the road. She sucks the night air in so hard, so fast, she makes the sound of a whooping crane. After several minutes she manages to catch her breath and that's when she turns around and looks at the garden's gateway.

Letty's standing in the gateway holding the horse's bridle. She's staring at the ground behind her mother, staring at the dead man and the trail of blood and brains. Her eyes have bugged out and her mouth has become frozen in a circle shaped by a silent scream.

Neola gently takes the reins from her daughter's limp hands and walks the horse forward until the cart's end is even with the gateway. She wraps the reins around one of the iron rings built into the garden wall for just such a purpose. She holds her tongue and waits it out, having no choice but to believe her daughter will soon come back from wherever her mind has taken her.

The horse has other ideas. Tossing his head, he whinnies and tries to walk away from the smell of blood and death, but the bit hurts him in the process. His eyes bulge and roll in panic as he tries to bolt. Ensuring he can't, but as gently as she can, Neola cinches the reins tighter.

The movement and sounds of the horse snap Letty out of her mindless ogling of the dead man. Her attention switches to her mother, her expression one of disgust. Neola breathes a sigh of relief and immediately goes on the offense by demanding, "Where's the plank to slide him on?"

"What?" Letty knows full well her mother never mentioned needing a plank until just now. Righteous anger overtakes her. With her hands on her hips, she leans towards her mother and lays the truth on her, "You never said anything about a plank. How on earth would I know about a plank? Am I a mind reader? What will you want next momma? A flying carpet? What about a red flying carpet to match the color of the blood you've spilled and managed to drag all over the place. Would you like me to get one of those, too?"

Letty's getting a little wound up.

Neola scolds, "Letty, just stop it! Time's running out. How else can we get him on the cart? Wishful thinking? Prayer? Come on girl. We're not strong enough to lift him up. And I think we'll need a lot more wood if we're to burn him to ash."

Neola shrinks a little in on herself. She's running out of steam. It's taking so much energy to convince Letty, and she only has so much game. A pitiful sigh of exhaustion escapes before Neola can suppress it. But giving up is not an option and so she pleads her case, "Please, please Letty, let's just get it done. Let's go to the mill and get a plank and a little more wood. Come on now, we need to finish this chore."

Neola turns her back on her daughter and walks away. Letty hesitates at first, but habit compels her to follow her mother. She hugs herself, suddenly feeling cold. The wind rises and in response the gathering clouds race across the face of the moon. The sky goes dark, then light, then dark, then light again in flickering, dizzying succession. It's otherworldly and makes her feel confused and unsteady. Letty feels bad about her back talking, so she tries for reconciliation, "You know, poppa had a big bag of coal for his forge. It burns awful hot. I wonder if we could use that?"

Neola's gives it to her. "You're just full of good ideas, aren't you? You get the bag of coal, and I'll get another armload of branches, and then we'll find that plank."

Letty catches up to her mother and takes hold of her hand. Neola gives Letty's hand a quick reassuring squeeze. They cross the road walking in matched strides, holding hands, the bad moment between them forgiven and forgotten. They face the mill and scan the area, looking for what they need. At the same moment, they notice a wide plank leaning against the windmill wall, next to a long, wooden ladder.

As one, they shout, "There it is, that's it!"

They let go of each other's hands and run for it, reach for it, and in their hurry, they bump butts and bump hips, and knock each other over. Neola's the first one up and by rights she takes possession of the plank. It's an obvious declaration of her winning the impromptu game. Chin up, she proudly drags her prize to the edge of the road and drops it on the ground.

Letty doesn't mind, her momma can have the win. She enters the mill and heads straight to the bag of coal. She twists the excess burlap at the top of the bag, making a handle of sorts, then picks the bag up and carries it to the plank. And then she bends her knees and picks the plank up. She can do it, but it's extremely awkward. She tucks the plank under one arm, but it wants to seesaw. She manages to find the balance and all while still holding the clunky bag of coal. A flush of pleasure washes over her, the acrobatics were a complicated game that she has just won.

Letty waddles her way across the road, under the weight of her load. Neola follows close behind with an enormous armload of wood. The hard, jagged branches scratch her face and hands, drawing blood, causing her tremendous discomfort and pain. But Neola doesn't care, she welcomes the pain. It's a small penance to pay for breaking the first commandment.

They drop everything on the road next to the cart. Neola grabs hold of the plank and together they walk to the end of the cart with the intention of building the loading ramp onto the cart's deck. And that's when the bloody corpse comes into view once again. He just never goes away. It never gets any better. He's still here, and he's still bloody dead.

The horse whinnies, tossing his head, pulling against the reins, still just as desperate as ever to get away from the smell of blood and death. And once again, Letty can't move. She's rooted to the spot, frozen. The sight of the corpse has made it all too real again, and it's all too much. And like a little child, Letty closes her eyes to hide from the sight.

Neola ignores her daughter and returns to the cottage to retrieve the dead man's possessions. She brings the hose, the boots, the belt, and the floppy brown hat outside, and drops them next to the corpse. She unloads the wood stored in the cart, and a bit more than half the straw. And then, by herself, she sets the plank in place.

"Help me, Letty. You need to help me pull him into the cart now," Neola demands.

Letty's eyes pop open and she squeaks out, "What? Me! You want me to touch that?" Letty points at the corpse. "No! No momma, no. You can't make me do it, I won't do it!"

"You have no choice, Letty. Do you want him to be found? Do you want us to all go to prison for theft or hang for murder? You could hang too, Letty. I'm sorry but it's true." Neola's hands and face are bruised and scratched from carrying the wood. She's splattered in blood and stew and what looks like the grey matter of human brains. She looks wild and crazed, not at all like what a mother should look like.

Letty's fear returns. The fear, along with being cold, brings on a case of the shivers. The shivers are so bad that even her teeth chatter. She rubs and hugs herself, desperate to warm up. Shoeless, no stockings, and still in her night clothes, she has become too cold for her own good.

Neola becomes aware of her daughter's state of undress for the first time since the death dealing battle. She takes pity on her and issues new orders. "Now listen to me Letty, I want you to go and get dressed. I want you to put your shoes on, and I want you to get your shawl. And then I want you to come back out here. I need you to be quick about getting dressed, don't you dare get distracted and make me come get you."

But Letty flat out refuses, declaring in no uncertain terms, "Momma, I can't, I just can't. Besides, even if I could get past that I don't think I'd be able to come back out here again." Snot oozes and tears flow down Letty's face as she points to the dead man. The corpse completely blocks the garden entrance and the full moon's harsh light is unfortunately still highlighting the blood and brain trail. Letty fixates on the sight and becomes immovable. She won't help, and she won't go.

Neola takes a long, hard look at the horrendous damage to the head of the man she has just murdered. She drops behind the cart and vomits. After a minute she's reduced to just dry heaving. After it stops she grabs hold of the top rail of the cart and pulls herself upright, back into Letty's view.

Impatient and angry, Neola resorts to sarcasm and says, "Alright, alright. I'm sorry, I'm sorry. I'm sorry. I'm sorry I even asked you for your help. I'll just do it all by myself. You just stand there and look pretty like you usually do."

One more time Neola grabs hold of the dead Stranger's bare ankles. And she succeeds in dragging him up the plank. She even manages to get his legs inside the cart. But she doesn't have the strength to pull him all the way in. His ass end has hung up on the top edge of the plank and stuck hard. She tries to wiggle him loose by shaking his feet to move his ass, but nothing she does gets his dead butt over that edge, his body won't bend that way, no one's does.

She stuffs more straw under the edge of the plank, hoping it will help him slide, but it doesn't work. She finally figures out that he should have been on his belly. He would have slid over that edge and into the cart no problem. But she did it all wrong, everything about tonight has been all wrong. And to drag him back down off the plank, flip him over and drag him back up again is beyond her now.

She really needs her daughter's help, and she doesn't have it. She gives up and drops the Stranger's legs with a thump so loud it manages to startle Letty. Neola stands with her hands on her hips, gasping for breath. It's just too hard for one person to do. Tears of pity wet her cheeks. Sobs powered by frustration escape. She swipes her snotty nose with the filthy sleeve of her bloody shirtwaist and waits.

Letty hesitates. Sighs. Gives up and gives in. It's clear her momma needs her help, and that's what Letty does best, she helps. She steps up on the hub of the wheel and throws her leg over the side of the cart, cleverly avoiding the bloody ramp and the bloody dead man. She stands straight as a rod and uses her superior height to look down on her mother.

Mother and daughter's eyes meet, and they become of one purpose. They each take an ankle and in perfect unison count out one, two, three, and on the go they yank with all their might. And this time the dead Stranger slides, but way too easy. In fact, he moves so surprisingly fast that Neola and Letty fall flat on their asses. It's such a shock they react by laughing. But suddenly, the laughing becomes the troubling kind of hysteria that soon leads to madness. Neola is taken aback. She recollects witnessing the mass hysteria that caused the death of several deckhands while she was travelling on her father's merchant sailing ship. She knows the danger is real. She attracts Letty's attention, shakes her head no, and covers her mouth. Puzzled, but trusting her mother, the daughter takes the cue and clamps her own mouth shut.

Now that they've sobered up, they stand up only to see the dead Stranger's head hanging over the edge of the cart, straight down, upside down, the plank having dropped onto the ground, useless now. The sight makes them laugh all over again, but just for a quick second. They grab hold of the dead Stranger's cold, clammy ankles and this time they manage to drag him all the way into the cart, finally finishing the horrible chore once and for all.

10

Letty

Now that the garden entrance has been freed of the corpse, Letty is willing to return to the cottage. She makes an exaggerated show of walking beside the path so her mother can see she wasn't being difficult, the bloody trail was so horribly gruesome it really did bother her.

At the cottage threshold Letty stops to survey the interior of her simple home, but the small fire her momma had built for light has burned out and everything in their home has now become vague shapes and shadows. And though she's fully capable of getting dressed in the dark, habit has Letty heading for the fireplace to rebuild the fire. But just as she gets within an arm's reach of the firewood stash, she steps on something that shouldn't be there. She takes a step back, bends down, and feels around. Her hand closes in on the handle of what just a short while ago she heard her momma call the prayer wheel.

She lays it against her heart and knows not why. After a moment, she makes an attempt to lay the prayer wheel on the corner of the table, but an invisible force intervenes and directs her hand to the table's center. One by one the invisible force pries her fingers loose of the handle until finally the prayer wheel drops from her grasp.

A sudden glint of silver catches her eye. It belongs to an unknown object levitating off the table. The prayer wheel and the silvered object suck together midair like magnets, noisy in their mating. And just as quick as they joined, they repel and drop back to the table hitting with a loud thud.

The sound of the thud knocks the memory of the mysterious force right out of her thoughts, but the memory of the object on the table remains. She knows it has no business being there, she clearly remembers everything sliding off the table during her poppa's battle.

Needing light to find out what could possibly be on the table, Letty returns to the task of building the fire. She feels around in the firewood stack and finds the butt ends of a few pieces of kindling. The wood's jammed in so tight she's forced to tug and wiggle the wood to set it free. The disruption causes the resident mice to rush from the stack. Their tiny, grasping feet scamper over her bare toes and she reacts with an ear-splitting shriek.

And then she feels silly. She knows full well there was no real reason for such a reaction, many a time she's felt the feet of the mice, it's just that she's so nervous tonight. She takes a steadying breath, then resumes building the fire. Once the fire's blazing, she locates and lights a candle stub and holds it aloft. All the combined light reveals a thick glistening pool of blood just a measly inch or so from her bare toes.

Letty screams a real scream this time and jumps back, her bare heel knocking against something that slides to the side. The glint and sparkle catch her eye, and she sees the crystal shard of the flower bowl for what it really is.

It's a death dealing weapon.

One wrong step could kill her. It's more than likely a deep cut would become infected and that's the real worry. She remembers the smell of her poppa's rotting leg. That same fate awaits her if she's not careful, and she's not been careful this night, not at all. Going barefoot tonight was not a good idea.

Letty scans the awful mess on the floor, looking for more hazards, understanding now that danger lurks everywhere. She spies the wicked, wicked tulip bulbs. They look too shiny and way too big. Desirable, yet somehow not. Letty lights the other candle stub and holds both candles aloft, increasing the overhead illumination.

Blood, brains, and tiny bits of glowing white skull make up a glistening trail all the way to the cottage door. There's so much blood, it's a wonder her poppa is even still alive. It's no wonder her mother killed the Stranger, he was hurting her poppa that bad.

And then Letty sees the trail of blood for what it really is. It's the same sort of track her momma made the night of the fire. That night her momma was dragging her poppa because she was saving his life. Tonight, her momma dragged a dead Stranger away from their home in hopes of saving the family from the gallows.

Sympathy fills Letty's eyes, blinding her. She blinks, blinks, blinks the tears away. Once her vision clears, her eyes just naturally gravitate to the two objects at the center of the table. She was right about the one being the prayer wheel. The other appears to be a knife inserted in a rather worn looking leather sheath.

A strange desire to use both objects to form a cross against her chest becomes a compulsion and so she does it, she forms the cross. Instantly, a rush of electricity fans out from her fluttering heart, zip zinging like arrows through her entire being until finally the charge blows out the top of her head and exits the tips of her toes. Letty is left with the strange notion that she needs to hide the objects from her mother.

Letty knows just where to hide them. She makes her way into her sleeping alcove and lays the prayer wheel and knife on the patchwork quilt covering her bed. A vague memory of tulip bulbs rolling under her privacy curtains becomes suddenly important. The lack of adequate light just makes her more determined to recover the bulbs. She drops to her knees and boldly sweeps the floor using one of her outstretched arms as the broom.

And in that way, she finds and gathers four tulip bulbs. She decides that's about enough and quits looking for more. She makes a tidy pile of the four bulbs, the prayer wheel, and the sheathed knife on her bed, not over thinking it, just doing it.

She turns to the rock wall behind her bed and with a well-practiced elbow punch she bumps a rock loose. A hidey hole is revealed. Letty discovered it quite by accident while bouncing on her bed one day shortly after they had moved from the room at the Village Inn to the larger, single room ancestral cottage. Curiosity compelled her to peer inside the cavity, but the angle was all wrong and she couldn't see to the bottom.

But it didn't matter, she was always up for a new game. Fearlessly, she stuck her hand in the hole and felt around. And that's when she discovered three lumpy gold rocks and a silk bag full of lots of something. The bag was made of a watered silk, the fabric a deep royal blue in color. It was the sort of silk fabric her grandfather had once brought home to sell to the royals and the wealthy. She promptly pulled the bag's drawstrings open and dumped a pile of sparkling gems into her lap. A large, flat bottomed transparent crystal was obviously the crown jewel.

Her eleven-year-old imagination took over. And after a few minutes of thinking about it, she became convinced she had found real treasure. Eager to share the happy news of the family's new-found wealth, Letty rushed to her mother's side and held out the smallest of the golden rocks and a few of the colored gems for her to examine. But her momma was too busy nursing her poppa's rotting leg to bother to take a good look.

Three times that day Letty tried to show her momma the treasure, and three times she was rebuffed.

But finally, on the fourth try, tired of being constantly interrupted in her nursing duties and no doubt distracted by her own pain caused from the burns on her own back, Neola gave the treasures a quick, dismissive glance and declared, "Yes, yes, they're pretty Letty, but that yellow rock is just fool's gold, and you must remember the Innkeeper's wife wearing a necklace made of the same colored-glass beads. Now I think you've bothered me enough times today about this and I'm tired of it. I tell you what. I'm giving the treasures to you, they're all yours, all the pretties, forever now and forevermore. I mean it, I really do. Now please promise me you will never ever bother me about the pretties again. And for God's sake, could you please just go outside and play for a while."

And so, Letty promised. It seemed the right thing to do since her momma wanted it so. But before Letty went outside to play, she closed her curtains and returned her treasures to the hidey hole. And that was when Letty realized she had forgotten to tell her momma about the hidey hole.

But it was too late now, her mother had forbidden her to speak of the treasures again. And after giving it some thought, Letty realized her mother was probably right. The yellow rocks were in the wall because it was a rock wall, and they were rocks. And the sparkling gemstones did resemble the glass beads strung on the necklace of the Inn keeper's wife. And even though the gems didn't have the necessary holes so they could be strung on a string and worn as a necklace, they were still pretty. Besides, one of her momma's favorite sayings has always been, "Finder keepers. Loser weepers." Letty loves that saying. It guarantees the pretties will always be hers.

And since that day, Letty has kept her promise to her mother while keeping the hidey hole a secret, too. She's also hidden a few other treasures in the hidey hole as well. Little kid things like the love poem from the boy at school and the exceedingly long red ribbon the haberdasher's son gave her as a parting gift before he left with his family for America.

She drops the prayer wheel, the sheathed knife, and the tulip bulbs in the hidey hole. Something crinkles as she leans on her pillow, and she remembers hiding the missive earlier that night. She adds it to the pile and replaces the rock.

Unexpectedly, Letty drops into a trance, her hands assuming the prayer position. Her body becomes so still she appears to be made of stone. But it doesn't last for long, her trance is soon disturbed by the sound of her mother yelling, "Letty! Letty! What's taking you so long? We need to go! Bring some matches and a candle with you. Hurry up now child, don't make me come and get you!"

Fortunately, Letty's daytime clothes are close by. But she gets in her own way as she rushes to stuff her arms in the sleeves of her shirtwaist. And when she throws her walking skirt over her head in the most normal of ways, it tangles and refuses to slide over her head. She finally stops with the struggle, relaxes, and shimmies her skirt into place. She buttons it, the clumsiness all gone, forgotten. Purpose returned, she buttons her shirtwaist, rolls on her stockings, slides on her leather footies, and slips on her wooden shoes. All together now, she collects her apron and shawl, a candle and a few matches, and heads for the door.

But halfway to the door she hears a moan, followed by a deep, shuddering groan. The sound resonates to her very marrow.

Her poppa is hurting. He needs her. She wants to help him, she really does. But by the sound of him, she can tell he's unconscious, and she knows she can do him no good. She's had lots and lots of practice watching her poppa fade in and out when his leg was still broken. It became so bad one day the doctor decided to cut it off. Of course, her momma wouldn't let the doctor do it. Instead, she kicked him out the door, telling the doctor to never, ever come back again. Then her momma fixed her poppa all right, nursed him night and day, and pretty much all by herself, too. It took a long, long time, but her momma never gave up and to this day, even though his leg healed crooked, and it caused him to limp, her poppa still has his leg.

And that's when Letty finally gets it. The real reason her mother is outside with the dead man and not nursing her poppa.

Her poppa can't be fixed.

Her mother shouts again, this time an obvious edge of panic in her voice. "Come on Letty, it's time to go! Get on out here right now!"

During Letty's absence, Neola had gone about the job of seeking retribution. She began the righteous act by piling the Stranger's possessions on top his body. Next, she shoved firewood and branches beneath him, raising his body off the cart's deck by a good foot. She followed by filling the voids with chunks of coal, twigs, and generous handfuls of straw. She stuffed coal in his pockets, then stuffed his shirt and pants with straw until he looked just like a scarecrow.

Then, for reasons she could not fathom, for she wasn't especially religious, she laid one line of coal across his chest, shoulder to shoulder, followed by another running from the center of his throat to the base of his pelvis. The making of the cross had made her smile, but not in a pretty way.

She made piles of coal on his heart and manhood and twisted pieces of coal into his unseeing eyes and his forever deaf ears. She scattered the last remaining bits of straw and twigs on top his unfeeling body, along with the rest of the firewood and the bloody plank. Finally, she retrieved a tin of kerosene from the mill and tucked it in at the back of the cart before untying the horse.

The cart is ready to burn, and she impatiently stamps her feet while holding the horse's reins. Neola's ready to go, just waiting for her daughter to join her.

And for her daughter's sake Neola attempts to wipe the ugly smile of triumphant revenge from her once pretty face. But the thought of reducing the Stranger to nothing, disappearing him for all time intercedes and the unpretty smile remains.

The urgent need to burn the Stranger is not Neola's only thought, though. Not at all. There's another, second thought pushing for dominance. It's a desire, really.

She wants her man back.

And she wants him now.

11

Green Smoke Woman

Letty exits the cottage and joins her mother. The setting moon's light extends the shadows of the skeletal oak tree across the road. Letty shivers at the sight, remembering her fears of a few hours ago and all that has happened since.

The atmosphere is heavy with the impending feeling of storm, the air super charged with the promise of night lightning. Bats fly crazy wild around the vanes of the windmill. Hungry, veering off at insane angles, they search for something, anything, on this most vile of nights.

An owl's single hoot, the harbinger of death is heard, adding yet another ominous layer to the already sinister feeling of the fading night.

Neola ignores the superstitious nonsense and leads the horse down the path towards the low spot with Letty following close behind. The wheels of the cart squeak, squeak, and the horse's hooves clip clop, creating simple music in their shared rhythm. When the path levels out Neola halts the horse and removes the harness. She slaps his rump hard and quick to startle him, and it does the job.

He runs off, desperate to be rid of the smell of blood and death and equally anxious to avoid another cruel slap. For a minute or so all is quiet. Then out of the deep dark of the lowland, the horse comes racing back. He's sucking air in and snorting thick mucus. Some of the mucus lands on Letty and Neola and causes them to flinch. The poor beast's eyes roll wild as he thunders by, heading up the gentle slope. He soon gains the road, and the sounds of his galloping hooves recede as he passes the cottage and the windmill on the way back to wherever he had come from all those long hours ago.

Neola shrugs she don't care and gets right on the job. She pours kerosene over the contents of the cart, once more giving especial attention to the dead man's heart and manhood, a gleeful, vindictive expression plastered across her once lovely face. She strikes a match against the metal hub of the cart's wheel and puts the flame to the fuel. The straw and twigs promptly roar up in a great ball of fire.

Letty and Neola jump back from the flames and the sudden heat. They retreat up the slope to a safe distance and sit down to watch the evidence burn. The moon has sunk so low in the sky almost everything is lost to shadow. Uninhabited marshland surrounds them, heavy with odor, mysterious and spooky. They hear a feral dog's triumphant howl as he takes down a rabbit, the rabbit's death scream sounding like that of a terrified woman, a sound truly dreadful to hear.

But the women don't care. This night, this endless night, has made them immune to simple, commonplace horror. And now all they really want is for the fire to burn hot and do its job of disappearing the wooden cart and the corpse of the Stranger.

Letty can't help but begin a game of spotting shapes in the flames, gaming is just part of her nature. Mother and daughter take turns naming the shapes of animals and such until suddenly, unexpectedly, the smoke coalesces into the shape of a woman spinning round and around. A ribbon of green smoke appears around her belly, undulating, snakelike in its form. Golden bangles encircle her wrists and ankles, and between her naked breasts odd little pouches swing from leather strings tied around her long, slender neck. Her hips gyrate to music they cannot hear, but the movement tempts them to stand up and move in concert with her. But of course, they don't. They still think it's just a game. A smoke and mirrors sort of game.

The green smoke woman gracefully raises her arms, and the precious gold bangles slither and slide toward her elbows. The firelight's reflection on the moving precious metal creates the shocking illusion of golden lava flowing down both her arms and into her heart. At the same time, directly over her head, her hands twist in odd patterns that somehow make sense but should not. One hand appears to drip blood, while in the other a small prayer wheel makes a sudden appearance. It's then she lifts her bowed head and reveals her moon face, her high round cheekbones, and her excited coal black eyes. A sly smile plays on her plump, heart shaped lips as her long, blue black hair lifts on the fire breeze.

Neola and Letty gasp as they realize they can no longer see through the smoke woman. She's become real flesh and blood and is no longer just an object in their game. At the very instance of their shared belief in her real physical presence, the green smoke woman stops dancing and lowers her arms. She makes a point of staring long and hard into Neola's surprised eyes. Then, the green smoke woman shakes her empty fist at Neola. An insane laugh escapes from her lips, then poof... she disappears in a puff of green smoke.

Mother and daughter turn and look at each other, their eyes all big with wonder. And then they ask each other at the same instance, "Did you see her? Did you hear her laugh?"

Neola shivers, an old memory surfacing. She whispers, "Oh my God, Letty. I've seen the green smoke woman before, I'm sure of it. It was the last time I voyaged with my father. We were moored at a dock near the mouth of the Indus River and my father had just hired a new deckhand. I was standing at the rail and watched the deckhand kiss her goodbye just before he boarded my father's ship. He was one of the strangest looking men I've ever seen. I couldn't stop looking at him. He had no hair, not even eyebrows. He was bare chested, very muscular, he carried not a single ounce of fat. His only clothing was a pair of white colored pantaloons. His skin was a deep honey color, so rich it glowed. It was his glow that first drew my gaze. He was unusually tall and graceful, he moved just like a cat, and he was so sure of himself. The green smoke woman caught me staring at him and waved her hands in the air. She was holding that same prayer wheel in one of her fists. Once she made sure she had my full attention, she looked me hard in the eye and shook her fist at me, exactly like she did right here just a moment ago. As young as I was, I knew it was a warning to stay away from him, although that would be near impossible as we would be sailing together for the next half year or so and be in close quarters, there would be no help for it. But it didn't really matter, that dock whore had nothing to worry about, she was being so stupidly silly. I never, ever could have loved him. I only ever had love eyes for your poppa."

Neola shuts down, lost to intimate memories of her life with her husband. But soon thoughts of the green smoke woman intrude, and Neola resurfaces and explains, "I remember now, he was a master seaman. We used to laugh at the insane pitching of the deck as we took care of the ship's business while hanging on for dear life. I loved the heavy weather, so did he. It was a ride, like a good game. Her man and I did have that in common. And I did love to watch him work the sails, his movements were so precise, so elegant. I spent hours sitting on the mast step watching him swing between the masts, pulling one line then another, trimming the sails just so. It was magic, I thought he was magic, I thought he could fly, he made the ship fly. My father bragged he could control the winds of a typhoon. I suppose he drowned along with my father when the ship sunk."

Neola's mind travels somewhere, but she doesn't share where. After a moment of quiet contemplation she continues, "Strange I would remember all that now, and how odd that we would both see his dock whore. What could it possibly mean? It was such a long time ago. I was just fifteen years old that year, about your age, the last time I sailed with my father, and then I came home for good and married your poppa the day I turned sixteen."

As she's speaking Neola's voice lifts with joy, and she smiles at the memory of her happy marriage and her love for Vonder. Her mind wanders away to dreams of their youth and the first blush of sexual love.

Letty frowns. It's been a little more than five years since her grandfather's merchant ship sunk and all hands were lost, including her grandfather's, then two months later her family's house and warehouse burnt to the ground, and her other grandparents died, too. Really, they all should have died. Everyone thought at the time it was a strange coincidence, a random act of God. But an even stranger coincidence is the green smoke woman holding the prayer wheel tonight of all nights. Letty remembers holding its identical twin in her hand along with four gigantic tulip bulbs just a little while ago.

What could it all mean? Letty knows it's not normal to see visions, especially shared visions. And the whole story of the green smoke woman happened so long ago, why would she suddenly appear now? And Letty's not even sure what a dock whore is, she's never heard that word before. It's all a strange puzzle in an even stranger night, and further proof nothing is normal anymore, normal appears to be gone for good.

The cart burns hot and fast. Neola makes a point of kicking the loose pieces back into the fire. Fortunately, a light wind carries the smell of a roasting human away. Soon there's nothing left but ash, but still the women remain in place, unmoving.

Slumped together shoulder to shoulder, the exhausted pair have fallen asleep while sitting up. Dawn's gentle light breaks over the eastern horizon, turning the sky a deep rosy red. The light soon wakes them, and they yawn and stretch. Disheveled and dirty, they rise, stiff from sitting on the cold, hard ground. They shake themselves loose, then take each other's hands before they head down the slope to see if their plan worked.

12

Tuesday Morning

Neola explodes with a triumphant shout, "We did it, Letty! We did it!" She lowers her voice and exclaims, "The cart and the Stranger are all gone. Well, except for this huge pile of ash. But rain's coming soon, and it looks like heavy rain. Can you smell it?"

Letty shakes her head no, so Neola points her finger towards the east and declares, "See the clouds piling up, becoming so dark and heavy looking? There's a whole lot of rain coming our way and that's good for us and our little problem here. You know how this low spot always floods. I think if we rake as much of the ash as we can into the marsh, in all the different directions, the rain will wash away what little is left on the path. Come on, now. Let's go to the garden shed and grab a couple of rakes and buckets. We need to get this done before the rain hits."

They trudge up the path and gain the road. It's a short walk to the gateway of the cottage garden. When they arrive, they find the garden gate wide open. It's no surprise, really. But what is worrisome is finding the cottage door standing wide open when it should have been closed. Neola can't resist giving Letty a hard look. They both know it was up to Letty to shut the door, she was the last one to leave the cottage. Neola shrugs and shakes her head no, there's no point in bothering to shut it now, they'll be back soon enough. They collect the rakes and buckets then head back to the ash pile. But before they reach the garden gate, they hear odd clicking noises, cringe-worthy scratching sounds, and menacing growls.

The sounds come from the dark recesses of the cottage. And then a sudden savage scream punctures the air. In response, the hair at the nape of the women's necks stands up while the hair on their forearms rubs backwards. Terrified, the women freeze in place. Then they melt, becoming weak in their knees but still capable of running for it, the sounds seeming too dangerous to confront.

And they do try to rush away. They really try hard. But they can't quite do it. A subtle, intangible feeling holds them in place. It's love, it's the feeling of love, love will not let them go. And it's love that compels them to face their fears. As one, they turn and silently tiptoe to the threshold of the door. Brave now, love winning. Mother and daughter, a serious force to be reckoned with, righteousness on their side. They spend a quick second planning the rescue of their man using pantomime to communicate.

As one, they leap through the doorway, screaming at the top of their lungs, swinging the rakes and buckets in front of them as makeshift weapons and shields. They surprise a red fox and her four kits in the act of licking and eating the blood, brains, and vegetable stew covering the cottage floor. The creatures freeze for a moment, then turn and stare at Letty and Neola. But not for too long. The kits and their mother suddenly scamper, going every which way, the instinctive behavior meant to deliberately confuse the perceived threat.

And seeing that it's only foxes, the women lose all fear and boldly run the critters round and around till the last little one scoots out the open door.

Seconds pass, maybe a minute or two. The women process what just happened. The last time they saw the mother fox, that nasty, feral creature, she was skulking, looking guilty. They both know what she's capable of, they've seen the carnage. That vile creature has ripped apart and sucked the life blood from their flock of chickens for far too many years now. And that vicious bitch was just here in the cottage right next to their defenseless man.

They come to the truth of it at the same moment. But before either one can decide what to do, they hear a deep, shuddering moan. Relieved, they drop the buckets and rakes and rush to Vonder's side, getting in each other's way, both anxious to examine him for signs of teeth marks, signs of blood sucking, and most especially, signs of rips to his vulnerable throat and guts. Blessed miracle, the mother fox had not yet done her dirty deed on the defenseless Vonder.

Seeing her husband this close, Neola needs him. She needs his touch. But she can't have it anymore, he's still alive, but already gone. She goes weak in the knees from the truth of it, and collapses across his chest, sobbing, brokenhearted. She tries to conjure him back to her, whispering words of want and need but nothing happens, nothing can.

Letty intervenes, as she must. She takes hold of her mother's shoulders and gives them a hard squeeze before she begs, "Momma. Momma. Come on momma, we need to clean up the pile of ash. It's evidence. Do you want us to go to jail or maybe even hang? Do you momma? How would that help poppa? Poppa will be alright by himself for a little while longer, you know he will."

Neola raises her head and turns her swollen, weeping eyes towards the irritating, whining noise. What could possibly be more important than her husband? Letty's close resemblance to Vonder momentarily confuses Neola. His intense blue eyes project from Letty's face, his corkscrew curls sprout from her head. It seems to be him, yet not. How can there be two of him? Neola shakes the tears from her eyes and realizes it's her own daughter she's looking at.

But Neola's still not willing to leave her husband's side just yet. Instead, she steals a moment more by admitting, "Yes, yes, I know. Someone will come looking this way, and it will be much too soon."

As she speaks, Neola's gaze returns to her comatose husband. She reaches out and gently strokes his cheek, then bends down and kisses him on his lips. In return, she's rewarded by the push of his warm breath against her face.

Trusting her mother will follow, Letty heads for the door. And Neola starts to follow, she does. But after two steps she hears the ancient siren song of a lover's pain, a moan so low it barely registers as sound, and she's stopped dead in her tracks.

Of course, she'll stay with her husband. She'll hold his hand, and never leave his side. She gives in to love, drops down deep into the feel of it, not at all sorry for the choice. She turns her back on her daughter and heads towards her husband.

And that's when Letty grips her mother's elbow and digs her fingernails in, deliberately causing her mother intense pain before she spins her back around and takes her by the chin. Letty looks long and deep into her mother's grieving eyes. And with that look, the daughter commands.

Letty releases her mother's face and hands her a rake and a bucket. And then she turns and walks away trusting her mother will follow. And Neola does, but still, she is reluctant.

As soon as they return to the ash heap, they tie their skirts in big knots well above their knees, then get to work raking the hot ash, spreading it out, pushing it into the marsh. It's not long before they see tendrils of smoke rising from the ground around them, but they think nothing of it until actual flames begin shooting out from under their wooden shoes.

In a panic, they scream and run into the marsh. They spend precious minutes stamping around in the stagnant water, making sure the fire is out before tromping back to the task of raking the ash.

The wind rises and blows the ash and soot around. Neola wipes her itchy face and leaves a streak across her upper lip. It looks just like a big black moustache and Letty gets the giggles, then outright laughs. She points to her mother's lips. Neola gets it and joins in. The tension dissipates, and they feel normal for exactly about one minute.

The blackened iron wheel rims present a separate problem and so they set them aside before raking the ash into the marsh land. As they rake, they find bits and pieces of metal and bits and pieces of something else. They rake the debris up the slope, trying to sort things out as they work. By the time they've finished, they've made several piles.

As if on cue, the wind rises. The sky darkens. Thick, black clouds cover the early morning sun. A boom of thunder, a strike of lightning, and the skies open. It rains so hard, so fast, an honest to God gulley washer occurs and they haven't the time to seek shelter.

Neola and Letty drop their rakes and just stand in it. They look up and let the warm rain wash over their ash covered faces. It feels so good they smile real smiles. Letty pretends to scrub the ash from her clothes. She slap-dashes scrubbing her armpits, then makes a point of twisting around, sticking her butt out and washing her privates.

Of course, her mother laughs. Soon enough the storm moves on. The blessed rain has given them a helping hand by dispersing the remaining ash into the lowland. The mother and daughter hold hands, almost happy, the nasty job of disappearing the Stranger good and done.

13

Crazy Momma

Letty stares at the pile of debris and comes to her senses. She might have turned a blind eye while raking the ash, but not now. The rain has washed the ash away and exposed the dead man's burnt bones. Letty whimpers as she pleads, "I won't touch that momma, I can't pick that up! Please don't make me do it, please don't, I won't do it momma, I just can't."

Neola takes pity. She pulls her daughter close and strokes her hair, pushing her tight curls behind her ears as she whispers, "I'll do it baby girl, you don't have to touch a thing, I'll take care of it."

The sun breaks free from behind a cloud at just that moment. Neola realizes the day is quickly passing. She pulls back and searches Letty's tear brightened eyes. And seeing that Letty has calmed down a bit Neola offers a refined, expanded solution, "First, we'll take care of the metal. I'll be the one to fill the buckets with the bits and pieces, and you can be the one to hide them at the mill. You can do that, right? Right? Of course, you can. It's just metal, after all."

Letty gives the tiniest nod of agreement. Neola accepts it as a yes and gets to work sorting through the mixed pile of metal and bones, culling out the pieces of metal, throwing them into the buckets. Soon, all that's left on the ground is the burnt bits of bones.

Letty has turned her back on her mother's gruesome task and has spent her time bouncing up and down on the metal rims, working at flattening them so they'll no longer resemble the shape of the cart's wheels. The rhythm of the bounce is so hypnotic Letty quickly becomes lost to it. Neola finishes the sorting and directs an impatient gaze at her daughter's back. Eventually, Letty feels the pressure of her mother's eyes and turns her head to see why. They make eye contact, each expressing frustration with just a look, but for the moment they hold their say.

Neola's the first to give in. She declares, " I've done my part. All the metal pieces are in the buckets. Now you need to do your job by taking the buckets away and hiding the metal at the mill. Find a spot away from the places we make use of. And then you come right back. And another thing, when you come back don't forget to bring the empty buckets with you. And Letty, don't you dare get distracted and make me come looking for you."

Letty drops her head and shields her eyes in a feeble attempt to avoid looking at the gruesome pile of bones. The ridiculous gesture makes it even more difficult for her to locate and pick up the buckets, but she doesn't care. She felt put out and wanted to make a show of it. She trudges up the path, the heavy buckets of metal slowing her down. And for the first time in her life she's wearing the terribly ugly sullen expression of an unhappy sixteen-year-old girl.

As she approaches the cottage gate, Letty hears muffled shouts of gibberish. It's her poppa crying out in pain and confusion. She enters the garden with the intention of going to his side to give him comfort, but she's been needing to use the outhouse since she woke up, and she's pretty sure she can't hold her shit any longer, so she makes a detour.

Relief is immediate, the gut cramps all but gone, but it's the sound of her piss splashing in the standing water below that provides Letty with the great idea to dump the metal pieces in the outhouse. The metal lands with a satisfying plop and sinks out of sight. It's enough to convince Letty that no one will ever suspect the cart's metal is in the outhouse hole. She leaves, and as always, the door slams shut behind her even without her touching it. She makes a quick stop at the well and pumps enough water to wash her hands and drink her fill. Her poppa is quiet for now, so she decides to leave him alone for a little while longer. Her sudden success at the outhouse makes her feel like her usual happy self when she has won a game and so she skips her way back to her mother, the two buckets swinging in time with her invigorated steps.

Surprised to see Letty return so soon, and in such good spirits, Neola makes the mistake of trying to use it to her advantage. She declares, "Well that was quick. But we still have the wheel rims to dispose of. And the bones need to be buried somewhere, but not in the garden where they might be found. I just don't know where to bury them, maybe you have an idea?"

The mention of the dead Stranger's bones immediately deflates Letty's happy high. Sudden, unreasonable anger takes over. She huffs a few times, otherwise speechless. Then she hangs her head and stares down at her feet while shaking her head no in response to her mother's question.

Neola takes note of her daughter's anger and chooses to ignore it. She begins the gruesome task of filling the buckets with the burnt bits of bones. She finds the jawbone and picks up all the loose teeth. She recovers long bones and short bones, finger bones and toe bones, rib bones, and of course, the pelvis. The snakelike pieces of the vertebrae are most impressive, the knee bones heavier than expected. All the bones are broken or crushed in some way or other, even the very marrow has been boiled out of them.

Neola slams the bones as hard as she can into the buckets. Some of them bounce back out. She likes when that happens because she gets to slam him all over again. By leaning the larger bones against a rock and slamming her foot down hard, she discovers she can bust the bones into several pieces. The breaking crack is satisfying, it pleases her. So much so, that she smiles. But it's an ugly smile, it distorts her pretty face in a frightening way.

After all, he deserves it and it makes her feel good to hold his burnt bones, his dead ass. She killed him. She's burned him. She's turned him to ash and burnt bits of nothing. He's become nothing. He's nothing now and he'll never be anything again. And Neola feels justified, she'd kill him all over again if she could. He tried to kill her man. He has killed her man. Vonder's as good as dead now, she can no longer pretend otherwise.

For Neola, time stops, she stops. The ache caused by the absence, the longing for Vonder has become too much to bear. His tender touch has been replaced instead by a black hole greedily devouring pieces of her heart. And it hurts, it hurts.

But then the moment passes, and time returns with purpose. Neola steps down on the Stranger's busted, burnt skull. Her heavy wooden shoes act as a sledgehammer and she busts the whole of his skull into fragments until she's sure he can never be put back together again. Finally, she's finished the job she started last night with the cast iron stew pot.

Letty watches as Neola devolves into violence. Her mother's sweet, loving face becomes so twisted with hatred that Letty turns away in fear, no longer able to recognize her own mother. She's seen her mother lose all control just twice before but both times it seemed to be for a good reason.

The first time was when she wrapped Letty in the marriage quilt and without warning threw her out the bedroom window into the dark unknown. The second time was last night when her mother beat her poppa's attacker to death with the stew pot. But now, well now her mother is stomping his skull to pieces but he's already long dead. It just makes no sense. Breaking human bones, it's not normal, it's sick, it's going full on crazy.

Taking a few steps back towards away, stopping just long enough to bend down and grab the flattened wheel rims, Letty heads up the gentle slope, out of her mother's view and out of harm's way. She enters the outhouse and quietly shuts the door and leans against it, holding it closed, deliberately hiding from her mother. She stares down the shit hole, seeing in her mind's eye the events of the last twelve hours.

The gruesome images become too much for her and needing a way to break her thoughts she throws the flattened wheel rims down the hole. And of course, shitty water spits out over the rim of the seat. She steps back, trying to get out of the splash zone but she's stopped by the closed door. And that little splash of shit water that lands on her filthy apron ignites her fury. She rushes from the outhouse and heads to the garden gate where she promptly proceeds to take her anger out on the poor old thing by slamming it shut then open, shut then open, shut then open. Finally, she stops. But her hands soon find a new purpose. They reach up and cover her ears to try to stop the memory of the sound of her mother cracking human bones. Will the sound ever fade from her ears, the image from her mind?

Letty works at calming down because she must, she's been given chores, she needs to finish the chores, she's a good girl, it's what she does, she does chores, she always does the chores. She needs to do chores. Reluctantly, she leaves the safety of the garden and heads back down the path, all the while dreading seeing her crazy momma again.

Oddly enough, her mother appears quite sane.

While Letty was gone, Neola managed to pack every bit of tooth and bone into the buckets. She kicks at the ground searching one final time for anything she might have missed but finds nothing. Satisfied, she looks up at her baby girl and smiles in a reassuring, calm manner.

Letty distrusts her mother's sudden change of mood, and she cautiously moves past Neola on her way to collect the tools and the empty kerosene can. Neola takes the hint and steps back, careful to keep her distance as she picks up the buckets of burnt bones. A heavy mist descends as the women make their way to the cottage.

Mother and daughter take the time to stop at the well and drink their fill. Then Neola fills the wash pan, and they clean up as they would normally do after a day of working in the garden. Letty dumps the wash water over the wall, then cleans the tools and stores them away in the garden shed. After closing the shed's doors, she heads to the mill to return the empty kerosene can.

Trusting Letty will properly put away all the tools and such, Neola has left her side and entered the cottage. Too tired to think straight and not knowing what else to do, she has brought the buckets of bones in with her and has set them down next to the doorway, tight up against the wall and out of the line of sight in case someone should happen to stop by. But really, no one can be allowed to enter their home until it is put to rights.

The day's light reveals the extent of the mess. The fox and her kits must have arrived just prior to Letty and Neola for it's clear they never had much of a chance to scavenge. The floor is still covered in chunks of cooked vegetables mixed in with the stew's gravy, clots of brain matter, and dried blood. Adding to the mess are withered flowers, shards of lethal cut crystal, fragments of bone from the skull, and the wicked, wicked tulip bulbs. Even the chairs are tipped on their sides and covered in blood.

Neola wants her life back. She pulls her chair up off the floor, sets it upright, and promptly sits her tired ass down on it. She's hungry and far, far beyond exhausted. She places her elbows on the old table, buries her face in her hands, and hides from all the horror. Ever so softly she weeps. Sorrow and exhaustion have finally merged into one and succeeded in beating her down to ground. She can no longer move her body., not even so much as her little finger. She sits as though she's already dead a dead woman, for she feels that alone.

And just as that secret, special light within her sad, sorry soul decides it's time now, well past time for it to go out, at that very moment of giving in and giving up, she feels the welcomed grip of a strong hand on her shoulder. She knows that grip well. She lifts her head and whispers, "Vonder?" Her face blooms with hope and love, and a wild joy overtakes her. She turns to look at the miracle God has given her. Her green eyes sparkle with anticipation, her truest smile appears for his eyes only.

But of course, it's not Vonder, it's only their daughter Letty.

Neola shudders and collapses with a sob so sad, so deep, so hopelessly hopeless that tears spring instantly to Letty's eyes. Neola makes a bad job of hiding her disappointment. Denied hope, anger pokes her hard. She hates herself for foolishly falling for the myth of divine interception when she has always known there is no such thing.

Letty knows what she just did. She gave her mother false hope and now her mother is a bit more broken. At first, Letty just stands there, her useless, guilty arms hanging at her sides. She stands silent and helpless. But as the moments pass it occurs to her what she could do to make it right.

"Momma," Letty declares. "Momma, listen. Listen to me. I'll clean up the mess. You eat some bread and butter and then go and take a nap, I know how tired you must be. Please just do it momma."

Not bothering to wait for permission, Letty retrieves last night's leftover bread, the crock of butter, a knife, and the nearly empty jar of honey, arranging it all on the cutting board. She carries it to the table and places it before her mother, then takes a few steps back, giving her mother plenty of room to breathe.

Neola takes stock of what Letty has offered. Her mouth waters with desire for the exquisite taste of the sweet, golden honey. Neola has never been able to resist honey, not ever and her empty stomach growls in anticipation, the growl so loud that even Letty can hear it. Neola takes the knife in hand and with deft movements she splits the bread horizontally, creating two enormous slices, one for her and one for Letty. She spreads the butter and honey on thick leaving just tiny bits of residue clinging to the sides of both the butter crock and the honey jar. Then she picks up the biggest piece and she eats it so fast she barely takes the time to chew it. God, but it did taste good. She stares at the left-over piece for maybe half a second. She knows it's not her piece, she understands it's for her daughter, but her mind goes somewhere wrong and gives her greed permission. She snatches Letty's piece and wolfs it down, never really trying to stop herself.

She looks at her daughter with a guilty expression, but it no longer matters. Letty's attention is centered on her comatose poppa. Neola breaks the silence by telling a little white lie. She declares, "Thank God, your poppa is still asleep because we need to clean the house, and we really need to pick up the tulip bulbs and hide them from whoever comes looking, because they will, they will surely come looking, and it will be soon."

Neola glances around and sees a charred remnant of the bundle's oilcloth cover at the outside edge of the far corner of the hearth. The enormous tulip bulbs are scattered everywhere. God, she hates the sight of those wicked things. If she were not so tired, she would step on each one and smash them into the floor just like she smashed the Stranger's burnt skull with her heavy, waterlogged wooden shoes.

The food settles down deep in Neola's belly, warming her from inside out. She struggles to keep her eyes open. Blind habit compels her to return the cutting board, the empty butter crock, and the empty honey jar to the shelf above the kitchen counter.

It's put her within arm's reach of her husband and their bed. She stares at him, her handsome man, her love, her heart. She watches as tremors roll up and down his beaten body.

She makes the hard choice and drags her tired self to Letty's bed, strips down to her chemise and drawers, rolls her filthy clothes into a tight ball and throws them as hard as she can at the plastered wall next to the firewood stack. The ball of bloody clothes busts loose on impact, spreading out, making yet one more mess.

And then Neola gives up, really gives up this time, simply does not care what happens anymore. She collapses on top of her daughter's quilt and falls into a deep, dreamless sleep.

14

Letty

Hovering over the remains of the battle are ten thousand flies. They scatter as Letty walks right through them. After she passes, the flies reassemble into a buzzing, undulating cloud floating just inches above the floor. Small groups descend and feast on the spilled stew and the stringy tendrils of grey brain matter. Once full, they lift off, then come back for more.

At the edge of the hearth Letty examines a large patch of dried blood. She knows it would become an ever-expanding, never-ending mess if she tried to clean it up using soap and water. Best to scrape the dried blood onto a sacrificial piece of wood shingle, or better yet, a piece of slate. And wouldn't that be fast and easy, then she could just toss it over the wall and forget about it. Her mind made up, Letty hurries to the scrap heap kept in the far corner of the garden. She scans the pile and picks out a large piece of slate with a thin, beveled edge, perfect for use as a dustpan. A few seconds later she recovers a smaller piece that can act as a scrapper. Her quick success qualifies as a win in her world, and she skips her way back to the cottage, happy for the moment.

The battle scene greets her. But it no longer bothers her, it's now become her new normal. And more surprisingly, she seems to have lost her revulsion at the sight of blood.

And isn't it about time? After all, she's been bleeding for a few days every month for well over two years now, so why would the sight of another's blood bother her? And her parents really need to stop calling her a baby girl. She stopped being their baby girl after the fire. Everyone knows she took care of all the chores. But that's not all she's done. Last night she helped her mother get rid of a dead body. Now that really finished off her childhood once and for all.

The ever-present embers make rebuilding the fire easy. Letty hangs a big pot of water on the crane then swings it over the flames. While waiting for the water to heat, she scrapes away at the dried pool of blood nearest the hearth. Flies land on her hands and her face. She constantly wiggles and shakes to dislodge them, but it does little good. She moves on to the dried pools of blood near the table, then finishes the chore of scraping blood at the threshold of the cottage door.

She's irritated by the sight of the buckets of bones tucked behind the opened door but realizes it's the perfect place to store the powdered blood. She does a careful balancing act as she settles the overloaded dustpan on the top of one of the buckets. The blood next to the burnt bones makes her realize she's looking at what's left of a whole man. The Stranger doesn't look like much of a threat now, not at all. Letty resists the impulse to laugh out loud, laughing at his death. It might tempt fate. For all she knows, it might even make her go crazy. Crazy like her momma.

She glances around the room looking for what to do next and spies the bloody bucket of water next to her parent's bed. She remembers bringing the water and a clean rag to her mother late last night. Her eyes just naturally gravitate to her poppa, and she takes a good long look at him.

Big mistake. All this time, she's been pretending her poppa would be alright. But now, she's not so sure. He looks shrunken, half the man he was just a day ago. His skin is a pasty blue-grey, and his breathing is too quick, and much too shallow. It's hard to believe he's even the same man she teased and called His Majesty at supper just last night. She moves to his side, leans down, and kisses his forehead, but he doesn't react. She picks his hand up and rubs it for a few minutes, trying to stimulate him, but he doesn't respond.

Letty remains calm. Her poppa's still breathing, and it gives her hope. She lays his hand on his heart, gives him a kiss on his clammy cheek, then whispers in his ear, "I love you, poppa. Momma loves you, too. We want you to wake up poppa, please wake up!"

Letty waits for a miracle, a divine intervention, but nothing happens. She gives up after a few minutes and picks up the bucket of bloody water. It needs to be dumped, so she hauls it outside. But instead of dumping it over the wall, she defiantly pours it over the garlic bed she helped her momma dig just twenty-four hours ago.

Her rebellious act breaks the long-standing rule of never, ever leaving human waste in the food garden. But Letty no longer cares about normal or rules for that matter. She'll dump her poppa's blood wherever she damn well pleases, he's a good man, why wouldn't his blood be good, too.

She stomps her way to the well and pumps half a bucket of water, then takes it back inside and sets it down on the floor next to the cast iron stew pot her mother used as the murder weapon. The bottom of the pot is covered in dried grey matter and short black hairs, while the inside still carries residue from last night's supper. Letty shoves the vile pot into the bucket of cold water.

She thought she was in control, but as soon as the pot settles to the bottom of the bucket her hands retract, retreat, and drop to her sides, then slide behind her back, desperate for physical distance from that unlikely instrument of death. She takes a step back, letting the pot soak for a minute, needing to build up courage so she can touch it again. A scant moment later she attacks the pot with exceptional vigor, scrubbing it inside and out with the help of the bloody rag.

At first, she gags as the rag grinds against the dried hair and gray matter. It feels bumpy when what she wants is a quick scrub, a slick slide off. She doesn't want to continue scrubbing, it's too awful. Still, it must be dealt with, and who else is there? Who else is paying attention to what needs to be done to keep them from going to prison or hanging? She glances at her father and remembers his words and understands his innocence. But her mother, she never expected that level of violence, the fury that lives within that tiny woman. So surprising, so sudden, and then her mother's unexpected collapse.

But Letty promised to take care of all the mess and that includes the murder pot. She fills a second bucket with half cold water, half hot, then adds soap and washes the pot all over again. Now she has two buckets of fouled water. She hauls them outside and this time she dumps them over the wall but doesn't bother to fling the slop water as far as she can. Now is not the time for childish games, she thinks that time might be done.

Seeing the chipped bones and the chunks of brains flow out with the fouled water really gets to Letty. Her knees go weak, and she grabs the top of the wall to keep from collapsing. She bends over, gags, then dry heaves. But just as soon as the gaging stops, she resumes her chores. She takes the empty buckets to the well and fills them each three quarters full, using the last little bit of the pump's runoff to rinse the sour taste from her mouth. She drinks a few mouthfuls of water, and it restores her enough that she's able to haul the heavy buckets of water back to the hearth. She adds hot water to one of the buckets and tosses in a bit of shaved soap along with the bloody rag.

She kneels on a thick towel and begins the task of wiping up all the blood, stew, and anything else that litters the cottage floor. While she works flies land in her hair, on her neck, and on her nose. They try to crawl in every orifice they can find. They even land on the corners of her eyes and try to suck her eye juice.

Letty's mind wanders as she goes about her task. She imagines a tail to flick the flies away. Wouldn't that be handy about now? She wiggles her butt and giggles at the thought of having a tail. A big, bushy white tail. How silly it would be to have such a tail. How would she sit down at the supper table? Would the tail poke out of a hole sewn into her skirt? She imagines her white, fluffy tail spread down over the back of the bench, swishing back and forth in time with each bite she takes of her supper. The vision reduces her to shoulder shaking laughter, but not for long, the bothersome flies bring her back to reality and the task of cleaning.

As Letty goes about scrubbing the floor, she stashes the tulip bulbs and the silver coins in her apron pocket. She sacrifices a wooden bowl so she can safely contain all the lethal shards of the crystal vase. Once all the pieces are recovered, she takes the wooden bowl to the outhouse and drops it down the hole. It splashes with an inevitable fountain of shitty water.

Curious, Letty peers down the hole and finds the wooden bowl floating, upright, the shards of glass still cradled inside. Unfortunately, the metal rims are poking a few inches above the watery shit soup. She finds it concerning, but she's not about to push them out of sight. And why should she bother? It's only her family using the outhouse.

She returns to the cottage and resumes cleaning. Finally, the floor, the hearth, and every leg and flat surface of the chairs and the table, the bench and the doorframe are spotlessly clean. The cottage becomes eerily quiet, the ten thousand flies having left in search of a new food source.

She dumps the last of the fouled wash water over the wall, then drinks her fill of water after rinsing and filling the buckets. Down to the bone tired, she still manages to haul the water to the kitchen. And then she stands still for a moment and gazes about the cottage, judging her work, finding it to be good until she closes the door and the two buckets of bones and the dustpan of powdered blood pops into view.

Somehow, she had forgotten all about them. She sighs, then nearly cries. It's exactly the kind of evidence that will put her in prison, maybe get her hanged, too. The fearsome thought pushes her to action and in a near panic she flings open the door, picks up the buckets and rushes outside, but carefully so as not to dislodge the dustpan of blood. The bones weigh more than she ever thought possible and as she approaches the gate the bucket's handles slowly slide from her grasp. The buckets land on the ground, but manage to stay upright, nothing spilling, not even the dustpan. She leans on the gate, too exhausted, too disheartened to move just yet. Besides, she has no idea what to do next. Her mother made it clear the bones were not to be buried in the garden. And with her luck they would probably float if she were to dump them down the outhouse hole. Besides, she can already imagine the arm bones reassembling, coming to life, reaching up and pulling her down into the stinking, brown shit soup.

She looks around, scanning the landscape for an idea. She catches sight of the vanes of the windmill wiggling back and forth in the light wind, the dog brake preventing them from spinning free. The resisting, resulting squeak, squeak, squeak gives her the seed of an idea. The idea grows and becomes her what to do. She lifts both buckets of bones, careful to maintain the balance of the dustpan and strides with renewed purpose to the ancient windmill.

Two centuries ago, her ancestors built the windmill using granite rock shot through with mica and quartz. At certain times of day, when the sun's rays hit the rocks at exactly the right angle the entire sunny side of the windmill comes alive with sparkles. It was during those moments that Letty would lose herself playing the game of another life. Sometimes she would imagine the windmill as a castle tower and pretend she was a princess awaiting her prince. At other times, the windmill's vanes would become the sails of her grandfather's merchant sailing ship and she would pretend she was fearlessly climbing the rigging as her mother once did, trimming the sails during a raging typhoon.

The sparkle is happening at just this moment, but for once Letty is not distracted. Instead, she boldly enters the windmill and walks directly to the granite grinding wheels. Their mass and purpose reinforce her decision. It's the right move, the fitting answer to disappearing the bones of the man who has so unjustly destroyed her family.

Letty carefully places the buckets near the levers that operate the grindstones. Then she lifts the dustpan off the bucket and lays it on the floor out of the way. As steady as she goes, Letty stands on her tippy toes and dumps the burnt bones into the hopper. Next, and in the exact order her poppa taught her, she drops a lever into a slot. The action causes a spindle to drop into the top grindstone. She listens for just the right moment between the squeak squeaks of the windmill's braked vanes and when she hears it, she slams a lever into the top groove on the spindle. She quickly follows that motion by pulling another lever out of its slot.

Immediately the squeak, squeak, squeak becomes a whoosh as the windmill's vanes are set free. The vane's rotation applies to the spindle, and in turn, the spindle transfers the energy to the top grindstone causing it to turn and grind against the fixed stone on the bottom. A low, growling, grinding noise fills the interior of the windmill.

And soon, what looks like dirty flour is pouring onto the mill's spotlessly clean stone floor. The flour fans out, scattering everywhere. This is unintended. The outlet chute should have had an empty bucket under it to catch the bone flour, but Letty forgot to put it there. The flow soon peters out to nothing. With all the strength Letty can muster she disengages the levers. The grindstones stop and the squeak, squeak, squeak of the restricted sails resumes. She pours the powdered blood into an empty bucket, then sweeps the spilled bone flour onto the dustpan and dumps it onto the blood, needing but just one bucket now.

And that's the moment Letty's ancient lizard brain decides to pop out of hiding. It's proud of her. It prods her until she laughs out loud. She's done it. She's reduced the Stranger to nothing, nothing. Nothing but burnt flour dust. She brags to no one at all, "Oh, this will do, and do very nicely,"

Out of nowhere comes a sudden gust of wind. It rustles the leaves of the old oak tree. The sound is one long, deep sigh, nature's lament for the dead. The sound shames her and pushes her into a deep state of melancholy.

She leaves the mill and heads for the cottage, failing once again to see the two vultures staring down on her from their perch at the crown of the massive oak tree. She drops the empty bucket at the well and returns the flagstone dustpan and scraper to the scrap heap. The bucket of ground bones needs to be hidden, but where?

Too tired to think it through she lets habit kick in. She brings the bucket inside the cottage and places it against the wall next to the door. It is, after all, what she would normally have done with a bucket of flour.

She feels all itchy, filthy dirty and is desperate to feel clean again. To that end, she builds up the fire and heats water, intending on taking a French bath just as soon as she possibly can. Her stomach hurts she's that hungry, and so she searches the kitchen cupboard for the piece of bread she knows her mother saved for her. It should be next to the butter and honey jars, but it's nowhere to be found. She decides the butter and honey will have to do for a quick meal but when she opens the containers, she finds them nearly empty.

Her crazy mother has left her with nothing ready to eat.

Letty's hunger is painful, unrelenting. A spoon is useless, so little is left. She slides her fingers around the interior walls and the bottoms of both containers, collecting the remnants of butter and honey, sucking on her fingers like a baby, needy, getting a moment of comfort from the simple act, sucking and licking, licking and sucking until she has consumed the very last drops of both the butter and the honey. Momentarily satiated, she looks up from the cupboard's counter and discovers her bath water is boiling.

Letty lights a fresh beeswax candle and places it near the center of the table. She slips off her water-logged wooden shoes, then tip toes quietly about the cottage pulling all the bed curtains closed. That done, she mixes a bucket of hot and cold water together to use for her bath, then reaches behind her back and unties her apron strings.

And that's when she feels them.

The wicked, wicked tulip bulbs.

She's forgotten all about them. She's been wearing a sack of tulip bulbs on her belly for so long, really for most of the day, that they have now become a part of her body. She removes her apron and hangs it on a hook near the fireplace. Curiosity gets the best of her, and she takes a single tulip bulb from the apron's pocket to examine.

The bulb is about the size and color of an apple, but the shape imitates that of a fat strawberry, especially the tip. Her hunger pains revive with a terrible vengeance as the enticing red glow of the bulb tempts her to eat it. Without overthinking it, she peels off the remaining bits of papery tunic. The bulb might harbor nearly invisible specks of diseased soil. So, just to be safe, she dips it in the pot of hot water and rinses it till she thinks it's clean enough. And then she bites the tip right off and chews it right up. Really just trying it, seeing if maybe it might be real food. The crunchy texture and the tangy, almost peppery taste make for an irresistible combination and Letty consumes the bulb in fast little bites. Almost immediately, a strange tingle ripples through her body. Her breasts swell and harden, and she just naturally cocks a hip.

The next moment, she feels overheated. She quickly strips off her outer clothes and is momentarily cooled. She resumes removing her clothes but at a bit more leisurely pace. As she unbuttons her chemise, top to bottom, her index finger traces a meandering path down her chest, circling between her breasts, teasing touching the nipples, chasing anticipation. She rolls her shoulders, and her chemise drops from her body.

One, undone button later, her underskirt follows. She steps out of it, then picks it up and without understanding why, she rubs the underskirt's coarse muslin fabric across her naked breasts, gasping as the cloth slides across her nipples, moaning as she rubs the fabric in circles over her round, firm butt cheeks. After a moment she tosses the underskirt, along with the chemise, onto the burgeoning laundry pile.

She would be nude but for her stockings and her thick leather footings. It's time they go. She slides the leather footings off and kicks them aside, then reaches down and starting high, using the long stroke down the inside of her thighs, she slips her thumbs under the tops of her garters and slowly pushes them down along with the stockings they were holding up, all the way down her long legs and off her little, pretty toes. She shakes them out and tosses them at the laundry pile. The stockings and garters flutter as they fall, landing exactly where they need to be. And just like that, Letty has won another game. Pleased with herself, a sultry smile blooms on her plump, pink lips.

Naked now, Letty struts over to the kitchen cupboard. Bending from the waist she opens the cupboard's lower door and removes two things from the shelf, a white porcelain dish containing a homemade bar of sweet-smelling soap and a soft, clean washcloth. She leaves the cupboard, cozies up to the fire and begins her French bath by first dipping the bar of soap and the washcloth into the bucket of hot water. The cleansing scent of lavender and something else is released, maybe a hint of rose, perhaps lily.

She soaps and scrubs every inch of her hands, her wrists, and all the way up to her elbows, washing the dirty deeds of the day away. Then she moves on and cleans every other bit of herself. The slippery, soapy washcloth further stimulates her skin. Waves of pleasure flow through her. Her nipples swell and harden, becoming separate beings begging to be rubbed. She's caught in the spell of a feeling she did not know existed and so she gives in, gently rubbing her swollen nipples round and around.

A tender ache begins between her legs, a need calling out. She drops her hand from her breast to her most private of places. The ache shows her what to do. She pushes and releases, pushes, and releases. And when that's not enough, she rubs up and down. Her fingers slip into a slick groove, and she discovers the little hard ball of her female sex. Her fingers make a motion that comes so naturally it's like she has always done this. Too soon, a throbbing convulsion overtakes her, and she can no longer bear to touch herself. A delicious full body shiver consumes her, leaving her limp and spent, barely able to stand. The lovely, luscious Letty had no idea her body could do this.

She wants to do it all over again.

She wants more.

She dumps the soapy water into the slop bucket, fills the bucket with clean warm water, and proceeds to rinse her entire body, hoping for an encore performance. But the feeling is not as intense, though she still feels pleasure. Her hair needs washing, and it's best done before the water cools. So, after dumping a few cups of the warm rinse water on her head, she massages the lavender scented soap through her curls. Eventually, she tires and leaning over the slop bucket she rinses her thick hair until the water is all used up.

And suddenly, just that quick, from head-to-toe, Letty feels clean. No blood, no brains, no greasy scent of roasting man clings to her. She's still dripping wet, though. She holds her arms out, tilts her head back and slowly spins as she air-dries in front of the fire. A wide, lazy smile plays on her plumped-up lips. She feels so good, oh so good.

Her body has never felt this alive. Her breasts and nipples tingle in a delicious way, a completely unexpected way. She wants to rub them again, against something, anything. She wants the feelings to never end.

A desperate need to fill the hole between her legs overtakes her and so she sticks her finger in and rubs it around until she finds a little flat spot with an entirely different texture. She barely rubs it round and around, it's no bigger than her little fingertip. She soon loses herself to a pulsing wave of euphoria. She senses a wetness between her legs, and she checks and finds a clear sticky fluid has leaked from the secret place of her monthly blood. The whole experience has left her so weakened she can barely stand.

And oddly enough she finds she's not in the least bit hungry. What's this? What happened to her hunger? And why was she overwhelmed with these odd, yet wonderful feelings? Could this be from eating the tulip bulb? It must be. It must be so, for she has never felt this way before.

She slides through the narrow gap between her curtains. From her storage chest she picks out a clean chemise and underskirt and slips them on, then gathers the clothes she will wear on the morrow. As she hangs her tomorrow clothes on the hooks next to the head of her bed her hands seem to take every opportunity to rub her breasts.

It seems especially hard to stop sliding her chemise over her tender nipples, it just feels so good.

Letty always assumed pleasure took two, but it's not true. A dreamy expression drifts across her satisfied face. Her body feels deliciously spent. She stretches in a lazy cat-like way, her arm inadvertently pushing the curtains further apart.

She looks through the gap into the room beyond. The usual night would have had her parent's sitting at the table maybe playing chess, maybe holding hands and whisper talking to one another, but usual is gone now. Strangely enough, as she pleasured herself, the awful truth of the last day had temporarily slipped from her mind. She replays her poppa's battle in her mind's eye and all that has happened since and she suddenly, desperately wants her momma.

She turns to her bed and looks down.

Her mother is laying on top of Letty's quilt, sound asleep. So incredibly beautiful, yet so disgustingly dirty.

The high Letty has enjoyed collapses under the full weight of her exhaustion. She crawls over her mother, careful not to disturb her, and slides under the quilt. Then she takes a deep breath, closes her eyes, and instantly falls into a deep, dreamless sleep.

15

Neola

Vonder moans and has a seizure. He moans again only this time louder. Muttered gibberish follows, then his hands clench into fists and he pounds the mattress. After a minute or so, he becomes rigid. A few minutes pass and then he relaxes. Drool slides from his slack lips. His eyelids open, but just briefly. The whites of his eyes have turned a hideous blood red while the blue of the iris has been swallowed by his oddly shaped, fully dilated pupils. The light of his loving, sweet-natured soul has now been trapped behind the dark curtain of impending death. Vonder's tortured sounds slowly nudge Neola awake. By the time she's fully conscious the cottage has become quiet. She knows something woke her, but she has no idea what it could have been. Through a gap in Letty's curtains, she sees the flickering flame of a candle placed near the center of the old battered table. A small fire is burning in the hearth, helping to further push back the darkness. As always, the soft light erases the poverty of their existence.

Neola rolls over and sits up, smells lavender, and sniffs it out. She finds Letty under the covers, curled up, deep in sleep, so recently bathed that her hair is still sopping wet. By contrast, Neola feels filthy dirty. Not just dirty in the usual way, but filthy in an immoral sense. She rubs her arms as if to rid herself of something corrupt, but it does little to change how she feels, so she stops doing it. She glances at her daughter to see if she has been bothered awake. But no, Letty's still sound asleep.

Something about Letty catches Neola's eye. She looks different, somehow matured. Neola realizes her daughter has the glow of a satisfied woman. It's as though the last twenty-four hours have been good for Letty, but how can that be?

Neola leaves the bed, slips through the curtains, then tiptoes to the hearth. As quietly as she can, she feeds the fire. It flares up and brightens the cottage, chasing the lingering shadows from the dim corners. She finds the entire cottage has been scrubbed clean, and everything has been put to rights. Letty did it, and all by herself. Neola is grateful, but then feels a bit of shame. It took a tremendous amount of work and a strong stomach to wash away all the blood and brains, the bits of scull. Her daughter is ever so helpful, ever so capable. She can always count on Letty to takes care of things.

Neola whispers, "Thank you, baby girl. Thank you."

Apparently, the one thing Letty didn't do is dump her own bath water. Neola slips her footwear on and takes care of it. She stops at the well on her way back to the cottage and refills the buckets. Then she carries the buckets of water back inside and promptly prepares a pot of water to heat for her bath. In all the days of her life she's never been this sticky and grimy and the only thing she cares about right now is having a French bath, the sooner the better.

But then the sudden sound of her husband's low moans changes her mind. She rushes to his side, crazy to be with him, hoping by some miracle he has revived. She yanks the bed curtains apart and drops to her knees. She's greeted by the full moon's light streaming in through the window. The moon's cold, white light highlights Vonder's horribly beaten and bruised face.

Neola needs to touch him, her one true love. She wants to nurse him back to health. More than anything she wants it to be true that she can nurse him back to life. She leans over him and puts her hand on his forehead to feel if it is hot or not.

Suddenly her wrist is grabbed and held tight by Vonder. His fingernails dig deep into her skin drawing blood. It hurts so bad she cries out in pain. She tries to pull free, but she can't. He's still unconscious, she knows he is, but he hangs on to her with more than his normal strength and doesn't let up or let go.

Neola understands Vonder's ancient lizard brain has slithered out of hiding, raised its ugly head, and taken control. She's experienced the strange phenomenon before while she was nursing injured men on her father's ship. She knows it won't last, it's just a protective reflex and has nothing to do with the real Vonder. She uses her free hand to break his grip, pulling one finger loose at a time. And as she does so, she whispers in his ear, "Easy, be easy now Vonder. It's me, Neola, I'm your wife. You know I would never, ever hurt you, so please stop hurting me, please let me go. I love you. You know I love you."

The instant she's free of his grip, she moves out of his reach, taking no chances with the vicious, ancient lizard brain. She takes a good long look at him. The cast of his skin is blue grey, a sure sign his heart and lungs are failing. She can't fix him, nor ease his suffering as he slowly exits their world. And because the sight of him hurts her own heart so much, she abandons him for the moment and returns to the fire.

A moment later, she slips out of her underthings and strips off her garters and stockings. The noxious odor of ripe body fluids hits her nose. Somehow the dead man has managed to foul even her underthings. Worse yet, he's still occupying space in her home. She hates him. Enraged, she throws the clothes at the burgeoning laundry pile.

Naked now, Neola appears transparent and luminous, her veins having tinged her snow-white skin barely blue. Her long auburn hair is all matted and tangled and she attacks it with the brush, dutifully giving it the customary one hundred strokes, all in preparation of washing it. She looks in the mirror, but gives no smile, for nothing happy lingers in her heart. Her heart is broken, and happiness cannot be held in a broken heart, and so it follows that happiness can no longer exist for her.

It's simple really. The Stranger has killed her happiness for all time. The revelation rolls through her, touching every cell, every atom, every bit of all of her being. It's the absence, the longing. She longs for what she had every moment of every day, all the days of her life. She needs Vonder's gentle, loving, knowing touch, his smile, his words and especially the sound of his sweet, sweet voice, but it's gone now, and just that quick.

She knows her real life is never coming back. Not now, not ever, how can it? She's committed the gravest of all sins, she willfully took a life and is forever after a murderer. Her mind spins, and the dark hole expands within her. It hurts her. It's constantly eating away at her heart now, and she can't stop it, not unless Vonder comes back and it would take a miracle from heaven to fix him, it would take divine intervention.

A bible lays on the shelf next to the box of essentials. It was a gift from the church deacon and meant to replace the one they lost in the fire. She understands the promise of solace that it offers, but she's disgusted by the sight of it now, and thinking out loud she declares, "Good book? I hardly think so. You're just a poorly written book full of violent, unjust, lustful stories. A real God doesn't need a book. And a real God would never have let my perfect Vonder be harmed. I don't think you're much of a God. I doubt you even exist."

And with that edict she throws the bible at the door with all her might. It hits with a dull thud, slides to the floor, and falls open to a page she will never, ever read again.

Vonder and Neola's hats and coats are hanging on the hooks under the shelf. With a trembling hand she reaches out and strokes her husband's bright blue hat, then buries her face in it, smelling his healthy man's smell, breathing in his essence. The realized loss twists her heart causing her acute physical pain. Grief becomes her one expression. She wants to melt away, sink into the ground and die. But she knows she can't. Not yet. She has a child to care for, Vonder's child. He would expect her to keep their child safe. And so, she will.

Neola returns to the hearth and slowly swings the crane holding the pot of boiling water away from the fire. Then she ladles hot water into the half-filled bucket of cold water until it's almost full. Using the same washcloth and soap as Letty, she washes her hands over, and over, and over again. Then by the light of the candle, she examines her murderous hands in minute detail. Imagines of the Stranger's blood and brains dripping from her fingertips overwhelm her. The hallucination is so real she develops vertigo and for a second, she really believes the room is falling over on its side and she starts to go with it. Just in time she grabs onto the edge of the table and manages to pull herself upright. She waits it out and a moment later the illusion passes, the room returns to normal, and she resumes the task of washing her murderous hands.

When Neola is finally satisfied her hands are truly clean, she moves on to the rest of her body, washing and rinsing each part of herself, including her filthy hair. The very last thing she washes is the hairbrush, for it has become fouled, too. As she dries off the rough towel rubs the large patch of scar tissue on her back. It causes her discomfort and a little bit of welcomed pain.

The dull ache reminds her of the fire that destroyed their way of life and killed Vonder's parents. And now after five hard years the bad luck has returned with a vengeance. The lightning that sparked the fire was considered an act of God, but all the trouble after Vonder found the bundle of tulip bulbs, is that just a mere coincidence? She thinks of the bad luck and when it started. Her own father's ship sunk, all the cargo and hands-on board lost. Two months later their own home and the nearby warehouse burnt to the ground, destroying their remaining wealth, killing Vonder's parents, nearly killing them all. And now a bundle of tulip bulbs has all but killed her husband, and she's gone mad and murdered a man. And if she's caught, she'll surely go to prison and hang for it. Letty might be jailed too, and even hanged for something she didn't do. Neola is beginning to think something sinister is trying to destroy their lives, but she has no idea what it could be or even why.

She's in a hurry now to be dressed. Her nakedness, her beautiful, lush body is an affront to her own sorrow. She opens the doors of the ancient wooden wardrobe and selects clean clothes based on how close they are to being a rag. She throws on a soft cotton chemise worn so thin it's become gauze, and slides on a pair of drawers in about the same condition. She slips on her plainest underskirt because she feels she doesn't deserve anything pretty. And all the while she's dressing, she's going about gathering her tomorrow clothes, including the everyday apron. She takes the long-sleeved cotton shirtwaist and the gabardine walking skirt to her daughter's alcove and hangs them on an empty hook next to Letty's next day clothes.

Habit compels her to take her apron to the usual hook next to the fireplace. She finds it already occupied by Letty's apron. It's concerning because her daughter's apron is so filthy it's obvious it should have been thrown in the laundry pile. Neola's too tired to deal with it and decides to just leave it there and hang her apron over it anyway. But as she does so, her hand brushes up against something hard and round buried deep inside Letty's apron pocket.

Curious, Neola reaches inside and pulls out an enormous tulip bulb. For some reason, the bulb makes her anxious. She finds an empty basket and dumps the entire contents of the apron's pocket into it. Then she sidles up to the table with the basket and sets it down exactly where her stew bowl would normally go. As she sorts through the contents, she counts out five silver coins and a total of sixteen tulip bulbs. She clearly remembers the last moments of fun she had with Vonder was when they were counting these very same tulip bulbs and shouting out the count at twenty-one. There's no doubt in her mind five tulip bulbs are missing.

Her mind blanks out, then last night's battle comes back to her in a flash. She vaguely remembers seeing a few tulip bulbs at the edge of the hearth. But Neola's tired and does the easy thing by assuming the missing tulip bulbs have been burnt.to ash. She has no idea what to do with the remaining bulbs and just glares at them until she realizes she can't take her eyes off them. The tulip bulbs seem to have captured her, and it incites her anger. Her anger builds until it slips into a rage so great her eyes beat with the rhythm of her heart. Each pulse becomes a push towards madness even as she wages a silent war with the tulip bulbs.

Suddenly, the robust health of the bulbs pisses her off and she picks one up and throws it as hard and as fast as she can at the crack in the door, pretending it's the Stranger she's hitting. After all, he was the one put that crack in her father's beautiful door by pounding so hard on it. Then she picks up another tulip bulb, and then a third, throwing them with all her might, as fast and as hard as she possibly can. The tulip bulbs bounce off, undamaged, and roll back to her, stopping at her bare feet, touching her toes, goading her on.

Frustrated beyond all common sense, overcome with fury and self-hate, she grabs two fistfuls of hair and pulls down hard on both sides of her head, needing to feel physical pain and succeeding, her frustration so great she pulls two small clumps of her hair loose from her scalp, the hair the color of a mortal wound.

The pain feels so good. The pain is a punishment of sorts. She hates this most horrible of days, this endless day, hopelessly endless. She slowly calms down as she chants the word why, why, why until why becomes whispers so quiet the word why becomes just breathing.

Calm now, and believing she has no other choice, she returns the tulip bulbs to the basket, then hangs the basket on the side of the kitchen cupboard in its usual spot. And so, once again, the wicked, wicked tulip bulbs are out of sight and have temporarily lost the power to entice, distract, and disturb the unwary.

16

Jacob Vandermeer

Neola retrieves the bag of money from under her mattress. The billfold is on top and so it naturally becomes the first thing she examines. It looks to be in good shape but well-handled. Made of the darkest of browns deeply oiled leather, the bifold billfold is marked with the initials J.V. stamped in gold on both sides. Neola has a vague memory of seeing the initials stamped on something else she handled last night. The Stranger's leather belt comes to mind, and she worries where it is for a moment, but then remembers throwing that damning piece of evidence on the funeral pyre.

The billfold's contents need a good looking at. She finds four folded documents but considers the possibility of a secret compartment. She massages the billfold feeling for anomalies and when she finds none, she tosses it on the fire. One by one, she unfolds the documents, flattens them, and stacks them. The top paper is a travel document stamped by the countries of China, Afghanistan, Tibet, India, Burma, Turkey, Italy, Spain, France, and England. The extent of his travels is truly astonishing. Because she was raised in the import export business, she recognizes that he was someone special, probably an important collector or trader of some desired commodity.

The second document is an open ticket for free passage on any of the Holland Shipping &Trading Company's ships to anywhere in the world, upon demand, authorized by the president of the Holland Horticultural Society. So, he was a field botanist employed by the Holland Horticultural Society. Thus, the tulip bulbs.

The third document is a receipt for six wooden crates transported on a Holland Shipping &Trading Company ship. She assumes the crates were brimming full of all manner of botanical specimens. Her possession of the documents is all the proof needed to hang her and put Letty in jail for years, or possibly hang Letty, too. Neola wads them into tight little balls and one by one she tosses them onto the fire. The last paper is an identity document. She reads his name out loud, "Jacob Vandermeer."

She can read no more. She hates him. The very sight of his name incites her rage She crumples the paper into the tightest of balls and pitches it onto the fire where it promptly whooshes and burns up in a furious explosion of light. But it's not enough. Her fists clench, and her nails dig so deep into the soft flesh of her palms they draw blood. It hurts her and she likes it. The pain makes her want to destroy him all over again. She looks around for him, but she can't find him. He's already gone. Frustrated, she looks for satisfaction elsewhere and realizes it's right in front of her.

She has all his money. Neola dumps the bag onto the table's top. A huge pile of banknotes and coins lay in front of her. Her ancient lizard brain momentarily slips to the surface and takes possession. Her once sweet lips contort into a twisted smile of greed. After all, it's been five long years since she has last seen anything close to this amount of wealth and it belongs to her now, it's all hers.

Finder keepers. Loser weepers.

A sudden single moan floats from her marriage bed and fills her ears. The human Neola, loving wife of Vonder, regains dominance. The money is not worth the loss of her love, the destruction of her family. No amount of money would ever be enough. Hot, heavy tears flow. She needs her man, so bad, so bad. She looks at him, hoping against hope, but he remains unconscious, still hovering on the brink of death, no reprieve for that man of hers, she knows it.

The fire pops. And just that quick Neola snaps back to the job of counting money. She separates the gold sovereigns, the gold and silver guilders, the pennies and the ha' pennies. The coins alone amount to several years of support if Letty's prudent. But the real shocker is the quantity of newly minted English banknotes. A small fortune is before her, enough to provide Letty with a secure start in some far away country.

Neola stuffs the coins and banknotes back in the bag along with the beat-up compass and the gold watch and chain. Not having a better idea, she hides the bag under the mattress again. While she's at the bed, Vonder has yet another seizure. It continues for what seems like forever before finally stopping. She takes a chance he won't grab her again and places her warm hand on his cool forehead, just needing to touch him again, to reassure herself he's still alive.

She returns to her chair just as a piece of pitch explodes with an especially loud pop. Startled, she jumps and cries out, unable to stop the involuntary reaction. She waits for a long moment, holding still, listening. expecting Letty to awaken, her husband to moan, but nothing happens no matter how hard she wishes it would. For the first time in her life Neola has no one to talk to. In the lonely stillness of the night, her mind begins to wander. She thinks back through the years remembering her strange family.

Vonder's mother was her mother, too. Her own mother's death made it so. Two days after giving birth to Neola, her mother died from bleeding out. Heartbroken, unable to care for his motherless newborn, Neola's father handed her off to Vonder's parents. Vonder was just nine-months old at the time and was still being breast fed, so it was easy for his mother to become Neola's wet nurse. She was a loving woman and comfortable with holding both babies in her arms at the same time. She sang to them as she fed them, the two babies just naturally snuggling, holding hands as they suckled from her generous breasts.

It was decided early on that Neola was not to call Vonder's parents momma and poppa, to do so would have been disrespectful. Instead, as soon as she could talk, she called them BeeBee and Howie. BeeBee held and hugged Neola throughout the day, every day, showing her by example how best to love and be loved. And Howie showed by example how best to be a helpmate.

It worked so well. Though not related, her father and BeeBee and Howie had equally inherited a centuries old import export business and were business partners And so, while Neola's father sailed the East Indian Archipelago and the South China Seas, buying and sometimes selling merchandise for the business, BeeBee and Howie ran the European marketing end of the business, maintaining a portion of the goods in the warehouse, all while caring for Neola as a well-loved guest.

She thinks back to her first trip on her father's merchant sailing ship. She was but five years old at the time and remembers falling in love with the movement of the ship as it slipped over the surface of the seas. The ocean's great swells seemed like just another way to breathe. Her little legs worked back and forth, up, and down, riding the rhythm of the pitching deck. She was a natural on the water, at home anywhere on the ship, no matter the weather. They docked at all manner of ports to buy merchandise, mostly tea and spices, but silk too, and other necessary wonderments, her father was good at that, finding special spices, finding special anything.

She saw many unusual sights, but it was the people that amazed her the most. As she walked about the bazaars, she saw people with blue black skin, their heads covered in thick wooly hair. She especially admired the child-sized women wrapped in vibrant colored silks. She loved their bare-naked bellies, the red dots between their eyebrows. Some had nose rings, and all wore multiple earrings, many dangling, some just hoops of gold. The bangles the women wore on their wrists and ankles made a delightful musical clanking with their every movement.

In her walkabouts, always accompanied by her father, she encountered hairy men with big beards and big noses. They wore elaborate headscarves and long white dresses. Sometimes they were accompanied by women so secret, so hidden by dark, loose clothing that only their eyes and hands were visible. Neola loved every minute of it, and the people in the crowds did too. They would pat her flaming red hair to put the fire out or gently stroke the white skin of her face to feel if it were snow or ice or maybe just white marble.

She loved to watch people from the rail of the ship when they were at dock. The dock whores were especially interesting, the clothes, the tricks to entice men so subtle, so clever. Young as she was, she caught on to the tricks. She waved at everyone just to see how many would wave back. Everyone always waved back. Because the voyages took so long to complete, her father allowed her just three trips in all. The last trip was the year she turned fifteen and her father added the South China Seas as a special present.

On that final trip, her father allowed her to leave the ship at every port, but only in his company, of course. They walked through all manner of bazaars and ate all kinds of delicious, regional food. She still caused a sensation but was able to politely turn away the curious hands. Her father was firm, but also fun loving, sharing his vast knowledge of different cultures with her, insisting she respect everyone, even the whores and the lepers. And of course, she understood she was to have no physical contact with anyone, except on the ship.

Her father tasked the ship's doctor with teaching Neola triage nursing. The deck hands were prone to accidents, often breaking legs or arms or heads, and so she became a competent nurse, nearly as skilled as the doctor.

Soon after returning from her final trip with her father, on the day of her sixteenth birthday, she married Vonder. The wedding was a joyous affair attended by everyone within a day's ride. Less than a year later she gave birth to their baby girl. They named her Letty, because the name meant joy. And they continued to make their home with his parents, happy to help run the home and import, export business.

But then one day word came her father's ship had sunk off the coast of west British India, near Karachi. They were told several waterspouts took down the ship. The twisting winds had been witnessed at a safe distance by another trader. Sadly, no one was left to be rescued. And then, two months later her home and warehouse burnt to the ground and her beloved BeeBee and Howie lost their lives, the inferno so hot they became nothing but piles of ash among piles of ash. Neola and Letty would have died too, but for Vonder's quick actions.

As she thinks on this, the timeline of the last five years, she puts it all together. Monday is the third time her family has been targeted in recent years with destruction. It could only be an old-fashioned foreign curse come to finish the job. And this time, the curse used tulip bulbs as the arrow and the Stranger as the bow to deliver the final, killing blows to her family.

Neola knows exactly where the wicked tulip bulbs are, but a vague memory of another object niggles at her mind. She breaths deep, trying to calm herself, but the injustice of it all reignites her rage. The anger stimulates Neola's natural fighting reflex. Memories surface of a past, life-threatening event she experienced on her father's ship when they sailed round the Cape of Good Hope during a horrendous storm's mountainous, collapsing hundred-foot seas. The curse is another such storm, and she vows to survive it or die trying.

Neola looks out the window above Letty's bed. Great clouds of bats are flying round and around the top of the windmill seemingly confused about the direction of tonight's foraging. A single hoot of an owl sounds, the ancient warning of impending death. Neola shivers, the superstition finally taking hold in her mind as truth.

She glances at her daughter. Letty's curled in the fetal position and staring back with great interest. Neola's surprised, then not. She wonders what Letty might have seen or heard but decides it makes no difference. The time has come to tell her daughter the truth about the Stranger and the bundle. Neola proceeds thoughtfully, carefully, as her husband would want her to.

"Letty, I'm glad you're awake. I need to tell you something about the Stranger and why he came to our home so late last night. He came to our door because he thought your poppa stole his valuable bundle of tulip bulbs. But your poppa did no such thing. Your poppa found the bundle on the road, he's not a thief. Your poppa is completely innocent. Never, ever forget that." Neola pauses, letting her words sink in.

After a moment she continues, "Somehow, the Stranger managed to find your poppa in only a few hours. I found it very odd that the empty cart was still hitched to the horse. It made me think he must have been close by, probably at the village stables, when he unloaded the crates and checked his cargo. When he discovered the bundle was missing, he didn't even bother to unhitch the horse before going in search of the bundle because the bundle was that valuable."

Neola sits all quiet for a minute, thinking of what it all means, putting the last pieces of the puzzle together.

"You know Letty, I think your poppa must have been the last

person to handle the crates, and that's why the Stranger suspected him. I think the Stranger must have asked the stable hand where the workman with a limp and a bright blue hat lived." Neola deliberately leaves her theory of the curse out of the explanation, hoping Letty's ignorance might be the saving grace of her.

Letty ponders her mother's words for a minute, then points to the hooks next to her parent's bed and says, "Momma, you best get rid of poppa's hat. Throw it on the fire right now. Burn it. We both know no one else has a bright blue hat like poppa, other people know it, too."

The noose of blind justice tightens just a little bit more around Neola's long, slender neck. It makes sense, she knows it's evidence. Neola removes her husband's hat from the hook and buries her face in it. She smells his smell. His very essence has been rubbed so deep into the felted wool that the hat has become a part of his physical self. She holds it against her face, breathing him in and out for so long her daughter finally begs her to stop.

But Neola finds it impossible to give up the hat that so intimately touched her man. The hat was a gift from the church to commemorate the day Vonder was able to walk again. It was a source of pride and accomplishment for Vonder, and he had made a point of wearing the hat every day. No one else had one like it, the blue dye used to make it was a special batch, far too costly for just ordinary people.

Sobbing, Neola collapses to her knees. Letty remains silent, waiting her mother out. Eventually, Neola comes to her senses and accepts the loss, knowing she must. She drops her husband's hat on the fire and together they watch it slowly melt into nothing but a memory.

Each grieves in her own way. Neola recovers first and gets practical. She heads to the kitchen cupboard to prepare for breakfast. She pours a few cups worth of cracked oats into a bowl, adds water, then places a heavy wooden lid on top the bowl to deter the ever-persistent mice.

She turns to her husband and catches him having a series of seizures. It hurts her, his seizures hurt her. All her bones ache all the time now. The black hole takes another bite from her heart. She feels it, the bite. Soon she will run out of heart and then what will become of Letty?

Neola knows it would be impossible to get any sleep next to her husband. And she needs sleep if she's to take care of their daughter. But more importantly, something evil is underfoot in their lives and she feels an urgent need to stay close to her daughter to protect her. Neola turns to Letty and begs, "May I sleep with you?"

In answer, Letty lifts the covers. Her mother takes the hint and slides in. They snuggle up close and tight, spooning. The daughter's arms wrap round the mother. Moonlight beams touch on the tears and amplify the hopelessly sad expressions of both the mother and daughter.

A feral dog's lonely howl for company pierces the night. An answering call carries up the hill from the hinterlands. The wild dogs yip back and forth, coming closer and closer to each other, creating the night's natural music, the rhythm of the call all the lullaby the mother and daughter need to fall into deep, dreamless sleep.

17

Wednesday, Daybreak

Dawn breaks, its gentle light filling the cottage. The mother and daughter wake and stretch. They sit up, swing their feet onto the floor and stand up all in one smooth move. They each take a curtain and pull it aside. At this moment in time they are twinning, and they both know it, and it makes them smile. They quickly dress, and when Letty puts on a clean apron, it reminds her of what she hid in her yesterday's apron.

"Momma," she says. "I hid the tulip bulbs in my apron's big pocket."

Letty's tongue is so swollen from biting it the night of the battle that Neola has a hard time understanding her. After a moment she parses it out and replies, "I know you did. I found them last night and put them in the basket that's hanging on the side of the kitchen cupboard. You bit your tongue, didn't you?"

Letty nods her head yes, but before she can explain Vonder moans and mutters. They turn to him, the hope obvious, but nothing has changed. He fails to wake. His eyes remain closed. However, there is a foul order emanating from his sick bed. Neola and Letty pinch their noses and breath through their mouths. They look in his direction, then look at each other.

"Letty, I need to clean your poppa. But I need you to understand he's not going to get better if he's unable to eat or drink. He'll soon die if he doesn't wake up and drink, and I don't know how to wake him up." With each word Neola's voice becomes softer, quieter. She shrinks in on herself, her life force diminished in tandem with her man's.

Letty takes hold of her mother's hands and says, "I'm sorry momma, I really am, but I'm so hungry I can't think of anything else. I haven't eaten in more than a day now. Is there anything ready to eat? And what ever happened to my slice of bread?"

Neola gives a little smile layered with guilt and admits, "I ate your piece of bread. Something came over me, and I found I couldn't stop myself. You poor thing, how about you build the fire up nice and hot, and you can cook the oats while I clean your poppa. First, we'll do our necessary and bring in some fresh water. Can you manage all that, baby girl?"

Letty nods her head yes, still mouth breathing so as not to smell the foul air.

The women go about their assigned tasks. Neola heats the water she'll need to clean her husband. She places a bucket of cold water, an empty bucket, and a washcloth within easy reach of the sickbed. It's best Letty doesn't see her father naked and vulnerable, lest it be her last memory of him, so she closes the curtains being especially careful to not leave a gap. Afraid of disturbing her husband's wounded head, Neola cuts the armhole and side seams of his shirt and undershirt and lifts the front pieces off, leaving the back pieces stuck to the sheet. Fortunately, his pants contain the worst of the mess even as she slides them off. She carefully lifts the pillow cradling his head as she pulls the sheet from under it, then gently lays the pillow down again once the sheet passes beyond his shoulders. The hardest struggle is to slip a towel under his ass as she slips the sheet past it. Then she's home free, hard parts over. The fouled clothes and the sheet are now in a tidy pile just waiting to be taken outside.

Slowly, ever so gently, Neola cleans every crevice of Vonder's bruised body, then she cleans him again, rinses him, and finally dries him with the roughest of towels, hoping to stimulate him and bring him back to her. And all the while she whispers softly to him about how pretty the day is, how sweet the flowers smell, and how she loves him so.

It's a struggle to lift his bulk while rolling a clean sheet beneath him, but she succeeds and even manages to slip the clean sheet under his pillow. She changes the cloth stuck to the back of his head, folding the fouled cloth without examining the contents, ignorance nurtures hope, and she could surely use some hope about now.

She dresses him in a clean nightshirt, cutting the back of the neck open before sliding the nightshirt up over his feet, legs, and ass. Then gently, slowly, she pulls the shirt up his back and chest, mindful of not moving his head. The cut fabric gives her just enough slack to stuff his arms into the sleeves. She finishes by buttoning the seven large mother of pearl buttons on the front of the nightshirt starting at the neck and going down.

Vonder's all clean, all good now. Normal, almost. But for the facial bruises, he really does look good to go from the front. Finally, she covers him with their wedding quilt and gently, longingly kisses his dried, cracked lips, hoping he will respond just one more time to her familiar touch.

Nothing happens. Vonder might still be alive, but he's already gone. She rolls back on her heels, thinking of this, but pulls the curtains back anyway, so Letty can see him, so she can see him, so they can both pretend he's part of the day.

While Neola was busy tending to her poppa, Letty drained the water off the oats and dumped them into the smallest of the cottage's cast iron cooking pots. Then she covered the oats with fresh cold water and swung the pot over the fire. She gathered the bowls and spoons and even refilled the jar of honey from the large crock stored in the windmill.

With nothing left to do until the oats are ready to eat, Letty sits down on the bench in her usual spot and makes a game of sticking her pinky finger in the honey then sucking on it. She's pretending it's a piece of hard candy bought at the village store, the kind her poppa used to bring home to her as a special treat. She sucks slow, making it last, then repeats, thinking of candy and little else.

Neola has taken the fouled clothing and sheet outside to the laundry tub. What she really wants to do is drop it all into the shit soup of the outhouse. She knows Vonder will never have need of them again, but she fears it would alarm their daughter, so instead she takes the time to rinse the fouled clothes and sheet in an old bucket they no longer use for house water. She transfers the sopping wet clothes into the laundry tub and dumps the shitty water down the outhouse hole. Then she pumps a bucket of water and pours it into the laundry tub careful to cover every inch of fabric. She hopes the cold water will help the body fluids and blood to soak out.

She uses lots of soap to thoroughly wash her hands before returning to the cottage, her nurse's training kicking in. She knows better than to allow disease to enter her home and fester. On her way into the cottage, she smells the sweet, cloying scent of lilies. Her BeeBee always stressed the importance of having a beautiful centerpiece on the table, and so Neola turns back and collects three white lilies and a few sprigs of spearmint. As soon as she goes inside the cottage, she retrieves a canning jar made of green glass from the top shelf of the kitchen cupboard. She adds a little water and adds the bouquet, crushing the spearmint leaves to release their clean odor. The simple arrangement looks lovely at the center of the table and the lingering sick room smell is soon overcome by the strong scent of lilies and spearmint.

Neola's last chore before eating breakfast is to haul the buckets of fouled water out of the house and dump and rinse them. And once again before entering the cottage, she washes her hands using plenty of soap.

Hunger has been pushing on Neola and she rushes to take her place at the table. The oats have long been ready, but Letty's good manners have made her wait for her mother to be present before eating. Now that Neola is comfortably seated, Letty fills the bowls and reclaims her seat at the table. Lacking milk or butter, they compensate by adding extra honey to the oats. After a few hurried mouthfuls, they look up at each other, guilty looks plastered across their faces. They've forgotten to say grace. Neola shrugs her shoulders and shakes her head no and that's the end of it, the boss has spoken. They resume eating until the pot has been scrapped clean.

The day is bumping up against noon and Neola explains how they must spend the rest of it. She says, "I'm sorry Letty, but we have no choice, I really must go to the village. Someone might be missing the Stranger and come looking for him. We need to find out if anyone suspects us. I'll need to spend a bit of time gossiping, so I'll have to sit at one of the little tables in the shop and have a cup of tea and a biscuit. I'm hoping the counter girl will tell me the news of the last few days. I plan on buying some cheese and butter and maybe a small piece of sausage to justify my visit, we need the butter anyway. I hate to ask this of you, you've already done so much, but the laundry needs to be done, and the firewood needs to be brought in. Could you do those chores by yourself? And would you wipe your poppa's face with a cold wet cloth and dribble a little water into his mouth every so often? I don't know how else we can help him."

Neola doesn't bother to wait for an answer, she just assumes Letty will do as she is told because she always has. Neola brings a cup of fresh water to her husband. She kneels at his side and leans the cup against his parched bottom lip, tipping it ever so slowly, hoping to see the swallow reflex. But instead, the water flows back out of his mouth and over his chin. The obvious sign of impending death is not lost on Neola. The rhythm of her breathing breaks, becoming hitches caught on choked sobs. She kisses his lips and cheeks, desperate to change his fate and not knowing how. Finally, she raises his limp hand to her face and lovingly, slowly rubs his fingertips across her lips, pretending for the moment that he knows exactly what he is doing.

She leaves his side and heads for the door. Letty comes out of her funk long enough to realize what a wild looking mess her mother has become. She jumps up from her seat at the table and grabs her mother by the elbow, stopping her before she opens the door.

Letty begs, "Momma, momma. You can't go yet. You haven't brushed your hair and put it in a bun. You always wear your hair in a bun when you go to the village. And where is your fancy going to town hat? And why are you still wearing that old work apron? That's not something you'd normally wear to the village. And another thing momma, how will you ever explain the scratches and bruises on your face and hands? You know how nosey that shop girl is. The first thing she'll want to know is how you got so hurt."

Neola looks in the mirror, and sure enough, she does look a little beat up, maybe used too hard. She takes off her old, stained apron and tosses it on her chair, too disheartened to bother to hang it in its usual spot. By the time she's finished giving her hair a hundred strokes and pinning it into a bun, she has thought up what she believes is a reasonable lie.

"Well," she says, "I'll just say I was working in the garden busy as usual with weeding when the rooster suddenly jumped down off the top of the wall and attacked me. His sharp claws were aimed straight at my face so I had no choice but to raise my arms and defend myself as best I could. Everyone knows a rooster can put out an eye, that's how mean they are. I think the shop girl will believe it. What do you think, Letty?" "It'll have to do. I don't really care about what story you tell. What I care about is you not being gone too long. I'm afraid to be alone with poppa, I really am. I'm afraid something might happen to him, and I wouldn't know what to do." Letty's voice cracks and wavers as she fights back sudden tears.

Letty's words hit Neola hard. It's a terrible thing she's asking her daughter to do. Letty's poppa might very well die while Neola's gone, but Neola really has no choice but to leave. She needs to know if the Stranger has been reported missing. The information might very well save Letty from prison or hanging. And saving Letty? Well, that's the most important, first and last thing both Vonder and her want.

But Neola still feels a need to apologize and so she says, "I'm sorry baby girl. I wish I could make it all go away. I wish with all my heart the Stranger had never come into our lives, but he did. I wish I could undo all that has happened to your poppa, but I can't. No one can. Not even God in heaven can turn back time."

A sudden look of puzzlement clouds Letty's face, but the look is quickly replaced by a glimmer of hope. A moment later Letty declares with complete confidence, "Momma, I believe God would fix poppa, if only he knew he needed to. So, I think what we need to do is to pray to God. Remember how we forgot to pray at breakfast? God might have noticed. I'm positive if we both pray all day long, as much as we can, God will hear us and fix poppa." Relief floods Letty's sweet face and she visibly brightens.

Neola turns away, not answering Letty, determined to hide her own loss of belief from her devout daughter. With the empty shopping basket in hand Neola heads for the door abruptly stops when she sees the bucket of bone flour. She points an accusing finger at the bucket and asks, "What is that?"

Letty stares stupidly at the bucket, her mind gone blank. A moment later, her memory clicks in and like any sixteen-year-old she does her best to explain and excuse, "Well," she says. "It's the bones momma. I ground them in the mill. Those nasty bones look just like dirty old flour now. I think I did a good job of it. But I don't know what to do with the tulip bulbs, they still look the same."

Neola's impressed. It's just one more example of how resourceful her daughter is. She thinks about what to do for a moment, then lays it all out, "Well, it's almost that time of year when people plant tulip bulbs. So, I want you to plant the bulbs in the new garlic bed we made the other day. Dig a narrow trench about one foot deep and one foot wide. Make it close to the path and make it about five feet long. Sprinkle the bone flour in, just like you would if you were using wood ash, then plant the tulip bulbs fat side down pointy top up. And be sure to space the bulbs evenly apart. Do it right now Letty, those tulip bulbs are all the proof they'd need to hang us."

Saying the word proof manages to jog Neola's memory. The worst sort of damning evidence is the money bag she hid late last night. No one must find it. Neola needs to take it with her when she leaves, but her gut instinct tells her to keep it a secret from Letty. If confronted, her daughter would likely spill the whole story. Letty's incapable of lying, she's just naturally an honest person, just like her poppa. Father and daughter so alike, both innocent, unworldly.

But not Neola. Neola is fully capable of lying, and easily when needs be. She learned the practical art of deception while traveling the High Seas with her father, when lying or hiding goods from the taxman or the pirate made all the difference between profit and loss, life or death.

Neola fetches the basket of tulip bulbs before she picks up the bucket of bone flour. Then she hands both to Letty, flings open the door, and pushes her daughter out. She slams the door shut so quick it hits Letty on her butt.

Letty trips forward a few steps, but it's not a problem, playing all those games after all those years while doing all those tedious chores has made it easy for Letty to catch her balance. But it is concerning, certainly puzzling, that her mother would shove her out of the house. She considers the possibility crazy momma in all her unpredictable and dangerous ways has reappeared. She decides it's best not to get on the wrong side of her momma right now. She marches her way to the garlic bed, drops the basket and bucket at the edge of the bed, then collects the planting spade from the garden shed.

Before digging the trench, she takes a good long look at the ground-up bones and the enormous tulip bulbs. A feeling of invincibility washes over her. And that's fine with her, she has a game for just that kind of moment. She stands ramrod straight, her chin parallel to the ground as she raises the little garden spade as high as she can in imitation of the photo she saw of the French Statue of Liberty. She holds the pose while counting to fifty, then spins round and around, high stepping over the imagined dropped chains as she raises the garden spade up and down, corkscrew curls bouncing in time as she celebrates her family's impending liberation from the crime scene evidence.

Meanwhile, inside the cottage, Neola retrieves the bag of money and tucks it into her shopping basket. But before she leaves, she gives Vonder a kiss goodbye. Earlier, when she was bathing him, he was cool to the touch. But not now. Now Vonder is radiating an unnatural level of heat. Neola wonders if this might be her husband's last moments and becomes torn between staying with her dying husband or saving her daughter from blind justice.

Neola retreats deep within herself and lets the choice be made. She lays a wet washcloth across her husband's forehead hoping it might cool him. It's all she can think to do. She takes a good, long look at her dying man, memorizing him, thinking maybe this is the last look she will ever have of her love while he's still drawing breath, and then she turns her back on him and leaves the cottage.

She strides down the walkway, clutching the basket tight against her chest, hiding the contents, ignoring her daughter until she has stepped through the garden entrance and onto the roadbed.

She takes several deep breaths to damp down her grief before turning to her daughter to say her goodbye. When she finally faces Letty, she finds her daughter wearing the relaxed look of a satisfied woman. It's the same look she saw Letty wearing last night while she was sleeping. It momentarily confuses Neola, but she leaves the wonder behind, she has no time for it.

Neola declares, "Letty, I'm leaving. But first I'm going to the mill to make sure the brake and lever are locked in place. I heard the vanes trying to turn in a gust of wind late last night, and that makes sense now that you've told me you made use of the grindstones yesterday."

Letty had politely ignored her mother's attempt at hiding the contents in the basket, but her mother's outrageous lie about the dog brake being improperly set suggests Letty is somehow incompetent. Challenged, she retorts, "Momma, you don't need to do that. Why would you do that? I can do that for you. What you need to do right now is leave so you can get back as quick as you can."

Neola deflects by insisting, "Letty, the windmill is far too important to allow it to be damaged by neglect. I need to double check the levers. I'll be sure and call you if I need any help. It does take a lot of strength to push the brake all the way in. You must remember how hard it was for your poppa to manage, especially when the wind was blowing."

Neola's grief, tinged with anger, has slipped out in the telling. But more importantly, she's talking way too fast and way too huffy in a self-serving sort of way. It's so unlike her mother that Letty's interest is tickled.

Some baser instinct compels Letty to slip off her noisy wooden shoes and secretly follow her mother to the windmill's door. But as she approaches the door, she changes her mind and peeks through the window instead. She watches as her mother pries a rock loose from the floor. When Neola steps back to set the stone aside, Letty's given a clear view of a hidey hole nearly identical to her own. And what a surprise it is. Letty had no idea her mother was hiding such a secret.

Neola pulls a plump leather bag from the depths of the basket, opens it, and takes out a handful of coins. She picks through the lot, selects one gold and three silver coins and drops them into the side pocket of her walking skirt. After returning the rejected coins to the bag and cinching the drawstrings tight, Neola does a dead drop of the bag into the hidey hole, all the while wearing an unpleasant smile upon her lips. Once Neola returns the stone to its proper place, she stands on it, rocking it back and forth until she feels it grind into position.

Grit remains behind, outlining the stone. It's obvious the stone has been recently moved. Neola spends precious moments sweeping the grit round and around until the tiny area blends in with the rest of the windmill's floor. Convinced her secret is safe she hurries to the door.

Letty anticipated her mother's exit and has made a quick getaway. By the time Neola emerges from the mill, pushing the bicycle, Letty is already back in the garden with her shoes on, waving goodbye.

It doesn't matter. Her mother's oblivious to the world around her. Without so much as a backward glance Neola hops on the bike and heads downhill in the direction of the village.

Letty watches her mother peddle out of sight, wondering all the while about that leather bag and how much money might be in it. Her mother probably got the money by picking the Stranger's pockets. Letty's has no problem with that. He owes them more than that for what he did to her poppa.

The chores call and Letty knots her skirt, tucks the ends of the knot into her waistband, and proceeds to dig a trench one foot deep and five feet long, just as she was told to do. When she's done digging the trench, she tips the bucket and shakes the contents out, directing it in a zig zag line, being creative in the garden for the first time ever. By accident, she spills a large pile of the blood and ground bones at the very beginning of the trench, but she leaves it, believing it's of no account.

The late morning sun feels good. She slips her shoes, the leather footies, and the stockings off and wiggles her bare toes in the freshly turned garden soil. Her toes wrap around a wet, wiggly worm and she laughs as she jumps away. A pair of small rosy headed birds swoop in and fly circles around her head, while two big blue birds sit in the puddle by the well and preen themselves pretty. Butterflies flit by as bees dip in and out of fall's spectacular show of orange and purple flowers.

The daily increase of the plants and the appearance of flowers is a magical mystery Letty never tires of. She loves the garden, and all its many plants and creatures. But most of all, she loves the sun and the gentle breeze caressing her skin, she makes a point to be outside and be free every day.

She decides to save a bulb to eat later, and why not? Eating the bulb last night made her feel good, even special, and it helped her forget all about the horror and sorrow she's just experienced. She picks out the biggest, brightest of the bulbs and drops it into her apron pocket before planting the remaining bulbs in the trench. She backfills and tamps down the soil, raking it smooth until it looks just like the garlic bed it was meant to be.

Without taking a break, she heads to the large cauldron resting on a grate at the center of the outdoor firepit. She fills the cauldron with water and builds a fire underneath it. The laundry tub is too heavy for her to dump, so she buckets the water out after first throwing her poppa's clothes onto the giant boulder rising out of the ground next to the firepit. After she refills the laundry tub with more cold water, she rinses her poppa's clothes, then tosses them back onto the boulder before emptying the tub again.

Letty begins to worry she'll not get her chores done before dark. She heads to the cottage grabbing the empty basket along the way. Once inside, she hangs the basket in its usual spot, then heads to the dirty laundry pile. She wraps her arms around the laundry and heads for the door, but just as she's about to exit the cottage she hears her name being called. It's so unexpected, she freezes.

Speaking in his normal, everyday voice, her poppa asks, "Letty, (a pause, then more quietly) Letty, is that you?" Hope leaps in Letty's heart. She drops the laundry and rushes to his side. She falls to her knees, takes both of his hands in hers, and whispers, "I'm here poppa. I'm right here." She waits for him to say more, but nothing happens.

Letty rubs her poppa's hands, hoping he will talk to her again, but he doesn't. His eyes remain closed, his face devoid of expression. After a moment she drops his hands and fetches a cup of water. She tips the water into his mouth, hoping he'll swallow, but the water just pours back out. She rewets the washcloth and lays it on his hot forehead, thinking the cold water will shock him into wakefulness, but it fails to work.

Still, Letty waits. She holds his hands in hers, stroking and squeezing them, but after a while she knows it's pointless. He's not responding. And so, she leaves his side, scoops up the laundry and heads back outside. She drops the dirty clothes into the tub and adds cold water. Then she thoroughly rinses them free of bloody yesterday, being deliberate about doing just that, serious for the moment, each garment examined, especially her poppa's cut clothes.

Her mother did a good job of that, it'll be easy for Letty to sew the shirt back together again when the pieces dry, really it would just take but a moment or two and then he can wear them again.

She changes the water in the laundry tub, this time adding equal parts hot and cold water and a generous amount of soap. One at a time, starting with the delicate underthings, she washes the clothes against the scrub board, squeezing the garments over the tub before throwing them onto the boulder. And once again, she buckets the fouled water out of the laundry tub. Then she refills the tub with hot and cold water and this time she dumps the entire load of washed laundry into the tub. Each garment is carefully rinsed before being tossed back on the boulder. She does one final rinse, once again laying the dripping clothes across that handy giant boulder, and for the final time she buckets the water out of the laundry tub.

And now comes the fun part of doing the laundry. Letty gets to hang the clothes on the clothesline using her poppa's special clothes pins. Her poppa spent a bit of time most everyday carving novelty clothespins to sell in a specialty market in Amsterdam, and it's thanks to him she always has an interesting, revolving supply to use. All the clothes pin tops have animal or bird themes. Some depict the head of a giraffe or a deer, others a lion or a bear, sometimes a turtle, a duck, or even an elephant. And although there are duplicates, none are exactly alike. Letty enjoys secret whispered conversations with the clothespin while hanging the laundry. It's just another of her many games.

Each animal has a distinct personality. The lion is fierce, the giraffe is aloof, the deer is nervous, the bear is boisterous, and the turtle is super serious. It's the elephant though, that she loves the best. The elephant is just naturally affectionate, always trying to wrap his trunk around her while whispering sweet nothings in her ear. Handling the animal clothespins improves Letty's mood and soon she is singing a sweet prayer for her poppa.

Once she's finished hanging the clothes, she fills and hauls two buckets of water into the cottage for the night's use. Then she refills the water pitcher, replaces the candle stubs with fresh candles, and fills the lantern with kerosene. And once again, the fire needs rebuilding. Letty is reminded of the need to replenish the firewood. The mere thought of more chores prompts her to sit down on the bench to rest a bit. Although she's not aware of doing it, she's been rubbing the tulip bulb she stashed in her apron pocket.

A single moan breaks the quiet of the cottage. The moan makes Letty anxious. And in turn, she becomes so aggressive in her fondling of the tulip bulb the papery tunic comes loose and falls away. The bulb feels somehow familiar, like her own earlobe. And oddly enough, touching the bare bulb makes her want to eat it even though she's not feeling especially hungry. She bites the tip of the tulip bulb off and chews it up anyway. Instantly, she feels stronger and a lot less anxious. She returns the partially eaten bulb to her pocket, deciding to save the rest for later, parsing out the feel good.

Suddenly, the silence is broken by the heart-wrenching sounds of her poppa's moans. They go on and on, in a deeply disturbing way. She's desperate to get the terrible sounds to stop, the moans hurt her, too. But all she can think to do is to bring her poppa another cup of cold, fresh water.

It puts her close enough to smell his foul breath and the stench of his rotting head wound. Letty pretends the air smells of sweet meadow grass instead. She drops to her knees and waves away the handful of flies surrounding his head. The motion brings back the memory of maggots eating the rotten flesh of her poppa's broken leg. Unfortunately, the image of maggots growing in her father's head wound, eating his brains, pops into her thoughts. She starts to gag but refuses to let it happen.

Instead, she leans in close and kisses his check. Then she coos, "I love you poppa, I will always love you." She rewets the washcloth and gently wipes his face and arms then rewets the cloth and lays it on his hot forehead. He fails to respond in any noticeable way. She dribbles water into his mouth, but he doesn't swallow, or even choke, the water just dribbles down his chin. She gives up her futile attempts at nursing and tucks the marriage quilt in around him instead.

Trying to nurse her comatose father is too much for her young heart and she seeks the help she has been told all her life is hers for the praying. She takes her poppa's hands in hers and prays out loud, "Please God, my Father in heaven, save my poppa, bring him back to us. I need him here, I really do. And God, why did you let this happen? Poppa has always believed in you. You know he has. And I believe in you, too. I believe you can fix my poppa. You are the good God in Heaven. You can do anything, perform any miracle, the minister told me so, and he has never, ever lied to me. So please God, please bring my poppa back to me. And, if you do it right now, I'll love you forever, I promise you I will."

During her prayer, Letty has tilted her head back so she's looking up at heaven, where she knows God is sitting on his golden throne. She finishes the prayer with a proper, sincere, "Amen." But for some reason she keeps repeating the word Amen. It's like the hiccups, but worse. Then suddenly, she can't lower her head. It feels like a pair of hands is holding her head back. She flails her arms over her head to free herself from the antagonist, but no one is there.

She inhales her saliva, along with her snot and tears. The wad of mucus sticks in the back of her throat and blocks her air flow. She can't breathe and panics, afraid now for her own life. Her heart races, the pace irregular, unnatural. Letty works at calming down, barely able to suck a thin stream of air through her nose. She manages to fill her lungs, then as fast and hard as she can she pushes the air out through her mouth.

The trick works. The hold on her head disappears and with all her might she hawks the wad of phlegm loose and spits it out onto the floor. Her breathing returns to normal, though ragged at first. All shaky, she stands up, steps back and examines her poppa. He's still unconscious, his skin is still a sickly shade blue grey. It's all the proof she needs to know that her prayer was not heard by God. She reaches in her pocket and fiddles with the tulip bulb again, lost in thought, thinking of how she nearly died a few moments ago. But mostly she thinks of saving her poppa. She resumes praying to God, but this time she does it slowly and silently and without the bribery inherent in her initial prayer. But still nothing happens. Nothing changes.

Twilight is soon to fall, and the firewood still needs to be brought in. Letty leaves the cottage and at the edge of the freshly dug garlic bed she slips on her footwear. A moment later she's crossing the road, walking through the flock of chickens as if they weren't even there.

Plenty of times she's watched her poppa move firewood using the wheelbarrow kept against the side of the windmill next to a wooden ladder. It's easy for her to handle empty, but once filled the wheelbarrow becomes heavy and awkward. She's forced to stop and rest several times on her way back to the cottage. It won't fit through the doorway, so she unloads the firewood one small armload at a time. After she returns the wheelbarrow to its usual spot she stops at the garden and pulls up enough carrots, beets and potatoes for the night's stew. Quite a few of the vegetables end up in pieces after she cuts the leaves and bad spots off. She rinses each piece under the spigot, and because she forgot to bring a basket, she drops the vegetables into her big apron pocket instead. The tulip bulb blends right in as it should. It's edible, after all.

Letty has managed to get all the chores done, and just before dark. She enters the cottage but on her way to the kitchen cupboard the firewood pile collapses, and a handful of mice spill out scampering this way and that. Normally, Letty would laugh about it, but not this time. This time, she leaps in the air and gives a good shriek, giving proof that nothing is usual anymore.

Letty's wound up tight, spooked good. It's horrible to be alone. Her poppa no longer counts as company anymore, he's barely breathing. She hugs herself and whimpers as she whispers to the uncaring walls, "I don't want to be alone anymore, being alone is so awful, I hate it, and I'm scared. I want you home momma, like normal. You need to come home right now and make all this bad stuff go away, make our life like it used to be. It's what a mother is supposed to do. It's true, it's your job, taking care of me is your most important chore. I know it is. Everyone knows it is. Now you just get home right now and do it.

18

Coming on to Dark

Letty hears the clip clop of horse's hooves and the squeak of turning wheels, the sound of an axel in desperate need of grease. It's an unexpected sound to hear this late in the day at this time of year. The field grain is weeks away from being harvested, so it's unlikely a farmer has come to use the grindstones. Besides, she was expecting her momma to quietly return on the bicycle. Letty recently learned the hard way that strangers can be dangerous. So, instead of going to the door and throwing it wide open in welcome as she normally would, she peeks out the window above her bed. Sure enough, a horse and wagon are slowly approaching the cottage. An official looking man and her mother occupy the single bench seat.

Her mother is sitting as far away from the old man as she can possibly get. She's clutching her shopping basket tight against her chest in a feeble attempt at hiding her breasts. The man is driving, and when they arrive at the garden gate, he pulls back hard on the horse's bit. The sudden pain brings the beast to a stop. The man engages the brake then climbs down from the wagon. He tethers the horse to an old hitching ring cleverly built into the garden wall.

And then he walks to the back of the wagon and drags Neola's bike from the wagon bed. He casually tosses it towards the garden wall as though it were nothing but a piece of junk. It hits the wall and falls over, but he just leaves it where it lays, it's really of no account to him. His one and only thought is to get back to the pretty little woman he left on the wagon seat so he can feel her up while he lifts her down.

Neola has other plans. As soon as the old man has his back to her, she looks directly at Letty's window and holds her index finger to her lips in the universal sign that signifies keep your mouth shut. That done, Neola jumps down from the wagon seat without waiting for the old man's help.

Denied the opportunity of manhandling that trim little waist of Neola's makes the old man foul tempered. And to show his displeasure he flings the garden gate open as hard as he can. The gate screeches in protest at the crude handling. The high-pitched sound raises the hair on the back of Letty's neck, and she is reminded once again of the events of Monday night. Fear takes hold in her heart and mind, and she gives the old man her full attention.

He enters the garden uninvited and glances around. His beady, piggy little eyes take in the clothes drying on the line, the outhouse, and the embers under the cauldron. The huge granite boulder stands out, the sparkling mica making it hard to miss. The closed doors of the garden shed beg opening, but what has really caught his eye is the freshly dug garden bed. It's nearly the size and shape of a grave. He considers what might lie beneath the newly turned soil, but a fragrance wafting on the gentle breeze steals his attention. He follows his nose to a lovely patch of lilies. They shine a ghostly white against the dark rock wall. He stares at the luminous lilies a little too long, apparently lost to a memory.

When the old man returns to the here and now, he finds it impossible to gaze upon the lovely Neola. Instead, he turns away and looks at the windmill. His eyes are irresistibly drawn to the crowns of the old oak tree. Two sets of glowing yellow eyes meet his. Vultures of a type he's never seen before in Holland are at roost. They seem to be examining him with great interest. He's glad to see the vultures. Their presence is living proof a large rotting carcass is somewhere nearby. He turns his back to them as they are no longer of any use now.

Without asking for Neola's permission, he enters the cottage. Letty has remained at the window, all stiff and unsmiling. He sees her but chooses to ignore her. Neola is behind him, close on his heels. She makes eye contact with Letty and puts her finger to her lips once again. He stops next to the battered old table and silently passes judgement as he gazes about the simple one room home.

Neola pleads, "Constable please. We don't know anything about a missing man or his bundle. I already told you. Can't you see? No one is here but my simple-minded daughter and my demented, disabled, bed-ridden husband."

A confused frown shades Letty's young, innocent face. She's not simple. She just can't talk right because she bit her tongue and it's swollen. And her poppa is not demented, instead he's been beaten to the edge of death by the Stranger. She ought to know, she saw the fight from beginning to end. But she keeps her mouth shut just like her momma told her to.

The Constable ignores Neola's pleas and instead demands, "Build that fire up and light that lantern. I need light to search your hovel. Come on now, get it done." He raises his right hand and snaps his fingers twice, punctuating his orders. Then he removes his black hat and places it carefully on the table in front of Vonder's empty chair. The hat's removal reveals a big bald patch on the top of his head that he's tried to hide with a pathetically thin comb-over.

Neola whines, "I don't understand why are you doing this to us? What exactly do you think is going on here?" All the while Neola is talking, she's poking the embers with a couple of pieces of kindling. When the tips catch fire, she drops the kindling onto the embers, then lays a few pieces of small firewood over the kindling in a crib pattern. Satisfied to leave the fire for now, she lights the candles on the mantle while Letty sets a match to the lantern's wick.

The Constable walks over and checks Vonder out. Neola's husband really does look demented, all slack jawed and comatose. It's obvious the man will never be a threat to anyone ever again, if in fact he ever was. He was known to be a cripple.

The Constable begins his search by looking under the table and then in the buckets. He pulls out the contents of the baskets on all the shelves, looking at everything carefully, shaking things out, leaving piles of their meager belongings on the floor. He shakes out the folds of all the linens and towels stored in the bench, throwing them into a messy heap on the floor. He opens the kitchen cupboard and checks every nook and cranny including looking inside and behind every cup and bowl. He checks the mantle, picking the delicate lotus vase up, dumping the flowers out, checking inside and underneath it. He finds nothing.

He examines everything sitting on Neola's little shelf, including looking behind the mirror. He dumps her box of essentials, her tiny, tidy keepsakes, her hairpins, her buttons and needles and threads, and he stirs the lot with his finger, just for spite, just because he can, hopelessly tangling everything. Just being nasty. He searches the clothes hanging under the shelf, spending extra time on Vonder's coat and vest. And again, he finds nothing. Disgusted, he throws the coat down on the floor and makes a point of walking on it as he makes his way to the woodpile.

He throws the wood haphazardly here and there, and again he finds nothing. He crosses the room and empties the sixteenth century wardrobe, throwing the hanging clothes on the floor but only after he's checked every pocket, hem, and seam of each garment. He's equally abusive with the couple's odd assortment of possessions on the shelves. He even goes so far as to try to pull the heavy walnut cupboard away from the wall so he can look behind it, but it refuses to budge.

The Constable has managed to work up quite a sweat, but so far, he's found nothing. He walks to the opposite side of the cottage and looks behind the drawing hanging above Letty's chest. Nothing there. He opens the lid of her chest and tips it on its side, checking underneath. He shakes out every article of clothing, even her unmentionables. He double checks every hem, seam, and pocket. And still, he finds nothing.

He searches Letty's clothing hanging on the hooks near the head of her bed and even takes the time to feel along the top and side seams of her privacy curtains, not needing to bother with the hem, for there's nothing there as they've long ago been split open. He pulls Letty's bed apart, checking for God knows what, shaking out the bedding and the pillows. He throws it all on the floor and then he finishes his search by upending both of Letty's mattresses, looking, looking, but once again, finding nothing of any interest to him.

Finally, the only place left to search is Vonder and Neola's marriage bed. And so, that's exactly where he goes. The exertion of searching has him all pumped up, and by the time he stops and stares down on the bedridden Vonder, the Constable seems to have grown in stature. An obvious sense of entitlement exudes from his every pore.

Letty shoves her fist into her mouth to keep from challenging him. Everyone knows a marriage bed is private, he must know that, too. She looks around her home. The old man has managed to make a mess of it and in such a short a time. She wonders if he's possessed by a fairytale demon, or could he be the actual devil the minister has always warned her about?

The Constable points to Vonder and asks, his voice dripping with suspicion, "What happened to him?"

Neola hesitates. Her gaze falls longingly, lovingly upon her husband, a single sob her first response. But Neola's no fool, Letty's freedom is at stake. She pulls herself together and comes up with an outrageously good lie, a lie based a bit on the truth.

She chokes out, "About a month ago, a rock from high up on the windmill came loose and hit my husband on the back of his head. Ever since he has been bedridden, and a few days ago he stopped eating and drinking. It's my fear sir, that if he doesn't wake up soon and drink some water, he will surely die."

The Constable juts his chin her way and asks, "Oh. So, it's just you and your daughter taking care of things right now, is that right Neola?"

"Did I not just tell you my husband has been bedridden for a month?" Neola exclaims, sudden anger flushing her face. "Of course, it's just my baby girl and me taking care of things. Who else is there? Our neighbors? The elderly Petersons? They can't help us, Vonder was the one that always helped them."

"Oh really, Neola? You've had no man to help you for the last month? Because someone told me they saw a man in a bright blue hat at the river dock the same day the missing botanist's ship docked and unloaded. That was just this past Monday. Your husband wears a bright blue hat, doesn't he? And the old people, the Petersons, said they saw your windmill sails turning yesterday. And don't they take a man's strength to work?" Done with his say, the Constable leans back on his heels, crosses his arms and waits for Neola's defense.

Quick on the uptake, Neola continues to righteously lie, "I hardly think so! Vonder lost his hat this past spring in the big windstorm. It was on a Sunday, and we were at church when the wind came up and blew his hat into the canal. It floated away so fast no one could catch it. Just ask around, everyone will tell you what happened. I suppose someone could have found the hat downstream and used it as their own. It was a good sturdy hat, sir. Extremely useful. You remember that terrible storm, don't you? It knocked down three trees in the village square. Everyone remembers that storm and all the damage it did, we all still talk about it every Sunday at church. But you don't go to our church, do you?"

Neola waits for a response, but the Constable just stands there stone-faced. She can't tell if he believes her or not and so she continues with her lies. "As for the windmill's sails moving, the dog brake slipped out of its slot during that sudden storm we had Tuesday morning. Even with the help of my baby girl it was all I could do to push the brake back on. I'm surprised anyone would have even noticed such a small thing. The vanes only turned for a moment. My husband was always the one to take care of the mill but now that he is bed-ridden, things are starting to fall apart."

Desperately wanting the Constable to lose interest in her man, Neola sacrifices herself by resorting to a trick she saw the whores on the docks do many a time. Pausing for added emphasis, she bends backwards just a bit, so her nipples thrust up and out in the Constable's general direction. She concludes her statement by suggestively adding, "My husband has been unable to do his duties for a long, long time now."

The Constable looks long and hard at Neola's perfect female form. Eventually, he clears his throat and orders, "Nevertheless Neola, I need to search your husband and the bed. You and your daughter will help me move him, and we will do it now."

The Constable grabs Vonder around his chest and pulls him upright. The women rush to form a litter of sorts. The Constable, still holding Vonder by his chest, lifts him and starts crab-walking him towards the table as the women awkwardly follow while maintaining a tenuous hold of each other's hands under Vonder's knees.

For no apparent reason, the Constable abruptly stops and declares, "We will lay him down right here, right now."

And that's exactly what happens. In one smooth motion they lay Vonder down upon the cold, hard floor. The blood drip dripping from the back of Vonder's head finally attracts the attention of the Constable. Neola notices his interest and silently prays with all her might to a God she no longer believes in that the Constable accepts her story of the rock hitting her husband's head.

The sight of her poppa's blood deeply disturbs Letty. She drops to her knees, covers her thighs with his discarded, disrespected coat, and scoots under his bloody head. Her lap provides a perfect cradle, the coat a perfect bandage to soak up the blood. She just naturally takes to stroking her poppa's forehead while humming an old lullaby she learned from him when she really was his little baby girl.

Meanwhile, the Constable proceeds to search under the marriage bed. He searches the sides and seams of the mattresses of the bed, and finally he searches along the wall of the bed, looking for any crevice or any possible hiding spot. He even shakes out the bedding and examines the pillows. To hurry things along Neola helps him move the mattresses to the floor. And still nothing is found.

Neola insists Vonder be returned to his bed. Reluctantly, the Constable agrees. Together, they put the mattresses back in place and remake the bed, all the while Neola struggles to hide her fear and anger, but most especially she fights to hold her tongue. The saddest moment comes when Letty must slide out from under her poppa's bleeding head. She's as gentle as she can be, kissing his forehead first, quickly whispering sorry sorry in both his ears.

The three assume their previous positions, but as they lift him Vonder has a massive seizure, twisting and jerking so violently they can barely keep from dropping him. His eyes snap open and he stares at something far, far away yet deep inside. The three people are irresistibly drawn to his glowing red eyes. A bright, white light shines deep within his dilated pupils. They can't stop staring at it. It shouldn't be there, but there it is. The light's so odd it sucks them in. Otherworldly, and yet somehow familiar. The three wonder and marvel at the feeling of love and hope the light radiates.

A subtle buzz and a certain weight in the air heralds a sense of peace descending upon them. They feel the lub dubs of their beating hearts, the blood pushing through their veins. They feel their very cells split apart and become atoms, and suddenly they are one with time.

Fear of death vanishes.

The three want to bask in the light of Vonder's mystical eyes forever, never to be parted. But alas, it's not to be. Vonder's eyes roll up as his eyelids close. The seizure abruptly stops. He relaxes, still held in their arms, and exhales a hitching, fractured slow, slow breath.

And then he dies.

The three people left standing, left alive, continue to hold him, frozen in place until their arms grow tired, and they realize the need to lay his dead weight down. They manage to lay him on the marriage bed, but then they freeze in place, the shock of his sudden death having robbed them of further movement and speech. For many long moments, the only sound to be heard is the popping of burning wood in the fireplace.

Letty is the one to make the first move. Sobbing, she collapses to the floor and begs God to bring her poppa back to life this very minute. She'll do anything, promise everything, but please God, just bring him back to her. But all her prayers, all the pleading is for naught. Her poppa remains dead.

The Constable just stands there with his mouth hanging open, unable to respond or move, staring stupidly at the man who has just died in his arms.

Neola turns on him. Her shoulders flatten and spread out. They become huge, the illusion of wings obvious, and she becomes that most feared of all creatures, the avenging angel.

Insane with rage, she shakes both fists at him. Through tightly clenched teeth she hisses, "You did this! You! You! You killed my husband. I'll see you rot in hell for what you've done this night. I promise you I will see you dead. I will step on you and smash you just like I watched you step on my husband's precious coat!"

Abruptly, Neola drops to her knees beside the bed and begs, "Vonder, Vonder. Come back, come back. Oh, please come back to me, don't leave me now. I don't want you to go, you can't go, please don't leave me here all alone." She takes his lifeless hand in hers and kisses each one of his still warm fingers, those very fingers that loved her every day every night. She gazes hopelessly, longingly at his empty, soulless face. And she comes to understand his touch is now forever gone. And it's this loss, the loss of his precious touch, that does her in and she becomes unhinged, losing all sense of fear.

She turns to the Constable and screams, "You did this! I told you not to move him! You killed him for nothing! You found nothing! You look at me when I'm talking to you mister, and you best listen to me this time!"

Neola jumps up and grabs the old man by his chin. She twists his face to hers so her hot breath can smother him, suck his oxygen away, maybe even kill him. She stamps her feet and shakes her finger. In fact, her whole body is vibrating as though she were on the verge of breaking into ten thousand pieces.

"Oh why, oh why did you have to move him? I told you not to. I hate you! I hate you! I want you dead, I want you to die!" Great heaving sobs wrack her body and break against her broken heart. The ever-expanding black hole takes another big bite from Neola's lovely, loyal being, tipping her mind closer to full-blown insanity.

The sudden wild scream of a wounded, enraged animal erupts from deep within Neola. She kicks the Constable in his shin over and over as hard and fast as she can. But it's not nearly enough hurt, so she takes to beating him with her clenched fists on his cold, cold heart.

He quickly gets tired of it and grabs her by both of her wrists. He pulls her close and holds her so tight she's unable to move. She struggles against his chest, trying to free her hands, trying to wiggle loose, but she can't, the Constable is too strong. And just as quickly as she attacked, she quiets and collapses, sobbing against the vile, heartless man.

He continues to hold her wrists up in the air and it's all that keeps Neola from dropping all the way to the floor. He gives her wrists a sharp upward yank and the accompanying pain in her shoulders brings her back to her senses. When she regains her feet, he releases his tight grip on her wrists. She stops crying and wipes the snot and tears from her face. And then she takes a step back and points at her dead husband.

Trembling, her voice raw with unbridled rage, she hisses, "You did this. You killed my husband. Now you get the hell out of my house right now. I want you out! Get out! Get out!" Neola stamps her foot and points at the open door, the color of her face matching the color of her hair, deep red, she is all of one terrible color now, the color of a mortal wound.

19

The Constable

The Constable refuses to retreat. He stiffens, sets his stance, and reasserts his authority by issuing new commands to the women, "Fetch the lantern and the candle. The both of you. We will search the windmill right now.

Neola can't believe the unmitigated gall of his demand. She protests by saying. "Oh no we won't. How dare you! My husband has just died."

The Constable insists, "It needs be done Neola. I need to know for certain that Vandermeer and his cart are not on the premises. After all, you had an English gold sovereign in your possession. Everyone knows your family lost everything to a fire five years ago and you never recovered your wealth. I find it all very odd that you suddenly have a gold coin, I really do."

The Constable has challenged Neola in the moment of her deepest grief, but she manages to rise to the challenge by saying, "You know full well I found that gold coin on the side of the road. I already told you so. It must have fallen through a hole in someone's pocket while they were walking down the road. Everyone walks everywhere in this flooded land. The glint of gold caught my eye, there's nothing more to it, and I just happened to be the lucky one that found it."

Neola has no idea of what he might find at the windmill. After all, it's where she told Letty to hide the metal pieces from the horse's cart. She's sure they'll both be arrested if he finds any evidence. She hates doing it, but to delay and confuse him, she resorts to using whore tricks once again. She bats her eyes, arches her back, and points her prominent nipples in the Constable's direction. To enhance the distraction, she adds another whore trick by rocking of her hips, but just barely.

He sees her moves and in response his mouth drops open and drool slips out. He visibly struggles to lift his eyes off her nipples as he retorts, "What a convenient story you've spun Neola. But the fact is, Jacob Vandermeer has gone missing after going in search of the thief that stole his valuable bundle of tulip bulbs. What interests me most was what the stableman had to say. He told me that when Vandermeer opened a crate in front of him he found a bundle missing. He suspected the thief was the man he hired at Miller's Landing. He described the man as having a pronounced limp and wearing a bright blue hat. The stableman guessed he was talking about your husband and pointed Vandermeer in your direction."

The Constable pauses, letting his words sink in, and then he continues, "Now initially, the stableman thought it was a terrible misunderstanding and it would be sorted out because your husband was known to be a real good Christian man. But when the horse returned alone, without Vandermeer or the cart, he found it concerning. And this is what gets me Neola, what makes me really wonder. Poor as your family has been these last five years, you suddenly have a gold coin. Vandermeer had money, too. Quite a bit, I hear. And maybe besides his money you have the missing bundle? Maybe the bundle's hidden in the windmill along with the cart? And that's exactly why we will go and search the windmill, and we will go and do it now."

To make his point, he slaps his black hat on his balding head and lifts the lantern off its hook. He grabs Neola by the wrist with his other hand and heads for the door, dragging her along with him. He looks back at Letty and demands, "Get up baby girl (she doesn't move), get up off that floor and bring a candle with you." Impatient, angry, he shouts, "Do it now, girl!"

Letty jumps up but doesn't make a move to join them. She saw how he grabbed hold of her momma and forced her against his fat old chest when she was beating on him. It was only after her momma calmed down that he let her go, but just a second later he grabbed her again, this time by the wrist. It was like he was tethering her momma to him, like she was nothing but an animal he owned. And her momma just took it, all meek and mild, giving in.

Seeing this, her mother's capitulation, convinces Letty she might be in real trouble, too. After all, she helped clean up the Stranger's death and she was the one that ground his bones to flour. Feeling anxious, she reaches in her apron pocket and fiddles with the tulip bulb for reassurance.

The Constable catches her in the act and asks, "What have you got in there, baby girl? Come on over here right now and empty your apron pockets on the table. Do it now, baby girl. Show me what you're hiding."

"There's nothing in my pocket but vegetables for supper, sir. Really sir, nothing at all out of the ordinary." Reluctantly, Letty obeys him and empties her apron pocket onto the table.

The Constable pokes his fingers among the vegetables. He pretends to examine each one with great care, even the ones cut into pieces, before picking up the huge, rosy-colored tulip bulb with the missing tip. He waves it in front of her face. "What's this?" he demands.

Letty promptly answers, "It's a type of root vegetable sir, like a little turnip."

The Constable regards Letty as though she really were a simple-minded child. He could barely understand her garbled response. He drops the tulip bulb back onto the table and declares, "Little turnip my ass."

Neola uses the moment to make a feeble attempt at slipping her wrist from the Constable's grip. He reacts by giving her wrist such a vicious twist she cries out in pain. But instead of letting her go, he pulls her closer as he drags her out the cottage entrance. Once they arrive at the road, he lets her go, convinced she's firmly under his control. And to prove him right, she follows him like a whipped dog as he strides towards the windmill. Letty follows at a safe distance, witness to his cruelty she's scared near to tears for her mother's safety.

Midway above the road a single bat flies, soon followed by thousands of bats erupting from the top of the windmill. They form a huge, undulating cloud over the moon, smothering the light. The temperature drops and the whole world takes on a sinister, dirty cast. But the living cloud cannot hold, and the bats fly off in all directions, seeking their nightly sustenance. The moon's light returns, and the landscape is once more revealed in cold, harsh detail. The secured, but nervous horse, disturbed by something seen yet not understood, stamps his feet and softly whinnies.

Down in the hinterlands, a wild dog howls and ancient memories of a lone wolf on the hunt ignites their lizard brains. They look over their shoulders, all three of them. Then they glance at one another and run for the windmill.

As they stumble across the windmill's threshold, the Constable grabs Neola by the wrist and gives such a hard, painful twist her knees buckle. He counters her collapse by pulling her wrist above her head, forcing her to recover her footing. Confident once again of her subservience, he relaxes the pressure on her wrist.

Fortunately, it coincides with the moment Neola sees the grindstones. She slides free of his grip, edging away from him until she is standing on her hidey hole stone. She fluffs her skirt all the while keeping her eyes locked on his, splitting his attention, deliberately befuddling.

And then just as the whores on the docks taught her, she leans against the grindstones and bends her knee ever so slightly, allowing the drape of her skirt to enhance the lovely shape of her leg. She wraps one arm over the brake lever and arches her back, once again displaying her nipples to their best advantage. With her free hand she strokes her hourglass curves, going high and then low a few times before stopping on the curve of her hip. Then she casually points her index finger at her mound of Venus, another trick she learned while watching the whores work the men on the docks. In a final attempt at distraction, Neola tosses her head in a come-hither sort of way, and pastes a pouty smile on her beautiful, deceitful face.

And all the while Neola's smoke and mirrors game plays out, Letty has been chewing on her bottom lip, worrying about the Stranger's money hidden under the rock her mother is standing on. It's the worst sort of evidence. Letty makes a show of looking up at the rafters, as if something were hidden there. She's hoping the Constable will follow her gaze, but he ignores her.

The Constable gives Neola a final, appreciative look, before raising the lantern and walking away from her. He struts around the tidy mill, examining every object, every nook and cranny. His eyes catch on a small white bit of something lying on the floor. Curious, he picks it up. It's so tiny he needs to squint at it to see what the hell it is. It appears to be a little bone.

Letty's horrified at the sight of the Stranger's little toe bone in the Constable's hand. They'll hang for sure if he figures out what he's holding. She quickly thinks up a lie and pantomimes what he should do as she shouts, "Drop it! Drop it! Drop it quick! Throw it down, sir, throw it down! It's a bat bone sir, we find them all the time on the floor. They fall from the bat roosts at the top of the mill. They have disease, sir. Terrible deadly disease. We don't ever touch them, not ever sir."

He understood her well enough to immediately drop the bone. He wipes his fingers on his trousers. Then he says, in the deepest, most authoritarian tone he can muster, "We're done here. We'll all go and have a look around the outside of the mill. Hurry up now."

20

Wednesday Night

Letty politely steps out of his way as the Constable exits the windmill. Neola follows behind him as though she were an obedient dog. He searches the entire perimeter of the mill but fails to find a cart or any other incriminating evidence. His lack of success does little to relieve the tension. All tired out, the three trudge their way back to the horse and wagon.

The Constable hands Neola the lantern and unties the horse. And then he leans in close, within a few inches of her face, and challenges her by once again asserting, "You had that gold coin Neola, and I don't believe for an instant the story you told me of how you found it. I'll be back in the morning to have a better look around. You can count on it."

Hearing his words makes Neola shrink in on herself. She looks to be on the verge of collapse. Letty takes the hint and wraps an arm around her mother's waist and guides her into the garden. Once inside, Letty slams the garden gate shut then leans her backside on it, and by that obvious gesture she takes command of the moment.

But the Constable doesn't see Letty take charge. He's too busy leading the horse around. As soon as the horse and wagon are pointed towards the village he climbs aboard the wagon and settles comfortably on the seat. He prods the horse's ass, and the horse slowly plods his way down the hill. The wagon passes out of sight, the noisy clip clop of the horse's hooves quickly fading away.

As he leaves Neola revives. She turns to Letty and asks, "Where did you hide the metal?"

Letty points to the outhouse.

Neola gets it, but she needs to make sure. So, she asks, "Did you really put the metal down the outhouse hole?"

"I know, I know, it's hard to believe I didn't do what you told me to do, momma. But I wanted to get it done quick, so I could take care of poppa. Anyway, it was a good thing I didn't hide the metal in the windmill. That horrible man might have noticed and made something of it. Did you know he was holding one of the Stranger's bones?"

Shocked, Neola says, " Oh no! No! I had no idea. I wondered what you were doing. You handled it perfectly. And not hiding the metal at the windmill was brilliant. I think you might have saved us. You are so wonderfully resourceful."

"But will it be alright momma?" The worry leaches from Letty's voice.

Neola hesitates. She takes a good, hard look at her daughter, seeing Vonder in the light blue eyes, the curly blond head of hair. She was never able to lie to Vonder and now the same holds true with her daughter. So, instead of outright lying Neola says, "Letty, you need to trust me, I'll make it right for you, I promise you I will. Have I ever broken a promise to you?"

Letty shakes her head no and bites her lip. They walk to the cottage holding hands. The door is unlatched, slightly ajar, and together they reach out and push it all the way open.

The moon beams stream through the open door and the cold

light illuminates the very dead Vonder. They see how still he is, his body like wax, no movement, never again, no pretense now, no wishful thinking will ever change the sad fact of his demise. The happy, gentle man they both loved is gone for good and they come to feel it now. Neola sets the lantern down and they hang on to each other as they sob their hearts out.

Suddenly, the gate gives an ear-splitting screech, and scared, the women jump. They continue to hang on to each other as they look over their shoulders to see what new horror has found them. It's the bad, bad Constable man. They think he's come back to get them and take them away. Unbidden, he boldly steps into the garden, trespassing once again. He glares at them as if he has caught them red handed doing something illegal. Though they're scared, they manage to stop crying, let go of each other, and turn and face him. They put their arms around each other's waists. It doubles their size and it's how they pretend they are a force to be reckoned with. It's all they can think of to do.

He surprises them by taking his hat off and holding it over his heart. He gives a good imitation of a pious nod before he says, "I'm deeply sorry for your loss, Neola, I truly am. I did not mean to cause your husband's death by moving him, but you must know he was going to die anyway. I just want you to know I'm not completely insensitive to your situation, and believe me, I do understand your current circumstances. Again, I am deeply sorry. I apologize if I have added to your pain in any way for it was not my intention. But Neola, you need to realize I will do the job for which I was tasked to do, and that job right now is to find Jacob Vandermeer. You can expect me first thing in the morning for you and I have unfinished business to take care of."

He strokes his moustache, making an obvious point of appraising her womanly attributes, assessing her worth in his scheme of things. He nods his head in some silent agreement with himself, then abruptly turns and walks out the gate, slamming it hard, as if he were locking them in. He walks past the windmill and down to the bottom of the hill to the horse he had left tied to a wild apple tree growing alongside the road. His dirty smirk expands into a cruel grin, the evil grin of a man who has played a rigged game.

Neola waits until she's sure he's really gone this time before spitting out, "He did it on purpose. He snuck up on us to scare us, Letty. I hate that man. I hate him so much, he is so bad, I never, ever want you to know how bad he truly is. He scares me, Letty. And I am so scared for you. Oh my God, he could ruin you for life." Tears stream down Neola's face as she cries out, "Oh God, I don't know what to do, I don't know what to do, I don't know what to do, what to do, what to do, what to do, what to do, what to do, what to do."

Neola's stuck. She needs to figure a way out but finds it impossible to tell the true story of what happened so that Letty carries no blame. No one must ever know how Letty helped disappear the corpse, it would ruin her for life. A long breath breaks loose from deep within her tiny frame, emptying her lungs, then her breathing becomes shallow and much, much too fast. And then she begins to pinch and hit her thighs. When the pain's not enough, she digs her nails into her palms drawing blood. The blood drips onto the threshold of their home and still it's not enough. Bone shaking sobs wrack her tiny frame until she finally collapses. She falls first to her knees, then topples onto her side, hugging her knees, wrapping herself tight, she's so tightly wound now, and bawling like the very world has come to an end.

Letty can't understand her mother's collapse. Her mother has always been the strong one, the boss of them all. At first, Letty just stands still, then she starts looking around. She looks at the moon, at the garden and at the outhouse. She looks everywhere and at everything until finally she runs out of things to look at and she turns her attention to the inside of her home.

The bad, bad Constable man has completely dismantled it. But before him, the Stranger destroyed it with his violence and his foul body fluids. That adds up to twice now, in just about two days, that her home has been trashed. Letty has had about enough of cleaning up messes someone else has made.

This latest stranger, the Constable, has thrown all their possessions onto the floor of the cottage. Letty figures since she was the one that cleaned up the last mess, this mess should rightly be taken care of by her mother. But her mother is currently lying on the floor, wrapped around herself, pretty much useless.

Letty does the only thing she can think to do. She kicks her mother hard in the ass, not once but twice, while demanding, "Stop it momma, stop it right now! You get up off that ground, you hear me! You need to do your fair share. It should be your turn to clean up the mess. Besides, you were the one that brought that bad man to our door today."

To punctuate her remarks, she kicks her mother in the ass again, but just once this time only twice as hard. Shocked, Neola stops crying. Her daughter's words shame her into action. She rolls onto her hands and knees and pulls herself upright with the help of the door frame. While brushing the grit from her clothes Neola admits, "Well, I guess I had that coming. I was feeling a bit sorry for myself, wasn't I? I think hunger is affecting me. Please tell me you started the stew or at least boiled some eggs. We could eat some cheese right now if only I knew what happened to it."

"What! What do you mean you have no idea what happened to the cheese, you had it and you let it go? How could you do that momma! And where is the butter and sausage? And for God's sake, when did you think I had time to cook? I spent all day doing the laundry and hauling the firewood and water. I tried to find the eggs. I wanted to eat a boiled egg too, but the hens are still hiding them.

And one more thing momma, did you forget that I was the one that took care of poppa while you were gone to town today?"

Letty pauses to catch her breath but gives up on the guilt filled rant when she notices her mother is staring at the marriage bed, her face vacant, yet somehow destroyed. Grief has not been kind, and Letty can barely recognize the face of the woman she has always called momma.

Letty desperately wants her momma back for the very selfish reason that she's afraid of being alone. She needs to distract her mother, but how?

The pile of vegetables on the table catches her eye. She finds it odd, but it almost seems the tulip bulb is tempting her to eat a little more of it. She retrieves it, but instead of taking a bite of it, she holds it out to her mother and declares, "We can eat this, momma! We can share it. I ate a whole one last night and it was so good, and in such a very strange way. And after I ate it, I was no longer hungry. We can eat this right now. It's food, it really is."

The movement manages to catch Neola's downcast eyes and she registers Letty's words. She's able to come back just enough to whisper, "You mean you ate a whole tulip bulb?" But her heart's not in it, not really. Neola could care less about the tulip bulb. What she wants to do is drop away from the here and now and fall into the same hole her husband has fallen into.

Letty takes hold of her mother's elbow and gives it a hard squeeze. The pain brings Neola back to the here and now and she proves it by making eye contact with Letty. Letty takes advantage of the connection and pushes her idea.

"Well, it does sound crazy, but these are crazy days, momma. And don't you think the tulip bulb looks a lot like an apple and a strawberry crossed together, maybe a little bit of a turnip thrown in? Just think of it that way, consider it a root vegetable. I'll eat half and you eat the other half. Eating it made me feel good. I think it will make you feel good, too. And besides, the tulip bulb is almost as big as an apple so there's plenty enough to share. Just trust me momma, do it, eat it."

Neola's memory sparks and she says, "I do trust you. But I noticed you looked different this morning. Maybe it had something to do with your eating the tulip bulb?"

"Maybe it did, momma, but I don't think eating it hurt me. I'm going to eat my half right now, I'm tired of being hungry." Letty eats her share in fast, little bites. Then she hands her mother the leftover half. Immediately Letty's hunger is gone, and she begins to flush. Suddenly she's unbearably hot.

Her mother follows suit and takes quick, little bites of her share. As soon as she finishes, she lets loose a burp then declares, "I don't think I could eat a steady diet of tulip bulbs. They taste a little too spicey and bitter." She burps again.

Neola's pale, blue-tinged skin suddenly flushes an odd shade of violet. Beads of sweat form on her forehead. She unbuttons her shirtwaist hoping it will be enough to cool her down but it's not nearly enough. Letty takes off her apron and unbuttons her shirtwaist but sweat is still rolling in rivulets down her flushed face. They rush to slip their shoes and leather footies off. They strip off their outer clothes in hopes that being nearly naked will cool them down. And it works. But as soon as they begin to relax the silence is disturbed with the sounds of a rhythmic thrumming coming from inside the wall above Letty's bed. It's reminiscent of music and something else.

It makes them feel like dancing and so they begin to dance their usual dance. But not for long. Like marionettes, they find themselves pulled this way and that, twirling round and around, all the while waving their arms above their heads. Their hands form intricate patterns that have no apparent meaning but feel familiar and right. Neola babbles all the while, the words sounding a bit like a foreign chant of a religious nature. Thankfully, the twirling dance soon slows until finally it stops altogether, along with the thrumming music.

Neola shakes her head, "Well, that was very strange, I felt like a puppet for a few minutes. And now I feel all tingly. like a hundred kisses are covering my body. Eating the tulip bulb did this? It's like magic. No wonder the Stranger wanted them back so badly. It might not even be about the money, maybe he knew how they made you feel if you ate one. Do you feel different too?"

Letty thinks for a moment, then replies, "Well, of course I do. But it was more powerful when I ate a whole tulip bulb. The bulb we split was missing its tip, so it was much smaller than the one I ate. And you being so little and all, a half a tulip bulb is probably equal to a whole bulb for me. It's like when we use herbs for medicine, the bigger the person, the bigger the dose. Makes sense, doesn't it?"

With new-found energy they go about putting the cottage back in order. They fold the linens and such and store them in their proper places. The odds and ends are returned to the boxes and baskets, and the clothing is hung in all the right areas. They rebuild the fire, put the stew pot on the crane, add water, and swing it over the fire. Letty throws a handful of barley in the pot, then goes about cutting the vegetables into small pieces. Neola does her part and drops the vegetables in the water along with some herbs, garlic, salt, and pepper. The stew simmers and soon a delightful aroma wafts throughout the simple, one room home.

Tonight, is the last night Neola will ever have with Vonder. She sits on the edge of their marriage bed and takes his hands in hers. Her gaze searches his face. She memorizes every pore, every whisker, the length of his mustache, the shape of his ears, and each blond curl on his head. Finally convinced he will never, ever be gone from her mind's eye she bends down and kisses him full on the lips. And then she whispers for the last time, "Goodnight my love."

She strokes his cheek, then gently covers his entire body, his face included, with the quilt they have slept under every night since their wedding night. She made the quilt from pieces of their childhood clothing, and she became a woman under the cover of it with his help. But now he has gone and died on her. He'll not be coming back, not ever. She comes to the truth of it and accepts his death.

She leaves his side and walks with purpose to the table. She holds her head high, her posture perfect, her natural elegance on full display. Despite all the tragedy, she's still the woman her beloved Bee-Bee taught her to be. She sits down on her usual chair and waits for her daughter to serve her.

Letty obliges by placing a full bowl of steaming stew in front of her mother before sitting down on the bench at her usual place with her own nearly overflowing bowl of stew. But before taking a bite, just to be sure, she looks up to meet her mother's grieving eyes. In silent agreement, they decide not to pray. The worst has happened and cannot be undone by prayers. They both know this and have no need to discuss it.

The women eat in companionable silence. Letty had the good luck of finding the cheese, butter, and sausage before the mice did. They drop a large pat of butter in their stew and have a thick slice of cheese as a side. They agree to save the sausage for another day, so Letty locks it away in the cupboard. For now, the cottage is warm and cozy. A soft gentle light infuses the home, pushing back the sad shadows.

Letty looks up from her bowl of stew and asks the dreaded question, "What about poppa? What do we do now?"

Neola replies, her voice weakened by sorrow, "We need to bury him, Letty. You know we do. Tomorrow, I suppose. But for now, we need to wash-up and go to bed. We need our sleep so we can gather our strength for what's to come."

Together, they put the food away and wash the dishes. Neola prepares the breakfast oats for their overnight soak. They bank the fire and blow out the candles, then take off their garters and stockings and climb onto Letty's bed. They crawl under the covers and wrap their arms around each other. Neola hums the lullaby Vonder used to sing to Letty when she really was a baby. It's the last thing Letty hears before falling asleep.

The ordeal of the last forty-eight hours has been too much for Neola, and it doesn't take long before she drops off into sleep, too. The mother and daughter sleep the sleep of the righteous and the loved, and of course, the very exhausted. A light wind comes up and rustles the leaves of the old oak tree, proving that in life there is always movement and change.

21

Thursday Morning

Slowly the women wake up and wipe the sleep fuzz from their eyes. Neola, ever the mother, inspects her baby girl and declares, "I think we need to brush our hair, Letty. We've not been attending to our own needs very well, have we? Did you even bother to brush your hair after you washed it?"

Letty shakes her head an emphatic no.

Neola continues, "I didn't think so. How about we spend some time brushing each other's hair. Don't you agree it will make us feel good." Letty bobs her head up and down in agreement, her corkscrew curls bouncing in time with the bobs. The sight makes Neola give a little laugh.

They climb out of bed and search out their clothes. Their natural playfulness suddenly comes alive, and they rush to see who can get dressed first. They race to slip the cotton shirtwaists on and race to button them up. Neither fumbles the delicate seed pearl buttons, so neither wins the first step of the spontaneous game. The game continues, and in tandem they throw the walking skirts over their heads, shimmy them into place, and button the waistbands, again at the same time.

The tie propels them to compete harder. They look each other in the eye before they bend over and roll on their stockings and garters. And when they have finished, they find they are still even. Finally, they slip on their leather footies and wooden shoes, all actions done as if they are of one mind, one body. They giggle at this twinning of motion, for the fact is, neither can claim victory in the race to dress, the game is an even draw.

Neola spins around and does a little hop and skip. Letty watches her mother's silly little dance. Life seems to be back to normal in this small moment.

Surprised by her own antics, Neola exclaims, " My goodness, I haven't felt like this since I was your age. My bones have stopped aching. I can't even feel my burn scars. And I feel twice as strong as I usually do. I wonder if the tulip bulb we ate did this. What do you think Letty?"

Neola turns towards her daughter for confirmation and finds her baby girl staring at her dead poppa. Letty appears paralyzed by grief. Neola's not sure what to do so she falls back on old habits and pleads, "Letty, I think it's time we say the Lord's Prayer for your father."

Neola begins the prayer by saying, "Our Father, who art in heaven, hallowed be Thy name. Thy kingdom come Thy will be done on earth as it is in heaven.... "

It's outrage that breaks Letty's paralysis and she gets physical. She shoves her mother and Neola trips backwards a few steps. Letty follows, stays right in front of Neola, gets right up tight against Neola's face. Letty screams, "Stop it! Stop it! Just stop it momma! You just stop saying that useless prayer right now. I'll never, ever say that lying prayer again, you can't make me."

Body shaking sobs follows Letty's tirade. Shocked, Neola stops mid-sentence. Letty's sobs soon become broken hitches that dwindle into sucking sniffles. Finally, she's able to speak again and she says, "Why would I pray to God, momma? Just think about it! God let my poppa die. And he did it after I prayed to him all day yesterday. He never even bothered to listen to me. He let death come into our home and take poppa. You know why he did that to us? He did it because we mean nothing to him. And that's why God means nothing to me. And now that poppa is dead, God is dead, too."

Neola was not expecting this reaction from her baby girl. Letty had never shown this degree of thoughtful anger before. The violence of the last few days has taken a heavy toll on her young heart. And God not saving Vonder, now that was the line crossed over. She knows now she should never have stopped Letty from running away. At least her daughter would still have the illusion of a caring God. But Neola allowed her own selfish needs to override Letty's best interests. It's just one more impulsive, bad choice she has made in the last few days and it's all beginning to pile up on her.

Neola stares out the window at the old stone windmill and the great oak tree. The two have stood together for well over two hundred years now. The same can no longer be said of her own family. Their life, once so perfect, is now forever lost. But Letty? Well Letty's life might still be salvageable.

To prepare for that outcome, Neola needs to clear up any loose ends, so she drops the toxic idea of praying and changing the subject she asks, "Letty, did you plant all the tulip bulbs? I know we ate one last night and you ate one the night before, but for the life of me I can't remember exactly how many bulbs were in the basket I gave you. Do you by any chance remember how many tulip bulbs you planted?"

Letty lets Neola's words hang in the air while she fusses with the fire. When she's satisfied with her efforts, she hangs the pot of oats on the hook and swings it over the flames. Then and only then does she bother to turn and face her mother.

"Momma," she declares. "You know I've always done whatever you've asked me to do.. So, of course I followed your directions when I planted the tulip bulbs. But just so there is no confusion I'll tell you exactly what I did. I dug the trench a foot wide, a foot deep, and a foot in from the edge of that new garlic bed we just dug this past Monday afternoon. I sprinkled the bone dust in the trench before I planted the tulip bulbs fat side down just like you said you wanted me to do. And no, I didn't bother to count them, why would I? You never told me to do that." Letty's glittering eyes dare her mother to push it further.

It breaks Neola's heart to see her daughter so bitter. Neola wants her willing daughter back again. Bitter's an ugly look on anyone, but most especially on someone as young as Letty. Neola knows it's up to her to change that look. she is the mother, after all. and she wants to see her little Letty pretty again She treads cautiously and begs oh so carefully, "Can I brush your hair? Please let me do it. It'll make us both feel so much better, I promise you it will. Please, please Letty, let me brush your hair. Come on baby girl, just let me do it."

As she pleads, Neola slowly moves in on Letty. She gently tucks her daughter's wild golden tendrils behind her ears, then caresses Letty's ear lobe, expanding the caresses to the area just behind her ear, on the thin skin of the scull, that most sensitive of spots. And it calms her daughter but not quite enough. Neola joins her breathing to Letty's, then slows her breathing down, helping Letty to slow down, exactly as Neola has done since the day her daughter was born. Letty leans her head into her mother's familiar caress and nods her head in agreement, all the while her anger dwindling to nothing.

The tangles have been set for too long and Neola's forced to use the wide toothed comb to untangle the budding dreadlocks. The comb has always been an instrument of pain and torture for Letty so Neola works as slowly and gently as she can, patiently grooming her daughter's difficult hair from the bottom up until Letty's tangles separate into a much longer version of Vonder's corkscrews curls.

Neola steps back and admires her daughter.

The personal attention has restored Letty's good nature. She gives her momma a big hug and a kiss on the cheek before declaring. "You were right momma. I feel so much better now. Thank you. And now I think it's your turn."

Neola's long hair is mostly loose curls, making it easy to brush. Her hair is a veritable pallet of reds. The soft morning light brightens some strands to pure ginger while the underlayer remains a rich shade of auburn. But it's the reddish orange of fire that's the most dominate shade of Neola's hair. Letty holds her mother's magnificent mane up in the air, away from Neola's graceful neck. She twists her mother's hair this way and that as she thoughtfully examines it. Finally, she asks, "Would you like me to braid your hair and pin it into a French chignon?"

Neola nods her head yes, unable to speak, grateful her sweet girl has come back to her. Letty braids then rolls Neola's hair into the complex French bun. Neola holds it in place while Letty fetches the hairpins from the essential box. It takes a bit of time for Letty to untangle the hairpins from the mess the Constable made of their essentials. But eventually she manages to get it done and return to her mother with the hair pins. Letty takes special care to pin the chignon low enough to hide the ugly raised scar on the back of Neola's neck. As a finishing touch Letty grabs her mother by the chin and kisses her full on the lips. She ends the kiss by smacking her lips together like she's just tasted something delicious. Her silly antic is followed by the loud sounds of her stomach rumbling. Neola's stomach follows with an even louder growl. They look at each other and dissolve into laughter.

Still giggling, Letty pokes her mother's tummy and says. "You just stay right there momma, and I'll serve us breakfast."

The two women share a quiet meal. No prayers, of course. Together, they wash the dishes and just as they finish the breakfast chores, they hear the clip clop of horse's hooves and the creaking of wagon wheels coming up the slope. That bad, bad Constable man has come back just like he warned them he would. They hear the wagon's wheels grind to a halt under the pressure of brakes being applied. Moments later a horrendous screech heralds the garden gate being violently pushed open.

The two women rush to the cottage door and fling it open. As one they block entry to their home by standing on the threshold. To further reinforce their defense, they link arms and grip the sides of the door frame. Instinct propels them to stand on their tippy toes, so they look even bigger. They glare straight ahead, set their pretty lips to fierce frowns and once more pretend they are a force to be reckoned with.

22

The Constable

The Constable walks right up to within a few steps of the women and declares, "Neola, I've come to help you bury your husband and then I will finish my looking around." And with that statement he uses his massive body to shoulder his way between the mother and daughter, casually and rudely splitting them apart as he once more enters their home without permission. He takes the few steps needed to arrive at the head of the marriage bed, that most private of places and stops. He stands with his hands on his hips, elbows poking out to the side, deliberately dominating the space as he glares down at the covered corpse of the very dead Vonder.

A scant moment later he asks, "Where do you want the cripple to be buried, Neola?"

Neola bites her tongue to keep from telling him to get the hell out. But it's not enough to stop the fury and hatred overtaking her. He should not have had such bad manners as to speak out loud the word cripple when talking about her beloved husband. Hearing the word takes her to the brink of violence, extreme violence, not unlike Monday night's violence. She turns her back on him so he can't see her murderous expression. She knows she's at war with him, and she needs to keep her one weapon, her attractiveness, foremost in his itty-bitty lizard brain, it's really her one and only weapon if she's to save Letty from prison.

"Come on Neola, let me help you. I know you have no one else." The Constable sneers, enormously pleased with himself at expressing the sad, obvious fact.

Upon hearing his latest heartless words, Neola shoves most of her fist in her mouth and bites down hard on it, desperate to staunch the angry retort trying to slip its way out. She knows she needs the help. She and Letty might have recently moved a corpse without help, but it was in an extremely disrespectful way and Vonder deserves more care than that insane Stranger whose head she smashed to nothing but mush. She'd like to turn the bad, bad Constable man's head into mush just about right now.

Neola tries to speak, but all she can do is squeak. Letty takes notice. She guesses her mother has succumbed once again to the family's penchant for being tongue tied and is no longer capable of responding to the Constable. But she can.

Letty pipes right up and declares, "Poppa loved sitting against the wall on the sunny side of the windmill. It's where he carved the animal heads on top his clothespins and where he read the books he was always borrowing from the butcher and the blacksmith. Sometimes I'd catch him just staring down the slope at the birds and the bees flitting and flying about the orchard trees. He'd be smiling and all relaxed."

"Alright then," the Constable acknowledges. Then after a brief pause, he says "You both know where the shovels are kept, go and get them. And then we will all take turns digging the grave. Hurry up now, we need to get it done, there's more to do here than just burying the dead cripple."

Letty and Neola exit the cottage, jaws set hard and tight. His constant use of the word cripple has made outright defiance inevitable. The Constable seems ignorant of their true expressions and possible bad intentions. He also seems unaware Letty's voice has returned to normal and can no longer be confused with that of a simple-minded girl.

Just past the bulk of the ancient windmill, while still on the road, the three people suddenly stop, struck by the natural beauty of the landscape spread before them. Dozens and dozens of apples, plum, and pear trees grow in staggered groves down the slope. Most of the trees are covered in fruit on the cusp of being ripe. Interspersed among the fruit trees, dense groves of filbert trees flourish, while walnut trees tower in the background. Current and gooseberry bushes grow in tangled clusters here and there, the summer leftovers feeding the insects, the insects in turn feeding the birds. Tiny meadows provide habitat for colonies of beehives, the source of Neola's beloved honey.

Letty breaks away from the others and walks to a spot next to the windmill wall. She pounds the ground with the tip of her shovel and announces, "This is the exact spot where my poppa liked to sit. He was happiest with the sun shining on his face and his back against the wall. Here is where we will bury my poppa. He would want this, I feel it. Don't you agree momma?"

No one bothers to pay attention to Letty. Instead, Neola has dropped her head into her hands and is silently crying while the Constable is busy examining the windmill's wall directly above Letty's head. And sure enough, the Constable spots a sizable hole indicating a missing rock. He does a quick search of the ground and locates the rock. It's big enough to kill a man, no doubt about it. Maybe Neola was telling the truth about her husband's injuries. He wishes her story were true as he is powerfully attracted to her. It would be unfortunate if he had to arrest her and lock her up because then she would be out of his reach. What he really wants to do is use her. She has no man now and will soon realize the need for one. He wants to be that one.

Letty interrupts the Constable's fantasy by making a big show of jumping on the top edge of the shovel and forcing it into the ground. She stands on the shovel's top edge, wiggling it a bit, loosening the soil. With all the purloined authority she can muster, she commands, "We will bury my poppa right here, and we will do it right now."

Letty works at digging the grave while the others stand by and watch. When she has dug down not quite two feet Neola taps her on the shoulder and takes the shovel from Letty's hands. Then Neola sets about the sad job of digging her beloved husband's grave.

The Constable leans on the spare shovel and gets comfortable as he watches the gorgeous Neola bend over and dig. Her vigorous movements cause the upper middle buttons on her shirtwaist to pop open and expose her cleavage. Her breasts are truly magnificent. So high, so round. The nipples strain against the tight fabric, pushing in and out with each thrust of the shovel. The physical exertion causes Neola's beautiful bun to loosen. Wonderful wisps of wavy red hair frame her perfect heart shaped face, the loose hairs just begging to be pulled.

He wants to pull them.

Neola's plump lips are pursed in the effort of digging. They look just like a heart to him. Or maybe more like a final kiss goodbye to her dead, demented husband. She must be so relieved the cripple is finally dead. Of course, she must hide how she really feels from her daughter. A small sheen of sweat appears on her upper lip.

He wants to lick it.

Between the two of them, the women have managed to dig down about to their waists. The grave is not yet deep enough, and not nearly wide enough, and the digging is taking far too long for the Constable's liking. It's time to finish it, to get it done.

The Constable takes over and soon his shovel is hitting a layer of rock. The rocks are heavy granite and nearly the size of one of Neola's laying hens. It's perfect timing the rocks have appeared. They can be stacked on top the grave to prevent the wild dogs from digging up the cripple's rotting corpse. To that end, he orders the women to pile the rocks at the opposite end of the grave from the dirt. He widens the grave as he digs, for he is a wide man and needs to go wide to have the room to go deep.

As often as possible the Constable sneaks looks at the widow. He tries to hand her all the rocks, so she will be the one to bend over. It gives him a chance to view her cleavage, maybe even her nipples. Digging dirt makes him hard, in every way a man can possibly want or be, and it feels so good, lucky him. He keeps at it. He takes off his hat and then his coat and it's Neola that takes them. He makes a show of rolling the sleeves of his shirt to his elbows, flexing his fat biceps. The last garment he removes is his vest. And once again Neola takes it. It pleases him no end that the widow has made such an obvious effort to take every garment he discards.

Neola wiggles her shoulders as she takes the clothes from him, making sure her breasts jiggle as she reaches for each garment. She promotes a promise in the direct look she gives him, and he believes it. He returns her look with an obscenely smug, superior, lecherous look of his own, but only for a second or so, not wanting to alert the baby girl of his true intentions.

Finally, the grave is well over seven feet deep and maybe, almost four feet wide. Plenty big enough for who it's for. He hands the shovel to Letty. And then he needs to get out. But he finds it to be impossible. Try as he might, he's not able to get a grip to hoist himself out. He's too short, he's too fat, he's far too deep and he's tired. Besides, the hole is much too wide. He needs help. He sees the grieving women standing over him and feels a sliver of fear pierce his selfish, calloused heart, that overly covetous heart of his. But he knows just enough to stand up straight, jut his chin out, and look formidable. He aims to stay in control. He is, after all, the man and that makes him the boss of them all.

He demands, "You there, baby girl, go get the ladder from the other side of the mill, I know it's there, I saw it laying on the ground near the wheelbarrow last night. You hurry up now girl, the day's getting away from us and we need to get your poppa buried."

Good girl that she is, Letty immediately obeys him. She walks off, soon disappearing around the wall of the windmill. A moment later she shouts, "Help! Help! I need help! Come here momma, I need your help!"

The baby girl's request angers the Constable. He doesn't want Neola out of his sight. His bulbous nose turns a shade of blue verging on deep purple. Frustrated, he rests his hands on his fat, wide hips and stares at his feet.

After a thoughtful pause, he looks up into the widow's glowing green eyes and says, "Go on Neola, go help your baby girl carry the ladder. Hurry up now, so we can finish burying your dead husband."

Because she knows he'll be watching her every move, Neola exaggerates the swing of her spectacular ass as she slowly walks away from the grave. And sure enough, the Constable backs up to keep her perfect form in view. He ends up stumbling and falling hard on his ass. It pisses him off, but he uses his anger to quickly recover his feet and when she passes from his field of vision, he's not worried. He knows she'll not only come back, but she'll come back soon. And that's because she has no real choice, he's the only man standing and he's the law. And when the gorgeous Neola walks back into his view, it'll be yet another excellent opportunity to watch her breasts bouncing in and out of her bodice. What a beautiful woman she is, and a widow woman at that. He can hardly believe his good fortune, the perfect timing that has brought him to this place, to this now, to this destiny.

Sure enough, Neola finds Letty awkwardly holding one end of the ladder, the other end stuck fast in the mud. So, it was true. Letty really did need her help. Neola thought it was just an excuse to walk away and leave that horrible man to die in the huge grave he had dug for himself. She likes the idea of leaving him. She likes the idea of him digging his own grave. Maybe a little too much.

Neola whispers in her daughter's ear, "How about we leave him where he is, and we just go. I have enough money saved up to get us by for a while. We can take his horse and wagon and go far, far away and start all over. Come on baby girl, how about we just go ahead and do it."

During the telling, Neola yanked on her daughter's arm so hard it caused Letty to let go of the ladder. The unexpected violence is a wake-up call for Letty, and she backs away from her mother, thinking she's gone crazy again. Neola is quick to realize her mistake. It was beyond foolish to encourage her daughter to be an accomplice to yet another crime.

Whatever had she been thinking?

The tension between the mother and daughter suddenly breaks when they hear the Constable's shouting that they need to come back right now. The note of pure panic in his voice is not lost on them.

The two women exchange looks. Sudden smirks bloom bold on their lips, the naked triumph of revenge fully on display, a righteous sight to behold. They both heard him, they both feel it, why try to hide it from each other? They revel in his fear. They've made him suffer. They've won a battle of sorts. Victory feels so good.

He yells again, this time he tries for absolute authority in his tone of voice, understanding his mistake, his sounding all needy and desperate. "Neola!" he shouts. "You get back here right now with that ladder, and you be quick about it, or there'll be hell to pay!"

Letty's humanity reasserts itself, prodded no doubt by the sound of authority she hears in his voice. After all, she's been trained all her life to obey when given an order to do a chore. A moment later Neola realizes she's lost all chance of corrupting her daughter's better instincts when Letty shouts. "Yes sir, we're coming sir. Just give us another minute, sir."

Letty picks the end of the ladder up from the ground. Her mother, compelled by guilt and shame, pulls the other end free of the muck. In silence, they walk the ladder to the gravesite and Letty is the one to drop her end into the pit. The Constable sets the legs of the ladder and quickly climbs out, a relieved expression on his blotchy red face. Then he pulls the ladder out of the grave and tosses it into the brush as if it were nothing more than a mere matchstick. He looks at Neola, suspicion in the look, and demands to know, "What took you so long to come back to me?"

Sweat pours off his forehead. The stench of fear permeates the air. That acrid odor, so unmistakable for what it is and what it means, is not lost on the mature, experienced Neola. However, Letty has no clue. She takes a step back, repelled. She innocently inquires, "What's that awful sour smell I'm smelling ?"

Neola ignores her daughter though she's tempted to tell her the truth. Instead, she replies to his question, "Well sir, the ladder was stuck so deep in the mud it took both of us to wiggle it loose. But we did it, didn't we baby girl? We would never fail you sir, never."

Letty follows her momma's lead and nods her head up and down several times in agreement all the while hoping the gesture will help her mother's lie take root. And it seems to do the trick.

And now it's time to bring Vonder to the graveside. Once more, the women follow the Constable across the road and through the garden gate. He stops next to the well, his face all pinched. He looks at Neola and says, "I need to use the outhouse. I think I might be in there a while. You two go on ahead. And Neola, you get your husband ready to move." He turns his back on the women and heads to the far corner of the walled garden where the outhouse stands. Letty and Neola turn towards each other exchanging worried looks. If he should happen to look down the shithole, he might see the burnt up twisted wagon wheel rims and figure out what happened to the Stranger.

The women cover their mouths, as if by hiding their lying lips they can hide the evidence from his eagle eyes. He opens the outhouse door and stands still for a good bit, looking, looking, his little pea brain spinning all the while. He gives a shrug and walks on in. The loud quick thump of the door slamming shut startles the women even though it's a sound they themselves make many times over the course of the day. The minutes stretch out as they wait for his reaction, but all they hear is a loud, disgusting grunt.

Neola begins to panic.

Desperate for an idea that would save her daughter from blind justice, Neola looks around the garden for a way out. Her eyes land on the freshly turned garlic bed. It's exactly the shape of a grave. And that's when it comes to her, the what to do.

Neola runs directly to the garden shed, pulls out the little planting spade, rushes to the garlic bed, and quick as she can she digs up four tulip bulbs. At the well, she rinses off the dirt, then peels the papery tunic free. She drops all but one of the bulbs into her apron pocket then she devours the one left in her hand. She takes a few deep breaths and failing to feel anything she consumes a second bulb, eating it just as fast as the first. She burps, burps, burps, until she forces herself not to.

Letty stares at her mother in utter disbelief.

Neola turns to her daughter. Motioning with her hands she shoos Letty towards the open cottage door. When Letty fails to move fast enough, Neola pushes her over the threshold. It causes Letty to stumble her way to the table. Her mother's odd actions have made

Letty unsure of what to do next. Guessing they will need a sheet for the burial shroud she lifts the lid on the storage bench.

Neola second guesses her and shakes her head no, then says, "We might as well wrap your poppa in the sheet he's lying on. The wedding quilt will be his burial shroud. I'd never be able to sleep under it without him, anyway. Your father and I were a love match, you know. Born to be together, never a doubt. I always knew I would marry your poppa and have you for my child. Remember how I made sure you were wrapped safely in the quilt before I threw you out the window? The quilt was the only possession that survived the fire."

Neola's once beautiful face twists with grief so deep it looks like an open wound that's exposed the bone. And as she stares down at the corpse of her one and only love tears crawl down her checks, but she forces herself to stop with the crying as she remembers through her grief her need to save their beautiful baby girl.

Letty hears her mother, really hears her. It finally dawns on Letty all that her mother has lost, all that loving, poof, snap of the finger, just like that gone. It's a bad spell, it's a bad dream, it's the worst possible nightmare come true.

And not knowing how to help her mother cope with her grief, that soul sucking emotion that feels like a deadly disease, she gets practical, changes the subject, and asks her mother, "But what about poppa's clothes? Shouldn't he be wearing real clothes for his burial? Shouldn't we prepare him in some way? It doesn't feel right to bury him in the ripped-up nightgown he died in, he's not asleep."

With the back of her hand, Neola wipes her eyes dry, pastes a phony smile on her face, and looks her daughter square in the eye. Because she could really use some time alone about right now, she says, " What a good idea. Can you get his clothes from the drying line? And bring in the other clothes, too. Would you do that right now, Letty? It's ever so important."Always obedient, ever helpful,

Letty goes to collect the laundry from the clothesline. As soon as her daughter is out of sight, Neola devours the remaining tulip bulbs. She's really starting to feel it now, curtains of colored lights are hanging around the room, moving with each breath she takes, some of the lights enter her mouth and expand inside making her feel all powerful. She knows it's not real, she needs to maintain. There's so much left to do. A buzz starts up in her belly. Then an odd thrumming fills her, and she's instantly reminded of the prayer wheel and the sounds it made when spinning.

And suddenly Neola becomes too hot. She takes her apron off and unbuttons her shirt waist. Her chemise is so old and thin it's become nothing but gauze. But that makes it the perfect fabric and garment for what she has in mind. She flushes her face free of the grief, smoothing her face back to the look of meaningless, unfeeling beauty. She takes the pins from her bun and shakes her head, loosening her hair, furthering the luscious look, making herself as ready as she possibly can.

Neola has never looked so desirable, or exuded such intense sexuality, but it's not meant for her beloved husband. He can't see her anymore. He's become a soulless corpse.

But still Neola whispers, "Forgive me, my love."

Letty quietly reenters the cottage with the clean, dry laundry draped across her arms. She lays it down on her own bed then quickly sorts through the pile. She puts her own clothes away in her storage chest, then puts her mother's clothes away in the old walnut wardrobe. Finally, she lays her poppa's clothes at his feet before making her way to the essential box to get the straight pins needed to hold her poppa's shirts while she sews them back together.

Neola is still standing next to the bed in the same spot, still staring down at her dead husband, her expression edging on empty. The black hole has nearly finished its work of consuming her heart.

Soon, very soon now, she knows she will die from the loss of her heart. No one can live without a heart, everyone knows this.

But Letty still needs to be saved, and Neola's trying to hold on, wanting to be the one that saves her. She turns her head towards their beautiful baby girl, so perfect, so right, but Neola is unable to make eye contact.

Letty takes note of her mother's disarrayed clothing, the missing apron, and especially the barely concealed breasts. She doesn't understand it and she doesn't like it. It's disrespectful to her poppa's memory. Letty's distaste turns to anger, and she grabs her mother by the shoulders and gives her a good hard shake.

Letty angrily blurts out, "What have you done momma? You ate too many bulbs, didn't you? How could you be so stupid! Look at you! You're almost naked. You need to cover your breasts. Do you want to give us away? Oh my God, what were you thinking? I just heard the outhouse door slam shut and he's coming. The Constable is coming, momma!"

Letty grabs her mother's chin and lifts her face, forcing her mother to make eye contact. As soon as they connect, Letty hisses, "Straighten up! And put that pretty face of yours back on. Your mouth is all twisted, your face is twitching something awful. You need to look normal, momma. You've got to fix your face right now!"

Neola (lightly sweating) says, "Alright, alright. I've got it Letty, I've got it. I know just what to do. You need to trust me about this Letty, just trust me. And I know you won't like it but I changed my mind about how we'll prepare your poppa. We'll skip dressing him in his clothes. Instead, we'll pull the bottom sheet up and over him, then we'll roll the quilt around him and tuck the ends in." Neola hesitates before adding, "Oh Letty, Letty. I love your poppa so much. I don't want him to go, I just can't let him go, I just can't."

Saying the word love breaks her even more, and Neola whisper-cries, "Don't leave me here alone without you, Vonder. Please don't go, I can't bear it. I can't live without you." Sobbing, she throws herself on Vonder's chest.

Letty has the sad task of pulling her mother off her dead poppa. Neola turns towards the cruel, heartless person who has so forcibly removed her from her man. She sees her husband's eyes staring back at her, framed by the familiar halo of blond curls. It's him but not.

It takes her a moment, but Neola finally wakes to the truth. The time has come to save their baby girl. And so, Neola pastes that death grin, that terrible phony smile back on her once pretty face, ready now to do the dirty deed.

23

Neola

Neola and Letty begin the sad job of winding the funeral shroud around Vonder's corpse. But before they've gotten very far, they hear the unexpected clip clop of horse's hooves and the rumble of rolling wagon wheels. Alarmed, yet curious, mother and daughter tip toe to the cottage door and poke their heads out just enough to see what's going on.

They find the Constable leading the horse in a tight turn at the end of the road. And damned if he doesn't move into the one area that affords him a view directly down the path to the low spot where they did the burning. Because his back is to the women, The Constable has no idea he's being watched and they silently urge him on, shooing him with their hands as though he were a chicken.

But all their shooing is for naught. The Constable stops exactly where they don't want him to. Something catches his eye, and he takes two steps forward and stares down the path. It becomes obvious to the women he's looking at the circle of ash left behind after the puddle of storm water evaporated. But he doesn't look for too long. The horse shakes its head, wanting nothing to do with the lingering odors of smoke and death rising from the path. The Constable seems to agree because he resumes leading the horse in the tight turn. Once the horse and wagon are finally headed towards the mill and the distant village, he walks the horse forward until the back of the wagon is aligned with the garden gate. It's then he halts the horse and loops the reins around the nearest hitching ring. To show the horse who's boss, he snugs the bridle so tight the bit digs into the tender flesh of the horse's jaw and draws blood. The pain is so intense it causes the horse to shudder. At the sight, the Constable smiles a satisfied smile.

He waddles his way over to the cottage door and he once again enters their home without permission. He catches the mother and daughter busy tucking the ends of a beautiful quilt around the dead cripple's head and feet. They've used the beautiful quilt as the funeral shroud. What a waste of good bedding. He would have stopped Neola from using it had he known that was her intention. When Neola becomes his wife, he'll not allow her to be so wasteful.

He wonders if the accident that crippled her husband had also affected his ability to perform his manly duties. It would explain why Neola looks like a woman needing a man's touch. Hell, she looks like she's begging for it. He could be the man to take care of her special needs. The sooner, the better. He has special needs, too.

Speaking in a gruff, but authoritarian tone, he declares, "Your husband had best be ready for burial because the time has come for the funeral to commence."

Handling Vonder's corpse has left the women choked with grief and unable to speak. It's all they can do to muster up enough good manners to nod their heads in agreement. The Constable takes a good, long look at Neola. She looks different. Loose. For God's sake, she's nearly half undressed. He becomes instantly, noticeably aroused. To hide his hardon he grabs the shrouded corpse around the chest and picks it up. The dead man's head covers his problem perfectly.

His sudden action has forced the women to rush into place and lock hands under Vonder's knees, creating a spontaneous litter of sorts. But before the women are securely in place, the Constable begins walking towards the door, aggressively pushing the women in front of him. The women stumble as they desperately try to keep from tripping on each other's feet. The women have no choice but to crabwalk the shrouded corpse out the door and up onto the wagon's deck without even one little rest. As one, they gently lay Vonder down.

What the women did just now, it puzzles the Constable. He knows most men would have laid the corpse on the end of the wagon deck, then stepped up, and picked the load up again. But not Neola and her baby girl. They had enough strength to step up under the load. He wonders if it has anything to do with Neola pulsing with an ungodly inner light. If he were a believer in the supernatural, he would consider her possessed. He'd like to possess her. The sooner, the better. God, but she is one fine looking little red-headed woman.

Unnerved by the excessive attention the Constable is paying to her mother's body, Letty tries to distract him by making a great show of unwrapping the horse's reins. She catches him looking her way, and believing she has his full attention she leads the horse and wagon down the road to just beyond the windmill, maneuvering the back of the wagon as close to the grave as she can get it. After tethering the horse to a nearby apple tree, she looks over her shoulder expecting to see her mother and the Constable right behind her.

But instead, they've remained at the garden gate. They have their backs to Letty and they are staring up at the roof of the cottage. And then Letty sees what they see. Two large vultures are perched on the ridgeline. Letty has a vague memory of seeing the vultures before. It was over by the windmill. They were each perched on their own branch near the crown of the old oak tree. She suddenly remembers it was on Monday night just before the Stranger appeared.

The mated pair of vultures return the couple's stares, then slowly spread their wings adding to the horror. A second set of enormous eyes magically appear above and behind their beady little yellow eyes. It's nature's magic, it's an optical illusion, the placement of color on individual feathers having created the effect, but the three people don't know that. They believe the illusion is real, they believe in the four eyes. Overcome by a nightmare come alive they temporarily freeze.

Then the hair on Letty's arms brushes backwards and she shivers uncontrollably. It breaks her free of her paralysis and she has a sudden, desperate need for the comfort of her mother and so she cries out, "Momma!"

The vultures answer Letty's cry by flapping their wings. It adds to the horror. But then only one of the vultures flies off the roof. It swoops down low enough that the tips of its wings brush against the astonished heads of everyone, including Letty's. And then the monstrous creature flies down the road in the direction of the village. The remaining vulture pulls its wings in tight to its body and settles down on the cottage ridgeline, looking for all the world like it has come to watch a great performance.

Neola ignores her daughter. She suddenly remembers seeing the vultures before. It was just five years ago. The vultures were perched in the big willow the night her home burnt to the ground. She saw the vultures while standing at her daughter's window. She was supposed to jump, but instead she froze in place, the multiple eyes having captured her as though she were the prey. It was the panic she heard in Vonder's voice that broke the hold the vultures had on her. Vonder saved her from burning to death that night, she's sure of it.

And then another, older memory rises to the surface of her mind. She's fifteen years old, on her father's ship, and the ship is tied to a dock in Karachi. This time the vultures are perched on a nearby wharf's pilings. As she stares at them, they spread their wings and reveal the extra sets of gigantic eyes. But before they had time to hypnotize her, she was distracted by the sight of her father's newest hire boarding the ship. And that's not all she remembers. The green smoke woman was there, too. She was kissing the new hire goodbye. At the time Neola assumed she was just another dock whore and totally interchangeable with any other whore.

The memory is more than seventeen years old. So why are the vultures here in Holland and why now? This is not their place. They should be in India along with the green smoke woman. They reek of a witch's magic, of old curses playing out in real time. The vultures are but one more sign of Gods out of control. Neola thinks on it, then finally nods her head yes, in some sort of silent agreement with the powers that be.

Full blown panic takes hold of Letty and she screams with all her might, "Momma, momma, momma!"

Neola is brought back to the present by her child's screams. Her baby girl needs her. She turns her back on the lone vulture, abandons the Constable, and in great haste she heads for her daughter.

And of course, that nasty old man follows close on Neola's heels as though she were nothing but a bitch dog in heat. In a cruel show of total domination, and in one hell of a hurry, he pushes between the two women, slaps his hands around Vonder's shrouded head and pulls with all his might, intent on dropping Vonder to the ground and dragging him to his grave.

Just in time, the outraged women swoop in and catch their beloved's shrouded feet before they hit the dirty ground. Neola and Letty pull up and try to pull back and it becomes an obscene sort of tug of war, Vonder's unfortunate dead body being the rope. The Constable quickly gives up as he realizes the indecency of the struggle, Besides, he intuitively knows the women will never, ever, ever give it up.

While everyone is catching their breath, Neola is deliberate in making eye contact with Letty. She tries to send a message by raising her eyebrows and looking at the Constable, then slowly rolling her eyes away and directing them at the pit. Letty doesn't get it. Neola repeats the eyeroll several times, but then gives up. Letty will never get it, she's a good girl. And to prove Neola right, Letty shakes her head no, but ever so slightly, but it's enough so her mother knows her confusion is for real.

They carry Vonder the short distance to the waiting grave and gently lay him down. The time has come for the last rites. The Constable breaks the silence by declaring, "I'll act as the presider. We will start the burial with the Lord's prayer." His words instantly set Letty off. Saying the Christian prayer would make God real again, and Letty can't have that. She won't do it. That false God died the moment her poppa died. To stop the Constable from continuing to speak Letty resorts to what worked so well for her as a small child. She throws a righteous temper tantrum, stamping her feet and slamming her fists against her thighs in time to the shouts of, "No, no, no, no, no!"

The Constable has grown tired of waiting to possess the luscious looking Neola, and he loses his temper. He takes aim at Letty's face intent on giving her a quick hard slap to shut her up but he stops just before his open palm connects with her jaw. His lecherous old eyes have suddenly caught sight of Letty's perky little unbound breasts bouncing in time with her foot stamps.

He studies her tall, lithe form and sees her for what she really is, a fully formed young woman. And although the girl is unusually tall, he somehow believed she was still a child, most likely because her face and figure are so completely different from her mother's. In fact, mother and daughter bear no resemblance to each other. And

Neola always calling her daughter a baby girl had only reinforced his notion that she was still but a child, albeit a somewhat retarded child at that. It dawns on him the baby girl is talking perfectly normal now. And now that he's taken a good, honest look at her, he decides she looks old enough to lay with a man. He could be that man.

Neola has caught sight of the Constable looking her daughter up and down. She watched the flicker of lust cross his fat face and knows exactly what it means. The man is nothing but a rutting animal, and Letty is not safe around him, not at all.

To deflect, Neola moves nearer to him, bouncing her ample breasts as she does so. She slowly licks her lips, and in her best imitation of the whores on the docks, she not so subtly runs her hands up and down her hips while pointing her index fingers towards her precious, valuable mound of Venus. Using the softest, lowest little girl voice she can muster, she suggests, "What my simple child means sir, is that after we properly lower her poppa into the grave, we will all say the Lord's prayer."

Distracted by Neola's considerable feminine wiles, the Constable forgets all about the tender, young Letty. Flustered, he reluctantly drags his eyes off Neola's luscious form and meeting her eyes, he says, "Right. Well, we could properly lower your dead husband into the grave if we had more help, but we don't. So, we'll have to make do and just roll him in." "What!" Neola asks. "What's this? Why did you say we need to roll him in? Where are the straps to lower him in with? And why on earth didn't you bring another man to help you?"

"Well, Neola," the Constable says, "Tuesday morning, just after dawn, the village was hit by a torrential downpour. It was Biblical in its proportions and so widespread. What a storm, so much water, in so little time. The dikes were breeched up and down the river from one village to the next. All the canals overflowed. Every man, woman, and child went right to work of repairing the damage. They had no choice they were all flooding out. Everyone is still working nonstop to patch the leaks and redirect the water. And I would have brought Vandermeer's son for assistance, he should have been waiting for me at the Inn so he could join me, but he was nowhere to be found."

The Constable's ever wandering eyes drop back down to Neola's precious mound of Venus. Actual drool seeps from the corner of his mouth. He licks his lips and leans towards her, breathing heavy.

His rotten breath makes Neola want to puke. But somehow, she manages to keep from doing it. She holds her ground long enough to demand, "What! Do you mean no one knows you're here? Not even your own wife? Why not?"

She's so pleased by his admission that a smile slips loose before she's able to suppress it. Fortunately, he's still lost to visions of possessing her and he fails to see it. By the time he manages to drag his eyes back to her face again, she's replaced the smile with a stern look.

The harsh look immediately puts him on the defense. And like the dog he is he goes there by saying. "Well now, the sad fact is I've lived alone for several years now, ever since the day my wife passed away. It was the horrible cough that took her. And I have no children. My wife was unable to bear a live child though we tried many times. So, that is why there was no one at home for me to tell."

Neola hides how pleased she is upon hearing this. She pretends concern and says, "Oh, my goodness. I had no idea. I am so sorry to hear about your wife. That is so sad for you. You must be so lonely. So, are you telling me no one knows you were at my place yesterday?

The Constable grows visibly irritated. After all, the questioning is delaying the burial and his imminent possession of Neola's precious mound of Venus. Frustrated, he snaps and says, "Who in the hell was there left to tell, Neola? The stupid shop girl? The ten-year old stable boy? I already told you how every able-bodied adult has been busy working on the canals for days now."

Neola can't help but push it, "Really? How curious. But why were you spying on me in the first place?

"Neola, I wasn't spying on you. It just so happens on Tuesday morning Vandermeer's son found me and asked if I would investigate his father's disappearance. His father had just been in London selling a collection of rare plants to the Kew Botanical Gardens. When he left England, he was carrying a significant amount of newly minted banknotes. He also told me his father made a practice of carrying gold coins in his pockets to use for trade. It didn't take me long to put it together after I saw you with the gold coin."

Neola bats her long lashes, and slowly, ever so slowly, arches her back. The movement draws his eyes to her nipples, the thin gauze of her chemise failing to conceal their plump perfection. She knows their power, and she uses it. She takes one more step towards him so he can feel the heat emanating from her body. And then she asks, "But do you have any real evidence? Have you found anything here?"

The Constable nods his head, looks her dead in the eye and says, "Why yes, yes I have."

"And what's that, that you've found?" Neola rocks her pelvis, but barely, just a suggestion of something yet to come. A promise. She watches him become confused and excited with obvious need. A twisted smile of victory blooms on her swelling lips.

"Neola, I think you know damn well what happened to Vandermeer, but I think we can work something out." And with that statement, the Constable winks at her.

Neola's breath quickens. Her chest expands and contracts, the nipples pushing in and out pulling the button placket away and apart. A naked nipple appears before his very eyes, colored a delicious, sweet pink, and it's all he can do to not reach out and tweak it, put his tongue on it and lick it.

Lust controls him and he has forgotten all about Letty's presence and the need to bury Neola's husband. A long silence ensues.

Letty breaks the stalemate by stamping her foot while shouting, "Stop it you two, just stop it right now!" She stamps her foot again, then drops to her knees next to her poppa's shrouded corpse. She pushes and shoves, grunting and crying, snot flying, loud and noisy. She tries her hardest to roll her poppa into the grave, but she can't quite do it. It's too awkward. She needs help.

The Constable sees his opportunity to once and for all get rid of Neola's husband. He makes a show of removing his black hat and placing it on the deck of the empty wagon. He joins Letty, his back to the widow. He stoops over Vonder's corpse, stretching his arms out to help roll the cripple's corpse into the grave, just a bit unbalanced because of being naturally top heavy.

Neola sees her chance. She picks up the heavy granite rock she so carefully picked out and set aside when they were digging the grave. In fact, the Constable had made a big show of handing it to her, making her bend so far over to reach for it, she feared she would fall in the grave and land on top of him. It was obvious he hoped her breasts would fall free of her clothing and he would get a real treat. She thought he was such an asshole, to try such a cheap trick at her husband's grave, but then she realized the potential of the knife-like edge on the rock and gave him an especially encouraging smile as she took it from him.

And now, her plan has all come together. As she looms over his bent back her shoulder blades expand, flaring out, the illusion of an avenging angel become physical fact. Justified in her righteous rage, perfect in her execution, she brings the axe-like edge of the rock straight down, splitting his skull nearly in two.

Chunks of bone and hair break loose and fall on her husband's shrouded corpse, even as the blood and brains spray and ooze from the back of the Constable's head, all the gore splattering on the truly magnificent breasts of the very naughty Neola. Her exertions have managed to pop the buttons off her chemise and now the fresh blood and brains of that lecherous old man drip, drip, drip from her exposed nipples.

And just as she expected the Constable very slowly topples over the body of her beloved husband and tumbles into the grave. He lands on his head, then rolls over onto his side and comes to rest in the fetal position. No doubt about it, that bad, bad, Constable man is a dead man now.

Neola tosses the rock in after him and wipes her hands against her skirt as if it were possible to clean them of this new crime, this latest of murders. "Good riddance to bad rubbish," she says to nobody at all. A ghastly grin spreads across her once beautiful face.

Letty's shocked and then strangely not. A heartbeat goes by. A silent moment, then another.

Letty recovers and screams, "What did you just do? Oh my God, what have you done? You just did it again momma! First you killed the Stranger and now you've killed the Constable. Oh my God, you just killed the Constable! Oh why, oh why, did you do it? At least you had a reason to kill the Stranger, he was trying to kill poppa. But the Constable, (she points at the grave) he was just trying to help us bury poppa. Didn't you see he was trying to help me, momma?"

Neola begs, "No, no Letty. Just listen to me! He knew something happened here. He was going to force me to be in bed with him, sleep with him, betray your poppa just to keep our secrets. I hated him. I begged him to not move your poppa, remember? But he did it anyway, didn't he? And now my Vonder is dead. My husband! He killed your poppa the same as that Stranger did. They both killed your poppa! So, of course I killed him just like I killed the Stranger. And I'd do it all over again if I had the chance."

Letty remains on her knees next to her poppa's corpse, her hands covering her ears, her head shaking no, no, no.

Neola continues, her voice losing strength, "Oh yes, oh yes I would. Believe it girl. They both deserved to die, they violated our home, they've destroyed our family."

Neola's perfect alabaster skin has turned an ugly shade of red and it's not from the exertions of the last few moments. She steps out of her wooden shoes and leather footies. Then unbuttons her skirt and underskirt and shakes them down to the ground. She slips off her unbuttoned shirt waist, dropping it, then steps out and away from all the bloody, brain spattered clothing, wearing nothing now but her unbuttoned chemise, drawers, stockings, and garters.

And still, she's too hot.

Neola's breathing becomes quick and shallow. She's shivers as though she were cold, even as she sweats. She knows she dare not slip away just yet, though it's what she wants to do. She has a secret to share with her daughter so big it will set Letty free, let her daughter walk right out of here and never look back. But just now it's flown out of Neola's head and into the clouds. She wants to catch it and bring it back. The clouds look so pretty, they seem to be breathing in and out in rhythm with her. The clouds look so soft and inviting she wants to float up and lay down on them and sleep forever after.

But something nags at Neola, keeping her present. She continues in a hurried, weakened voice, "I meant to tell you something, but I can't remember what it is. I'm terribly sorry."

Letty nods her head yes, trying to stay calm so as not to miss a single word least they be her momma's last.

Neola continues, her voice verging on a whisper, "Something is terribly wrong with me. I'm hot and cold all at the same time and it feels like a bird is trapped in my chest trying to beat its way out." Neola suddenly chokes and blood gushes from her nose, pours over her lips and over her bare breasts, adding to the escalating horror.

Letty rises from her kneeling position next to the corpse of her poppa. The Constable's splattered blood and brains drip from her backside. Oblivious to the gruesome mess she cannot see, frightened over what she perceives is happening, she grabs her mother by the shoulders and looks deep into Neola's tortured eyes.

Desperate to quickly bring everything back to normal, Letty takes a steadying breath to slow her escalating panic and asks, "Momma, did you eat more tulip bulbs after I went to get the laundry? You did, didn't you? Tell me how many you ate momma."

"I ate four," Neola whispers. "I ate enough to get the job done. It was the only way I could think of to keep you safe. The bulbs gave me added strength and helped me confuse that awful old man. Listen to me baby girl, you did nothing wrong. Nothing. You are free now. I made sure you would be free. I did it for you, Letty. But I need to die now. I want to die, I do. I already feel dead inside without my Vonder."

Letty shakes her head no, no, denying her mother's words.

"Yes, yes Letty. Your poppa was my heart, and I can't feel him anymore. He's gone now and taken my heart with him. I can't live without a heart, no one can."

And with that, Neola collapses to her knees and falls on her side on top of the shrouded corpse of her beloved husband. Bubbles of blood float out of her mouth and pop, spraying fine blood droplets into the air. Neola holds her hands out as though to catch something fluttering in the wind. She whispers, "Oh the stars, the stars, I never knew."

Neola's smile becomes sweet, her face nearly the face of four days ago until suddenly it dissolves into a fearsome sight as blood gushes out her nose and flows over her chin. Reaching out as if to grasp a hand, she says in a voice filled with awe, "Vonder my love, is that you?"

Slowly Neola expels her last breath as she rolls onto her belly. Husband and wife belly to belly now. Her death collapse, a final embrace of her man.

Letty stares in horror at her dead mother lying on top of her dead poppa. She can't wrap her mind around it. Ever so slowly she comes to an understanding. Her momma acted the way she did so she could kill the Constable. And then the tulip bulbs killed her. A perfect solution for her mother. She wanted to die, she even welcomed it, it brought her back to her man, it was death gave her back her heart.

Letty's thinking now, thinking hard. The real weapon of death is the wicked, wicked tulip bulbs. The tulip bulbs have managed to kill them all, all except for her.

Letty drops to her knees and kisses her dead mother's bloody lips. She picks up her mother's murderous hands and tenderly kisses each finger. It's the only thing she can think to do. It's what she saw her mother do with her dead poppa and it's the only act that makes any sense now. But Letty knows there's more to it. Her mother sacrificed herself to make sure Letty would be free of blame, free to live, to have a chance.

Letty whispers, "Thank-you momma, thank-you."

24

William

Letty leans back on her haunches, her face tipped to heaven, but there is no heaven, only sky. And then the loss hits her. She lets loose a banshee wail, but it's too late to warn, death's evil deeds having already taken the living. She clutches both hands together, knuckle to knuckle, meshed over her heart, trying to put the broken pieces back together again. Down on her knees, she rocks back and forth as she sobs, "No, no, no."

She has no idea what comes next, nor what to do to make next happen.

The unexpected crunch of footsteps on gravel breaks through her grief. A shadow falls upon her and she looks over her shoulder. A young man stares down at her from a few feet away. Letty is close enough to see his dark five o'clock shadow and his soft brown eyes. She knows who he is without asking, for he is the spitting image of his dead father.

The intruder proclaims, "I can't believe what I just heard. Oh my God! I hope you know I saw what just happened here." He points at the dead bodies. The sight compels him to lower his voice, an ingrained sense of decency demanding it, though he continues with his accusations. "I know your mother killed my father, too. She did, didn't she? I heard her say as much, so don't you dare lie to me about it."

It's a bad move on his part to tell her what to do or say. She's had about enough of being bullied by total strangers. In fact, she's had about enough of strangers. Killers, violators of her home, there's nothing good about strangers showing up. And this newest stranger is proving to be no different having so callously interrupted her private grieving.

Letty's not quite scared. But she is on the ground on her knees and defenseless. It's possible he might suddenly attack her just like his father suddenly attacked her poppa. She needs to be able to defend herself, but how?

Her poppa's favorite bit of advice suddenly springs to mind. It was his belief the first and best weapon of defense is confidence. Letty proudly lifts her head and stares the intruder dead in the eyes. Her glowing, glittering, wolf-like eyes temporarily render him paralyzed and harmless. Letty keeps her blood-stained mouth shut tight and waits him out, intuitively understanding that she is now the one with all the advantage.

A long moment passes. No one moves, no one can. But eventually, the intruder frowns. He'd expected an argument, but the girl failed to give him one. Flustered by her lack of a defensive posture, he changes tactics, lowers his voice, and asks. "But what I don't get is why. Why would your mother murder two people? And why did your mother just drop dead? And who is the person rolled up in that quilt lying at the edge of that huge grave?"

He stops talking and points a shaking finger at the shrouded corpse. Then hesitantly, fearfully, he asks, "Is that my father? It is, isn't it? What on earth have you people done to him? Oh my God, what is wrong with you people?"

Letty pulls her head back, then hisses through clenched teeth, "What's wrong with my people? What is wrong with you? If you were close enough to hear, why didn't you lend a hand with my poppa's burial?"

This time it's her turn to point a finger at the shrouded corpse. She says "That's my poppa, not yours. And why didn't you stop my momma from killing the Constable? What good are you? You're no better than your crazy, murderous father, always jumping to conclusions!"

All the while Letty is having her say, she's regaining her feet until she is fully upright and face to face with this newest threat to her young life. And once again, for several long moments there is silence.

Then the young man takes a step back, giving ground. On the defensive, he speaks first and says, "If you must know, I arrived just in time to see your mother pick up a rock and smash it into the back of the Constable's head, but I was too far away to stop her from doing it. I am terribly sorry."

Letty hears the truth in the simple words. She nods her head in agreement and whispers, "I am too."

Surprised by her response, the sad sound of it, he feels a need to further explain himself. So, he tells her, "I would have been here sooner but because of the storm, all the horses and bicycles were in use. So, I had to walk all the way here. By the time I arrived at the Bridge of Sighs a layer fog had formed but I kept walking anyway. Then, when I arrived at a huge pile of old ash, I continued to follow what I thought was the right road. But after walking for what seemed like quite a distance the road bent around and became a dead end in the marshland, so I was forced to back track. Oddly enough, the moment I arrived back at the old ash heap the fog lifted and I saw another road, the right road I thought, so I followed it. Then of all things, the fog returned just as I approached a flat granite boulder by the side of the road. The fog was so thick, I couldn't see my own hand in front of my face. My sense of direction abandoned me, and I turned round and around wondering which way to go. I felt so foolish I just stood for a while. Finally, the fog lifted ever so slightly, and I saw an overgrown lane next to the boulder. After a short walk I ended up at the house of a run-down old farm. An old couple were standing in front of the house staring at their front door. Somehow it had come off its hinges. The old man was looking all dismayed and helpless, and the old woman was crying. They told me they were sitting at the table having tea when they heard something big slam into the house. Of course, I had no choice but to stay and help them. And it shouldn't have taken long to rehang the door, but the old man kept getting in the way, he wanted to be useful, but he's not capable of fixing things on his own anymore, he hasn't any strength left, old age has taken it. They should move to the village where they can be looked after, don't you think?"

He waits for her to agree, needing her to tell him he at least did something right by helping the elderly neighbors. But she keeps quiet and once again waits him out.

He sighs, looks puppy dog sad for a second, then resumes his story, "I left immediately after fixing the door, I even refused a cup of tea. I backtracked to the main road and found the fog had lifted. The old man told me to take a right at the end of his lane and keep walking till I arrived at a windmill, so that's what I did. But when I got close enough to see your windmill, a giant vulture landed a few feet in front of me. I had no choice but to stop. And then the vulture did something very strange. He walked towards me with his wings fully opened. He was so huge he filled the road! He was trying to get me to back up. When I wouldn't, he jumped in my face with his talons aimed straight at my eyes and forced me to take a step back. I believed he was trying to keep me away from a dead, rotting animal he was feasting on. I thought he would soon give up once I was beyond the immediate area, but he stayed in front of me and for every ten steps or so forward that I took, he drove me back one or two. But I toughed it out. The vulture finally flew off when I reached the bottom of your little slope." The young man stops to catch his breath.

Letty immediately challenges his story. "I hardly think that's true! Sudden fog! Disappearing roads! A wicked, vicious, giant bird! Do you really expect me to believe all that? It sounds like a poorly made-up fairy tale to me." Letty has forgotten all about seeing the vultures earlier that day, let alone seeing them perched in the old oak tree on Monday night before the Stranger appeared.

Sudden anger flushes the young man's face. How dare a girl covered in blood, standing before three dead people, one of them her own murderess mother, call him a liar. He sputters and stammers as he protests, "But I'm telling you the truth! It all happened just the way I said. And really, I should not have been walking at all. The Constable should have picked me up this morning. I was waiting for him, standing on the side of the road near the stables, but he drove right by me like a man possessed. He failed to even acknowledge me! Thank God the stable boy was close by and guessed where he was going. That was why I was able to find your place, but also why I was too late to stop your murderous mother. I really am so sorry, I found it a horrible thing to see, her killing that man."

Letty's impressed with his ability to talk nonstop while telling a story, but it was exhausting to pay that much attention with her heart so heavy with grief. And is he really that nice that he would stop to help the elderly Peterson's? She really doubts it. After all, he is the son of a murderer. Of course, he'd be a liar too. And then Letty's mind trips on itself. She turns her face away from his for just a moment. She thought it was a horrible thing to witness her mother kill two men this week too. She's become the daughter of a double murderess. Odd how she forgot that important fact. She feels a bit of shame over her own self-righteousness, but not enough to let him off the hook. She remains silent and once more waits him out.

Before long, the young man gives in and asks, "Well, where is my father? You do know where he is, don't you? I heard your mother say she killed the Stranger. She was talking about my father, wasn't she? Tell me, is my father dead?"

Letty gives him a good long look. He's so young he barely needs to shave. She guesses he's only a few years older than she is. He looks so desperately sad she feels pity for him. She wants to tell him what happened. Besides, who else can she tell?

And clearly, it's her turn. So, she tells him as much of the truth as she deems safe. "Your father was here. He came to our home Monday night and pounded so hard on our door he caused the wood to split. My poppa opened the door to him anyway, but before my poppa could welcome him in as one would normally do, your father accused my poppa of being a thief. Then he grabbed my poppa by the throat. My poppa rightly defended himself from your father's insane attack. They fought until they ended up at the fireplace with your father on top. Then your father took to bashing my poppa's head on the stone edge of the hearth. He was killing my poppa! That was when my momma hit your father on the back of his head with a cast iron cooking pot. I watched her do it and I watched your father's brains and blood spill out from the back of his crushed skull. He was good and dead alright, but you need to realize my momma was only defending my poppa."

The young man's soft brown eyes tear up, so Letty stops for a moment and waits, giving him time to absorb the horrible manner of his father's death. When she sees his left shoulder shrug just a little, the acceptance obvious, she picks up where she left off.

"My poppa was no thief," she says. "He found a bundle of tulip bulbs laying on the road after your father drove off. He was going to return the bundle in the morning, but he never had the chance.

Instead, your father beat him senseless, and he never woke up again. He died last night. And now my momma is dead, too. Everyone's dead except for you and me."

The young man thinks it over, then admits, "Well, your story might well be true. If my father believed his bundle had been stolen, he would have moved heaven and earth to get the bundle back for it contained the rarest of tulip bulbs. He spent years trying to find those bulbs. The bulbs are worth a small fortune. But of course, he would have punished the thief even if the bulbs were worthless. He hated thieves. He had no tolerance for thieves of any kind. But excuse me, it sounds like four people have died, but I count only three people lying dead in front of me and not one of them seems to be my father. I need you to tell me right now where he is."

His deep bass voice and his use of an authoritarian tone remind Letty of that demon, that devil, that bad, bad Constable man. She's had about enough of that. The young man might deserve an answer, but she's not about to be ordered around. She's not afraid of him, nor afraid of any consequences, not anymore, not after what she has seen and done these last few days. Still, she offers up a little bit more of the truth.

She admits, "He's nowhere, he's not here. There is no body. We burnt him up. He was burnt with the cart, and now there is nothing left of him. The heavy rains we had early Tuesday morning washed his ashes out over the marsh. We burnt him at the low spot down over the hill at the end of the path." Letty points her finger towards the general direction of where his father had gotten to, all the while avoiding the subject of her grinding his father's bones to flour.

Visibly outraged, the young man exclaims, "What? You cremated him? How could you? Why on earth would you do that? What kind of a monster are you?" Now he has taken to shouting and waving his arms as though to keep her away from him, as though she were about to burn him up too. He sputters and spits as he walks backwards in a frantic attempt at putting distance between them. He looks to be on the verge of losing control, not unlike how his own father looked the night he beat her poppa down to the edge of death.

Her pity passes, her anger reignites. Vibrating with raw emotion, she walks towards him waving her arms, trying to look huge and intimidating, just like her momma taught her to. And all the while she's shouting, "Me! You think I'm a monster? Now I ask you, what kind of a man attacks someone who opens the door to him? Your father was a monster first! He started this awful mess, didn't he?"

The full glory of self-righteous fury descends. The red-faced young man, the blood soaked, tear-stained young woman, stand puffed up and glaring at one another. They remain silent and alert as they digest the truth of each other's words.

Time passes, understanding dawns.

Letty finally breaks the silence. "He's dead, he really is. My momma thought we would all go to jail or be hanged if his body were found so she burned him up and I helped her do it, I did. I did it for my family. I can't explain why she killed the Constable, her doing that was just so sudden, so full-on crazy. I'm sorry, I really am. I wish I could bring them all back, but you know dead is dead. But most of all, I wish I had never, ever set eyes on your father, or those evil tulip bulbs."

They become still and separate, diminished, dropped down deep into their own private grief. Four days ago, they had family. Now, no family, all gone, just gone. Gone like bones ground to dust and buried deep in the garlic bed never to see the light of day, nor mentioned to anyone ever, ever, ever again.

The young man's habitual shrug defines the moment he accepts his father's death. Most of his childhood had been spent with his father absent. He assumed his father would die in the most remote and dangerous of deserts, jungles, or mountains, all in pursuit of plants for the great Horticultural Societies of Europe. An avalanche or a flood, a bug or snake bite, or more horribly, most likely, a lingering infection would have, should have caused his death. But no. Instead, on the soil of his own home country, a mere woman, a very tiny woman with hair like fire and skin like snow killed him dead and she didn't even leave a body to bury, she was that mad.

Letty can see how affected he is, and her heart softens. She reaches out to him and takes hold of his hands. As they look at each other something starts between them. A recognition of their unique circumstances. Both orphans now, no family left. He pulls his hands loose and wraps his arms around her. She leans in and accepts the embrace. They sob in each other's arms until they become tired of crying. They release each other, and he takes a step back. He examines her bloody, tired face and comes to a life changing decision.

25

William and Letty

The young man informs Letty, "You know we need to bury all the dead. We should do it now, before it gets dark. We'll do it together."

Letty nods her head yes, the lump in her throat prevents her from responding. She turns away from him and gazes down upon her dead parents. She no longer has a mother or a father. It was all so sudden. In just two days she's lost hem both. It somehow makes perfect sense. Her mother's last act was to reach out and touch her husband, her last breath was used to say his name. The love so obvious, of course her mother had to die. Letty's strained expression is replaced by one of loving acceptance.

The young man watches the progression of thoughts flicker across the girl's bloody face. He feels a compulsion to ease her suffering. Clearly, she has had a bad time of it and none of it is her fault. He heard her mother say as much, and he believes it's true. It just feels right, her innocence. But something holds him back from telling her he believes in her. Instead, he says, "I think it best to roll your mother in first, then your father. This grave is plenty big enough for three. Why is it so big? I hope the Constable dug most of it. He did, didn't he? It looks like he might have been trying to impress your mother with his manliness. Do you think he was?"

Letty shakes her pretty head up and down, her blond curls bouncing every which way, naturally distracting. "Yes, why yes, I guess he was. He looked at my mother like he was undressing her, and in front of my poppa, too. He was doing it all the time, from when he first arrived at our home when my poppa was still alive. He looked at me that same way just before my momma killed him. He acted like he owned us. I heard him tell my momma they would work something out, and then he winked at her. It really upset my momma. What did he mean by all that, do you know?"

" I don't know, William replies. "Life is just life. There's no sense to most of it." The realization the girl is an innocent comes as a pleasant surprise. He's spent his whole life in the city and knows things he wished he did not know.

William begins the burial by tossing the Constable's formal black hat in first, followed by Neola's pile of clothes. Together, they roll Neola off her husband towards the edge of the grave. It's easy to do because she's so tiny and she's still pliable. In fact, she's still warm to the touch. It takes one more push to get her to fall off the edge into the grave. She lands in opposition to the Constable, bent in the fetal position, her head at his feet. Together, in death, they form a perfect yin yang symbol. The symbolism is not lost on the young man. His tutors had instructed him on the philosophy behind the meaning of Yin and Yang, as well as the merits of cremation as opposed to the somewhat barbaric European practice of burial. He's glad his own father is not part of the grave, but he has no intention of sharing that thought with the girl.

Letty just thinks it's a fortunate happenstance that there is still plenty of room left for her poppa. They roll her shrouded father into the grave. He lands face up, on top, fitting above and between the two corpses below. The force of her beloved husband's impact lifts Neola's right arm, and it flies up and lands across his torso, her hand flattening and covering his heart in one final, eternal embrace. The two young people, the orphans, witness this natural blessing of sorts, this final act of a great, true love, and it makes a lasting impression on their untested, innocent hearts.

And then the young man, remembering his proper church upbringing, proclaims, "It's time to say a prayer."

But on hearing the word prayer, Letty recoils, gives him a sharp, hard look, then just as quickly drops her glance. In an odd way she doesn't want him to see how much she hates the word prayer. She knows she's forever done with blind faith and prayers, but it's personal and no explanation will ever be given to anyone, especially not to the son of the man that killed her poppa. But she also knows it's not acceptable to be irreligious in decent society and so she hides her distaste as best she can. But she knows he's right about one thing. This is the time to say goodbye to her parents, and so she solemnly declares, "Poppa, momma, I am so sorry for how things turned out. I know there was no help for what happened, it was all a terrible misunderstanding. I'll never, ever forget how you both loved each other and how you loved me, too. I'll love you both all the days my life. And momma, you were magnificent, you did right by me and poppa. Goodnight you two lovebirds, sleep tight."

The young people just naturally make eye contact. Letty intuits his silent ask and reluctantly nods her head yes. The young man acknowledges the untimely death of the Constable by saying the all-inclusive, "God rest all your souls, Amen." Then he picks up the shovel and starts shoveling dirt on top of the bodies. Young and strong, he shovels with the power and speed of the righteous and the wronged.

Letty remembers the horse and fetches two buckets of water from the well. She tucks one bucket under the horse's mouth and holds it steady against her knee until his long greedy tongue has slurped every droplet of water. The horse needs food as well, so she extends his lead so he can move around and feed on the lush grasses growing beneath the tree. But the horse ignores the grass, instead pulling a few green apples off the tree's limbs to eat. Letty leans the second bucket of water against the base of the tree so it's within easy reach should the horse need it.

Now that her chore is done, she has time to watch the young man fling dirt. He seems to be a nice young man. She remembers hearing her momma telling her poppa that all the young men had emigrated to the colonies or America and that was the reason Letty was destined to become a sacred sister. Well, it appears her momma was wrong about that. Not all the young men have gone away. Letty's looking at an attractive young man right now.

The young man has worked so fast the dirt pile is now more than half gone. His doing most of the work just doesn't feel right. It's made Letty uncomfortable. Watching others work just isn't normal and lately, she's had far too much of not normal. She makes her presence felt by nudging him. Then she begs, "Let me do it. I need to do it. It should be my chore. I should be the one burying my parents, not you."

He hesitates, thinking it over, then hands her the shovel and stands back, well out of the arc of her swing, not quite sure of her intentions yet. Letty ignores him. She pushes the shovel as hard as she can into the dwindling pile of dirt and starts shoveling. She works with a wild fury, her mouth twisting in a wedded expression of madness and grief. Sobs try to escape, but Letty manages to suck the sobs back in. It doesn't take long before Letty slows down. The young man takes notice and taps her on the shoulder. She smiles an exhausted smile of thanks as he slips the shovel's handle from her loosened grip.

By now, the dirt level is at the top of the grave but by the time he's finished shoveling the remaining dirt the grave has become a sizable mound. And still the grave is not finished. William rests for a moment, then politely informs her, "I know you're tired, but we need to cover the dirt with the rocks that are piled at the other end of the grave. It'll keep any animals from digging the grave apart. It has to be done now, I'm terribly sorry."

Letty nods her head in agreement. She knows it's true. She's heard the feral dogs late at night running the screaming rabbits down to ground. The snarls and growls as the dogs rip the poor creatures apart is especially horrible to hear. Worse yet, she knows the dogs are scavengers, and would dig up the grave for an easy meal. Eager to protect her parents from such a fate, she's the first to pick up a rock and throw it on the grave. The young man follows suit, and a noisy flurry of tossed rocks ensues. Twilight ends the moment the burial is complete but as yet the moon has not made much of an appearance, the cloudy sky adding to the darkness. It's time to go, but after they take just a few steps towards the cottage they see a shooting star cross the night sky. A single bat follows the same path, but then it veers off, swoops down, and passes between them. Startled, the young man reaches out and pulls Letty to his side. Perfect timing on his part. What follows is the wind on their skin of ten thousand beating bat wings as the gruesome creatures fly past en masse in pursuit of nightly nourishment.

Instinctively they duck and run while still holding hands. Letty guides the young man into the garden, closing the gate behind them, and for just this once the gate hinges barely give a squeak. She leads him to the garden shed and prepares the wash water. It's become so dark she feels the need to guide his hands into the washbasin. She soaps his hands, then leaves him to wash and rinse his face. The intimacy comes so naturally, they fail to even notice it as such.

She's first to enter the dark cottage, pulling him along behind her by his wet hand. He waits at the open door while she lights a candle and the kerosene lantern. Once the room is bathed in light, he shuts the door and approaches her.

Somehow, Letty knows the next moment is important. She looks directly at the earnest young man and nods her head yes, inviting him to speak.

The young man clears his throat, holds a hand over his heart, and with a smidgen of pride says, "I am William. William Vandermeer of the Amsterdam Vandermeer's."

A small laugh escapes Letty. It's so absurd, it really is. After all, they've just witnessed a murder and a suicide by poisoning and have just buried three people. And it was all done without properly introducing themselves.

The sweet, young woman finally minds her manners and proudly announces, "And I am Letty. Letty Miller. Both my parents had the same last name though they were not related by blood. Almost everyone in this area is named Miller, that's why the Wharf is named Miller Wharf, but my mother's family is the only family with the grindstone windmill in all the region.

William resurrects the fire and Letty places last night's leftover vegetable stew on the crane's hook and pushes it over the flames. They each take a place at the table. William just naturally chooses Vonder's chair and after a brief hesitation Letty takes Neola's. They glance at one another and in sync they reach out and join hands. A sweet, gentle peace descends upon them. They should hate each other, but they don't. It's simple really. Their parent's actions belong to their parents.

Last night's leftover food quickly comes to a boil. Letty ladles the stew into bowls and hands one to William. She places the butter between them and slices two pieces of cheese, handing him the thickest slice. She brings the pitcher of cool, fresh water to the table and fills their cups. Quenching their thirst becomes a spur of the moment contest, and they drink without stopping until the cups are empty, and they are water drunk. And although they both know the drinking contest was a tie, they each shout "I won!" They argue and laugh over who really was the winner for way too long, enjoying the challenge, the give and take, and especially the looking deeply into each other's eyes until hunger finally compels them to give the win to the other.

And then they attack the food. Fast and sloppy for the first few bites, they shovel it in, then remember each other again. They fight and flirt over the butter and cheese. But soon, every morsel of food that was in the stew pot has been scrapped up and eaten. They do the washup and put the leftover crocks of butter and cheese in the cupboard, being mindful about closing and locking the cupboard door against the ever-present onslaught of the little mice.

That done, they realize that they are done with all the business between them. The laying of blame, the confessions, the burying, it's all over now. They've done their duty and it's time they part company.

An awkwardness descends and they get in each other's way. Their bodies become all jutting elbows, tripping feet, shy heads hanging down. They look away, they steal glances. They take a few steps back and away from each other, giving each other plenty of space, respecting free will.

He doesn't want to leave her. She doesn't want him to go. It's not the fear of being alone. It's the wanting to stay with each other. They pause, wondering what to do next.

Letty's the first to speak and she begs, with no hint of shame, "Please sleep here. Please, please. I want you to stay, I really do."

William looks deep into her beautiful eyes, those wolf eyes with the black ring around the blue and he literally gasps for air. He speaks spontaneously from the whole of his being as he says, "Of course, I'll stay. I really want to, I do, I do."

Letty looks around the cottage and her gaze lands on her parent's empty bed. The bed is fouled with the stench of shit and piss and death. It would be wrong to ask William to sleep there. Unconsciously, she directs the full force of her luscious, young body at William, pulling her shoulders back, displaying her perky breasts to full advantage while she just naturally accentuates her waist and hips with the help of the careful placement of her hands. She unconsciously copies her mother's trick of batting her eyelashes as she says, "Momma and I slept in my bed the last few nights, we could sleep there, too." She points to her bed and they both look at the cozy place. They'll fit nicely.

Suddenly, the good manners that have been so carefully bred into William raise their hands, grab him, and try to hold him back. Letty looks to be barely sixteen years old. It might be a bad idea to sleep in the same bed as the virginal Letty. It would change her life forever and he would be the cause. There would be no going back if he slept with her.

Letty notices his hesitation and can't imagine why. She takes a step towards him, their lips on the verge of touching. They suck in each other's air and their lips just naturally slip into a kiss. The kiss becomes a hundred more, a thousand. They cover each other's ears and eyelids, necks, and chins, hungry for more, kissing each other clean, making each other brand new.

They fall onto her bed and move on to the rest of each other. Exploring by touch, removing each other's clothes. And although they are virgins, they instinctively know what to do. Letty guides his fingertip till he feels the round ball of her female sex. He quickly finds the right motion and it's good for her. But there's more. His finger just naturally slips inside a hole and rubs up against a spot the texture of his very own earlobe. Perfectly round, flat, high up on top, and just a half a finger in. The texture is so different it fascinates him, and he slowly rubs it, round and around.

On his first try he's found the circle of love, the secret pleasure spot of all women. It excites Letty, so it excites him, too. And then she's had enough of his finger. She becomes desperate for something else to be rubbed inside and she knows just where it is. She climbs on top of him and slides him in, then keeps on sliding him in then out, rocking on him, till she brings them to climax. A great shudder overtakes them, and they cry out and collapse, thoroughly spent and mutually satisfied.

They lay on their sides, not believing it, how good they feel, all sweaty but not minding as they hold each other. They spend time learning each other's eyes, each other's faces. In tiny movements, they push the hair back from each other's flushed foreheads. They keep doing the gazing and gentle stroking until they fall asleep, wrapped tight in each other's arms as if they are of one body, one soul.

26

Friday Dawn

The rosy glow of morning's first light wakes the young lovers. They gaze into each other's eyes and blush. As she finger-combs his hair, he pulls one of her curls, wanting nothing so much as to see the bounce of it after it's pulled straight and let go.

The curl is surprisingly long and by the time he has it pulled perfectly straight his elbow bumps up against the rock wall behind him and dislodges a stone. The stone falls onto the bed and rolls up against his bare ass. The cold of the stone piques William's interest and he turns around to see the cause of his discomfort.

It's nothing but a rock. But above the rock is a hole in the wall. It looks like a contrived hidey-hole. William peers inside it. A familiar-looking leather sheath holding an equally familiar knife greets his eyes. An official looking missive is laying beneath the knife and propped against the back wall of the hidey hole is an object that appears to be the very prayer wheel his father described in his final letter to William. Worst of all, nestled among the pile of evidence, are four enormous tulip bulbs.

William swings his legs over the side of the bed and sits up. He briefly holds his head between his hands and squeezes with all his might. The nightmare has returned and taken on new meaning. He confronts it head on by asking Letty, "Why are my father's possessions hiding in this hole above your bed?

Letty freezes. She can't help it. She becomes tongue-tied, the family trait once more rearing its useless head.

Her silence scares him. Her being all feisty and equal and all yesterday, and her freezing up now, her shrinking in on herself, it looks like guilt to him. He grabs her by her naked shoulders and shakes her, but gently, not really wanting to hurt her. He's not someone who hurts people, but she needs to know how serious this matter is.

He blurts out, "Did you help kill my Father? You did, didn't you? And you were the one that hid everything in this hidey hole, weren't you? All this belonged to my father, I know it all did. I want you tell me the truth now, and don't you dare try to lie to me!"

Letty covers her face, trying to hide and be as small as she can possibly be. She wants to crawl onto her dead momma's lap. She wants her dead poppa to pick her up and hold her above this mess she made for herself. This is all so hard and twisted. Nothing is turning out right and true. She just wants to crawl into the hidey hole and hide. But she can't. She's too big.

Her heart drops, her tummy rolls, and she feels like retching. She forgot all about hiding his father's possessions, she really did. A wrinkle of confusion creases her brow as she ponders what is what and how to say it. Still unable to speak, she gives a tiny nod of agreement.

William scoots away from her. Oh, the horror of it all. He just spent last night loving his father's murderer, willingly sleeping next to her. He has no idea how to process it, and now he becomes the one struck dumb.

Letty would like to help him with his little problem. She really enjoyed their night together and would like it to continue. She forces herself to make sound and manages to squeak out an explanation, "I didn't kill your father, nor did I help kill him. But I was the one that put your father's property in the hidey hole."

William shakes his head, obviously confused. Finally, he asks, "But why on earth would you do that?"

"I don't know why," Letty says. "What I mean is, I just felt like doing it. The cottage was a big mess. And my mother was acting all crazy, wanting to burn everything in sight. Anyway, I was alone for a few minutes and when I picked up the knife and the prayer wheel a strange, tingling sensation came over me, and I just knew I had to save them, and hide them. And you know what? Now I know why. I saved them for you. They're your treasures William. They all belong to you."

She perks up and smiles a happy smile. She understands the compulsion now, amazed that something so good has finally come out of that night of pure hell. She reaches into the hidey hole and pulls out the missive and hands it to him. She retrieves the rest of his father's possessions and makes a show of laying each one on the bed next to his bare-naked thigh.

A bit more subdued, Letty continues, "The other things in there, what I left behind, they're mine. My parents never knew about my secret hidey hole. And my mother never knew about my hiding the four tulip bulbs. She thought they rolled into the fire and burned up. She thought I just kept two tulip bulbs. And those two bulbs are gone for good because I ate one and shared the other with my momma. I was alone when I ate the whole bulb. It made me feel funny, but good, like when you and I were touching. It also made me strong. The next night Momma and I split the second bulb, but the effect was not as powerful. Yesterday my momma ate four bulbs. She did it to make sure she would be strong enough to deal with the Constable. And it worked, she gave that man the business."

Letty stops speaking for a moment, the death of her mother

made real once again. But she pulls herself back from the brink of grief, takes a deep breath and continues, "Believe me, my momma would have destroyed all your father's possessions had she known they still existed. She might even have tried to kill you. Vengeance was on her mind all the time. My poppa was her heart, she was his body and soul and together they made a whole person. They always said this to each other, and they meant it. My momma just went crazy when she lost her heart."

William picks the missive up and looks at it. The Holland Horticultural Society's name is dominate on the masthead. His father was never without the missive, no matter what country he traveled to, no matter how far he went. It was his father's constant companion. William hates it. He could quote it verbatim. When his father was home, he forced William to read it many, many times to prove the merit of his absence. William lays it aside, not needing to read it ever again.

He picks up the tulip bulbs and examines them. So, it's true. His father had finally found what he was after. Three of the tulip bulbs are blushed red, and one is blushed yellow, and all are of an unusual size, and all are in good condition. It's obvious they are something special, undoubtedly unique in all of Holland.

William shares his amazement with Letty by exclaiming, "My God, these bulbs are twice as big as normal, they look like a cross between an apple and a strawberry."

Letty gives him the old side eye before replying, "Exactly what I thought. They even have juice like a strawberry, and they have the same shape to the tip, but they do chew up like an apple. They taste kind of hot and spicy. They change how you feel when you eat them, not only physical sensations but also emotions. Eating too many tulip bulbs killed my momma. They're pure poison. I hate them. I never, ever want to see them again!"

Sudden anger erupts inside Letty, and needing a physical release for her rage, she grabs the tulip bulbs and throws the lot as fast and hard as she can, not even bothering to aim. The bulbs hit the base of the bench and bounce a few times, then roll back to her bed, undamaged.

The young lovers stare at the tulip bulbs for a few heartbeats then collapse into fits of laughter. It's downright ridiculous how quickly the evil things returned to their feet. There's no getting away from those wicked, wicked tulip bulbs.

William fiddles with the cylinder of the tiny prayer wheel. One of the panels pops open and the corner of a piece of paper pokes out. He stares at it not knowing what to do until Letty nudges him with her elbow. He takes the hint and pulls on the paper. The spindle turns and the paper unspools and separates into two pieces that flutter down before coming to rest on William's lap. The top piece of paper is a map depicting an area in Central Asia marked in the King's English as Notch Pass. The whole of the map is a beautiful work of art, the landmarks embellished with gold, green and black ink. William has no idea what to do with it for now, and neither does Letty, so he refolds it and winds it back onto the spindle for safe keeping.

And then William does a double take upon examining the remaining piece of paper. He exclaims, "Oh my God, Letty. This is my father's handwriting. It really is. This letter is from my father!"

They exchange happy glances. William (his voice suddenly serious) proceeds to read the message out loud.

"My dearest William,

The bundle is full of the origin tulip bulbs, the very ones I've been searching for all these years. The bulbs are called Shangri-La and when consumed they have a powerful aphrodisiac and hallucinogenic effect and will instantly increase physical strength. I personally would never eat more than one. I collected the bulbs west of the Tien San Mountain Region in central western Asia. A beautiful Shaman woman named Lotus was growing them on a terrace high above the throat of an extinct volcano. They were in full bloom when I collected them, only red and yellow flowers, no other colors, they are the real deal, there's no doubt. I believe she was also a witch of some sort and I suspect she put a spell on me, for she surely had me doing her bidding. She was too eager to give me the bulbs and tried to refuse payment for them. She also insisted I take the prayer wheel, but now I am wary of it for it has a spin opposite of all the others. I'm not exactly sure what that means but please don't play with it, don't spin it. I don't think it's a toy. The academics in Holland are aware the prayer wheels of the region have a distinctive octagonal shape and they will undoubtedly accept it as proof of the location of the origin tulip bulbs. Of course, the map I've included is proof as well. But, if for some reason you are unable to sell the bulbs right away, you must plant them in the home garden, pointy side up. But first, sprinkle cattle bone dust and blood underneath the base of the bulbs. Plant them at least six times as deep as they are long. They will winter over and still be marketable. If you are reading this, then I am probably dead, and all that I have is now yours. But beyond all that, I need you to understand one important truth. Your mother's death was never your fault, it was only ever the fault of the thief. I understand that now. Please forgive me for treating you the way that I did after your mother died. It was wrong of me. I know that now and I am terribly sorry, especially for our lost time. Take care of yourself. Love and allow yourself to be loved. And remember, you can never change the past, so tread lightly. Your loving father, Jacob Vandermeer."

The young people absorb the meaning of the words. William's perpetual frown slowly disappears as the heavy weight of years of guilt is lifted from his being. Letty lets her silence express her sympathy.

William flips the paper over. A message written in green ink covers the entire page. The script is precise and tiny, and very feminine. They bump heads in their haste to read it. Together, they read out loud.

"Woman with hair like fire and skin like snow, my gods have arranged for you to spin my personal prayer wheel. And when you do it, and you surely will, it will activate my prayer. Many years ago, I warned you to leave my husband alone. It was the first day my husband boarded your father's ship. But you didn't take it to heart. I know because my husband bragged about how you openly admired him while he worked the sails. He told me how brave you were in heavy weather, how natural you were on deck. How you loved to play games and make him laugh. How you were a real woman, not scared of the water like I was. By the time the voyage ended my husband had become obsessed with you. And all the years after that, whenever he was home on leave, I would hear him whisper your name in his sleep. But I said nothing, not even when he stole my things and gave them to your father to give to you. I wanted our love to come back like it was in the beginning. I was sure it would if only I had a child, but he was so rarely home. And when he was home, he rarely touched me in that way. The end for us came the day I woke before he did and saw the size of his morning wood. Of course, I took advantage. I sat on him and slid him home. As he woke to the unexpected pleasure, he called your name, not mine. When he opened his eyes, he saw it was me, not you, and he pushed me off like I was a diseased whore. And then he beat his chest and begged your forgiveness, not mine. And that's the day I knew my husband had to die. It was also the day we went our separate ways. My husband moved full-time onto your father's ship, and I returned to my ancestral home. And then I called upon all my Gods for help. They obliged by whipping up the storm that sunk your father's ship. But my husband's death was not enough. It was really you who had caused all the trouble, you who had cursed my marriage and made me an unloved, childless wife. So, I asked my Gods to hunt you down and burn you to nothing but a pile of ash. They were happy to oblige, they love me. I even sent my pet vultures to witness your destruction. But somehow, you managed to escape. After a few years, my ancient ones were able to find you again. Then they found a lonely, greedy man and sent him to my door to do my bidding. I put that fool under a spell and sent him to your door to deliver your death to you. My pet vultures have followed that fool and will be my eyes as I watch you die. And this time I know you will die, because this time my curse is powered by greed, and greed always, always kills."

The young couple absorb the meaning of the written words, then exchange a nervous glance. Letty begs, "My mother's dead, so that ends the curse, right? Right?"

William shrugs, unwilling to promise the lovely Letty what he cannot know. They both try to reread the message out loud again, but the words disappear faster than they can be read. The last of the words disappear in a puff of green smoke.

Letty remembers seeing green smoke recently. It was during the cremation of William's father and the burning of the cart. A naked dancing woman, her belly hidden behind a snake-like ribbon of green smoke, magically appeared in the cremation flames. And when the woman disappeared, it was in a huge puff of green smoke identical in color to the one they just witnessed.

Letty guesses the woman was the sailor's wife checking in on them, using her magic powers to do so. The letter and the memory convince Letty the curse is real, but for some unknown reason she's been spared for now. She takes the hint and pleads,

" William, I need to leave the cottage. All the violence and death are just too much. And I am done with all the crying, I need new places, new spaces, so I can be happy. Besides, I wonder if I would even be safe if I stayed."

William believes her. Of course, she would never be able to live alone among the ghosts, the gruesome manner of her family's death would always present. The memory would eat at her, killing her spirit bit by bit, day by day. But Letty not being safe? He thinks she might be overreacting.

He knows all about losing family. He lost his mother years ago in a terrible accident, a day he will never, ever forget. He was but a small child walking between his parents, holding onto their hands as they crossed a busy intersection in Amsterdam, when a thief came out of nowhere and grabbed his mother's purse. He pulled her into the path of an oncoming freight wagon, but the thief realized the danger and suddenly let go of the purse, twirling out of the way in the nick of time.

The suddenness of the thief's release made his mother stumble on the uneven cobblestones. She fell to her knees, and was crushed by the horse's hooves, then crushed again as the wagon wheels rolled over her. It was a sickening sound, a horrible sight. It was a terrible death. His mother hung on to her life for three days, in the worst of agonies, the doctors unable to relieve her suffering.

The thief escaped unharmed and was never seen again though William's father spent all his free time searching the streets and the slums for any sign of him. His father insisted that if he had been the one next to his wife his proximity would have deterred the thief or at the very least, he would have been able to prevent her being dragged to her death. His father never said it out loud, he didn't need to, William knew it was really his fault his mother was dead.

By her absence, William came to understand his mother was the glue that held their family together. After they buried her, his father could barely look at William, the reason obvious. Resentment and guilt were the only emotions his father was able to share. The mere sight of the word thief in the newspaper would send his father into a violent rage resulting in the breaking of whatever object lay near at hand. Or worse yet, deep depression lasting for days, then weeks.

The night finally came when his father could no longer stand to sleep in the same house as William. The next day, a few hours after sunrise, his father left his post as the Professor of Botany at the University of Amsterdam and returned to the field, pursuing and collecting unique botanical specimens, spending most of his time traveling in Asia, and in that way, he legitimately avoided spending time with his son. William was left in the care of housekeepers, private schools, and finally an apprenticeship. His father rarely returned home and when he did, he was no better than before.

The last time William saw his father was well over three years ago and now he will never see him again. But at least he knows his father had stopped blaming him for his mother's death, although his father's hatred of thieves persisted until his dying day. It is, after all, the pursuit of a thief that killed his father in the end.

Letty's right of course. They need to leave, and they need to do it now. Not shy about their nakedness, they get up and get dressed. William quickly stuffs the letter and prayer wheel, the watch and the compass, and the four tulip bulbs into his trouser pockets. Letty pulls clean clothes from her storage chest and quickly dresses. She stuffs yesterday's dirt encrusted clothes into the bottom of the biggest basket the family own.

They run outside and take turns doing their necessary. They finish up by washing their hands at the garden shed's counter, scooting in close, touching hips. The basket holding the clothespins is conveniently sitting on the shelf above the wash pan and Letty retrieves it and picks out the animal pairs, wiggling them in the air, making a game, pretending to make them dance their way into her apron pocket.

It makes William laugh. She laughs, too. She holds her favorite pair, the elephants, an extra-long moment just to see if William will admire them as much as she does. He obliges by whistling his appreciation. She drops them into her pocket, pleased that he thinks the elephants are something special, too.

Done now with their morning necessary they hurry back inside. Letty heads to the basket she had begun packing and drops the clothespins on top of the towel covering her dirty laundry. And then she moves on to the kitchen. She takes the cheese and sausage from the cupboard and hands them over to William. He had already anticipated the need to cook and was busy building a small, hot fire.

Letty returns to her sleeping alcove and rolls her thick feather quilt around her pillow. It'll make an awkward bundle unless it's bound and tied. Instead of string, she decides to use the long red ribbon the haberdasher's son gave her all those years ago. She dips her hand in the hidey hole and feels around for it, but instead of finding the ribbon her fingers bump into her pretties. William's presence has made her just a little bit distracted and she had forgotten all about her treasures. She slips the fool's gold into one skirt pocket and the drawstring bag into the other, then she retrieves the ribbon and winds and twists it around the bedding, making the ribbon cross on both sides so it becomes a real bundle.

The last thing left in the hidey hole is the love poem given to her by the boy at church. She leaves it there. She has no use for it now for she's sure she'll never see him again. He's been long gone to America for over two years now. Out of habit, she replaces the rock in the wall and once again the hidey hole becomes invisible.

There's lots to pack and Letty moves on to the next item of importance, a pencil sketch hanging above her chest. It's one of her few possessions and she's not about to leave it behind. The subject of the sketch is the ancestral windmill, the old oak tree and the cottage. An artist named Vincent drew it for her. Her poppa had stumbled upon Vincent wandering in the hinterlands. He was lost and soaked to the skin. Her poppa brought him home to the cottage and in between eating and sleeping by the fire Vincent tutored Letty on the finer points of sketching with pen and ink. Three days later, he deemed her exceptionally talented, and then he left. They never saw nor heard of him again. Letty smiles at the memory, then slips the drawing into her sketch book. She stows the book inside the cherrywood box holding her art supplies. After considering the possibilities of the ink pot spilling and ruining her clothes, she settles the art box under the dirty laundry at the bottom of the basket.

She makes the hard choice to leave her cumbersome storage chest behind. The sad truth is, it's a real piece of furniture and not a traveling trunk. She unloads her meager pile of clothes and packs them all in the basket. They barely fit. She covers the clothes with a folded sheet, making sure to tuck the edges in tight so nothing can be lost.

And still there is more to pack. She starts filling a second basket. Her heavy woolen winter cape goes on the bottom, followed by all the garters and stockings and anything of her mother's that might fit Letty's larger frame along with the two fancy party aprons. From the shelf by her parent's bed, she takes the carved walnut box her poppa made for her momma's essentials, double wraps it in two kitchen towels, and packs it in the basket, too.

Under the shelf, hanging on hooks, are her father's vest and her mother's black cashmere shawl. Letty hugs them, she can't help herself. She breathes in her poppa's woodsy smell, her mother's scent of lavender and lily.

When she finally comes up for air, she decides to take them with her and packs them in the basket on top of the box of essentials. She tucks the hairbrush, the comb, and all the hair ribbons in around the edges. And that's the last of the personals. She covers the contents with a sheet and throws her own shawl over her shoulders before tying her momma's fancy hat around her neck.

She stops long enough to eat a thick slice of cheese and a cooked sausage before returning to the packing up of her life. She eats while standing, her eyes roaming about the cottage looking for anything else that might be of use in her new life. William sits quietly at the table, watching her, admiring her efficiency as he slowly munches up every bit of available food.

Letty locates her family's largest water bucket. Chance has it empty, but not for long. She drops the enameled dish pan in it, then looks around for a cooking pot to add to it. She reaches for the very pot her momma used as the weapon to murder William's father but stops short of touching it. It dawns on her that using the pot after knowing how genuinely nice William is, especially after making such sweet and satisfying pleasure with him, well it would just be wrong. Besides, it's made of cast iron and it's too heavy to travel with.

She needs a smaller pot, an innocent pot not associated with death. She kneels on the floor and looks through the bottom shelf of the kitchen cupboard. Way in the back is a copper pot with a tight-fitting lid. She remembers seeing it years ago and her momma telling her to never mind about it, it might be pretty, but it was way too small for their family's needs. But it's perfect for Letty's. She takes it out of the cupboard and drops it inside the wash pan. Then she removes the lid and drops the small tin boiler inside the copper pot.

But Letty's left holding the copper pot's lid wondering what to do with it. She decides to keep it, - she might need it. It looks like it will fit between the pots and the basket if it's on edge. But as she begins to slide it into place, she catches sight of a yellowed piece of paper stuck inside the lid.

Intrigued, Letty gently peels the fragile paper out from under the rolled rim and unfolds it. It's an old note to her mother from her grandfather. For William's benefit, and because she can't help but play a game, she imitates her grandfather's gruff voice as she reads it out loud.

"Congratulations, you have found another important clue my darling daughter, just like I knew you would. This time I've hidden quite a few gold coins in my most favorite of secret hidey holes. I know you know where because I showed you the spot when you were but six years old. But in case you have forgotten, here is another clue. The sun is a golden orb, and no matter what time of day you stand still in this spot it will always heat your red head. The rain will go away and come again another day but have no fear the water will always be here. Good luck! The gold is yours if you can find it. I hope you do." Love you forever always, your adoring poppa.

Mostly for William's benefit, Letty explains, "My grandfather's letter is part of the game my momma played with him. And although my momma never found this letter, I believe she most probably found the hidden treasure because one of her daily habits was to search the premises." And that's about all she has to say about that to William.

But she keeps thinking about it on her own. Letty loves a good game, but the clue means nothing to her. Her own little hidey hole lacks a relationship to the sun or rain. But still, the gold coins could have been hidden in the hidey hole and her mother or someone else could have found the coins, leaving the bag of useless glass and the lumpy chunks of fool's gold behind because they knew they had no real value. That explanation makes the most sense.

She lets it go, just wanting to finish packing and leave this bad luck place behind. She picks up where she left off and adds two beautifully carved wooden bowls and a couple of not so special, but unbreakable, enameled metal cups (useful for hot or cold liquids) to the kitchen bucket. She shoves the cutting board in, its narrow size allows for an easy fit. She wraps her various soaps for various uses in dishrags and drops them into the voids. She wraps up enough cutlery for two and includes the small ladle and the bread and meat knife before wedging the bundle behind the cutting board so tight it barely wiggles. She adds the sharpening stone, and gathers the salt and pepper containers, the cheese and butter crocks and the honey jar. She wraps each one separate in a linen dish towel or a washcloth according to its size. She adds a few wooden spoons into the voids, then covers the traveling kitchen with the best bath towel the family owns.

Satisfied she has the basics packed, she carries the bucket to the door where William has been patiently waiting and asks, "William, would you carry the kitchen bucket and my bedding to the wagon for me please?"

"Of course. I'd be more than happy to carry anything you want me to," William replies. He's just as anxious to leave as she is. And he proves it by practically running to the bed to grab the bedding bundle. After he tucks the bedding under his arm he rushes back to the door and picks up the kitchen bucket. He stops long enough to make a gracious little bow in Letty's direction as he declares, "After you, my lovely little Letty."

Letty takes one last look around, her eyes glittering with unshed tears. She lifts her hand and wiggles her fingers as she says goodbye to her ancestral home. William follows close on her heels as she walks out the door. The warmth and cleansing power of the golden rays of the morning sun wash over her and bring a bright smile to her pretty face. But when the disturbed dirt of the newly turned garlic bed comes into view her smile disappears and she suddenly stops. William can't stop his forward movement in time and bumps into her backside. The bump knocks Letty forward a few steps and she drops both baskets. Letty doesn't care. She rushes to the garden shed and throws open the door. She grabs the little planting spade then hurries to the garlic bed and promptly proceeds to dig up the remaining wicked, wicked tulip bulbs.

Alarmed, William cries out, "Letty, whatever are you doing! You're touching them! Don't you dare touch them! I don't want you to touch them! You of all people should know better than to take those evil tulip bulbs in your hands again, why on earth did you ever do that?"

"Why?" Letty says. "Why? Because they belong to you, William. Each one of those tulip bulbs is yours. I refuse to let the curse of greed win this time. My poppa wanted to return them to your father. I heard him say a much, so I am standing in for my father. And then the scales will be balanced between us, and I want that more than anything. Don't you?" She looks at him for confirmation while she continues to rinse all eight bulbs free of dirt. Forgoing permission, she proceeds to stuff the bulbs into every vest and coat pocket he has, and he just stands there and lets her.

When she's done, he looks like he has the distended tits of the Peterson's deaf old bitch collie. Letty points at him and giggles.

William gets the joke and laughs, too. Then he declares, "Alright, alright. I'll take them. But once I sell them, we are forever done with tulip bulbs. Agreed?"

Letty quickly replies. "Agreed."

Her hands need washing and so she dips a bit of water from the rain barrel into the old wash pan. She needs to go deep to reach the water. The water level seems extremely low considering the deluge that struck Tuesday morning. As the sun beats down on her head, warming it, she is reminded of her grandfather's clue and can't help but whisper, " Rain, rain go away come again another day."

It's such a silly thought to have right now, but just in case, she peers into the bottom of the barrel hoping to see the glint of gold. But all she sees is the barrel's black wooden bottom magnified through a foot of rainwater. It's muddy around the outside of the barrel's base and she knows the mud wasn't there yesterday. And the bottoms of several of the barrel's staves are a rotten black, glistening with moisture. The barrel has apparently sprung a leak and needs repaired, but Letty no longer cares. For the last time she uses her poppa's gritty soap to wash her hands and she knows it. She picks up the baskets and takes the lead as they walk towards the horse and wagon. William follows close behind. With each step Letty's smile grows till by the time they reach the horse and wagon she's grinning from ear to ear. But her smile disappears as they load her possessions onto the wagon deck. Something nags at Letty, distracting her. She scans the landscape trying to get an idea of what it could possibly be. Her searching gaze passes over the entrance to the windmill, then abruptly swings back. Stunned, she realizes what she has forgotten and what she must do.

27

Letty and William

Letty laughs, then shouts, "Come on William! Come with me!" She grabs him by the hand and drags him behind her, laughing all the while, skipping with wild joy. The real Letty has reappeared in all her natural exuberance.

William allows himself to be pulled along. Letty is so suddenly free and easy. Even her corkscrew curls are joyous, bouncing this way and that, a visual delight. He falls a little bit more in love with her.

They enter the windmill holding hands, but Letty lets go when they arrive at the grindstones. She studies the floor before she bends down and pries loose a large, grey-colored stone from the floor. Another hidey hole pops into view. Letty removes the same money bag she watched her momma hide late Wednesday morning. Triumphant, she waves the bag back and forth in front of William's astonished eyes.

With a giggle, and a graceful curtsy, she proclaims, "Voila! Voila! For you, my majesty, always for you."

He takes the bag from her, and his hands drop from the unexpected weight. He lifts it up and down, judging the true weight and the potential value. Excited by all the possibilities, he at first fumbles the drawstring, delaying the opening of the bag. He takes a deep, calming breath and teases the strings apart, then reaches inside and pulls out a thick wad of English banknotes. The quantity is truly astonishing, but when he peers inside the bag he's greeted by the sight of his father's compass and watch. It makes his father's death real once again. He's overcome with feelings of deep sadness, and he forgets all about the wad of paper money he's holding in his hand.

But soon enough, the considerable pile of mostly gold coins lying beneath his father's watch and compass catches his eye. The money is life changing, no doubt about it. But it's the honesty of the lovely Letty that he finds priceless. She could have kept the money for herself, and he never would have known. He looks at her and thinks she's the real treasure. He wants her love more than he wants the money, but he's happy to have both.

Letty elaborates, "I wasn't supposed to know about the bag of money. That's probably why I forgot all about it. But it belongs to you. It's your father's money. I think my mother must have picked your father's pockets after he died, that's how everything ended up in the bag. She never knew I watched her hide it. But it's all for the good. Now I'm able to give you all your father's possessions, his money, and the tulip bulbs. It's everything, I'm sure of it now. It's all I can do. And now we are truly even, William. Greed will not win this time. I won't let it."

William stuffs the banknotes back in the bag, carefully cinches the bag shut, and stuffs the precious bag in the deep inside pocket of his coat. And all the while he seems to be considering something of a deeply personal nature.

Finally, he exclaims "Oh my God, Letty. This bag contains a small fortune. And if I sell my household goods and the contents of the crates and the tulip bulbs, it will be more than enough for me to leave Holland and emigrate to America. Thank you. Thank you. This is a godsend, a final, farewell gift from my father. He always knew I wanted to go to America, and now I can, I'm finally free to go. And it's all thanks to you, Letty. You've made it all possible."

Letty had failed to anticipate this result. He's leaving her. She forces her face to go blank. She should have expected it. After all, he is his father's son. And that man cared more for money than life. Why would William be any different? And now that he has all the valuable tulip bulbs and the big bag of money it would make sense for him to just leave her behind and never look back.

Still, she had to give him his property. It's what a good girl would do, and she's always been a good girl, it just comes natural to her. But maybe just this once she should have tried to be a bad girl and held something back for herself? She leans away from him, making the parting of ways possible.

William guesses why she's pulled back. He takes her hands in his and pulls her close. Then he whispers breathes into her sad, solemn face, "Come with me Letty. Be my wife. We'll be each other's family."

Letty instantly, wholeheartedly, wants this too. She nods her head yes and leans in for the kiss to seal the deal. William obliges. A few minutes later, after coming up for air, they share a joyous smile and a bit of a laugh, comfortable with each other once again.

William replaces the stone. He takes Letty's hand, and they fairly skip their way to the horse and wagon. He shortens the lead and secures the horse to the wagon. They climb aboard and settle in the seat as close to each other as they can possibly get, the length of their thighs tight against each other's, their hips joined with no space between, touching, touching, feeling the young love, the belly flutters. They grin at each other, tip their heads back and laugh, joy filling their youthful hearts, their tinkling laughter carried on the light, warm breeze.

William turns to Letty and asks, "Are you sure you don't want to take anything else with you, to help you remember your life here with your parents? Maybe some family heirlooms? There's plenty of room left in the wagon and I can help you if it's heavy."

Letty thinks on it, but not for long. She asks, "Well, could we take my big storage chest? The inlay on the lid is made of all kinds of exotic woods and mother *of pearl shells. Everyone says what a beautiful work of art it is, and it's quite useful, too. My poppa made it especially for me. It's a real piece of furniture and not the traveling trunk people would normally use. But I love it. I 'd like to take it with us to America. I think between the two of us we can easily manage to carry it."

They jump off the wagon, making a game of who's first to hit the ground. It's a tie, of course. William wraps the horse's reins around the same old tree limb as before. They grab hands and run back to the cottage. And that's when William finally sees the crack in the door made by his father's pounding fists. He rubs his finger on the crack, feeling the depth of the break, feeling the power of his father's anger.

Letty takes a step back, giving William plenty of space. She understands the importance of William touching one of the last things his father had ever touched. The crack in the door is also the final proof William needs to accept her story of his father's death.

After a moment, he opens the door. Letty enters first and leads him to her storage chest. They find it surprisingly easy to lift, but they manage to tangle with the privacy curtains as they carry it away from the wall. As William untangles himself, he takes note of the exquisite embroidery stitched on the royal blue fabric and decides it's far too fine to be left behind for the mice, the moths, or the thieves.

He looks at Letty with a question in his eyes. She answers yes with a nod of her head. William unhooks one end of the curtain rod, and the curtains slide down and land in a silken puddle on the floor.

He does the same thing to the set of curtains servicing the marriage bed.

As they set about folding them, William notices the stitching on the hems is loose every six inches or so and the usual lead curtain weights are missing. He mimes Letty why? She shrugs she don't know. She's never really thought about it. They finish folding the curtains and pack them away in the chest.

Letty's eyes are irresistibly drawn to the flower vase sitting on the mantle. It's precious and lovely. She remembers when her mother had found it hidden in the garden shed several months after they moved in. It would make for a beautiful family heirloom, and so Letty decides to take it with her. But the second she picks it up she realizes the color of the vase is the exact same shade of green as the green smoke woman. Even the intertwined flowers painted on the vase are all lotus blossoms, and according to William's father, Lotus was the name of the Shaman witch.

Letty throws the vase as hard and as fast as she can at the back wall of fireplace. It explodes and shatters into a thousand pieces, never to be put back together again.

Startled, William just stares at her, secretly wondering if she had suddenly gone mad like her momma. He doesn't want any part of that, and he quickly asks, "That was unexpected, what possessed you to destroy such a beautiful vase?"

"It was green, exactly like the letter's smoke. I'm sure it was from Lotus, the Shaman witch." Letty says matter-of-factually. "I had to destroy it. I almost took it with us, it made me want to. I think it was part of the curse, a way of tracking my family. I feel sure we need to get rid of the prayer wheel, too. And we need to do it as soon as we possibly can. The people who want to buy the bulbs need to take it, too. Please, please promise me you'll make them take it."

Relieved, William nods his head yes. It's exactly what he thinks they should do, too.

So young and happy they are, so evenly matched, they lift the chest up as though it weighed nothing at all and walk it all the way out the door, down the path through the garden gate, across the road, and to the horse and wagon. Somehow, they manage to avoid banging it up as they sling it onto the deck of the wagon bed.

Not so William's knee. Unfortunately, Letty's pocket full of rocks happened to swing with the movement and slam into the side of his knee. The sudden pain caused him to grab hold of the side of the wagon to keep from crumpling to the ground. William succeeded in not swearing however, always the sign of a true gentleman.

William grits his teeth, takes a few deep breaths, and gathers his thoughts. When the pain finally subsides, he points at her skirt and politely inquires, "Whatever are you hiding in your pocket?"

Letty knows something just happened, but she's not quite sure what. Worse, she finds she's become tongued tied again.

He puts his full weight on his leg, but a sharp pain causes his knee to buckle. He catches hold of the wagon's sideboard and takes the weight off his injured leg for a moment. This time he demands, his voice all gruff, "Whatever it is you are hiding from me Letty, you need to show it to me right now."

She can tell by the way he grabbed his knee that she has hurt her nice young man and, in turn, upset him. She also knows he's the only available young man in the region, she heard her mother say as much Monday night, and that's why she needs to keep him. Besides, she likes him. She needs to make it all right with him again.

Her voice breaks free, and she explains in the sweetest, sincerest of tones, "William, I wasn't hiding anything from you, at least not on purpose. I just have a few keepsake treasures in my pockets. That's all, nothing more. After we get settled on the wagon seat, I'll show you everything, I promise."

William tries to put weight on his leg again. This time his knee takes it, the pain greatly reduced. He unties the horse, and they clamber back on board. They take their places on the bench seat and just naturally scooch in close and snuggle up against each other. William rubs his knee while making a point to smile at Letty and nod his encouragement.

She returns the smile, and then explains, "Our real home, our fancy home, burnt to the ground when I was eleven years old. I had nothing after the fire. People gave us used clothes, but they weren't pretty, and I was used to having pretty. So, when I discovered the keepsakes in the bottom of the hidey hole, I was so excited. Once again, I had pretty. But I also thought they were real treasures so I immediately showed them to my momma, thinking she would think they were real treasures, too. But instead, she told me the rocks were called fool's gold and worthless and that the gems I held in my hands were nothing but glass and crystals and didn't I remember seeing the same baubles strung on the fancy necklaces the inn keeper's wife always wore. She told me to stop bothering her about it, she needed to care for poppa so he wouldn't lose his leg and I should just keep my pretties to myself from now on. So that's what I did. But now that they've hurt you, you've earned the right to see them. So, close your eyes, hold out your hands, and wait for a big surprise."

William happily obliges his soon-to-be wife by cupping his hands and closing his eyes. Letty drops the rocks into his waiting hands. Then, from the other pocket, she removes the drawstring bag, opens it, and pours a stream of colored glass baubles onto her lap. She throws her hands up in the air and exclaims, "Voila! Voila! Open your eyes to a big surprise!"

William does as he is told. He looks back and forth between what is in his hands and what is in Letty's lap, his eyes round with amazement. He says not one word, though his mouth keeps opening and closing. Letty becomes increasingly worried. What if he thinks she is too much of a child to be his wife? Maybe he thinks she is simple, not a suitable match for his educated mind? She should have kept her treasures a secret. All that colored glass, pretending the fool's gold was special, she looked like a simpleton. Oh why, oh why, did she have to share everything? When will she ever learn?

William comes to his senses, lets out a low whistle, and declares, "Oh my God Letty, these aren't just any pretty old rocks in my hands, these are real gold nuggets. No wonder my knee still hurts. And all those glass beads laying in your lap? They're precious gems, not glass! I see emeralds, Burmese rubies, and celestial sapphires. And my God, that thing that looks like a huge sparkling cut crystal! It isn't glass, it's not a crystal! It's a real diamond, an Indian diamond. I can tell by the cut. It looks to be well over forty carats. It's worth a king's ransom. I know it is, it's what I do, I've been an apprentice to the king's jeweler for the past five years, so I know what I'm talking about. I'm positive each one is a real gem, even without my jeweler's loupe to confirm. I'll just bet your grandfather brought this treasure back from India and hid it for your mother to find. You did say he liked to play hide and seek with your mother."

Letty tries to reply but no words come out, she just stutters. Not quite tongue-tied, but close. She's having a really hard time processing what William just told her. Her eyes keep blinking, and she can't stop them. She's become stuck.

William gets it and asks, "You never knew, did you? Your pretties are worth a small fortune, more than enough for you to be independent. You're rich, Letty. You're rich!"

Letty's surprise quickly turns to sadness. If only her mother had paid attention when Letty first showed her the pretty treasures all those years ago. It would have rescued them from abject poverty. But really, the truth was at the time her poppa's survival was all the treasure her momma ever wanted.

But at least now Letty won't be a beggar when she leaves this cursed and no doubt haunted place. And best of all, she now has free choice. And it's all thanks to her seafaring grandfather. He sure liked to play games and hide things. She's always loved a good game, too. Maybe the love of a game is a family trait, like being tongue-tied. And it just so happens she has an idea for a brand-new game right now.

William can almost see Letty's mind spinning, thinking of all the what ifs. He knows the exact moment she realizes she has her own money and what real independence means, it's that obvious. He doesn't hold it against her, it's what he would think, too. But what he doesn't know is what path she will choose. Will she stay with him, or will she go?

Letty looks him straight in his love-struck eyes and with the utmost, deepest regret she can muster, she sighs and says, "William, (again she pauses, sighing wistfully, dragging the moment out) will you marry me?"

She waits a few heartbeats and explodes with laughter. She really had him going. It was clear in the worried expression so blatantly displayed on his handsome young face. No doubt about it, it's a love match struck between them. And best of all, early in their love though it is, she already knows how best to tease him. So much fun is in store for them, she just knows it.

William lets out his breath. Relieved, overjoyed, he exclaims, "What? What? What did you just say? Did you just ask me to marry you? You did. You did. You did, you funny little tease. Well, of course I'll marry you. I always wanted a wife that was rich."

They look at each other side eye, then bust out laughing. It's been so much fun but now it really is time to go. Letty returns the treasures to her pockets. She recently reinforced all her skirt's seams and feels confident her new-found wealth is secure. A silly thought suddenly pops into her mind. She's now become a walking around hidey hole. It's such a naughty thought it makes her giggle. She thinks of last night's pleasuring and blushes. She looks to William to see if he's noticed.

But William is busy pulling on the reins, directing the horse and wagon towards the village. A variable wind starts up and swings the garden gate back and forth. The motion causes the gate's hinges to squeak, squeak, squeak in a high soprano. Meanwhile at the windmill, the dog brake slips loose, and the sails start ever so slowly to turn in a measured whoop, whoop, whoop. The tenor sound is followed by the grindstones grinding out a thumping bass beat.

All the sounds combine as a farewell song to the lovely Letty and her nice young man.

But Letty and William are unable to hear the goodbye song. The young lovers have turned their backs on the past and are intent on the road ahead.

28

Early spring. Ice encrusted patches of snow dot the grounds of the abandoned cottage. The boards below the false bottom of the rain barrel have rotted through and gold coins have spilled out onto the snow. But there's no one to see. The property is taboo now, the locals believe the four violent deaths have made it forever haunted. The squeaking hinges of the garden gate seem to be calling out to someone, anyone to come latch it shut, but no one comes, no one dares to.

A scrawny fox sniffs the scorched earth at the bottom of the path. She smells the faint odor of food and follows it up the hill. As the path becomes the road the smell of roasted meat and blood intensifies. Excited now, the fox sprints her way through the garden to a pile of disturbed dirt at the base of three enormous tulip flowers, each petal the color of a mortal wound. The fox pounces on the loose dirt and begins to dig. Soon, she has unearthed a large pile of powdered blood mixed in with ground up burnt bones. She cocks her head from side to side as she mulls it over. At almost the same instant the babies in her belly give her a vicious kick and her empty stomach rumbles in response. Decision made, the fox with the red fur coat devours the last remaining bits of the burnt botanist.

Reading Group Guide for the novel

TULIP

for more information on purchasing copies of the novel TULIP

google tulipthenovel.com

email @aldmpublishing.com

ALDM Publishing P.O. Box 104, Quilcene, Wa. 98376

POSSIBLE DISCUSSION QUESTIONS ;

1. *What was your initial reaction to the book?*

2. *Of the seven main characters, who was your favorite? Your least favorite?*

3. *The Botanist and Vonder paid a steep price for jumping to conclusions. What other choice could each man have made? Did they both have free will?*

4. *Vonder took charge of the evacuation once he discovered the staircase was on fire, but Neola was tasked with the final save. What would you have done differently?*

5. *Lotus sacrificed her father, Neola sacrificed herself. Whose sacrifice was greater? When the story ends are they finally even? How so?*

6. *Is justice so blind Letty would hang for what she did? Why did Letty go along with her mother's delusion?*

7. *It took years for Lotus to act against her husband's emotional infidelity. Why so long? Would you have waited so long?*

8. *Why do Letty and Neola lose their Christian religion in just four day*

while Lotus clings to her ancient Deities years after the second curse fails? Is the death of God during crisis the norm?

9. Why was Neola so quick to act so slutty? Why did her father allow her to see whores working the docks? If Neola had been a boy instead, would watching whores have been more appropriate?

10, The tulip bulbs have unusual properties, capable of increasing strength and endurance while acting as a powerful aphrodisiac and hallucinogen. Both Neola and Lotus use the bulbs as weapons yet when Letty consumes a bulb she experiences pleasure. Why the different reactions?

11. Letty is sixteen. Why do her parents still call her baby girl? In what way do nicknames hinder or help people?

12. Neola accused the Constable of murder. Was it justified?

13. What incident cemented Letty and William's equality?

14. Do you believe in curses? Why or why not?

15. Does playing hide and seek with family treasure seem like a normal family game? The family lived a hard scrabble life. Why were they so playful? Would you be?

16. Was there a plot twist you loved? Or one you hated?

17. How do you feel about the ending?

18. If TULIP was made movie into a movie who would you want to play the main characters? Do you think unknown actors would better represent the story?

Acknowledgements

I wish to thank David Thompson, Jennifer Takai, Al Wagner, Jean Joseph, and Stephanie River for taking the time to read the many drafts of the novel TULIP.

And special thanks to Vicki Jean Sturges for her proofreading and editing of the novel TULIP, I never could have done it without you. But as with all things TULIP, the final editing choices were decided by me, the author, Alice L. Lumbard.

When my partner, Tim Batey, bought me a kitchen timer it solved the problem of under cooked, over cooked. and outright burned to ash meals. Tim, you were the first to know the story and watching your physical reaction while I read it out loud was not only a great source of delight for me but also a great part of the writing and editing process.

The tulip bulbs really do originate in the region mentioned in the novel TULIP, as does the tree that produces the apple. Diamonds and other gemstones are also abundant within the same region, thus their inclusion in. the novel TULIP.

ABOUT THE AUTHOR

The author, Alice L Lumbard, shares a home with a dog, a cat, and her partner of more than twenty two years, Tim Batey. They live near the little town of Quilcene, Washington on the Olympic Peninsula. The majestic Olympic mountains provide the backdrop for her simple home, a salt water beach full of oysters and clams is just a mere mile away. Reading has always been the author's number one passion, travelling by pickup truck and commercial fishing vessel being a close second. She credits an intense conversation with the author and professor Jack Cady and a proof reading and editing college course with giving her the confidence to write and seek publication. Tulip is her debut novel.

CPSIA information can be obtained
at www.ICGtesting.com
Printed in the USA
BVHW030253011021
617907BV00007B/197